The Phantom Ship

by

Captain Marryat

Double 9
BOOKS

The phantom ship
by Captain Marryat

Copyright © 2024

All Rights reserved.

ISBN: 978-93-65789-04-1

Published by

DOUBLE 9 BOOKS

2/13-B, Ansari Road
Daryaganj, New Delhi – 110002
info@double9books.com
www.double9books.com
Tel. 011-40042856

ABOUT THE AUTHOR

Captain Frederick Marryat (an early innovator of the sea story) was a British Royal Navy Officer and novelist. He gained the Royal Human Society's gold medal for bravery, before leaving the services in 1830 to write books. He is mainly remembered for his stories of the sea, many written from his own experiences. He started a series of adventure novels marked by a brilliant, direct narrative style and an absolute fund of incident and fun. These have The King's Own (1830), Peter Simple (1834), and Mr. Midshipman Easy (1836). He also created a number of children's books, among which The Children of the New Forest (1847), a story of the English Civil Wars is a classic of children literature. A Life and Letters was processed by his daughter Florence (1872). He is recognized also for a broadly used system of maritime flag signalling known as Marryat's Code. Familiar for his adventurous novels, his works are known for their representation of deep family bonds and social structure beside naval action. Marryat died in 1848 at the age of fifty.

CONTENTS

Chapter One

About the middle of the seventeenth century, in the outskirts of the small but fortified town of Terneuse, situated on the right bank of the Scheldt, and nearly opposite to the island of Walcheren, there was to be seen in advance of a few other even more humble tenements, a small but neat cottage, built according to the prevailing taste of the time. The outside front had, some years back, been painted of a deep orange, the windows and shutters of a vivid green. To about three feet above the surface of the earth, it was faced alternately with blue and white tiles. A small garden, of about two rods of our measure of land, surrounded the edifice; and this little plot was flanked by a low hedge of privet, and encircled by a moat full of water, too wide to be leaped with ease. Over that part of the moat which was in front of the cottage-door was a small and narrow bridge, with ornamented iron handrails, for the security of the passenger. But the colours, originally so bright, with which the cottage had been decorated, had now faded; symptoms of rapid decay were evident in the window-sills, the door-jambs, and other wooden parts of the tenement and many of the white and blue tiles had fallen down and had not been replaced. That much care had once been bestowed upon this little tenement, was as evident as that latterly it had been equally neglected.

The inside of the cottage, both on the basement and the floor above, was divided into two larger rooms in front, and two smaller behind; the rooms in front could only be called large in comparison with the other two, as they were little more than twelve feet square, with but one window to each. The upper floor was, as usual, appropriated to the bedrooms; on the lower, the two smaller rooms were now used only as a wash-house and a lumber-room; while one of the larger was fitted up as a kitchen, and furnished with dressers, on which the metal utensils for cookery shone clean and polished as silver. The room itself was scrupulously neat; but the furniture as well as the utensils, were scanty. The boards of the floor were of a pure white, and so clean that you might have laid anything down without fear of soiling it. A strong deal table, two wooden-seated chairs, and a small easy couch, which had been removed from one of the bedrooms upstairs, were all the moveables which this room contained. The other front room had been fitted up as a parlour; but what might be the style of its furniture was now unknown, for no eye had beheld the contents of that room for nearly seventeen years, during which it had been hermetically sealed, even to the inmates of the cottage.

The kitchen, which we have described, was occupied by two persons. One was a woman, apparently about forty years of age, but worn down by pain and suffering. She had evidently once possessed much beauty: there were still the regular outlines, the noble forehead, and the large dark eye; but there was a tenuity in her features, a wasted appearance, such as to render the flesh transparent; her brow, when she mused, would sink into deep wrinkles, premature though they were; and the occasional flashing of her eyes strongly impressed you with the idea of insanity. There appeared to be some deep-seated, irremoveable, hopeless cause of anguish, never for one moment permitted to be absent from her memory: a chronic oppression, fixed and graven there, only to be removed by death. She was dressed in the widow's coif of the time; but although clean and neat, her garments were faded from long wear. She was seated upon the small couch which we have mentioned, evidently brought down as a relief to her, in her declining state.

On the deal table in the centre of the room sat the other person, a stout, fair-haired, florid youth of nineteen or twenty years old. His features were handsome and bold, and his frame powerful to excess; his eye denoted courage and determination, and as he carelessly swung his legs, and whistled an air in an emphatic manner, it was impossible not to form the idea that he was a daring, adventurous, and reckless character.

"Do not go to sea, Philip; oh, promise me *that*, my dear child," said the female, clasping her hands.

"And why not go to sea, mother?" replied Philip; "what's the use of my staying here to starve?—for, by Heaven! it's little better, I must do something for myself and for you. And what else can I do? My uncle Van Brennen has offered to take me with him, and will give me good wages. Then I shall live happily on board, and my earnings will be sufficient for your support at home."

"Philip—Philip, hear me. I shall die if you leave me. Whom have I in the world but you? O my child, as you love me, and I know you *do* love me, Philip, don't leave me; but if you will, at all events do not go to sea."

Philip gave no immediate reply; he whistled for a few seconds, while his mother wept.

"Is it," said he at last, "because my father was drowned at sea that you beg so hard, mother?"

"Oh, no—no!" exclaimed the sobbing woman. "Would to God—"

"Would to God what, mother?"

"Nothing—nothing. Be merciful—be merciful, O God!" replied the mother, sliding from her seat on the couch, and kneeling by the side of it, in which attitude she remained for some time in fervent prayer. At last she resumed her seat, and her face wore an aspect of more composure.

Philip, who during this, had remained silent and thoughtful, again addressed his mother.

"Look ye, mother. You ask me to stay on shore with you, and starve,— rather hard conditions:— now hear what I have to say. That room opposite has been shut up ever since I can remember—why, you will never tell me; but once I heard you say, when we were without bread and with no prospect of my uncle's return—you were then half frantic, mother, as you know you sometimes are—"

"Well, Philip, what did you hear me say?" inquired his mother, with tremulous anxiety.

"You said, mother, that there was money in that room which would save us; and then you screamed and raved, and said that you preferred death. Now, mother, what is there in that chamber, and why has it been so long shut up? Either I know that, or I go to sea."

At the commencement of this address of Philip, his mother appeared to be transfixed, and motionless as a statue; gradually her lips separated, and her eyes glared; she seemed to have lost the power of reply; she put her hand to her right side, as if to compress it, then both her hands, as if to relieve herself from excruciating torture: at last she sank, with her head forward, and the blood poured out of her mouth.

Philip sprang from the table to her assistance, and prevented her from falling on the floor. He laid her on the couch, watching with alarm the continued effusion.

"Oh! mother—mother, what is this?" cried he, at last, in great distress.

For some time his mother could make him no reply; she turned further on her side, that she might not be suffocated by the discharge from the ruptured vessel, and the snow-white planks of the floor were soon crimsoned with her blood.

"Speak, dearest mother, if you can," repeated Philip in agony; "What shall I do?—what shall I give you? God Almighty! what is this?"

"Death, my child, death!" at length replied the poor woman, sinking into a state of unconsciousness.

Philip, now much alarmed, flew out of the cottage, and called the neighbours to his mother's assistance. Two or three hastened to the call; and as soon as Philip saw them occupied in restoring his mother, he ran as fast as he could to the house of a medical man, who lived about a mile off;—one Mynheer Poots, a little, miserable, avaricious wretch but known to be very skilful in his profession. Philip found Poots at home, and insisted upon his immediate attendance.

"I will come—yes, most certainly," replied Poots, who spoke the language but imperfectly; "but, Mynheer Vanderdecken, who will pay me?"

"Pay you! my uncle will, directly that he comes home."

"Your uncle, de Skipper Vanbrennen: no, he owe me four guilders, and he has owed me for a long time. Besides his ship may sink."

"He shall pay you the four guilders, and for this attendance also," replied Philip in a rage; "come directly,—while you are disputing, my mother may be dead."

"But, Mr Philip, I cannot come, now I recollect. I have to see the child of the Burgomaster at Terneuse," replied Mynheer Poots.

"Look you, Mynheer Poots," exclaimed Philip, red with passion; "you have but to choose,—will you go quietly, or must I take you there? You'll not trifle with me."

Here Mynheer Poots was under considerable alarm, for the character of Philip Vanderdecken was well known.

"I will come by-and-by, Mynheer Philip, if I can."

"You'll come now, you wretched old miser," exclaimed Philip, seizing hold of the little man by the collar, and pulling him out of his door.

"Murder! murder!" cried Poots, as he lost his legs, and was dragged along by the impetuous young man.

Philip stopped, for he perceived that Poots was black in the face.

"Must I then choke you, to make you go quietly? for, hear me, go you shall, alive or dead."

"Well, then," replied Poots, recovering himself, "I will go, but I'll have you in prison to-night: and, as for your mother, I'll not—no, that I will not—Mynheer Philip, depend upon it."

"Mark me, Mynheer Poots," replied Philip, "as sure as there is a God in heaven, if you do not come with me, I'll choke you now; and when you arrive, if you do not your best for my poor mother, I'll murder you there. You know that I always do what I say, so now take my advice, come along quietly, and you shall certainly be paid, and well paid—if I sell my coat."

This last observation of Philip, perhaps, had more effect than even his threats. Poots was a miserable little atom, and like a child in the powerful grasp of the young man. The doctor's tenement was isolated, and he could obtain no assistance until within a hundred yards of Vanderdecken's cottage; so Mynheer Poots decided that he would go—first, because Philip had promised to pay him, and secondly, because he could not help it.

This point being settled, Philip and Mynheer Poots made all haste to the cottage; and on their arrival, they found his mother still in the arms of two of her female neighbours, who were bathing her temples with vinegar. She was in a state of consciousness, but she could not speak; Poots ordered her to be carried up stairs and put to bed, and pouring some acids down her throat, hastened away with Philip to procure the necessary remedies.

"You will give your mother that directly, Mynheer Philip," said Poots, putting a phial into his hand; "I will now go to the child of the Burgomaster, and will afterwards come back to your cottage."

"Don't deceive me," said Philip, with a threatening look.

"No, no, Mynheer Philip, I would not trust to your uncle Vanbrennen for payment, but you have promised, and I know that you always keep your word. In one hour I will be with your mother; but you yourself must now be quick."

Philip hastened home. After the potion had been administered, the bleeding was wholly stopped; and in half an hour, his mother could express her wishes in a whisper. When the little doctor arrived, he carefully examined his patient, and then went down stairs with her son into the kitchen.

"Mynheer Philip," said Poots, "by Allah! I have done my best, but I must tell you that I have little hopes of your mother rising from her bed again. She may live one day or two days, but not more. It is not my fault, Mynheer Philip," continued Poots, in a deprecating tone.

"No, no; it is the will of Heaven," replied Philip, mournfully.

"And you will pay me, Mynheer Vanderdecken?" continued the doctor after a short pause.

"Yes," replied Philip in a voice of thunder, and starting from a reverie. After a moment's silence, the doctor recommenced:

"Shall I come to-morrow, Mynheer Philip? You know that will be a charge of another guilder: it is of no use to throw away money or time either."

"Come to-morrow, come every hour, charge what you please; you shall certainly be paid," replied Philip, curling his lip with contempt.

"Well, it is as you please. As soon as she is dead the cottage and the furniture will be yours, and you will sell them of course. Yes, I will come. You will have plenty of money. Mynheer Philip, I would like the first offer of the cottage, if it is to let."

Philip raised his arm in the air as if to crush Mynheer Poots, who retreated to the corner.

"I did not mean until your mother was buried," said Poots, in a coaxing tone.

"Go, wretch, go!" said Philip, covering his face with his hands, as he sank down upon the blood-stained couch.

After a short interval, Philip Vanderdecken returned to the bedside of his mother, whom he found much better; and the neighbours, having their own affairs to attend to, left them alone. Exhausted with the loss of blood, the poor woman slumbered for many hours, during which she never let go the hand of Philip, who watched her breathing in mournful meditation.

It was about one o'clock in the morning when the widow awoke. She had in a great degree recovered her voice, and thus she addressed her son:—

"My dear, my impetuous boy, and have I detained you here a prisoner so long?"

"My own inclination detained me, mother. I leave you not to others until you are up and well again."

"That, Philip, I shall never be. I feel that death claims me; and O my son, were it not for you, how should I quit this world rejoicing! I have long been dying, Philip,—and long, long have I prayed for death."

"And why so, mother?" replied Philip, bluntly; "I've done my best."

"You have, my child, you have: and may God bless you for it. Often have I seen you curb your fiery temper—restrain yourself when justified in wrath—to spare a mother's feelings. 'Tis now some days that even hunger has not persuaded you to disobey your mother. And, Philip, you must have thought me mad or foolish to insist so long, and yet to give no reason. I'll speak—again—directly."

The widow turned her head upon the pillow, and remained quiet for some minutes; then, as if revived, she resumed:

"I believe I have been mad at times—have I not, Philip? And God knows I have had a secret in my heart enough to drive a wife to frenzy. It has oppressed me day and night, worn my mind, impaired my reason, and now, at last, thank Heaven! it has overcome this mortal frame: the blow is struck, Philip—I'm sure it is. I wait but to tell you all,—and yet I would not,—'twill turn your brain as it has turned mine, Philip."

"Mother," replied Philip, earnestly, "I conjure you, let me hear this killing secret. Be heaven or hell mixed up with it, I fear not. Heaven will not hurt me and Satan I defy."

"I know thy bold, proud spirit, Philip,—thy strength of mind. If any one could bear the load of such a dreadful tale, thou couldst. My brain, alas! was far too weak for it; and I see it is my duty to tell it to thee."

The widow paused as her thoughts reverted to that which she had to confide; for a few minutes the tears rained down her hollow cheeks; she then appeared to have summoned resolution, and to have regained strength.

"Philip, it is of your father I would speak. It is supposed—that he was—drowned at sea."

"And was he not, mother?" replied Philip, with surprise.

"O no!"

"But he has long been dead, mother?"

"No,—yes,—and yet—no," said the widow, covering her eyes. Her brain wanders, thought Philip, but he spoke again:

"Then where is he, mother?"

The widow raised herself, and a tremor visibly ran through her whole frame, as she replied—

"In *Living Judgment* ."

The poor woman then sank down again upon the pillow, and covered her head with the bedclothes, as if she would have hid herself from her own memory. Philip was so much perplexed and astounded, that he could make no reply. A silence of some minutes ensued when, no longer able to bear the agony of suspense, Philip faintly whispered—

"The secret, mother, the secret; quick, let me hear it."

"I can now tell all, Philip," replied his mother, in a solemn tone of voice. "Hear me, my son. Your father's disposition was but too like your own;—O may his cruel fate be a lesson to you, my dear, dear child! He was a bold, a daring, and, they say, a first-rate seaman. He was not born here, but in Amsterdam; but he would not live there, because he still adhered to the Catholic religion. The Dutch, you know, Philip, are heretics, according to our creed. It is now seventeen years or more that he sailed for India, in his fine ship the Amsterdammer, with a valuable cargo. It was his third voyage to India, Philip, and it was to have been, if it had so pleased God, his last, for he had purchased that good ship with only part of his earnings, and one more voyage would have made his fortune. O! how often did we talk over what we would do upon his return, and how these plans for the future consoled me at the idea of his absence, for I loved him dearly, Philip,—he was always good and kind to me! and after he had sailed, how I hoped for his return! The lot of a sailor's wife is not to be envied. Alone and solitary for so many months, watching the long wick of the candle and listening to the howling of the wind—foreboding evil and accident—wreck and widowhood. He had been gone about six months, Philip, and there was still a long dreary year to wait before I could expect him back. One night, you, my child, were fast asleep; you were my only solace—my comfort in my loneliness. I had been watching over you in your slumbers: you smiled and half pronounced the name of mother; and at last I kissed your unconscious lips, and I knelt and prayed—prayed for God's blessing on you, my child, and upon him too—little thinking, at the time, that he was so horribly, so fearfully *cursed* ."

The widow paused for breath, and then resumed. Philip could not speak. His lips were sundered, and his eyes riveted upon his mother, as he devoured her words.

"I left you and went down stairs into that room, Philip, which since that dreadful night has never been re-opened. I sate me down and read, for the wind was strong, and when the gale blows, a sailor's wife can seldom sleep. It was past midnight, and the rain poured down. I felt unusual fear,—I knew not why, I rose from the couch and dipped my finger in the blessed water, and I crossed myself. A violent gust of wind roared round the house and alarmed me still more. I had a painful, horrible foreboding; when, of a sudden, the windows and window-shutters were all blown in, the light was extinguished, and I was left in utter darkness. I screamed with fright— but at last I recovered myself, and was proceeding towards the window that I might reclose it, when whom should I behold, slowly entering at the casement, but—your father,—Philip!—Yes, Philip,—it was your father!"

"Merciful God!" muttered Philip, in a low tone almost subdued into a whisper.

"I knew not what to think,—he was in the room; and although the darkness was intense, his form and features were as clear and as defined as if it were noon-day. Fear would have inclined me to recoil from,—his loved presence to fly towards him. I remained on the spot where I was, choked with agonising sensations. When he had entered the room, the windows and shutters closed of themselves, and the candle was relighted—then I thought it was his apparition, and I fainted on the floor.

"When I recovered I found myself on the couch, and perceived that a cold (O how cold!) and dripping hand was clasped in mine. This reassured me, and I forgot the supernatural signs which accompanied his appearance. I imagined that he had been unfortunate, and had returned home. I opened my eyes, and beheld my loved husband and threw myself into his arms. His clothes were saturated with the rain; I felt as if I had embraced ice—but nothing can check the warmth of woman's love, Philip. He received my caresses but he caressed not again: he spoke not, but looked thoughtful and unhappy. 'William—William,' cried I; 'speak, to your dear Catherine.'

"'I will,' replied he, solemnly, 'for my time is short.'

"'No, no, you must not go to sea again; you have lost your vessel but you are safe. Have I not you again?'

"'Alas! no—be not alarmed, but listen? for my time is short. I have not lost my vessel, Catherine, *but I have lost* !—Make no reply, but listen; I am not dead, nor yet am I alive. I hover between this world and the world of spirits. Mark me.'

"'For nine weeks did I try to force my passage against the elements round the stormy Cape, but without success; and I swore terribly. For nine weeks more did I carry sail against the adverse winds and currents, and yet could gain no ground and then I blasphemed,—ay, terribly blasphemed. Yet still I persevered. The crew, worn out with long fatigue, would have had me return to the Table Bay; but I refused; nay, more, I became a murderer—unintentionally, it is true, but still a murderer. The pilot opposed me, and persuaded the men to bind me, and in the excess of my fury, when he took me by the collar, I struck at him; he reeled; and, with the sudden lurch of the vessel, he fell overboard, and sank. Even this fearful death did not restrain me; and I swore by the fragment of the Holy Cross, preserved in that relic now hanging round your neck, that I would gain my point in defiance of storm and seas, of lightning, of heaven, or of hell, even if I should beat about until the Day of Judgment.'

"'My oath was registered in thunder, and in streams of sulphurous fire. The hurricane burst upon the ship, the canvass flew away in ribbons; mountains of seas swept over us, and in the centre of a deep o'erhanging cloud, which shrouded all in utter darkness, were written in letters of livid flame, these words— *Until the Day of Judgement* .'

"'Listen to me, Catherine, my time is short. *One hope* alone remains, and for this am I permitted to come here. Take this letter.' He put a sealed paper on the table. 'Read it, Catherine, dear, and try if you can assist me. Read it, and now farewell—my time is come.'

"Again the window and window-shutters burst open—again the light was extinguished, and the form of my husband was, as it were, wafted in the dark expanse. I started up and followed him with outstretched arms and frantic screams as he sailed through the window;—my glaring eyes beheld his form borne away like lightning on the wings of the wild gale, till it was lost as a speck of light, and then it disappeared. Again the windows closed, the light burned, and I was left alone!

"Heaven, have mercy! My brain!—my brain!—Philip!—Philip!" shrieked the poor woman; "don't leave me—don't—don't—pray don't!"

During these exclamations the frantic widow had raised herself from the bed, and, at the last, had fallen into the arms of her son. She remained there some minutes without motion. After a time Philip felt alarmed at her long quiescence; he laid her gently down upon the bed, and as he did so her head fell back—her eyes were turned—the widow Vanderdecken was no more.

Chapter Two

Philip Vanderdecken, strong as he was in mental courage, was almost paralysed by the shock when he discovered that his mother's spirit had fled; and for some time he remained by the side of the bed, with his eyes fixed upon the corpse, and his mind in a state of vacuity. Gradually he recovered himself; he rose, smoothed down the pillow, closed her eyelids, and then clasping his hands, the tears trickled down his manly cheeks. He impressed a solemn kiss upon the pale white forehead of the departed, and drew the curtains round the bed.

"Poor mother!" said he, sorrowfully, as he completed his task, "at length thou hast found rest,—but thou hast left thy son a bitter legacy."

And as Philip's thoughts reverted to what had passed, the dreadful narrative whirled in his imagination and scathed his brain. He raised his hands to his temples, compressed them with force, and tried to collect his thoughts, that he might decide upon what measures he should take. He felt that he had no time to indulge his grief. His mother was in peace: but his father—where was he?

He recalled his mother's words—"One hope alone remained." Then there was hope. His father had laid a paper on the table—could it be there now? Yes, it must be—his mother had not had the courage to take it up. There was hope in that paper, and it had lain unopened for more than seventeen years.

Philip Vanderdecken resolved that he would examine the fatal chamber—at once he would know the worst. Should he do it now, or wait till daylight?—but the key, where was it? His eyes rested upon an old japanned cabinet in the room: he had never seen his mother open it in his presence: it was the only likely place of concealment that he was aware of. Prompt in all his decisions, he took up the candle, and proceeded to examine it. It was not locked; the doors swung open, and drawer after drawer was examined, but Philip discovered not the object of his search; again and again did he open the drawers, but they were all empty. It occurred to Philip that there might be secret drawers, and he examined for some time in vain. At last he took out all the drawers, and laid them on the floor, and lifting the cabinet off its stand he shook it. A rattling sound in one corner told him that in all probability the key was there concealed. He renewed his attempts to discover how to gain it, but in vain. Daylight now streamed through the casements, and Philip had not desisted from his attempts: at last, wearied out, he resolved to force the back panel of the cabinet; he descended to the kitchen, and returned with a small chopping-knife and hammer, and was on his knees busily employed forcing out the panel, when a hand was placed upon his shoulder.

Philip started: he had been so occupied with his search and his wild chasing thoughts, that he had not heard the sound of an approaching footstep. He looked up and beheld the Father Seysen, the priest of the little parish, with his eyes sternly fixed upon him. The good man had been informed of the dangerous state of the widow Vanderdecken, and had risen at daylight to visit and afford her spiritual comfort.

"How now, my son," said the priest: "fearest thou not to disturb thy mother's rest? and wouldst thou pilfer and purloin even before she is in her grave?"

"I fear not to disturb my mother's rest, good father," replied Philip, rising on his feet, "for she now rests with the blessed. Neither do I pilfer or purloin. It is not gold, I seek although if gold there were, that gold would now be mine. I seek but a key, long hidden, I believe, within this secret drawer, the opening of which is a mystery beyond my art."

"Thy mother is no more, sayest thou, my son? and dead without receiving the rites of our most holy church! Why didst thou not send for me?"

"She died, good father, suddenly, most suddenly, in these arms, about two hours ago. I fear not for her soul, although I can but grieve you were not at her side."

The priest gently opened the curtains, and looked upon the corpse. He sprinkled holy water on the bed, and for a short time his lips were seen to move in silent prayer. He then turned round to Philip.

"Why do I see thee thus employed? and why so anxious to obtain that key? A mother's death should call forth filial tears and prayers for her repose. Yet are thine eyes dry, and thou art employed upon an indifferent search while yet the tenement is warm which but now held her spirit. This is not seemly, Philip. What is the key thou seekest?"

"Father, I have no time for tears—no time to spare for grief or lamentation. I have much to do, and more to think of than thought can well embrace. That I loved my mother, you know well."

"But the key thou seekest, Philip?"

"Father, it is the key of a chamber which has not been unlocked for years, which I must—will open; even if—"

"If what, my son?"

"I was about to say what I should not have said. Forgive me, Father; I meant that I must search that chamber."

"I have long heard of that same chamber being closed: and that thy mother would not explain wherefore, I know well for I have asked her, and have been denied. Nay, when, as in duty bound, I pressed the question, I found her reason was disordered by my importunity, and, therefore, I abandoned the attempt. Some heavy weight was on thy mother's mind, my son, yet would she never confess or trust it with me. Tell me, before she died, hadst thou this secret from her?"

"I had, most holy father."

"Wouldst thou not feel comfort if thou didst confide to me, my son? I might advise, assist—"

"Father, I would indeed—I could confide it to thee, and ask for thy assistance—I know 'tis not from curious feeling thou wouldst have it, but from a better motive. But of that which has been told it is not yet manifest whether it is as my poor mother says, or but the phantom of a heated brain. Should it indeed be true, fain would I share the burthen with you—yet little you might thank me for the heavy load. But no—at least not now—it must not, cannot be revealed. I must do my work—enter that hated room alone."

"Fearest thou not?"

"Father, I fear nothing. I have a duty to perform—a dreadful one, I grant; but, I pray thee, ask no more; for like my poor mother, I feel as if the probing of the wound would half unseat my reason."

"I will not press thee further, Philip. The time may come when I may prove of service. Farewell, my child; but I pray thee to discontinue thy unseemly labour, for I must send in the neighbours to perform the duties to thy departed mother, whose soul I trust is with its God."

The priest looked at Philip; he perceived that his thoughts were elsewhere; there was a vacancy and appearance of mental stupefaction, and as he turned away, the good man shook his head.

"He is right," thought Philip, when once more alone; and he took up the cabinet, and placed it upon the stand. "A few hours more can make no difference: I will lay me down, for my head is giddy."

Philip went into the adjoining room, threw himself upon his bed, and in a few minutes was in a sleep as sound as that permitted to the wretch a few hours previous to his execution.

During his slumbers the neighbours had come in, and had prepared everything for the widow's interment. They had been careful not to wake the son, for they held as sacred the sleep of those who must wake up to sorrow. Among others, soon after the hour of noon, arrived Mynheer Poots; he had been informed of the death of the widow, but having a spare hour, he thought he might as well call, as it would raise his charges by another guilder. He first went into the room where the body lay, and from thence he proceeded to the chamber of Philip, and shook him by the shoulder.

Philip awoke, and, sitting up, perceived the doctor standing by him.

"Well, Mynheer Vanderdecken," commenced the unfeeling little man, "so it's all over. I knew it would be so; and recollect you owe me now another guilder, and you promised faithfully to pay me; altogether, with the potion, it will be three guilders and a half—that is, provided you return my phial."

Philip, who at first waking was confused, gradually recovered his senses during this address.

"You shall have your three guilders and a half, and your phial to boot, Mr Poots," replied he, as he rose from off the bed.

"Yes, yes; I know you mean to pay me—if you can. But look you, Mynheer Philip, it may be some time before you sell the cottage. You may not find a customer. Now, I never wish to be hard upon people who have no money, and I'll tell you what I'll do. There is a something on your mother's neck. It is of no value—none at all, but to a good Catholic. To help you in your strait I will take that thing, and then we shall be quits. You will have paid me, and there will be an end of it."

Philip listened calmly: he knew to what the little miser had referred,— the relic on his mother's neck; that very relic upon which his father swore the fatal oath. He felt that millions of guilders would not have induced him to part with it.

"Leave the house," answered he, abruptly. "Leave it immediately. Your money shall be paid."

Now Mynheer Poots, in the first place, knew that the setting of the relic, which was in a square frame of pure gold, was worth much more than the sum due to him: he also knew that a large price had been paid for the relic itself, and, as at that time such a relic was considered very valuable, he had no doubt but that it would again fetch a considerable sum. Tempted by the sight of it when he entered the chamber of death, he had taken it from the neck of the corpse, and it was then actually concealed in his bosom, so he replied, — "My offer is a good one, Mynheer Philip, and you had better take it. Of what use is such trash?"

"I tell you no," cried Philip, in a rage.

"Well, then, you will let me have it in my possession till I am paid, Mynheer Vanderdecken—that is but fair. I must not lose my money. When you bring me my three guilders and a half and the phial, I will return it to you."

Philip's indignation was now without bounds. He seized Mynheer Poots by the collar, and threw him out of the door. "Away immediately," cried he, "or by—"

There was no occasion for Philip to finish the imprecation. The doctor had hastened away with such alarm, that he fell down half the steps of the staircase, and was limping away across the bridge. He almost wished that the relic had not been in his possession; but his sudden retreat had prevented him, even if so inclined, from replacing it on the corpse.

The result of this conversation naturally turned Philip's thoughts to the relic, and he went into his mother's room to take possession of it. He opened the curtains—the corpse was laid out—he put forth his hand to untie the black ribbon. It was not there. "Gone!" exclaimed Philip. "They hardly would have removed it—never would. It must be that villain Poots—wretch! but I will have it, even if he has swallowed it, though I tear him limb from limb!"

Philip darted down the stairs, rushed out of the house, cleared the moat at one bound and, without coat or hat, flew away in the direction of the doctor's lonely residence. The neighbours saw him as he passed them like the wind; they wondered, and they shook their heads. Mynheer Poots was not more than half way to his home for he had hurt his ankle. Apprehensive of what might possibly take place, should his theft be discovered, he occasionally looked behind him; at length, to his horror, he beheld Philip Vanderdecken at a distance, bounding on in pursuit of him. Frightened almost out of his senses, the wretched pilferer hardly knew how to act; to stop and surrender up the stolen property was his first thought, but fear of Vanderdecken's violence prevented him; so he decided on taking to his heels, thus hoping to gain his house, and barricade himself in, by which means he would be in a condition to keep possession of what he had stolen, or at least to make some terms ere he restored it.

Mynheer Poots had need to run fast, and so he did, his thin legs bearing his shrivelled form rapidly over the ground; but Philip, who, when he witnessed the doctor's attempt to escape, was fully convinced that he was the culprit, redoubled his exertions, and rapidly came up with the chase. When within a hundred yards of his own door, Mynheer Poots heard the bounding steps of Philip gain upon him, and he sprang and leaped in his agony. Nearer and nearer still the step, until at last he heard the very breathing of his pursuer; and Poots shrieked in his fear, like the hare in the jaws of the greyhound. Philip was not a yard from him; his arm was outstretched when the miscreant dropped down paralysed with terror; and the impetus of Vanderdecken was so great, that he passed over his body, tripped and after trying in vain to recover his equilibrium, he fell and rolled over and over. This saved the little doctor; it was like the double of a hare. In a second he was again on his legs, and before Philip could rise and again exert his speed, Poots had entered his door and bolted it within. Philip was, however, determined to repossess the important treasure; and as he panted, he cast his eyes around to see if any means offered for his forcing his entrance into the house. But as the habitation of the doctor was lonely, every precaution had been taken by him to render it secure against robbery; the windows below were well barricaded and secured, and those on the upper story were too high for any one to obtain admittance by them.

We must here observe, that although Mynheer Poots was,—from his known abilities, in good practice, his reputation as a hard-hearted, unfeeling miser was well established. No one was ever permitted to enter his threshold, nor, indeed, did any one feel inclined. He was as isolated from his fellow-creatures as was his tenement, and was only to be seen in the chamber of disease and death. What his establishment consisted of no one knew. When he first settled in the neighbourhood, an old decrepit woman occasionally answered the knocks given at the door by those who required the doctor's services; but she had been buried some time, and ever since all calls at the door had been answered by Mynheer Poots in person, if he were at home, and if not, there was no reply to the most importunate summons. It was then surmised that the old man lived entirely by himself, being too niggardly to pay for any assistance. This Philip also imagined; and as soon as he had recovered his breath, he began to devise some scheme by which he would be enabled not only to recover the stolen property, but also to wreak a dire revenge.

The door was strong and not to be forced by any means which presented themselves to the eye of Vanderdecken. For a few minutes he paused to consider, and as he reflected, so did his anger cool down, and he decided that it would be sufficient to recover his relic without having recourse to violence. So he called out in a loud voice—

"Mynheer Poots, I know that you can hear me. Give me back what you have taken, and I will do you no hurt; but if you will not, you must take the consequence, for your life shall pay the forfeit before I leave this spot."

This speech was indeed very plainly heard by Mynheer Poots; but the little miser had recovered from his fright, and, thinking himself secure, could not make up his mind to surrender the relic without a struggle; so the doctor answered not, hoping that the patience of Philip would be exhausted, and that by some arrangement, such as the sacrifice of a few guilders, no small matter to one so needy as Philip, he would be able to secure what he was satisfied would sell at a high price.

Vanderdecken, finding that no answer was returned, indulged in strong invective, and then decided upon measures certainly in themselves by no means undecided.

There was part of a small stack of dry fodder standing not far from the house, and under the wall a pile of wood for firing. With these Vanderdecken resolved upon setting fire to the house, and thus, if he did not gain his relic, he would at least obtain ample revenge, he brought several armfuls of fodder and laid them at the door of the house, and upon that he piled the faggots and logs of wood, until the door was quite concealed by them. He then procured a light from the steel, flint, and tinder which every Dutchman carries in his pocket, and very soon he had fanned the pile into a flame. The smoke ascended in columns up to the rafters of the roof, while the fire raged below. The door was ignited, and was adding to the fury of the flames, and Philip shouted with joy at the success of his attempt.

"Now, miserable despoiler of the dead—now, wretched thief, now you shall feel my vengeance," cried Philip, with a loud voice. "If you remain within, you perish in the flames; if you attempt to come out, you shall die by my hands. Do you hear, Mynheer Poots—do you hear?"

Hardly had Philip concluded this address, when the window of the upper floor furthest from the burning door was thrown open.

"Ay,—you come now to beg and to entreat;—but no—no," cried Philip—who stopped as he beheld at the window what seemed to be an apparition, for instead of the wretched little miser, he beheld one of the loveliest forms Nature ever deigned to mould—an angelic creature, of about sixteen or seventeen, who appeared calm and resolute in the midst of the danger by which she was threatened. Her long black hair was braided and twined round her beautifully-formed head; her eyes were large, intensely dark, yet soft; her forehead high and white, her chin dimpled, her ruby lips arched and delicately fine, her nose small and straight. A lovelier face could not be well imagined; it reminded you of what the best of painters have sometimes, in their more fortunate moments, succeeded in embodying, when they would represent a beauteous saint. And as the flames wreathed and the smoke burst out in columns and swept past the window, so might she have reminded you in her calmness of demeanour of some martyr at the stake.

"What wouldst thou, violent young man? Why are the inmates of this house to suffer death by your means?" said the maiden, with composure.

For a few seconds Philip gazed, and could make no reply; then the thought seized him that in his vengeance, he was about to sacrifice so much loveliness. He forgot everything but her danger, and seizing one of the large poles which he had brought to feed the flame, he threw off and scattered in every direction the burning masses, until nothing was left which could hurt the building but the ignited door itself; and this, which as yet—for it was of thick oak plank—had not suffered very material injury, he soon reduced, by beating it, with clods of earth, to a smoking and harmless state. During these active measures on the part of Philip, the young maiden watched him in silence.

"All is safe now, young lady," said Philip. "God forgive me that I should have risked a life so precious. I thought but to wreak my vengeance upon Mynheer Poots."

"And what cause can Mynheer Poots have given for such dreadful vengeance?" replied the maiden, calmly.

"What cause, young lady? He came to my house—despoiled the dead—took from my mother's corpse a relic beyond price."

"Despoiled the dead!—he surely cannot—you must wrong him, young sir."

"No, no. It is the fact, lady,—and that relic—forgive me—but that relic I must have. You know not what depends upon it."

"Wait, young sir," replied the maiden; "I will soon return."

Philip waited several minutes, lost in thought and admiration: so fair a creature in the house of Mynheer Poots! Who could she be? While thus ruminating, he was accosted by the silver voice of the object of his reveries, who, leaning out of the window held in her hand the black ribbon to which was attached the article so dearly coveted.

"Here is your relic, sir," said the young female; "I regret much that my father should have done a deed which well might justify your anger: but here it is," continued she, dropping it down on the ground by Philip; "and now you may depart."

"Your father, maiden! can he be *your* father?" said Philip, forgetting to take up the relic which lay at his feet.

She would have retired from the window without reply, but Philip spoke a again—

"Stop, lady, stop one moment, until I beg your forgiveness for a wild, foolish act. I swear by this sacred relic," continued he, taking it from the ground and raising it to his lips, "that had I known that any unoffending person had been in this house, I would not have done the deed, and much do I rejoice that no harm hath happened. But there is still danger, lady; the door must be unbarred, and the jambs, which still are glowing, be extinguished, or the house may yet be burnt. Fear not for your father, maiden; for had he done me a thousand times more wrong, you will protect each hair upon his head. He knows me well enough to know I keep my word. Allow me to repair the injury I have occasioned, and then I will depart."

"No, no; don't trust him," said Mynheer Poots, from within the chamber.

"Yes, he may be trusted," replied the daughter; "and his services are much needed for what could a poor weak girl like me, and a still weaker father, do in this strait? Open the door, and let the house be made secure." The maiden then addressed Philip—"He shall open the door, sir, and I will thank you for your kind service. I trust entirely to your promise."

"I never yet was known to break my word, maiden," replied Philip; "but let him be quick, for the flames are bursting out again."

The door was opened by the trembling hands of Mynheer Poots, who then made a hasty retreat upstairs. The truth of what Philip had said was then apparent. Many were the buckets of water which he was obliged to fetch before the fire was quite subdued; but during his exertions neither the daughter nor the father made their appearance.

When all was safe, Philip closed the door, and again looked up at the window. The fair girl made her appearance, and Philip, with a low obeisance, assured her that there was then no danger.

"I thank you, sir," replied she—"I thank you much. Your conduct, although hasty at the first, has yet been most considerate."

"Assure your father, maiden, that all animosity on my part hath ceased, and that in a few days I will call and satisfy the demand he hath against me."

The window closed, and Philip, more excited but with feelings altogether different from those with which he had set out, looked at it for a minute, and then bent his steps to his own cottage.

Chapter Three

The discovery of the beautiful daughter of Mynheer Poots had made a strong impression upon Philip Vanderdecken, and now he had another excitement to combine with those which already overcharged his bosom. He arrived at his own house, went upstairs, and threw himself on the bed from which he had been roused by Mynheer Poots. At first, he recalled to his mind the scene we have just described, painted in his imagination the portrait of the fair girl, her eyes, her expression, her silver voice, and the words which she had uttered; but her pleasing image was soon chased away by the recollection that his mother's corpse lay in the adjoining chamber, and that his father's secret was hidden in the room below.

The funeral was to take place the next morning, and Philip, who, since his meeting with the daughter of Mynheer Poots, appeared even to himself not so anxious for immediate examination of the room, resolved that he would not open it until after the melancholy ceremony. With this resolution he fell asleep; and, exhausted with bodily and mental excitement, he did not wake until the next morning, when he was summoned by the priest to assist at the funeral rites. In an hour all was over; the crowd dispersed, and Philip, returning to the cottage, bolted the door that he might not be interrupted, and felt happy that he was alone.

There is a feeling in our nature which will arise when we again find ourselves in the tenement where death has been, and all traces of it have been removed. It is a feeling of satisfaction and relief at having rid ourselves of the memento of mortality, the silent evidence of the futility of our pursuits and anticipations. We know that we must one day die, but we always wish to forget it. The continual remembrance would be too great a check upon our mundane desires and wishes; and, although we are told that we ever should have futurity in our thoughts, we find that life is not to be enjoyed if we are not permitted occasional forgetfulness. For who would plan what rarely he is permitted to execute, if each moment of the day he thought of death? We either hope that we may live longer than others, or we forget that we may not.

If this buoyant feeling had not been planted in our nature, how little would the world have been improved even from the Deluge! Philip walked into the room where his mother had lain one short hour before, and unwittingly felt relief. Taking down the cabinet, he now recommenced his task; the back panel was soon removed, and a secret drawer discovered; he drew it out, and it contained what he presumed to be the object of his search, — a large key with a slight coat of rust upon it, which came off upon its being handled. Under the key was a paper, the writing on which was somewhat discoloured; it was in his mother's hand, and ran as follows: —

"It is now two nights since a horrible event took place which has induced me to close the lower chamber, and my brain is still bursting with terror. Should I not, during my lifetime, reveal what occurred, still this key will be required, as at my death the room will be opened. When I rushed from it I hastened upstairs, and remained that night with my child; the next morning I summoned up sufficient courage, to go down, turn the key and bring it up into my chamber. It is now closed till I close my eyes in death. No privation, no suffering, shall induce me to open it, although in the iron cupboard under the buffet farthest from the window, there is money sufficient for all my wants; that money will remain there for my child, to whom, if I do not impart the fatal secret, he must be satisfied that it is one which it were better should be concealed, — one so horrible as to induce me to take the steps which I now do. The keys of the cupboards and buffets were, I think, lying on the table, or in my work-box, when I quitted the room. There is a letter on the table — at least I think so. It is sealed. Let not the seal be broken but by my son, and not by him unless he knows the secret. Let it be burnt by the priest, — for it is cursed; — and even should my son know all that I do, oh, let him pause, — let him reflect well before he breaks the seal, — for 'twere better he should know NO MORE!"

"Not know more!" thought Philip, as his eyes were still fixed upon the paper. "Yes, but I must and will know more, so forgive me dearest mother, if I waste no time in reflection. It would be but time thrown away, when one is resolved as I am."

Philip pressed his lips to his mother's signature, folded up the paper and put it into his pocket; then taking the key, he proceeded downstairs.

It was about noon when Philip descended to open the chamber; the sun shone bright, the sky was clear, and all without was cheerful and joyous. The front door of the cottage being closed, there was not much light in the passage when Philip put the key into the lock of the long-closed door, and with some difficulty turned it round. To say that when he pushed open the door he felt no alarm would not be correct; he did feel alarm, and his heart palpitated; but he felt more than was requisite of determination to conquer that alarm, and to conquer more, should more be created by what he should behold. He opened the door, but did not immediately enter the room: he paused where he stood, for he felt as if he was about to intrude into the retreat of a disembodied spirit, and that that spirit might reappear. He waited a minute, for the effort of opening the door had taken away his breath, and, as he recovered himself, he looked within.

He could but imperfectly distinguish the objects in the chamber, but through the joints of the shutters there were three brilliant beams of sunshine forcing their way across the room, which at first induced him to recoil as if from something supernatural; but a little reflection reassured him. After about a minute's pause, Philip went into the kitchen, lighted a candle, and, sighing deeply two or three times as if to relieve his heart, he summoned his resolution, and walked towards the fatal room. He first stopped at the threshold, and, by the light of the candle, took a hasty survey. All was still: and the table on which the letter had been left, being behind the door, was concealed by its being opened. It must be done, thought Philip: and why not at once? continued he, resuming his courage; and, with a firm step, he walked into the room and went to unfasten the shutters. If his hand trembled a little when he called to mind how supernaturally they had last been opened, it is not surprising. We are but mortal, and we shrink from contact with aught beyond this life. When the fastenings were removed and the shutters unfolded, a stream of light poured into the room so vivid as to dazzle his eyesight; strange to say, this very light of a brilliant day overthrew the resolution of Philip more than the previous gloom and darkness had done; and with the candle in his hand, he retreated hastily into the kitchen to re-summon his courage, and there he remained for some minutes with his face covered, and in deep thought.

It is singular that his reveries at last ended by reverting to the fair daughter of Mynheer Poots, and her first appearance at the window; and he felt as if the flood of light which had just driven him from the one, was not more impressive and startling than her enchanting form at the other. His mind dwelling upon this beauteous vision appeared to restore Philip's confidence; he now rose and boldly walked into the room. We shall not describe the objects it contained as they chanced to meet the eyes of Philip, but attempt a more lucid arrangement.

The room was about twelve or fourteen feet square, with but one window; opposite to the door stood the chimney and fireplace, with a high buffet of dark wood on each side. The floor of the room was not dirty, although about its upper parts spiders had run their cobwebs in every direction. In the centre of the ceiling hung a quicksilver globe, a common ornament in those days, but the major part of it had lost its brilliancy, the spiders' webs enclosing it like a shroud. Over the chimney-piece were hung two or three drawings, framed and glazed, but a dusty mildew was spotted over the glass, so that little of them could be distinguished. In the centre of the mantelpiece was an image of the Virgin Mary, of pure silver, in a shrine of the same metal, but it was tarnished to the colour of bronze or iron; some Indian figures stood on each side of it. The glass doors of the buffets on each side of the chimney-piece were also so dimmed that little of what was within could be distinguished: the light and heat which had been poured into the room, even for so short a time, had already gathered up the damp of many years, and it lay as a mist, and mingled with the dust upon the panes of glass: still here and there a glittering of silver vessels could be discerned, for the glass doors had protected them from turning black, although much dimmed in lustre.

On the wall facing the window were other prints, in frames equally veiled in damp and cobwebs and also two bird-cages. The bird-cages Philip approached, and looked into them. The occupants, of course, had long been dead; but at the bottom of the cages was a small heap of yellow feathers, through which the little white bones of the skeletons were to be seen, proving that they had been brought from the Canary Isles; and, at that period, such birds were highly valued. Philip appeared to wish to examine everything before he sought that which he most dreaded, yet most wished, to find. There were several chairs round the room: on one of them was some linen; he took it up. It was some that must have belonged to him when he was yet a child. At last, Philip turned his eyes to the wall not yet examined (that opposite the chimney piece), through which the door was pierced, and behind the door as it lay open, he was to find the table, the couch, the work-box, and the FATAL LETTER. As he turned round, his pulse, which had gradually recovered its regular motion, beat more quickly, but he made the effort, and it was over. At first he examined the walls, against which were hung swords and pistols of various sorts but chiefly Asiatic bows and arrows, and other implements of destruction. Philip's eyes gradually descended upon the table and little couch behind it, where his mother stated herself to have been seated when his father made his awful visit. The work-box and all its implements were on the table, just as she had left them. The keys she mentioned were also lying there, but Philip looked, and looked again; there was no letter, he now advanced nearer, examined closely — there was none that he could perceive, either on the couch or on the table — or on the floor. He lifted up the work-box to ascertain if it was beneath — but no. He examined among its contents, but no letter was there. He turned over the pillows of the couch, but still there was no letter to be found. And Philip felt as if there had been a heavy load removed from his panting chest. "Surely, then," thought he, as he leant against the wall, "this must have been the vision of a heated imagination. My poor mother must have fallen asleep, and dreamt this horrid tale. I thought it was impossible, at least I hoped so. It must have been as I suppose; the dream was too powerful, too like a fearful reality,—partially unseated my poor mother's reason." Philip reflected again, and was then satisfied that his suppositions were correct.

"Yes, it must have been so, poor dear mother! how much thou hast suffered; but thou art now rewarded, and with thy God."

After a few minutes (during which he surveyed the room again and again with more coolness, and perhaps some indifference, now that he regarded the supernatural history as not true), Philip took out of his pocket the written paper found with the key, and read it over,—"The iron cupboard under the buffet farthest from the window."

"'Tis well." He took the bunch of keys from off the table, and soon fitted one to the outside wooden doors which concealed the iron safe. A second key on the bunch opened the iron doors; and Philip found himself in possession of a considerable sum of money, amounting, as near as he could reckon, to ten thousand guilders, in little yellow sacks.

"My poor mother!" thought he; "and has a mere dream scared thee to penury and want, with all this wealth in thy possession?" Philip replaced the sacks, and locked up the cupboards, after having taken out of one, already half emptied, a few pieces for his immediate wants. His attention was next directed to the buffets above, which with one of the keys, he opened; he found that they contained china, and silver flagons, and cups of considerable value. The locks were again turned, and the bunch of keys thrown upon the table.

The sudden possession of so much wealth added to the conviction, to which Philip had now arrived that there had been no supernatural appearance, as supposed, by his mother, naturally revived and composed his spirits; and he felt a reaction which amounted almost to hilarity. Seating himself on the couch, he was soon in a reverie, and, as before reverted to the lovely daughter of Mynheer Poots indulging in various castle-buildings, all ending, as usual, when we choose for ourselves, in competence and felicity. In this pleasing occupation he remained for more than two hours, when his thoughts again reverted to his poor mother and her fearful death.

"Dearest, kindest mother!" apostrophised Philip aloud, as he rose from his leaning position, "here thou wert, tired with watching over my infant slumbers, thinking of my absent father and his dangers, working up thy mind and anticipating evil, till thy fevered sleep conjured up this apparition. Yes, it must have been so; for see here, lying on the floor, is the embroidery, as it fell from thy unconscious hands, and with that labour ceased thy happiness in this life. Dear, dear mother!" continued he; a tear rolling down his cheek as he stooped to pick up the piece of muslin, "how much hast thou suffered when—God of Heaven!" exclaimed Philip, as he lifted up the embroidery, starting back with violence, and overturning the table, "God of Heaven, and of Judgment, there is—there *is*," and Philip clasped his hands, and bowed his head in awe and anguish, as in a changed and fearful tone he muttered forth—"the LETTER!"

It was but too true,—underneath the embroidery on the floor had lain the fatal letter of Vanderdecken. Had Philip seen it on the table when he first went into the room, and was prepared to find it, he would have taken it up with some degree of composure: but to find it now, when he had persuaded himself that it was all an illusion on the part of his mother; when he had made up his mind that there had been no supernatural agency; after he had been indulging in visions of future bliss and repose, was a shock that transfixed him where he stood and for some time he remained in his attitude of surprise and terror. Down at once fell the airy fabric of happiness which he had built up during the last two hours; and as he gradually recovered from his alarm, his heart filled with melancholy forebodings. At last he dashed forward, seized the letter, and burst out of the fatal room.

"I cannot, dare not, read it here," exclaimed he: "no, no, it must be under the vault of high and offended Heaven, that the message must be received." Philip took his hat, and went out of the house; in calm despair he locked the door, took out the key, and walked he knew not whither.

Chapter Four

If the reader can imagine the feelings of a man who, sentenced to death, and having resigned himself to his fate, finds himself unexpectedly reprieved; who, having recomposed his mind after the agitation arising from a renewal of those hopes and expectations which he had abandoned, once more dwells upon future prospects, and indulges in pleasing anticipations: we say, that if the reader can imagine this, and then what would be that man's feelings when he finds that the reprieve is revoked, and that he is to suffer, he may then form some idea of the state of Philip's mind when he quitted the cottage.

Long did he walk, careless in which direction, with the letter in his clenched hand, and his teeth firmly set. Gradually he became more composed: and out of breath with the rapidity of his motion, he sat down upon a bank, and there he long remained, with his eyes riveted upon the dreaded paper, which he held with both his hands upon his knees.

Mechanically he turned the letter over; the seal was black. Philip sighed:— "I cannot read it now," thought he, and he rose and continued his devious way.

For another half-hour did Philip keep in motion, and the sun was not many degrees above the horizon. Philip stopped and looked at it till his vision failed. "I could imagine that it was the eye of God," thought Philip, "and perhaps it may be. Why, then, merciful Creator, am I thus selected from so many millions to fulfil so dire a task?"

Philip looked about him for some spot where he might be concealed from observation—where he might break the seal, and read this mission from a world of spirits. A small copse of brushwood, in advance of a grove of trees, was not far from where he stood. He walked to it, and sat down, so as to be concealed from any passers by. Philip once more looked at the descending orb of day, and by degrees he became composed.

"It is thy will," exclaimed he; "it is my fate, and both must be accomplished."

Philip put his hand to the seal,—his blood thrilled when he called to mind that it had been delivered by no mortal hand, and that it contained the secret of one in judgment. He remembered that that one was his father; and that it was only in the letter that there was hope,—hope for his poor father, whose memory he had been taught to love, and who appealed for help.

"Coward that I am, to have lost so many hours!" exclaimed Philip; "yon sun appears as if waiting on the hill, to give me light to read."

Philip mused a short time; he was once more the daring Vanderdecken. Calmly he broke the seal, which bore the initials of his father's name, and read as follows:—

"To *Catherine* .

"One of those pitying spirits whose eyes rain tears for mortal crimes has been permitted to inform me by what means alone my dreadful doom may be averted.

"Could I but receive on the deck of my own ship the holy relic upon which I swore the fatal oath, kiss it in all humility, and shed one tear of deep contrition on the sacred wood, I then might rest in peace.

"How this may be effected, or by whom so fatal a task will be undertaken, I know not. O Catherine, we have a son— but, no, no, let him not hear of me. Pray for me, and now, farewell.

" *I. Vanderdecken* ."

"Then it is true, most horribly true," thought Philip; "and my father is even now *In Living Judgment* . And he points to me,—to whom else should he? Am I not his son, and is it not my duty?"

"Yes, father," exclaimed Philip aloud, falling on his knees, "you have not written these lines in vain. Let me peruse them once more."

Philip raised up his hand; but although it appeared to him that he had still hold of the letter, it was not there—he grasped nothing. He looked on the grass to see if it had fallen—but no, there was no letter, it had disappeared. Was it a vision?—no, no, he had read every word. "Then it must be to me, and me alone, that the mission was intended. I accept the sign.

"Hear me, dear father,—if thou art so permitted,—and deign to hear me, gracious Heaven—hear the son who, by this sacred relic, swears that he will avert your doom, or perish. To that will he devote his days; and having done his duty, he will die in hope and peace. Heaven, that recorded my rash father's oath, now register his son's upon the same sacred cross, and may perjury on my part be visited with punishment more dire than his! Receive it, Heaven, as at the last I trust that in thy mercy thou wilt receive the father and the son: and if too bold, O pardon my presumption."

Philip threw himself forward on his face, with his lips to the sacred symbol. The sun went down, and the twilight gradually disappeared; night had, for some time, shrouded all in darkness, and Philip yet remained in alternate prayer and meditation!

But he was disturbed by the voices of some men, who sat down upon the turf but a few yards from where he was concealed. The conversation he little heeded; but it had roused him and his first feeling was to return to the cottage, that he might reflect over his plans; but although the men spoke in a low tone, his attention was soon arrested by the subject of their conversation, when he heard the name mentioned of Mynheer Poots. He listened attentively, and discovered that they were four disbanded soldiers, who intended that night to attack the house of the little doctor, who had, they knew, much money in his possession.

"What I have proposed is the best," said one of them; "he has no one with him but his daughter."

"I value her more than his money," replied another; "so, recollect before we go, it is perfectly understood that she is to be my property."

"Yes, if you choose to purchase her, there's no objection," replied a third.

"Agreed; how much will you in conscience ask for a paling girl?"

"I say five hundred guilders," replied another.

"Well, be it so, but on this condition, that if my share of the booty does not amount to so much, I am to have her for my share, whatever it may be."

"That's very fair," replied the other: "but I'm much mistaken if we don't turn more than two thousand guilders out of the old man's chest."

"What do you two say — is it agreed — shall Baetens have her?"

"O yes," replied the others.

"Well, then," replied the one who had stipulated for Mynheer Poots's daughter, "now I am with you heart and soul. I loved that girl, and tried to get her, — I positively offered to marry her, but the old hunks refused me, an ensign, an officer; but now I'll have revenge. We must not spare him."

"No, no," replied the others.

"Shall we go now, or wait till it is later? In an hour or more the moon will be up,—we may be seen."

"Who is to see us? unless, indeed, some one is sent for him. The later the better, I say."

"How long will it take us to get there? Not half an hour if we walk. Suppose we start in half an hour hence, we shall just have the moon to count the guilders by."

"That's all right. In the meantime, I'll put a new flint in my lock, and have my carbine loaded. I can work in the dark."

"You are used to it, Jan."

"Yes, I am,—and I intend this ball to go through the old rascal's head."

"Well, I'd rather you should kill him than I," replied one of the others, "for he saved my life at Middleburgh, when every one made sure I'd die."

Philip did not wait to hear any more; he crawled behind the bushes until he gained the grove of trees, and passing through them, made a détour, so as not to be seen by these miscreants. That they were disbanded soldiers, many of whom were infesting the country, he knew well. All his thoughts were now to save the old doctor and his daughter from the danger which threatened them; and for a time he forgot his father, and the exciting revelations of the day. Although Philip had not been aware in what direction he had walked when he set off from the cottage, he knew the country well; and now that it was necessary to act, he remembered the direction in which he should find the lonely house of Mynheer Poots: with the utmost speed he made his way for it, and in less than twenty minutes he arrived there out of breath.

As usual, all was silent, and the door fastened. Philip knocked, but there was no reply. Again and again he knocked, and became impatient. Mynheer Poots must have been summoned, and was not in the house; Philip therefore called out so as to be heard within, "Maiden, if your father is out, as I presume he must be, listen to what I have to say—I am Philip Vanderdecken. But now I overheard four wretches, who have planned to murder your father, and rob him of his gold. In one hour, or less, they will be here, and I have hastened to warn and to protect you, if I may. I swear upon the relic that you delivered to me this morning, that what I state is true."

Philip waited a short time, but received no answer.

"Maiden," resumed he, "answer me, if you value that which is more dear to you than even your father's gold to him. Open the casement above, and listen to what I have to say. In so doing there is no risk; and even if it were not dark, already have I seen you."

A short time after this second address, the casement of the upper window was unbarred, and the slight form of the fair daughter of Mynheer Poots was to be distinguished by Philip through the gloom.

"What wouldst thou young sir, at this unseemly hour? and what is it thou wouldst impart, but imperfectly heard by me, when thou spokest this minute at the door?"

Philip then entered into a detail of all that he had overheard, and concluded by begging her to admit him, that he might defend her.

"Think, fair maiden, of what I have told you. You have been sold to one of those reprobates, whose name I think they mentioned was Baetens. The gold, I know, you value not; but think of thine own dear self—suffer me to enter the house, and think not for one moment that my story is feigned. I swear to thee, by the soul of my poor dear mother, now, I trust, in heaven, that every word is true."

"Baetens, did you say, sir?"

"If I mistook them not, such was the name; he said he loved you once."

"That name I have in memory—I know not what to do, or what to say: my father has been summoned to a birth, and may be yet away for many hours. Yet how can I ope the door to you—at night—he not at home—I alone? I ought not—cannot—yet do I believe you. You surely never could be so base as to invent this tale."

"No—upon my hopes of future bliss I could not, maiden! you must not trifle with your life and honour, but let me in."

"And if I did, what could you do against such numbers?"

"They are four to one—would soon overpower you, and one more life would be lost."

"Not if you have arms; and I think your father would not be left without them. I fear them not—you know that I am resolute."

"I do indeed—and now you'd risk your life for those you did assail. I thank you, thank you kindly, sir—but dare not ope the door."

"Then, maiden, if you'll not admit me, here will I now remain; without arms, and but ill able to contend with four armed villains; but still, here will

I remain and prove my truth to one I will protect 'gainst any odds—yes, even here!"

"Then shall I be thy murderer!—but that must not be. Oh! sir—swear, swear by all that's holy, and by all that's pure, that—you do not deceive me."

"I swear by thyself, maiden, than all to me more sacred!"

The casement closed, and in a short time a light appeared above. In a minute or two more the door was opened to Philip by the fair daughter of Mynheer Poots. She stood with the candle in her right hand, the colour in her cheeks varying—now flushing red, and again deadly pale. Her left hand was down by her side, and in it she held a pistol half concealed. Philip perceived this precaution on her part, but took no notice of it; he wished to re-assure her.

"Maiden!" said he, not entering, "if you still have doubts—if you think you have been ill advised in giving me admission—there is yet time to close the door against me; but for your own sake I entreat you not. Before the moon is up, the robbers will be here. With my life I will protect you, if you will but trust me. Who indeed could injure one like you?"

She was indeed (as she stood irresolute and perplexed from the peculiarity of her situation, yet not wanting in courage when it was to be called forth) an object well worthy of gaze and admiration. Her features thrown into broad light and shade by the candle which at times was half extinguished by the wind—her symmetry of form and the gracefulness and singularity of her attire—were matter of astonishment to Philip. Her head was without covering, and her long hair fell in plaits behind her shoulders; her stature was rather under the middle size, but her form perfect; her dress was simple but becoming, and very different from that usually worn by the young women of the district. Not only her features but her dress would at once have indicated to a traveller that she was of Arab blood, as was the fact.

She looked in Philip's face as he spoke—earnestly, as if she would have penetrated into his inmost thoughts; but there was a frankness and honesty in his bearing, and a sincerity in his manly countenance, which re-assured her. After a moment's hesitation she replied—

"Come in, sir; I feel that I can trust you."

Philip entered. The door was then closed and made secure.

"We have no time to lose, maiden," said Philip: "but tell me your name, that I may address you as I ought."

"My name is Amine," replied she, retreating a little.

"I thank you for that little confidence; but I must not dally. What arms have you in the house, and have you ammunition?"

"Both. I wish that my father would come home."

"And so do I," replied Philip, "devoutedly wish he would, before these murderers come; but not, I trust, while the attack is making, for there's a carbine loaded expressly for his head, and if they make him prisoner, they will not spare his life, unless his gold and your person are given in ransom. But the arms, maiden—where are they?"

"Follow me," replied Amine, leading Philip to an inner room on the upper floor. It was the sanctum of her father, and was surrounded with shelves filled with bottles and boxes of drugs. In one corner was an iron chest, and over the mantelpiece were a brace of carbines and three pistols.

"They are all loaded," observed Amine, pointing to them, and laying on the table the one which she had held in her hand.

Philip took down the arms and examined all the primings. He then took up from the table the pistol which Amine had laid there, and threw open the pan. It was equally well prepared. Philip closed the pan, and with a smile observed:—

"So this was meant for me, Amine?"

"No—not for you—but for a traitor, had one gained admittance."

"Now, maiden," observed Philip, "I shall station myself at the casement which you opened, but without a light in the room. You may remain here, and can turn the key for your security."

"You little know me," replied Amine. "In that way at least I am not fearful: I must remain near you and reload the arms—a task in which I am well practised."

"No, no," replied Philip, "you might be hurt."

"I may. But think you I will remain here idly, when I can assist one who risks his life for me? I know my duty, sir, and I shall perform it."

"You must not risk your life, Amine," replied Philip; "my aim will not be steady if I know that you're in danger. But I must take the arms into the other chamber, for the time is come."

Philip, assisted by Amine, carried the carbines and pistols into the adjoining chamber; and Amine then left Philip, carrying with her the light.

Philip, as soon as he was alone, opened the casement and looked out—there was no one to be seen; he listened, but all was silent. The moon was just rising above the distant hill, but her light was dimmed by fleecy clouds, and Philip watched for a few minutes; at length he heard a whispering below. He looked out, and could distinguish through the dark the four expected assailants, standing close to the door of the house. He walked away softly from the window, and went into the next room to Amine, whom he found busy preparing the ammunition.

"Amine, they are at the door, in consultation. You can see them now without risk. I thank them, for they will convince you that I have told the truth."

Amine, without reply, went into the front room and looked out of the window. She returned, and laying her hand upon Philip's arm, she said—"Grant me your pardon for my doubts. I fear nothing now but that my father may return too soon, and they seize him."

Philip left the room again, to make his reconnoissance. The robbers did not appear to have made up their mind—the strength of the door defied their utmost efforts, so they attempted stratagem. They knocked, and as there was no reply, they continued to knock louder and louder: not meeting with success, they held another consultation, and the muzzle of a carbine was then put to the keyhole, and the piece discharged. The lock of the door was blown off, but the iron bars which crossed the door within, above and below, still held it fast.

Although Philip would have been justified in firing upon the robbers when he first perceived them in consultation at the door, still there is that feeling in a generous mind which prevents the taking away of life, except from stern necessity; and this feeling made him withhold his fire until hostilities had actually commenced. He now levelled one of the carbines at the head of the robber nearest to the door, who was busy examining the effect which the discharge of the piece had made, and what further obstacles intervened. The aim was true, and the man fell dead, while the others started back with surprise at the unexpected retaliation. But in a second or two a pistol was discharged at Philip, who still remained leaning out of the casement, fortunately without effect; and the next moment he felt himself drawn away, so as to be protected from their fire. It was Amine, who, unknown to Philip, had been standing by his side.

"You must not expose yourself, Philip," said she, in a low tone.

"She called me Philip," thought he, but made no reply.

"They will be watching for you at the casement now," said Amine. "Take the other carbine, and go below in the passage. If the lock of the door is blown off, they may put their arms in, perhaps, and remove the bars. I do not think they can, but I'm not sure; at all events, it is there you should now be, as there they will not expect you."

"You are right," replied Philip, going down.

"But you must not fire more than once there; if another fall, there will be but two to deal with, and they cannot watch the casement and force admittance too. Go—I will reload the carbine."

Philip descended softly and without a light. He went up to the door, and perceived that one of the miscreants, with his arm through the hole where the lock was blown off, was working at the upper iron bar, which he could just reach. He presented his carbine, and was about to fire the whole charge into the body of the man under his raised arm, when there was a report of fire-arms from the robbers outside.

"Amine has exposed herself," thought Philip, "and may be hurt."

The desire of vengeance prompted him first to fire his piece through the man's body, and then he flew up the stairs to ascertain the state of Amine. She was not at the casement; he darted into the inner room, and found her deliberately loading the carbine.

"My God! how you frightened me, Amine. I thought by their firing that you had shown yourself at the window."

"Indeed I did not; but I thought that when you fired through the door they might return your fire, and you be hurt; so I went to the side of the casement and pushed out on a stick some of my father's clothes, and they who were watching for you fired immediately."

"Indeed, Amine! who could have expected such courage and such coolness in one so young and beautiful?" exclaimed Philip, with surprise.

"Are none but ill-favoured people brave, then?" replied Amine, smiling.

"I did not mean that, Amine—but I am losing time. I must to the door again. Give me that carbine, and reload this."

Philip crept down stairs that he might reconnoitre, but before he had gained the door he heard at a distance the voice of Mynheer Poots. Amine, who also heard it, was in a moment at his side with a loaded pistol in each hand.

"Fear not, Amine," said Philip, as he unbarred the door, "there are but two, and your father shall be saved."

The door was opened, and Philip, seizing his carbine, rushed out; he found Mynheer Poots on the ground between the two men, one of whom had raised his knife to plunge it into his body, when the ball of the carbine whizzed through his head. The last of the robbers closed with Philip, and a desperate struggle ensued—it was however, soon decided by Amine stepping forward and firing one of the pistols through the robber's body.

We must here inform our readers that Mynheer Poots, when coming home, had heard the report of fire-arms in the direction of his own house. The recollection of his daughter and of his money—for to do him justice he did love her best—had lent him wings; he forgot that he was a feeble old man and without arms; all he thought of was to gain his habitation. On he came, reckless, frantic, and shouting, and rushed into the arms of the two robbers, who seized and would have despatched him, had not Philip so opportunely come to his assistance.

As soon as the last robber fell, Philip disengaged himself and went to the assistance of Mynheer Poots, whom he raised up in his arms and carried into the house as if he were an infant. The old man was still in a state of delirium from fear and previous excitement.

In a few minutes, Mynheer Poots was more coherent.

"My daughter!" exclaimed he—"my daughter! where is she?"

"She is here father, and safe," replied Amine.

"Ah! my child is safe," said he, opening his eyes and staring. "Yes, it is even so—and my money—my money—where is my money?" continued he, starting up.

"Quite safe, father."

"Quite safe—you say quite safe—are you sure of it?—let me see."

"There it is, father, as you may perceive, quite safe—thanks to one whom you have not treated so well."

"Who—what do you mean?—Ah, yes, I see him now—'tis Philip Vanderdecken—he owes me three guilders and a half, and there is a phial—did he save you—and my money, child?"

"He did, indeed at the risk of his life."

"Well, well, I will forgive him the whole debt—yes, the whole of it; but—the phial is of no use to him—he must return that. Give me some water."

It was some time before the old man could regain his perfect reason. Philip left him with his daughter, and, taking a brace of loaded pistols, went out to ascertain the fate of the four assailants. The moon, having climbed above the bank of clouds which had obscured her, was now high in the heavens, shining bright, and he could distinguish clearly. The two men lying across the threshold of the door were quite dead. The others, who had seized upon Mynheer Poots, were still alive, but one was expiring and the other bled fast. Philip put a few questions to the latter, but he either would not or could not make any reply; he removed their weapons and returned to the house, where he found the old man attended by his daughter, in a state of comparative composure.

"I thank you, Philip Vanderdecken—I thank you much. You have saved my dear child, and my money—that is little, very little—for I am poor. May you live long and happily!"

Philip mused; the letter and his vow were, for the first time since he fell in with the robbers, recalled to his recollection, and a shade passed over his countenance.

"Long and happily—no, no," muttered he, with an involuntary shake of the head.

"And I must thank you," said Amine, looking inquiringly in Philip's face. "O, how much have I to thank you for!—and indeed I am grateful."

"Yes, yes, she is very grateful," interrupted the old man; "but we are poor—very poor. I talked about my money because I have so little, and I cannot afford to lose it; but you shall not pay me the three guilders and a half—I am content to lose that, Mr Philip."

"Why should you lose even that, Mynheer Poots?—I promised to pay you, and will keep my word. I have plenty of money—thousands of guilders, and know not what to do with them."

"You—you—thousands of guilders!" exclaimed Poots. "Pooh, nonsense, that won't do."

"I repeat to you, Amine," said Philip, "that I have thousands of guilders: you know I would not tell you a falsehood."

"I believed you when you said so to my father," replied Amine.

"Then, perhaps, as you have so much, and I am so very poor, Mr Vanderdecken—"

But Amine put her hand upon her father's lips, and the sentence was not finished.

"Father," said Amine, "it is time that we retire. You must leave us for to-night, Philip."

"I will not," replied Philip; "nor, you may depend upon it, will I sleep. You may both to bed in safety. It is indeed time that you retire—good night, Mynheer Poots. I will but ask a lamp, and then I leave you—Amine, good night."

"Good night," said Amine, extending her hand, "and many, many thanks."

"Thousands of guilders!" muttered the old man, as Philip left the room and went below.

Chapter Five

Philip Vanderdecken sat down at the porch of the door; he swept his hair from his forehead, which he exposed to the fanning of the breeze; for the continued excitement of the last three days had left a fever on his brain which made him restless and confused. He longed for repose, but he knew that for him there was no rest. He had his forebodings—he perceived in the vista of futurity a long-continued chain of danger and disaster, even to death; yet he beheld it without emotion and without dread. He felt as if it were only three days that he had begun to exist; he was melancholy, but not unhappy. His thoughts were constantly recurring to the fatal letter—its strange supernatural disappearance seemed pointedly to establish its supernatural origin, and that the mission had been intended for him alone; and the relic in his possession more fully substantiated the fact.

"It is my fate, my duty," thought Philip. Having satisfactorily made up his mind to these conclusions, his thoughts reverted to the beauty, the courage, and presence of mind shown by Amine. "And," thought he, as he watched the moon soaring high in the heavens, "is this fair creature's destiny to be interwoven with mine? The events of the last three days would almost warrant the supposition. Heaven only knows, and Heaven's will be done. I have vowed, and my vow is registered, that I will devote my life to the release of my unfortunate father—but does that prevent my loving Amine?—No, no; the sailor on the Indian seas must pass months and months on shore before he can return to his duty. My search must be on the broad ocean, but how often may I return? and why am I to be debarred the solace of a smiling hearth?—and yet—do I right in winning the affections of one who, if she loves, would, I am convinced, love so dearly, fondly truly—ought I to persuade her to mate herself with one whose life will be so precarious?—but is not every sailor's life precarious, daring the angry waves, with but an inch of plank 'tween him and death? Besides, I am chosen to fulfil a task—and if so, what can hurt me, till in Heaven's own time it is accomplished? but then how soon, and how is it to end?—in death! I wish my blood were cooler, that I might reason better."

Such were the meditations of Philip Vanderdecken, and long did he revolve such chances in his mind. At last the day dawned, and as he perceived the blush upon the horizon, less careful of his watch he slumbered where he sat. A slight pressure on the shoulder made him start up and draw the pistol from his bosom. He turned round and beheld Amine.

"And that pistol was intended for me," said Amine, smiling, repeating Philip's words of the night before.

"For you, Amine?—yes, to defend you, if 'twere necessary, once more."

"I know it would—how kind of you to watch this tedious night after so much exertion and fatigue! but it is now broad day."

"Until I saw the dawn, Amine, I kept a faithful watch."

"But now retire and take some rest. My father is risen—you can lie down on his bed."

"I thank you, but I feel no wish for sleep. There is much to do. We must to the burgomaster and state the facts, and these bodies must remain where they are until the whole is known. Will your father go, Amine, or shall I?"

"My father surely is the more proper person, as the proprietor of the house. You must remain; and if you will not sleep, you must take some refreshment. I will go in and tell my father; he has already taken his morning's meal."

Amine went in, and soon returned with her father, who had consented to go to the burgomaster. He saluted Philip kindly as he came out; shuddered as he passed on one side to avoid stepping over the dead bodies, and went off at a quick pace to the adjacent town, where the burgomaster resided.

Amine desired Philip to follow her, and they went into her father's room, where, to his surprise, he found some coffee ready for him—at that time a rarity, and one which Philip did not expect to find in the house of the penurious Mynheer Poots; but it was a luxury which, from his former life, the old man could not dispense with.

Philip, who had not tasted food for nearly twenty-four hours, was not sorry to avail himself of what was placed before him. Amine sat down opposite to him, and was silent during his repast.

"Amine," said Philip at last, "I have had plenty of time for reflection during this night, as I watched at the door. May I speak freely?"

"Why not?" replied Amine. "I feel assured that you will say nothing that you should not say, or should not meet a maiden's ear."

"You do me justice, Amine. My thoughts have been upon you and your father. You cannot stay in this lone habitation."

"I feel it is too lonely; that is for his safety—perhaps for mine—but you know my father—the very loneliness suits him—the price paid for rent is little, and he is careful of his money."

"The man who would be careful of his money should place it in security— here it is not secure. Now, hear me, Amine. I have a cottage surrounded, as you may have heard, by many others, which mutually protect each other. That cottage I am about to leave—perhaps for ever; for I intend to sail by the first ship to the Indian seas."

"The Indian seas! why so?—did you not last night talk of thousands of guilders?"

"I did, and they are there; but, Amine, I must go—it is my duty. Ask me no more, but listen to what I now propose. Your father must live in my cottage; he must take care of it for me in my absence; he will do me a favour by consenting, and you must persuade him. You will there be safe. He must also take care of my money for me. I want it not at present—I cannot take it with me."

"My father is not to be trusted with the money of other people."

"Why does your father hoard? He cannot take his money with him when he is called away. It must be all for you—and is not then my money safe?"

"Leave it then in my charge, and it will be safe; but why need you go and risk your life upon the water, when you have such ample means?"

"Amine, ask not that question. It is my duty as a son, and more I cannot tell, at least at present."

"If it is your duty I ask no more. It was not womanish curiosity—no, no—it was a better feeling, I assure you, which prompted me to put the question."

"And what was that better feeling, Amine?"

"I hardly know—many good feelings perhaps mixed up together— gratitude, esteem, respect, confidence, good-will. Are not these sufficient?"

"Yes, indeed, Amine, and much to gain upon so short an acquaintance; but still I feel them all, and more, for you. If, then, you feel so much for me, do oblige me by persuading your father to leave this lonely house this day, and take up his abode in mine."

"And where do you intend to go yourself?"

"If your father will not admit me as a boarder for the short time I remain here, I will seek some shelter elsewhere; but if he will, I will indemnify him well—that is, if you raise no objection to my being for a few days in the house?"

"Why should I? Our habitation is no longer safe, and you offer us a shelter. It were, indeed, unjust and most ungrateful to turn you out from beneath your own roof."

"Then persuade him, Amine. I will accept of nothing, but take it as a favour; for I should depart in sorrow if I saw you not in safety.—Will you promise me?"

"I do promise to use my best endeavours—nay, I may as well say at once it shall be so; for I know my influence. Here is my hand upon it. Will that content you?"

Philip took the small hand extended towards him. His feelings overcame his discretion; he raised it to his lips. He looked up to see if Amine was displeased, and found her dark eye fixed upon him, as once before when she admitted him, as if she would see his thoughts—but the hand was not withdrawn.

"Indeed, Amine," said Philip, kissing her hand once more, "you may confide in me."

"I hope—I think—nay, I am sure I may," at last replied she.

Philip released her hand. Amine returned to her seat and for some time remained silent, and in a pensive attitude. Philip also had his own thoughts, and did not open his lips. At last Amine spoke.

"I think I have heard my father say that your mother was very poor—a little deranged; and that there was a chamber in the house which had been shut up for years."

"It was shut up till yesterday."

"And there you found your money? Did your mother not know of the money?"

"She did, for she spoke of it on her death-bed."

"There must have been some potent reasons for not opening the chamber."

"There were."

"What were they, Philip?" said Amine, in a soft and low tone of voice.

"I must not tell, at least I ought not. This must satisfy you—'twas the fear of an apparition."

"What apparition?"

"She said that my father had appeared to her."

"And did he, think you, Philip?"

"I have no doubt that he did. But I can answer no more questions, Amine. The chamber is open now, and there is no fear of his re-appearance."

"I fear not that," replied Amine, musing. "But," continued she, "is not this connected with your resolution of going to sea?"

"So far will I answer you, that it has decided me to go to sea; but I pray you ask no more. It is painful to refuse you, and my duty forbids me to speak further."

For some minutes they were both silent, when Amine resumed—

"You were so anxious to possess that relic, that I cannot help thinking it has connection with the mystery. Is it not so?"

"For the last time, Amine, I will answer your question—it has to do with it; but now no more."

Philip's blunt and almost rude manner of finishing his speech was not lost upon Amine, who replied:—

"You are so engrossed with other thoughts, that you have not felt the compliment shown you by my taking such interest about you, sir?"

"Yes, I do—I feel and thank you too, Amine. Forgive me, if I have been rude; but recollect, the secret is not mine—at least, I feel as if it were not. God knows, I wish I never had known it, for it has blasted all my hopes in life."

Philip was silent; and when he raised his eyes, he found that Amine's were fixed upon him.

"Would you read my thoughts, Amine, or my secret?"

"Your thoughts, perhaps—your secret I would not; yet do I grieve that it should oppress you so heavily as evidently it does. It must, indeed, be one of awe to bear down a mind like yours, Philip."

"Where did you learn to be so brave, Amine?" said Philip, changing the conversation.

"Circumstances make people brave or otherwise; those who are accustomed to difficulty and danger fear them not."

"And where have you met with them, Amine?"

"In the country where I was born, not in this dank and muddy land."

"Will you trust me with the story of your former life, Amine? I can be secret, if you wish."

"That you can be secret, perhaps, against my wish, you have already proved to me," replied Amine, smiling; "and you have a claim to know something of the life you have preserved. I cannot tell you much, but what I can will be sufficient. My father, when a lad, on board of a trading vessel, was taken by the Moors, and sold as a slave to a Hakim, or physician, of their country. Finding him very intelligent, the Moor brought him up as an assistant, and it was under this man that he obtained a knowledge of the art. In a few years he was equal to his master; but, as a slave, he worked not for himself. You know, indeed it cannot be concealed, my father's avarice. He sighed to become as wealthy as his master, and to obtain his freedom; he became a follower of Mahomet, after which he was free, and practised for himself. He took a wife from an Arab family, the daughter of a chief whom he had restored to health, and he settled in the country. I was born; he amassed wealth, and became much celebrated; but the son of a Bey dying under his hands was the excuse for persecuting him. His head was forfeited, but he escaped; not, however, without the loss of all his beloved wealth. My Mother and I went with him; he fled to the Bedouins, with whom we remained some years. There I was accustomed to rapid marches, wild and fierce attacks, defeat and flight, and oftentimes to indiscriminate slaughter. But the Bedouins paid not well for my father's services, and gold was his idol. Hearing that the Bey was dead, he returned to Cairo, where he again practised. He was allowed once more to amass until the heap was sufficient to excite the cupidity of the new Bey; but this time he was fortunately made acquainted with the intentions of the ruler. He again escaped, with a portion of his wealth, in a small vessel, and gained the Spanish coast; but he never has been able to retain his money long. Before he arrived in this country he had been robbed of almost all, and has now been for these three years laying up again. We were but one year at Middleburg, and from thence removed to this place. Such is the history of my life, Philip."

"And does your father still hold the Mahomedan faith, Amine?"

"I know not. I think he holds no faith whatever: at least he hath taught me none. His god is gold."

"And yours?"

"Is the God who made this beautiful world, and all which it contains—the God of nature—name him as you will. This I feel, Philip, but more I fain would know; there are so many faiths, but surely they must be but different paths leading alike to heaven. Yours is the Christian faith, Philip. Is it the true one? But every one calls his own the true one, whatever his creed may be."

"It is the true and only one, Amine. Could I but reveal—I have such dreadful proofs—"

"That your own faith is true: then is it not your duty to reveal these proofs? Tell me, are you bound by any solemn obligations never to reveal?"

"No, I am not; yet do I feel as if I were. But I hear voices—it must be your father and the authorities—I must go down and meet them."

Philip rose and went down stairs. Amine's eyes followed him as he went and she remained looking towards the door.

"Is it possible," said she, sweeping the hair from off her brow, "so soon,—yes, yes, 'tis even so. I feel that I would sooner share his hidden woe—his dangers—even death itself were preferable with him, than ease and happiness with any other. And it shall be strange indeed if I do not. This night my father shall move into his cottage; I will prepare at once."

The report of Philip and Mynheer Poots was taken down by the authorities, the bodies examined, and one or two of them recognised as well-known marauders. They were then removed by the order of the burgomaster. The authorities broke up their council, and Philip and Mynheer Poots were permitted to return to Amine. It will not be necessary to repeat the conversation which ensued: it will be sufficient to state that Poots yielded to the arguments employed by Amine and Philip, particularly the one of paying no rent. A conveyance for the furniture and medicines was procured, and in the afternoon most of the effects were taken away. It was not, however, till dusk that the strong box of the doctor was put into the cart, and Philip went with it as a protector. Amine also walked by the side of the vehicle, with her father. As it may be supposed, it was late that night before they had made their arrangements, and had retired to rest.

Chapter Six

"This, then, is the chamber, which has so long been closed," said Amine, on entering it the next morning long before Philip had awakened from the sound sleep produced by the watching of the night before. "Yes, indeed, it has the air of having long been closed." Amine looked around her, and then examined the furniture. Her eyes were attracted to the birdcages: she looked into them:— "Poor little things!" continued she, "and here it was his father appeared unto his mother. Well, it may be so,—Philip saith that he hath proofs; and why should he not appear? Were Philip dead, I should rejoice to see his spirit,—at least it would be something. What am I saying—unfaithful lips, thus to betray my secret?—The table thrown over:— that looks like the work of fear; a workbox, with all its implements scattered,—only a woman's fear: a mouse might have caused all this; and yet there is something solemn in the simple fact that, for so many years, not a living being has crossed these boards. Even that a table thus overthrown could so remain for years seems scarcely natural, and therefore has its power on the mind. I wonder not that Philip feels there is so heavy a secret belonging to this room—but it must not remain in this condition—it must be occupied at once."

Amine, who had long been accustomed to attend upon her father, and perform the household duties, now commenced her intended labours.

Every part of the room, and every piece of furniture in it, were cleaned; even the cobwebs and dust were cleared away, and the sofa and table brought from the corner to the centre of the room; the melancholy little prisons were removed; and when Amine's work of neatness was complete, and the sun shone brightly into the opened window, the chamber wore the appearance of cheerfulness.

Amine had the intuitive good sense to feel that strong impressions wear away when the objects connected with them are removed. She resolved, then, to make Philip more at ease; for, with all the fire and warmth of blood inherent in her race, she had taken his image to her heart, and was determined to win him. Again and again did she resume her labour, until the pictures about the room, and every other article, looked fresh and clean.

Not only the birdcages, but the workbox and all the implements, were removed; and the piece of embroidery, the taking up of which had made Philip recoil as if he had touched an adder, was put away with the rest.

Philip had left the keys on the floor. Amine opened the buffets, cleaned the glazed doors, and was busy rubbing up the silver flagons, when her father came into the room.

"Mercy on me!" exclaimed Mynheer Poots; "and is all that silver?—then it must be true, and he has thousands of guilders; but where are they?"

"Never do you mind, father; yours are now safe, and for that you have to thank Philip Vanderdecken."

"Yes, very true; but as he is to live here—does he eat much—what will he pay me? He ought to pay well, as he has so much money."

Amine's lips were curled with a contemptuous smile, but she made no reply.

"I wonder where he keeps his money; and he is going to sea as soon as he can get a ship? Who will have charge of his money when he goes?"

"I shall take charge of it, father," replied Amine.

"Ah—yes—well—we will take charge of it. The ship may be lost."

"No, *we* will not take charge of it, father: you will have nothing to do with it. Look after your own."

Amine placed the silver in the buffets, locked the doors, and took the keys with her when she went out to prepare breakfast, leaving the old man gazing through the glazed doors at the precious metal within. His eyes were rivetted upon it, and he could not remove them. Every minute he muttered, "Yes, all silver."

Philip came down stairs; and as he passed by the room, intending to go into the kitchen, he perceived Mynheer Poots at the buffet, and he walked into the room. He was surprised as well as pleased with the alteration. He felt why and by whom it was done, and he was grateful. Amine came in with the breakfast, and their eyes spoke more than their lips could have done; and Philip sat down to his meal with less of sorrow and gloom upon his brow.

"Mynheer Poots," said Philip, as soon as he had finished, "I intend to leave you in possession of my cottage, and I trust you will find yourself comfortable. What little arrangements are necessary, I will confide to your daughter previous to my departure."

"Then you leave us, Mr Philip, to go to sea? It must be pleasant to go and see strange countries—much better than staying at home. When do you go?"

"I shall leave this evening for Amsterdam," replied Philip, "to make my arrangements about a ship; but I shall return, I think, before I sail."

"Ah! you will return. Yes—you have your money and your goods to see to; you must count your money. We will take good care of it. Where is your money, Mr Vanderdecken?"

"That I will communicate to your daughter this forenoon, before I leave. In three weeks, at the furthest, you may expect me back."

"Father," said Amine, "you promised to go and see the child of the burgomaster; it is time you went."

"Yes, yes—by-and-by—all in good time; but I must wait the pleasure of Mr Philip first: he has much to tell me before he goes."

Philip could not help smiling when he remembered what had passed when he first summoned Mynheer Poots to the cottage; but the remembrance ended in sorrow and a clouded brow.

Amine, who knew what was passing in the minds of both her father and Philip, now brought her father's hat, and led him to the door of the cottage; and Mynheer Poots, very much against his inclination—but never disputing the will of his daughter—was obliged to depart.

"So soon, Philip?" said Amine, returning to the room.

"Yes, Amine, immediately; but I trust to be back once more before I sail; if not, you must now have my instructions. Give me the keys."

Philip opened the cupboard below the buffet, and the doors of the iron safe.

"There, Amine, is my money. We need not count it, as your father would propose. You see that I was right when I asserted that I had thousands of guilders. At present they are of no use to me, as I have to learn my profession. Should I return some day, they may help me to own a ship. I know not what my destiny may be."

"And should you not return?" replied Amine, gravely.

"Then they are yours, as well as all that is in this cottage, and the cottage itself."

"You have relations, have you not?"

"But one, who is rich—an uncle, who helped us but little in our distress, and who has no children. I owe him but little—and he wants nothing. There is but one being in this world who has created an interest in this heart, Amine, and it is you. I wish you to look upon me as a brother. I shall always love you as a dear sister."

Amine made no reply. Philip took some more money out of the bag which had been opened, for the expenses of his journey, and then locking up the safe and cupboard, gave the keys to Amine. He was about to address her when there was a slight knock at the door, and in entered Father Seysen, the priest.

"Save you my son; and you, my child, whom as yet I have not seen. You are, I suppose, the daughter of Mynheer Poots?"

Amine bowed her head.

"I perceive, Philip, that the room is now opened; and I have heard of all that has passed. I would now talk with thee, Philip, and must beg this maiden to leave us for a while alone."

Amine quitted the room; and the priest, sitting down on the couch, beckoned Philip to his side. The conversation which ensued was too long to repeat. The priest first questioned Philip relative to his secret; but on that point he could not obtain the information which he wished. Philip stated as much as he did to Amine, and no more. He also declared his intention of going to sea, and that, should he not return, he had bequeathed his property—the extent of which he did not make known—to the doctor and his daughter. The priest then made inquiries relative to Mynheer Poots, asking Philip whether he knew what his creed was, as he had never appeared at any church, and report said that he was an infidel. To this Philip, as usual, gave his frank answer, and intimated that the daughter, at least, was anxious to be enlightened, begging the priest to undertake a task to which he himself was not adequate. To this request Father Seysen, who perceived the state of Philip's mind with regard to Amine, readily consented. After a conversation of nearly two hours, they were interrupted by the return of Mynheer Poots, who darted out of the room the instant he perceived Father Seysen. Philip called Amine, and having begged her as a favour to receive the priest's visits, the good old man blessed them both and departed.

"You did not give him any money, Mr Philip?" said Mynheer Poots, when Father Seysen had left the room.

"I did not," replied Philip; "I wish I had thought of it."

"No, no—it is better not—for money is better than what he can give you; but he must not come here."

"Why not, father," replied Amine, "if Mr Philip wishes it? It is his own house."

"O yes, if Mr Philip wishes it; but you know he is going away."

"Well, and suppose he is—why should not the Father come here? He shall come here to see me."

"See you, my child!—what can he want with you? Well, then, if he comes, I will not give him one stiver—and then he'll soon go away."

Philip had no opportunity of further converse with Amine; indeed he had nothing more to say. In an hour he bade her farewell in presence of her father, who would not leave them, hoping to obtain from Philip some communication about the money which he was to leave behind him.

In two days Philip arrived at Amsterdam, and having made the necessary inquiries, found that there was no chance of vessels sailing for the East Indies for some months. The Dutch East India Company had long been formed, and all private trading was at an end. The Company's vessels left only at what was supposed to be the most favourable season for rounding the Cape of Storms, as the Cape of Good Hope was designated by the early adventurers. One of the ships which were to sail with the next fleet was the Ter Schilling, a three-masted vessel, now laid up and unrigged.

Philip found out the captain, and stated his wishes to sail with him, to learn his profession as a seaman; the captain was pleased with his appearance, and as Philip not only agreed to receive no wages during the voyage, but to pay a premium as an apprentice learning his duty, he was promised a berth on board as the second mate, to mess in the cabin; and he was told that he should be informed whenever the vessel was to sail. Philip having now done all that he could in obedience to his vow, determined to return to the cottage; and once more he was in the company of Amine.

We must now pass over two months, during which Mynheer Poots continued to labour at his vocation, and was seldom within doors, and our two young friends were left for hours together. Philip's love for Amine was fully equal to hers for him. It was more than love,—it was a devotion on both sides, each day increasing. Who indeed could be more charming, more attractive in all ways than the high-spirited, yet tender Amine? Occasionally the brow of Philip would be clouded when he reflected upon the dark prospect before him; but Amine's smile would chase away the gloom and as he gazed on her, all would be forgotten. Amine made no secret of her attachment; it was shown in every word, every look, and every gesture. When Philip would take her hand, or encircle her waist with his arm, or even when he pressed her coral lips, there was no pretence of coyness on her part. She was too noble, too confiding; she felt that her happiness was centred in his love, and she lived but in his presence. Two months had thus passed away, when Father Seysen, who often called, and had paid much attention to Amine's instruction, one day came in as Amine was encircled in Philip's arms.

"My children," said he, "I have watched you for some time:— this is not well. Philip, if you intend marriage, as I presume you do, still it is dangerous. I must join your hands."

Philip started up.

"Surely I am not deceived in thee, my son," continued the priest in a severe tone.

"No, no, good Father; but I pray you leave me now: to-morrow you may come, and all will be decided. But I must talk with Amine."

The priest quitted the room, and Amine and Philip were again alone. The colour in Amine's cheek varied and her heart beat, for she felt how much her happiness was at stake.

"The priest is right, Amine," said Philip sitting down by her. "This cannot last;—would that I could ever stay with you; how hard a fate is mine! You know I love the very ground you tread upon, yet I dare not ask thee to wed to misery."

"To wed with thee would not be wedding misery, Philip," replied Amine, with downcast eyes.

"'Twere not kindness on my part, Amine. I should indeed be selfish."

"I will speak plainly, Philip," replied Amine. "You say you love me,—I know not how men love,—but this I know, how I can love. I feel that to leave me now were indeed unkind and selfish on your part; for, Philip, I—I should die. You say that you must go away—that fate demands it,—and your fatal secret. Be it so;—but cannot I go with you?"

"Go with me, Amine—unto death?"

"Yes, death; for what is death but a release? I fear not death, Philip; I fear but losing thee. Nay, more; is not your life in the hands of Him who made all? then why so sure to die? You have hinted to me that you are chosen—selected for a task;—if chosen, there is less chance of death; for until the end be fulfilled, if chosen, you must live. I would I knew your secret, Philip: a woman's wit might serve you well: and if it did not serve you, is there no comfort, no pleasure in sharing sorrow as well as joy with one you say you dote upon?"

"Amine, dearest Amine, it is my love, my ardent love alone, which makes me pause; for, O Amine, what pleasure should I feel if we were this hour united? I hardly know what to say, or what to do. I could not withhold my secret from you if you were my wife, nor will I wed you till you know it. Well, Amine, I will cast my all upon the die. You shall know this secret, learn what a doomed wretch I am, though from no fault of mine, and then you yourself shall decide. But remember my oath is registered in heaven, and I must not be dissuaded from it: keep that in mind, and hear my tale,—then if you choose to wed with one whose prospects are so bitter, be it so,—a short-lived happiness will then be mine, but for you, Amine—"

"At once the secret, Philip," cried Amine, impatiently.

Philip then entered into a detail of what our readers are acquainted with. Amine listened in silence; not a change of feature was to be observed in her countenance during the narrative. Philip wound up with stating the oath which he had taken. "I have done," said Philip, mournfully.

"'Tis a strange story, Philip," replied Amine: "and now hear me;—but give me first that relic,—I wish to look upon it. And can there be such virtue—I had nigh said, such mischief—in this little thing? Strange; forgive me, Philip,—but I've still my doubts upon this tale of *Eblis*. You know I am not yet strong in the new belief which you and the good priest have lately taught me. I do not say that it *cannot* be true: but still, one so unsettled as I am may be allowed to waver. But, Philip, I'll assume that all is true. Then, if it be true, without the oath you would be doing but your duty; and think not so meanly of Amine as to suppose she would restrain you from what is right. No, Philip, seek your father, and, if you can, and he requires your aid, then save him. But, Philip do you imagine that a task like this, so high, is to be accomplished at one trial? O! no; if you have been so chosen to fulfil it, you will be preserved through difficulty and danger until you have worked out your end. You will be preserved and you will again and again return;—be comforted—consoled—be cherished—and be loved by Amine as your wife. And when it pleases Him to call you from this world, your memory, if she survive you, Philip, will equally be cherished in her bosom. Philip, you have given me to decide;—dearest Philip, I am thine."

Amine extended her arms, and Philip pressed her to his bosom. That evening Philip demanded his daughter of the father, and Mynheer Poots, as soon as Philip opened the iron safe and displayed the guilders, gave his immediate consent.

Father Seysen called the next day and received his answer—and three days afterwards, the bells of the little church of Terneuse were ringing a merry peal for the union of Amine Poots and Philip Vanderdecken.

Chapter Seven

It was not until late in the autumn that Philip was roused from his dream of love (for what, alas! is every enjoyment of this life but a dream?) by a summons from the captain of the vessel with whom he had engaged to sail. Strange as it may appear, from the first day which put him in possession of his Amine, Philip had no longer brooded over his future destiny; occasionally it was recalled to his memory, but immediately rejected, and, for the time, forgotten. Sufficient he thought it, to fulfil his engagement when the time should come; and though the hours flew away, and day succeeded day, week week, and month month, with the rapidity accompanying a life of quiet and unvarying bliss, Philip forgot his vow in the arms of Amine, who was careful not to revert to a topic which would cloud the brow of her adored husband. Once, indeed, or twice, had old Poots raised the question of Philip's departure, but the indignant frown and the imperious command of Amine (who knew too well the sordid motives which actuated her father, and who, at such times, looked upon him with abhorrence) made him silent, and the old man would spend his leisure hours in walking up and down the parlour with his eyes riveted upon the buffets, where the silver tankards now beamed in all their pristine brightness.

One morning, in the month of October, there was a tapping with the knuckles at the cottage door. As this precaution implied a stranger, Amine obeyed the summons.

"I would speak with Master Philip Vanderdecken," said the stranger, in a half-whispering sort of voice.

The party who thus addressed Amine was a little meagre personage, dressed in the garb of the Dutch seaman of the time, with a cap made of badger-skin hanging over his brow. His features were sharp and diminutive, his face of a deadly white, his lips pale, and his hair of a mixture between red and white. He had very little show of beard—indeed, it was most difficult to say what his age might be. He might have been a sickly youth early sinking into decrepitude, or an old man, hale in constitution, yet carrying no flesh. But the most important feature, and that which immediately riveted the attention of Amine, was the eye of this peculiar personage—for he had but one; the right eye-lid was closed, and the ball within had evidently wasted away; but his left eye was, for the size of his face and head, of unusual dimensions, very protuberant, clear and watery, and most unpleasant to look upon, being relieved by no fringe of eyelash either above or below it. So remarkable was the feature, that when you looked at the man, you saw his eye and looked at nothing else. It was not a man with one eye, but one eye with a man attached to it; the body was but the tower of the lighthouse, of no further value, and commanding no further attention, than does the structure which holds up the beacon to the venturous mariner; and yet, upon examination, you would have perceived that the man, although small, was neatly made; that his hands were very different in texture and colour from those of common seamen; that his features in general, although sharp, were regular; and that there was an air of superiority even in the obsequious manner of the little personage, and an indescribable something about his whole appearance which almost impressed you with awe. Amine's dark eyes were for a moment fixed upon the visitor, and she felt a chill at her heart for which she could not account, as she requested that he would walk in.

Philip was greatly surprised at the appearance of the stranger, who, as soon as he entered the room, without saying a word sat down on the sofa by Philip in the place which Amine had just left. To Philip there was something ominous in this person taking Amine's seat; all that had passed rushed into his recollection and he felt that there was a summons from his short existence of enjoyment and repose to a life of future activity, danger, and suffering. What peculiarly struck Philip was, that when the little man sat beside him, a sensation of sudden cold ran through his whole frame. The colour fled from Philip's cheek, but he spoke not. For a minute or two there was a silence. The one-eyed visitor looked round him, and turning from the buffets, he fixed his eyes on the form of Amine, who stood before him; at last the silence was broken by a sort of giggle on the part of the stranger, which ended in—

"Philip Vanderdecken—he! he!—Philip Vanderdecken, you don't know me?"

"I do not," replied Philip, in a half angry tone.

The voice of the little man was most peculiar—it was a sort of subdued scream, the notes of which sounded in your ear long after he had ceased to speak.

"I am Schriften, one of the pilots of the Ter Schilling," continued the man; "and I'm come—he! he!"—and he looked hard at Amine—"to take you away from love,"—and looking at the buffets—"he! he! from comfort, and from this also," cried he, stamping his foot on the floor as he rose from the sofa—"from terra firma—he! he!—to a watery grave perhaps. Pleasant!"

continued Schriften, with a giggle; and with a countenance full of meaning he fixed his one eye on Philip's face.

Philip's first impulse was to put his new visitor out of the door; but Amine, who read his thoughts, folded her arms as she stood before the little man, and eyed him with contempt, as she observed:—

"We all must meet our fate, good fellow; and, whether by land or sea, death will have his due. If death stare him in the face, the cheek of Philip Vanderdecken will never turn as white as yours is now."

"Indeed!" replied Schriften, evidently annoyed at this cool determination on the part of one so young and beautiful; and then fixing his eye upon the silver shrine of the Virgin on the mantelpiece—"You are a Catholic, I perceive—he!"

"I am a Catholic," replied Philip; "but does that concern you? When does the vessel sail?"

"In a week—he! he!—only a week for preparation—only seven days to leave all—short notice!"

"More than sufficient," replied Philip, rising up from the sofa. "You may tell your captain that I shall not fail. Come, Amine, we must lose no time."

"No, indeed," replied Amine, "and our first duty is hospitality: Mynheer, may we offer you refreshment after your walk?"

"This day week," said Schriften, addressing Philip, and without making a reply to Amine. Philip nodded his head, the little man turned on his heel and left the room, and in a short time was out of sight.

Amine sank down on the sofa. The breaking-up of her short hour of happiness had been too sudden, too abrupt, and too cruelly brought about for a fondly doting, although heroic woman. There was an evident malignity in the words and manner of the one-eyed messenger, an appearance as if he knew more than others, which awed and confused both Philip and herself. Amine wept not, but she covered her face with her hands as Philip, with no steady pace, walked up and down the small room. Again, with all the vividness of colouring, did the scenes half forgotten recur to his memory. Again did he penetrate the fatal chamber—again was it obscure. The embroidery lay at his feet, and once more he started as when the letter appeared upon the floor.

They had both awakened from a dream of present bliss, and shuddered at the awful future which presented itself. A few minutes was sufficient for Philip to resume his natural self-possession. He sat down by the side of his

Amine, and clasped her in his arms. They remained silent. They knew too well each other's thoughts; and, excruciating as was the effort, they were both summoning up their courage to bear, and steeling their hearts against, the conviction that, in this world, they must now expect to be for a time, perhaps for ever, separated.

Amine was the first to speak: removing her arm; which had been wound round her husband, she first put his hand to her heart, as if to compress its painful throbbings, and then observed —

"Surely that was no earthly messenger, Philip! Did you not feel chilled to death when he sat by you? I did as he came in."

Philip, who had the same thought as Amine, but did not wish to alarm her, answered confusedly —

"Nay, Amine, you fancy — that is, the suddenness of his appearance and his strange conduct have made you imagine this; but I saw in him but a man who, from his peculiar deformity, has become an envious outcast of society — debarred from domestic happiness, from the smiles of the other sex; for what woman could smile upon such a creature? His bile raised at so much beauty in the arms of another, he enjoyed a malignant pleasure in giving a message which he felt would break upon those pleasures from which he is cut off. Be assured, my love, that it was nothing more."

"And even if my conjecture were correct, what does it matter?" replied Amine. "There can be nothing more, nothing which can render your position more awful, and more desperate. As your wife, Philip, I feel less courage than I did when I gave my willing hand. I knew not then what would be the extent of my loss; but fear not, much as I feel here," continued Amine, putting her hand to her heart — "I am prepared, and proud that he who is selected for such a task is my husband." Amine paused. "You cannot, surely, have been mistaken, Philip?"

"No! Amine, I have not been mistaken, either in the summons, or in my own courage, or in my selection of a wife," replied Philip, mournfully, as he embraced her. "It is the will of Heaven."

"Then may its will be done," replied Amine, rising from her seat. "The first pang is over. I feel better now, Philip. Your Amine knows her duty."

Philip made no reply; when, after a few moments, Amine continued —

"But one short week, Philip —"

"I would it had been but one day," replied he; "it would have been long enough. He has come too soon — the one-eyed monster."

"Nay, not so, Philip. I thank him for the week—'tis but a short time to wean myself from happiness. I grant you, that were I to teaze, to vex, to unman you with my tears, my prayers, or my upbraidings (as some wives would do, Philip), one day would be more than sufficient for such a scene of weakness on my part, and misery on yours. But, no, Philip, your Amine knows her duty better. You must go like some knight of old to perilous encounter, perhaps to death; but Amine will arm you, and show her love by closing carefully each rivet to protect you in your peril, and will see you depart full of hope and confidence, anticipating your return. A week is not too long, Philip, when employed as I trust I shall employ it—a week to interchange our sentiments, to hear your voice, to listen to your words (each of which will be engraven on my heart's memory), to ponder on them, and feed my love with them is your absence and in my solitude. No! no! Philip; I thank God that there is yet a week."

"And so do I, then, Amine! and, after all, we knew that this must come."

"Yes! but my love was so potent, that it banished memory."

"And yet, during our separation, your love must feed on memory, Amine."

Amine sighed. Here their conversation was interrupted by the entrance of Mynheer Poots, who, struck with the alteration in Amine's radiant features, exclaimed, "Holy prophet! what is the matter now?"

"Nothing more than what we all knew before," replied Philip; "I am about to leave you—the ship will sail in a week."

"Oh! you will sail in a week?"

There was a curious expression in the face of the old man as he endeavoured to suppress, before Amine and her husband, the joy which he felt at Philip's departure. Gradually he subdued his features into gravity, and said—

"That is very bad news, indeed."

No answer was made by Amine or Philip, who quitted the room together.

We must pass over this week, which was occupied in preparations for Philip's departure. We must pass over the heroism of Amine, who controlled her feelings, racked as she was with intense agony at the idea of separating from her adored husband. We cannot dwell upon the conflicting emotions in the breast of Philip, who left competence, happiness, and love, to encounter danger privation, and death. Now, at one time, he would almost resolve to remain, and then at others, as he took the relic from his bosom, and remembered his vow registered upon it, he was nearly as anxious to depart. Amine, too, as she fell asleep in her husband's arms, would count the few hours left them; or she would shudder, as she lay awake and the wind howled, at the prospect of what Philip would have to encounter. It was a long week to both of them, and, although they thought that time flew fast, it was almost a relief when the morning came that was to separate them; for, to their feelings, which, from regard to each other, had been pent up and controlled they could then give vent; their surcharged bosoms could be relieved; certainty had driven away suspense, and hope was still left to cheer them and brighten up the dark horizon of the future.

"Philip," said Amine, as they sat together with their hands entwined, "I shall not feel so much when you are gone. I do not forget that all this was told me before we were wed, and that for my love I took the hazard. My fond heart often tells me that you will return; but it may deceive me—return you *may*, but not in life. In this room I shall await you; on this removed to its former station, I shall sit; and if you cannot appear to me alive, O refuse me not, if it be possible, to appear to me when dead. I shall fear no storm, no bursting open of the window. O no! I shall hail the presence even of your spirit. Once more: let me but see you—let me be assured that you are dead—and then I shall know that I have no more to live for in this world, and shall hasten to join you in a world of bliss. Promise me, Philip."

"I promise all you ask, provided Heaven will so permit; but, Amine," and Philip's lips trembled, "I cannot—merciful God! I am indeed tried, Amine, I can stay no longer."

Amine's dark eyes were fixed upon her husband—she could not speak—her features were convulsed—nature could no longer hold up against her excess of feeling—she fell into his arms, and lay motionless. Philip, about to impress a last kiss upon her pale lips, perceived that she had fainted.

"She feels not now," said he, as he laid her upon the sofa; "it is better that it should be so—too soon will she awake to misery."

Summoning to the assistance of his daughter Mynheer Poots, who was in the adjoining room, Philip caught up his hat, imprinted one more fervent kiss upon her forehead, burst from the house, and was out of sight long before Amine had recovered from her swoon.

Chapter Eight

Before we follow Philip Vanderdecken in his venturous career, it will be necessary to refresh the memory of our readers, by a succinct recapitulation of the circumstances that had directed the enterprise of the Dutch towards the country of the East, which was now proving to them a source of wealth, which they considered as inexhaustible.

Let us begin at the beginning. Charles the Fifth, after having possessed the major part of Europe, retired from the world for reasons best known to himself, and divided his kingdoms between Ferdinand and Philip. To Ferdinand he gave Austria and its dependencies; to Philip, Spain; but to make the division more equal and palatable to the latter, he threw the Low Countries, with the few millions vegetating upon them, into the bargain. Having thus disposed of his fellow-mortals much to his own satisfaction, he went into a convent, reserving for himself a small income, twelve men, and a pony. Whether he afterwards repented his hobby, or mounted his pony is not recorded; but this is certain—that in two years he died.

Philip thought (as many have thought before and since) that he had a right to do what he pleased with his own. He therefore took away from the Hollanders most of their liberties: to make amends, however, he gave them the Inquisition; but the Dutch grumbled, and Philip, to stop their grumbling, burnt a few of them. Upon which the Dutch, who are aquatic in their propensities, protested against a religion which was much too warm for their constitutions. In short, heresy made great progress; and the duke of Alva was despatched with a large army to prove to the Hollanders that the Inquisition was the very best of all possible arrangements, and that it was infinitely better that a man should be burnt for half an hour in this world than for an eternity in the next.

This slight difference of opinion was the occasion of a war which lasted about eighty years, and which, after having saved some hundreds of thousands the trouble of dying in their beds, at length ended in the Seven United Provinces being declared independent.—Now we must go back again.

For a century after Vasco de Gama had discovered the passage round the Cape of Good Hope, the Portuguese were interfered with by other nations. At last the adventurous spirit of the English nation was roused. The passage to India by the Cape had been claimed by the Portuguese as their sole right: they defended it by force. For a long time no private company ventured to oppose them, and the trade was not of that apparent value to induce any government to embark in a war upon the question. The English adventurers, therefore, turned their attention to the discovery of a north-west passage to India, with which the Portuguese could have no right to interfere, and in vain attempts to discover that passage the best part of the fifteenth century was employed. At last they abandoned their endeavours, and resolved no longer to be deterred by the Portuguese pretensions.

After one or two unsuccessful expeditions, an armament was fitted out and put under the orders of Drake. This courageous and successful navigator accomplished more than the most sanguine had anticipated. He returned to England in the month of May, 1580, after a voyage which occupied him nearly three years; bringing home with him great riches, and having made most favourable arrangements with the king of the Molucca Islands.

His success was followed up by Cavendish and others, in 1600. The English East India Company, in the meanwhile, received their first charter from the government and had now been with various success carrying on the trade for upwards of fifty years.

During the time that the Dutch were vassals to the crown of Spain, it was their custom to repair to Lisbon for the productions of the East, and afterwards to distribute them through Europe; but when they quarrelled with Philip, they were no longer admitted as retailers of his Indian produce: the consequence was that, while asserting and fighting for their independence, they had also fitted out expeditions to India. They were successful; and in 1602 the various speculators were, by the government, formed into a company, upon the same principles and arrangement as those which had been chartered in England.

At the time, therefore, to which we are reverting, the English and Dutch had been trading in the Indian seas for more than fifty years; and the Portuguese had lost nearly all their power, from the alliances and friendships which their rivals had formed with the potentates of the East, who had suffered from the Portuguese avarice and cruelty.

Whatever may have been the sum of obligation which the Dutch owed to the English for the assistance they received from them during their struggle for independence, it does not appear that their gratitude extended beyond the Cape; for, on the other side of it, the Portuguese, English, and Dutch fought and captured each other's vessels without ceremony; and there was no law but that of main force. The mother countries were occasionally called upon to interfere; but the interference up to the above time had produced nothing more than a paper war; it being very evident that all parties were in the wrong.

In 1650 Cromwell usurped the throne of England, and the year afterwards, having, among other points, vainly demanded of the Dutch satisfaction for the murder of his regicide ambassador, which took place in this year, and some compensation for the cruelties exercised on the English at Amboyne some thirty years before, he declared war with Holland. To prove that he was in earnest, he seized more than two hundred Dutch vessels and the Dutch then (very unwillingly) prepared for war. Blake and Van Tromp met, and the naval combats were most obstinate. In the "History of England" the victory is almost invariably given to the English, but in that of Holland to the Dutch.—By all accounts, these engagements were so obstinate, that in each case they were both well beaten. However, in 1654, peace was signed; the Dutchman promising "to take his hat off" whenever he should meet an Englishman on the high seas—a mere act of politeness, which Mynheer did not object to, as it *cost nothing*. And now, having detailed the state of things up to the time of Philip's embarkation, we shall proceed with our story.

As soon as Philip was clear of his own threshold he hastened away as though he were attempting to escape from his own painful thoughts. In two days he arrived at Amsterdam, where his first object was to procure a small, but strong, steel chain to replace the ribbon by which the relic had hitherto been secured round his neck. Having done this, he hastened to embark with his effects on board of the Ter Schilling. Philip had not forgotten to bring with him the money which he had agreed to pay the captain, in consideration of being received on board as an apprentice rather than a sailor. He had also furnished himself with a further sum for his own exigencies. It was late in the evening when he arrived on board of the Ter Schilling, which lay at single anchor, surrounded by the other vessels composing the Indian fleet. The captain, whose name was Kloots, received him with kindness, showed him his berth, and then went below in the hold to decide a question relative to the cargo, leaving Philip on deck to his own reflections.

And this, then, thought Philip, as he leaned against the taffrail and looked forward—this, then, is the vessel in which my first attempt is to be made. First and—perhaps last. How little do those with whom I am about to sail imagine the purport of my embarkation? How different are my views from those of others? Do *I* seek a fortune? No! Is it to satisfy curiosity and a truant spirit? No! I seek communion with the dead. Can I meet the dead without danger to myself and these who sail with me? I should think not, for I cannot join it but in death. Did they surmise my wishes and intentions, would they permit me to remain one hour on board? Superstitious as seamen are said to be, they might find a good excuse, if they knew my mission, not only for their superstition, but for ridding themselves of one on such an awful errand. Awful indeed! and how to be accomplished? Heaven alone, with perseverance on my part, can solve the mystery. And Philip's thoughts reverted to his Amine. He folded his arms, and entranced in meditation, with his eyes raised to the firmament, he appeared to watch the flying scud.

"Had you not better go below?" said a mild voice, which made Philip start from his reverie.

It was that of the first mate, whose name was Hillebrant, a short, well-set man of about thirty years of age. His hair was flaxen, and fell in long flakes upon his shoulders, his complexion fair, and his eyes of a soft blue: although there was little of the sailor in his appearance, few knew or did their duty better.

"I thank you," replied Philip; "I had, indeed, forgotten myself, and where I was: my thoughts were far away. Good night, and many thanks."

The Ter Schilling, like most of the vessels of that period, was very different in her build and fitting from those of the present day. She was ship-rigged, and of about four hundred tons burden. Her bottom was nearly flat, and her sides fell in (as she rose above the water), so that her upper decks were not half the width of the hold.

All the vessels employed by the Company being armed, she had her main deck clear of goods, and carried six nine-pounders on each broadside; her ports were small and oval. There was a great spring in all her decks,— that is to say, she ran with a curve forward and aft. On her forecastle another small deck ran from the knight-heads, which was called the top-gallant forecastle. Her quarter-deck was broken with a poop, which rose high out of the water. The bowsprit staved very much, and was to appearance almost as a fourth mast: the more so, as she carried a square spritsail and sprit-topsail. On her quarter-deck and poop-bulwarks were fixed in sockets implements of warfare now long in disuse, but what were then known by the names of cohorns and patteraroes; they turned round on a swivel, and were pointed by an iron handle fixed to the breech. The sail abaft the mizzen-mast (corresponding to the driver or spanker of the present day) was fixed upon a lateen-yard. It is hardly necessary to add (after this description) that the dangers of a long voyage were not a little increased by the peculiar structure of the vessels, which (although with such top hamper, and so much wood above water, they could make good way before a favourable breeze) could hold no wind, and had but little chance if caught upon a lee-shore.

The crew of the Ter Schilling was composed of the captain, two mates, two pilots, and forty-five men. The supercargo had not yet come on board. The cabin (under the poop) was appropriated to the supercargo; but the main-deck cabin to the captain and mates, who composed the whole of the cabin mess.

When Philip awoke the next morning, he found that the topsails were hoisted, and the anchor short-stay apeak. Some of the other vessels of the fleet were under weigh and standing out. The weather was fine and the water smooth? and the bustle and novelty of the scene were cheering to his spirits. The captain, Mynheer Kloots, was standing on the poop with a small telescope, made of pasteboard, to his eye, anxiously looking towards the town. Mynheer Kloots, as usual, had his pipe in his mouth, and the smoke which he puffed from it for time obscured the lenses of his telescope. Philip went up the poop ladder and saluted him.

Mynheer Kloots was a person of no moderate dimensions, and the quantity of garments which he wore added no little to his apparent bulk. The outer garments exposed to view were, a rough fox-skin cap upon his head, from under which appeared the edge of a red worsted nightcap; a red plush waistcoat, with large metal buttons; a jacket of green cloth, over which he wore another of larger dimensions of coarse blue cloth, which came down as low as what would be called a spencer. Below he had black plush breeches, light-blue worsted stockings, shoes, and broad silver buckles; round his waist was girded, with a broad belt, a canvas apron, which descended in thick folds nearly to his knee. In his belt was a large broad-bladed knife in a sheath of shark's skin. Such was the attire of Mynheer Kloots, captain of the Ter Schilling.

He was as tall as he was corpulent. His face was oval, and his features small in proportion to the size of his frame. His grizzly hair fluttered in the breeze, and his nose (although quite straight) was, at the tip, fiery red from frequent application to his bottle of schnapps, and the heat of a small pipe which seldom left his lips, except for *him* to give an order, or for *it* to be replenished.

"Good morning, my son," said the captain, taking his pipe out of his mouth for a moment. "We are detained by the supercargo, who appears not over-willing to come on board; the boat has been on shore this hour waiting for him, and we shall be last of the fleet under weigh. I wish the Company would let us sail without these *gentlemen*, who are (*in my opinion*) a great hinderance to business; but they think otherwise on shore."

"What is their duty on board?" replied Philip.

"Their duty is to look after the cargo and the traffic, and if they kept to that it would not be so bad; but they interfere with everything else and everybody, studying little except their own comforts; in fact, they play the king on board, knowing that we dare not affront them, as a word from them would prejudice the vessel when again to be chartered. The Company insist upon their being received with all honours. We salute with five guns on their arrival on board."

"Do you know anything of this one whom you expect?"

"Nothing, but from report. A brother captain of mine (with whom he has sailed) told me that he is most fearful of the dangers of the sea, and much taken up with his own importance."

"I wish he would come," replied Philip; "I am most anxious that we should sail."

"You must be of a wandering disposition, my son: I hear that you leave a comfortable home, and a pretty wife to boot."

"I am most anxious to see the world," replied Philip; "and I must learn to sail a ship before I purchase one, and try to make the fortune that I covet." (Alas! how different from my real wishes, thought Philip, as he made this reply.)

"Fortunes are made, and fortunes are swallowed up too, by the ocean," replied the captain. "If I could turn this good ship into a good house, with plenty of guilders to keep the house warm, you would not find me standing on this poop. I have doubled the Cape twice, which is often enough for any man; the third time may not be so lucky."

"Is it so dangerous, then?" said Philip.

"As dangerous as tides and currents, rocks and sand-banks, hard gales and heavy seas, can make it, —no more! Even when you anchor in the bay, on this side of the Cape, you ride in fear and trembling, for you may be blown away from your anchor to sea or be driven on shore among the savages, before the men can well put on their clothing. But when once you're well on the other side of the Cape, then the water dances to the beams of the sun as if it were merry, and you may sail for weeks with a cloudless sky and a following breeze, without starting tack or sheet, or having to take your pipe out of your mouth."

"What ports shall we go into, Mynheer?"

"Of that I can say but little. Gambroon, in the Gulf of Persia, will probably be the first rendezvous of the whole fleet. Then we shall separate: some will sail direct for Bantam, in the island of Java; others will have orders to trade down the Straits for camphor, gum, benzoin, and wax; they have also gold and the teeth of the elephant to barter with us: there (should we be sent thither) you must be careful with the natives, Mynheer Vanderdecken. They are fierce and treacherous, and their curved knives (or creeses, as they call them) are sharp and deadly poisoned. I have had hard fighting in those Straits both with Portuguese and English."

"But we are all at peace now."

"True, my son; but when round the Cape, we must not trust to papers signed at home; and the English press us hard, and tread upon our heels wherever we go. They must be checked; and I suspect our fleet is so large and well appointed in expectation of hostilities."

"How long do you expect your voyage may occupy us?"

"That's as may be: but I should say about two years;—nay, if not detained by the factors, as I expect we shall be, for some hostile service, it may be less."

"Two years," thought Philip, "two years from Amine!" and he sighed deeply, for he felt that their separation might be for ever.

"Nay, my son, two years is not so long," said Mynheer Kloots, who observed the passing cloud on Philip's brow. "I was once five years away, and was unfortunate, for I brought home nothing, not even my ship. I was sent to Chittagong, on the east side of the great Bay of Bengala, and lay for three months in the river. The chiefs of the country would detain me by force; they would not barter for my cargo, or permit me to seek another market. My powder had been landed and I could make no resistance. The worms ate through the bottom of my vessel and she sank at her anchors. They knew it would take place, and that then they would have my cargo at their own price. Another vessel brought us home. Had I not been so treacherously served, I should have had no need to sail this time; and now my gains are small, the Company forbidding all private trading. But here he comes at last; they have hoisted the ensign on the staff in the boat; there— they have shoved off. Mynheer Hillebrant, see the gunners ready with their linstocks to salvo the supercargo."

"What duty do you wish me to perform?" observed Philip. "In what can I be useful?"

"At present you can be of little use, except in those heavy gales in which every pair of hands is valuable. You must look and learn for some time yet; but you can make a fair copy of the journal kept for the inspection of the Company, and may assist me in various ways, as soon as the unpleasant nausea, felt by those who first embark, has subsided. As a remedy, I should propose that you gird a handkerchief tight round your body so as to compress the stomach, and make frequent application of my bottle of schnapps, which you will find always at your service. But now to receive the factor of the most puissant Company. Mynheer Hillebrant, let them discharge the cannon."

The guns were fired, and soon after the smoke had cleared away, the boat, with its long ensign trailing on the water, was pulled alongside. Philip watched the appearance of the supercargo—but he remained in the boat until several of the boxes with the initials and arms of the Company were first handed on the deck; at last the supercargo appeared.

He was a small, spare, wizen-faced man with a three-cornered cocked-hat, bound with broad gold lace, upon his head, under which appeared a full-bottomed flowing wig, the curls of which descended low upon his shoulders. His coat was of crimson velvet, with broad flaps: his waistcoat of white silk, worked in coloured flowers, and descending half-way down to his knees. His breeches were of black satin, and his legs were covered with white silk stockings. Add to this, gold buckles at his knees and in his shoes, lace ruffles to his wrists, and a silver-mounted cane in his hand, and the reader has the entire dress of Mynheer Jacob Janz Von Stroom, the supercargo of the Honourable Company, appointed to the good ship Ter Schilling.

As he looked round him, surrounded at a respectful distance, by the captain, officers, and men of the ship, with their caps in their hands, the reader might be reminded of the picture of the "Monkey who had seen the world," surrounded by his tribe. There was not, however, the least inclination on the part of the seamen to laugh, even at his flowing, full-bottomed wig: respect was at that period paid to dress; and although Mynheer Von Stroom could not be mistaken for a sailor, he was known to be the supercargo of the Company, and a very great man. He therefore received all the respect due to so important a personage.

Mynheer Von Stroom did not, however, appear very anxious to remain on deck. He requested to be shown into his cabin, and followed the captain aft, picking his way among the coils of ropes with which his path was encumbered. The door was opened, and the supercargo disappeared. The ship was then got under weigh, the men had left the windlass, the sails had been trimmed, and they were securing the anchor on board, when the bell of the poop-cabin (appropriated to the supercargo) was pulled with great violence.

"What can that be?" said Mynheer Kloots (who was forward), taking the pipe out of his mouth. "Mynheer Vanderdecken, will you see what is the matter?"

Philip went aft, as the pealing of the bell continued, and opening the cabin door, discovered the supercargo perched upon the table and pulling the bell-rope, which hung over its centre, with every mark of fear in his countenance. His wig was off, and his bare skull gave him an appearance peculiarly ridiculous.

"What is the matter, sir?" inquired Philip.

"Matter!" spluttered Mynheer Von Stroom—"call the troops in with their firelocks. Quick, sir. Am I to be murdered, torn to pieces, and devoured? For mercy's sake, sir, don't stare, but do something—look, it's coming to the table! O dear! O dear!" continued the supercargo, evidently terrified out of his wits.

Philip, whose eyes had been fixed on Mynheer Von Stroom, turned them in the direction pointed out, and much to his astonishment perceived a small bear upon the deck, who was amusing himself with the supercargo's flowing wig, which he held in his paws, tossing it about and now and then burying his muzzle in it. The unexpected sight of the animal was at first a shock to Philip; but a moment's consideration assured him that the animal must be harmless, or it never would have been permitted to remain loose in the vessel.

Nevertheless, Philip had no wish to approach the animal, whose disposition he was unacquainted with, when the appearance of Mynheer Kloots put an end to his difficulty.

"What is the matter, Mynheer?" said the captain. "O! I see: it is Johannes," continued the captain, going up to the bear, and saluting him with a kick, as he recovered the supercargo's wig. "Out of the cabin, Johannes! Out, sir!" cried Mynheer Kloots, kicking the breech of the bear till the animal had escaped through the door. "Mynheer Von Stroom, I am very sorry,—here is your wig. Shut the door, Mynheer Vanderdecken, or the beast may come back, for he is very fond of me."

As soon the door was shut between Mynheer Von Stroom and the object of his terror, the little man slid off the table to the high-backed chair near it, shook out the damaged curls of his wig, and replaced it on his head; pulled out his ruffles, and, assuming an air of magisterial importance, struck his cane on the deck, and then spoke.

"Mynheer Kloots, what is the meaning of this disrespect to the supercargo of the puissant Company?"

"God in Heaven! no disrespect, Mynheer;—the animal is a bear, as you see; he is very tame, even with strangers. He belongs to me. I have had him since he was three months old. It was all a mistake. The mate, Mynheer Hillebrant, put him in the cabin, that he might be out of the way while the duty was carrying on, and he quite forgot that he was here. I am very sorry, Mynheer Von Stroom; but he will not come here again, unless you wish to play with him."

"Play with him! I! supercargo to the Company, play with a bear! Mynheer Kloots, the animal must be thrown overboard immediately."

"Nay, nay; I cannot throw overboard an animal that I hold in much affection, Mynheer Von Stroom; but he shall not trouble you."

"Then, Captain Kloots, you will have to deal with the Company, to whom I shall represent this affair. Your charter will be cancelled, and your freight-money will be forfeited."

Kloots was, like most Dutchmen, not a little obstinate, and this imperative behaviour on the part of the supercargo raised his bile. "There is nothing in the charter that prevents my having an animal on board," replied Kloots.

"By the regulations of the Company," replied Von Stroom, falling back in his chair with an important air, and crossing his thin legs, "you are required to receive on board strange and curious animals, sent home by the governors and factors to be presented to crowned heads,—such as lions, tigers, elephants, and other productions of the East;—but in no instance is it permitted to the commanders of chartered ships to receive on board, on their own account, animals of any description, which must be considered under the head and offence of private trading."

"My bear is not for sale, Mynheer Von Stroom."

"It must immediately be sent out of the ship, Mynheer Kloots. I order you to send it away,—on your peril to refuse."

"Then we will drop the anchor again, Mynheer Von Stroom, and send on shore to head-quarters to decide the point. If the Company insists that the brute be put on shore, be it so; but recollect, Mynheer Von Stroom, we shall lose the protection of the fleet, and have to sail alone. Shall I drop the anchor, Mynheer?"

This observation softened down the pertinacity of the supercargo: he had no wish to sail alone, and the fear of this contingency was more powerful than the fear of the bear.

"Mynheer Kloots, I will not be too severe; if the animal is chained, so that it does not approach me, I will consent to its remaining on board."

"I will keep it out of your way as much as I can; but as for chaining up the poor animal, it will howl all day and night and you will have no sleep, Mynheer Von Stroom," replied Kloots.

The supercargo, who perceived that the captain was positive and that his threats were disregarded, did all that a man could do who could not help himself. He vowed vengeance in his own mind, and then, with an air of condescension, observed—"Upon those conditions, Mynheer Kloots, your animal may remain on board."

Mynheer Kloots and Philip then left the cabin; the former, who was in no very good humour, muttering as he walked away—"If the Company send their *monkeys* on board, I think I may well have my *bear*." And pleased with his joke, Mynheer Kloots recovered his good humour.

Chapter Nine

We must allow the Indian fleet to pursue its way to the Cape with every variety of wind and weather. Some had parted company; but the rendezvous was Table Bay, from which they were again to start together.

Philip Vanderdecken was soon able to render some service on board. He studied his duty diligently, for employment prevented him from dwelling too much upon the cause of his embarkation, and he worked hard at the duties of the ship, for the exercise procured for him that sleep which otherwise would have been denied.

He was soon a favourite of the captain, and intimate with Hillebrant, the first mate; the second mate, Struys, was a morose young man, with whom he had little intercourse. As for the supercargo, Mynheer Jacob Janz Von Stroom, he seldom ventured out of his cabin. The bear, Johannes, was not confined, and therefore Mynheer Von Stroom confined himself; hardly a day passed that he did not look over a letter which he had framed upon the subject, all ready to forward to the Company; and each time that he perused it he made some alteration, which he considered would give additional force to his complaint, and would prove still more injurious to the interests of Captain Kloots.

In the mean time, in happy ignorance of all that was passing in the poop-cabin, Mynheer Kloots smoked his pipe, drank his schnapps, and played with Johannes. The animal had also contracted a great affection for Philip, and used to walk the watch with him.

There was another party in the ship whom we must not lose sight of—the one-eyed pilot, Schriften, who appeared to have imbibed a great animosity towards our hero, as well as to his dumb favourite the bear. As Philip held the rank of an officer, Schriften dared not openly affront, though he took every opportunity of annoying him, and was constantly inveighing against him before the ship's company. To the bear he was more openly inveterate, and seldom passed it without bestowing upon it a severe kick, accompanied with a horrid curse. Although no one on board appeared to be fond of this man, everybody appeared to be afraid of him, and he had obtained a control over the seamen which appeared unaccountable.

Such was the state of affairs on board the good ship Ter Schilling, when, in company with two others, she lay becalmed about two days' sail to the Cape. The weather was intensely hot, for it was the summer in those southern latitudes, and Philip, who had been lying down under the awning spread over the poop, was so overcome with the heat, that he had fallen asleep. He awoke with a shivering sensation of cold over his whole body, particularly at his chest, and, half-opening his eyes, he perceived the pilot, Schriften, leaning over him, and holding between his finger and his thumb a portion of the chain which had not been concealed, and to which was attached the sacred relic. Philip closed them again, to ascertain what were the man's intentions: he found that he gradually dragged out the chain, and, when the relic was clear, attempted to pass the whole over his head, evidently to gain possession of it. Upon this attempt Philip started up and seized him by the waist.

"Indeed!" cried Philip, with an indignant look, as he released the chain from the pilot's hand.

But Schriften appeared not in the least confused at being detected in his attempt: looking with his malicious one eye at Philip, he mockingly observed—

"Does that chain hold her picture?—he! he!"

Vanderdecken rose, pushed him away, and folded his arms.

"I advise you not to be quite so curious, Master Pilot, or you may repent it."

"Or perhaps," continued the pilot quite regardless of Philip's wrath, "it may be a child's caul, a sovereign remedy against drowning."

"Go forward to your duty, sir," cried Philip.

"Or, as you are a Catholic, the finger-nail of a saint; or, yes, I have it—a piece of the holy cross."

Philip started.

"That's it! that's it!" cried Schriften, who now went forward to where the seamen were standing at the gangway.

"News for you, my lads!" said he; "we've a bit of the holy cross aboard, and so we may defy the devil!"

Philip, hardly knowing why, had followed Schriften as he descended the poop-ladder, and was forward on the quarterdeck, when the pilot made this remark to the seamen.

"Ay! ay!" replied an old seaman to the pilot; "not only the devil, but the Flying Dutchman to boot."

"Flying Dutchman," thought Philip, "can that refer to—?" and Philip walked a step or two forward, so as to conceal himself behind the mainmast, hoping to obtain some information, should they continue the conversation. In this he was not disappointed.

"They say that to meet with him is worse than meeting with the devil," observed another of the crew.

"Who ever saw him?" said another.

"He has been seen, that's sartain, and just as sartain that ill luck follows the vessel that falls in with him."

"And where is he to be fallen in with?"

"O! they say that's not so sartain—but he cruises off the Cape."

"I should like to know the whole long and short of the story," said a third.

"I can only tell what I've heard. It's a doomed vessel; they were pirates, and cut the captain's throat, I believe."

"No! no!" cried Schriften, "the captain is in her now—and a villain he was. They say that, like somebody else on board of us now, he left a very pretty wife, and that he was very fond of her."

"How do they know that, pilot?"

"Because he always wants to send letters home when he boards vessels that he falls in with. But, woe to the vessel that takes charge of them!—she is sure to be lost, with every soul on board!"

"I wonder where you heard all this," said one of the men. "Did you ever see the vessel?"

"Yes, I did!" screamed Schriften; but, as if recovering himself, his scream subsided into his usual giggle, and he added, "but we need not fear her, boys; we've a bit of the true cross on board." Schriften then walked aft as if to avoid being questioned, when he perceived Philip by the mainmast.

"So, I'm not the only one curious?—he! he! Pray did you bring that on board, in case we should fall in with the Flying Dutchman?"

"I fear no Flying Dutchman," replied Philip, confused.

"Now I think of it, you are of the same name; at least they say that his name was Vanderdecken—eh?"

"There are many Vanderdeckens in the world besides me," replied Philip who had recovered his composure; and having made this reply, he walked away to the poop of the vessel.

"One would almost imagine this malignant one-eyed wretch was aware of the cause of my embarkation," mused Philip; "but no! that cannot be. Why do I feel such a chill whenever he approaches me? I wonder if others do; or whether it is a mere fancy on the part of Amine and myself. I dare ask no questions.—Strange, too, that the man should feel such malice towards me. I never injured him. What I have just overheard confirms all; but there needed no confirmation. Oh, Amine! Amine! but for thee, and I would rejoice to solve this riddle at the expense of life. God in mercy check the current of my brain," muttered Philip, "or my reason cannot hold its seat!"

In three days the Ter Schilling and her consorts arrived at Table Bay, where they found the remainder of the fleet at anchor waiting for them. Just at that period the Dutch had formed a settlement at the Cape of Good Hope, where the Indian fleets used to water and obtain cattle from the Hottentot tribes who lived on the coast, and who for a brass button or a large nail would willingly offer a fat bullock. A few days were occupied in completing the water of the squadron, and then the ships, having received from the Admiral their instructions as to rendezvous in case of parting company, and made every preparation for the bad weather which they anticipated, again weighed their anchors and proceeded on their voyage.

For three days they beat against light and baffling winds, making but little progress; on the third, the breeze sprang up strong from the southward, until it increased to a gale, and the fleet were blown down to the northward of the bay. On the seventh day the Ter Schilling found herself alone, but the weather had moderated. Sail was again made upon the vessel, and her head put to the eastward, that she might run in for the land.

"We are unfortunate in thus parting with all our consorts," observed Mynheer Kloots to Philip, as they were standing at the gangway; "but it must be near meridian, and the sun will enable me to discover our latitude. It is difficult to say how far we may have been swept by the gale and the currents to the northward. Boy, bring up my cross-staff, and be mindful that you do not strike it against anything as you come up."

The cross-staff at that time was the simple instrument used to discover the latitude, which it would give to a nice observer to within five or ten miles. Quadrants and sextants were the invention of a much later period. Indeed, considering that they had so little knowledge of navigation and the variation of the compass, and that their easting and westing could only be computed by dead reckoning, it is wonderful how our ancestors traversed the ocean in the way they did, with comparatively so few accidents.

"We are full three degrees to the northward of the Cape," observed Mynheer Kloots, after he had computed his latitude. "The currents must be running strong; the wind is going down fast, and we shall have a change, if I mistake not."

Towards the evening it fell calm, with a heavy swell setting towards the shore; shoals of seals appeared on the surface, following the vessel as she drove before the swell; the fish darted and leaped in every direction, and the ocean around them appeared to be full of life as the sun slowly descended to the horizon.

"What is that noise we hear?" observed Philip; "it sounds like distant thunder."

"I hear it," replied Mynheer Kloots. "Aloft there, do you see the land?"

"Yes," replied the man after a pause in ascending the topmast shrouds. "It is right ahead—low sand-hills, and the sea breaking high."

"Then that must be the noise we hear. We sweep in fast with this heavy ground-swell. I wish the breeze would spring up."

The sun was dipping under the horizon, and the calm still continued: the swell had driven the Ter Schilling so rapidly on the shore that now they could see the breakers which fell over with the noise of thunder.

"Do you know the coast, pilot?" observed the captain to Schriften, who stood by.

"Know it well," replied Schriften; "the sea breaks in twelve fathoms at least. In half an hour the good ship will be beaten into toothpicks, without a breeze to help us." And the little man giggled as if pleased at the idea.

The anxiety of Mynheer Kloots was not to be concealed; his pipe was every moment in and out of his mouth. The crew remained in groups on the forecastle and gangway, listening with dismay to the fearful roaring of the breakers. The sun had sunk down below the horizon, and the gloom of night was gradually adding to the alarm of the crew of the Ter Schilling.

"We must lower down the boats," said Mynheer Kloots to the first mate, "and try to tow her off. We cannot do much good, I'm afraid; but at all events the boats will be ready for the men to get into before she drives on shore. Get the tow ropes out and lower down the boats, while I go in to acquaint the supercargo."

Mynheer Von Stroom was sitting in all the dignity of his office, and, it being Sunday, had put on his very best wig. He was once more reading over the letter to the Company, relative to the bear, when Mynheer Kloots made his appearance, and informed him in a few words that they were in a situation of peculiar danger, and that in all probability the ship would be in pieces in less than half an hour. At this alarming intelligence, Mynheer Von Stroom jumped up from his chair, and in his hurry and fear knocked down the candle which had just been lighted.

"In danger! Mynheer Kloots!—why the water is smooth and the wind down! My hat—where is my hat and my cane? I will go on deck. Quick! A light—Mynheer Kloots, if you please to order a light to be brought; I can find nothing in the dark. Mynheer Kloots, why do you not answer? Mercy on me! he is gone and has left me."

Mynheer Kloots had gone to fetch a light, and now returned with it. Mynheer Von Stroom put on his hat, and walked out of the cabin. The boats were down, and the ship's head had been turned round from the land: but it was now quite dark and nothing was to be seen but the white line of foam created by the breakers as they dashed with an awful noise against the shore.

"Mynheer Kloots, if you please, I'll leave the ship directly. Let my boat come alongside—I must have the largest boat for the Honourable Company's service—for the papers and myself."

"I'm afraid not, Mynheer Von Stroom," replied Kloots; "our boats will hardly hold the men as it is, and every man's life is as valuable to himself as yours is to you."

"But, Mynheer, I am the Company's supercargo. I order you—I will have one—refuse if you dare."

"I dare, and do refuse," replied the captain, taking his pipe out of his mouth.

"Well, well," replied Mynheer Von Stroom, who now lost all presence of mind—"we will, sir—as soon as we arrive—Lord help us!—we are lost. O Lord! O Lord!" And here Mynheer Von Stroom, not knowing why, hurried down to the cabin, and in his haste tumbled over the bear Johannes, who crossed his path, and in his fall his hat and flowing wig parted company with his head.

"O! mercy! where am I? Help—help here! for the Honourable Company's supercargo!"

"Cast off there in the boats, and come on board," cried Mynheer Kloots, "we have no time to spare. Quick now, Philip, put in the compass, the water, and the biscuit; we must leave her in five minutes."

So appalling was the roar of the breakers, that it was with difficulty that the orders could be heard. In the mean time Mynheer Von Stroom lay upon the deck, kicking, sprawling, and crying for help.

"There is a light breeze off the shore," cried Philip, holding up his hand.

"There is, but I'm afraid it is too late. Hand the things into the boats, and be cool, my men. We have yet a chance of saving her, if the wind freshens."

They were now so near to the breakers that they felt the swell in which the vessel lay becalmed turned over here and there on its long line, but the breeze freshened and the vessel was stationary! The men were all in the boats, with the exception of Mynheer Kloots, the mates, and Mynheer Von Stroom.

"She goes through the water now," said Philip.

"Yes, I think we shall save her," replied the captain: "steady as you go, Hillebrant," continued he to the first mate, who was at the helm. "We leave the breakers now—only let the breeze hold ten minutes."

The breeze was steady, the Ter Schilling stood off from the land, again it fell calm, and again she was swept towards the breakers; at last the breeze came off strong, and the vessel cleaved through the water. The men were called out of the boats; Mynheer Von Stroom was picked up along with his hat and wig, carried into the cabin, and in less than an hour the Ter Schilling was out of danger.

"Now we will hoist up the boats," said Mynheer Kloots, "and let us all, before we lie down to sleep, thank God for our deliverance."

During that night the Ter Schilling made an offing of twenty miles, and then stood to the southward; towards the morning the wind again fell, and it was nearly calm.

Mynheer Kloots had been on deck about an hour, and had been talking with Hillebrant upon the danger of the evening, and the selfishness and pusillanimity of Mynheer Von Stroom, when a loud noise was heard in the poop-cabin.

"What can that be?" said the captain; "has the good man lost his senses from the fright? Why, he is knocking the cabin to pieces."

At this moment the servant of the supercargo ran out of the cabin.

"Mynheer Kloots, hasten in—help my master—he will be killed—the bear!—the bear!"

"The bear! what Johannes?" cried Mynheer Kloots. "Why, the animal is as tame as a dog. I will go and see."

But before Mynheer Kloots could walk into the cabin, out flew in his shirt the affrighted supercargo. "My God! my God! am I to be murdered?— eaten alive?" cried he, running forward, and attempting to climb the fore-rigging.

Mynheer Kloots followed the motions of Mynheer Von Stroom with surprise, and when he found him attempting to mount the rigging, he turned aft and walked into the cabin, when he found to his surprise that Johannes was indeed doing mischief.

The panelling of the state cabin of the supercargo had been beaten down, the wig boxes lay in fragments on the floor, the two spare wigs were lying by them, and upon them were strewed fragments of broken pots and masses of honey, which Johannes was licking up with peculiar gusto.

The fact was, that when the ship anchored at Table Bay, Mynheer Von Stroom, who was very partial to honey, had obtained some from the Hottentots. This honey his careful servant had stowed away in jars, which he had placed at the bottom of the two long boxes, ready for his master's use during the remainder of the voyage. That morning, the servant fancying that the wig of the previous night had suffered when his master tumbled over the bear, opened one of the boxes to take out another. Johannes happened to come near the door, and scented the honey. Now, partial as Mynheer Von Stroom was to honey, all bears are still more so, and will venture everything to obtain it. Johannes had yielded to the impulse of his species, and, following the scent, had come into the cabin, and was about to enter the sleeping berth of Mynheer Stroom, when the servant slammed the door in his face; whereupon Johannes beat in the panels, and found an entrance. He then attacked the wig-boxes, and, by showing a most formidable set of teeth, proved to the servant, who attempted to drive him off, that he would not be trifled with. In the meanwhile, Mynheer Von Stroom was in the utmost terror: not aware of the purport of the bear's visit, he imagined that the animal's object was to attack him. His servant took to his heels after a vain effort to save the last box, and Mynheer Von Stroom, then finding himself alone, at length sprang out of his bed-place, and escaped, as we have mentioned, to the forecastle, leaving Johannes master of the field, and luxuriating upon the *spolia opima*. Mynheer Kloots immediately perceived how the case stood. He went up to the bear and spoke to him, then kicked him, but the bear would not leave the honey, and growled furiously at the interruption. "This is a bad job for you, Johannes," observed Mynheer Kloots; "now you will leave the ship, for the supercargo has just grounds of complaint. Oh, well! you must eat the honey, because you will." So saying, Mynheer Kloots left the cabin, and went to look after the supercargo, who remained on the forecastle, with his bald head and meagre body, haranguing the men in his shirt, which fluttered in the breeze.

"I am very sorry, Mynheer Von Stroom," said Kloots, "but the bear shall be sent out of the vessel."

"Yes, yes, Mynheer Kloots; but this is an affair for the most puissant Company—the lives of their servants are not to be sacrificed to the folly of a sea-captain. I have nearly been torn to pieces."

"The animal did not want you; all he wanted was the honey," replied Kloots. "He has got it, and I myself cannot take it from him. There is no altering the nature of an animal. Will you be pleased to walk down into my cabin until the beast can be secured? He shall not go loose again."

Mynheer Von Stroom who considered his dignity at variance with his appearance, and who perhaps was aware that majesty deprived of its externals was only a jest, thought it advisable to accept the offer. After some trouble with the assistance of the seamen, the bear was secured and dragged away from the cabin, much against his will, for he had still some honey to lick off the curls of the full-bottomed wigs. He was put into durance vile, having been caught in the flagrant act of burglary on the high seas. This new adventure was the topic of the day, for it was again a dead calm, and the ship lay motionless on the glassy wave.

"The sun looks red as he sinks," observed Hillebrant to the captain, who with Philip was standing on the poop; "we shall have wind before to-morrow, if I mistake not."

"I am of your opinion," replied Mynheer Kloots. "It is strange that we do not fall in with any of the vessels of the fleet. They must all have been driven down here."

"Perhaps they have kept a wider offing."

"It had been as well if we had done the same," said Kloots. "That was a narrow escape last night. There is such a thing as having too little as well as having too much wind."

A confused noise was heard among the seamen, who were collected together and, looking in the direction of the vessel's quarter, "A ship! No—Yes, it is!" was repeated more than once.

"They think they see a ship," said Schriften, coming on the poop. "He! he!"

"Where?"

"There in the gloom!" said the pilot, pointing to the darkest quarter in the horizon, for the sun had set.

The captain, Hillebrant, and Philip directed their eyes to the quarter pointed out, and thought they could perceive something like a vessel. Gradually the gloom seemed to clear away, and a lambent pale blaze to light up that part of the horizon. Not a breath of wind was on the water—the sea was like a mirror—more and more distinct did the vessel appear, till her hull, masts, and yards were clearly visible. They looked and rubbed their eyes to help their vision, for scarcely could they believe that which they did see. In the centre of the pale light, which extended about fifteen degrees above the horizon, there was indeed a large ship about three miles distant; but although it was a perfect calm, she was to all appearance buffeting in a violent gale, plunging and lifting over a surface that was smooth as glass, now careening to her bearing, then recovering herself. Her topsails and mainsail were furled, and the yards pointed to the wind; she had no sail set, but a close-reefed foresail, a storm staysail, and trysail abaft. She made little way through the water, but apparently neared them fast, driven down by the force of the gale. Each minute she was plainer to the view. At last she was seen to wear, and in so doing, before she was brought to the wind on the other tack, she was so close to them that they could distinguish the men on board: they could see the foaming water as it was hurled from her bows; hear the shrill whistle of the boatswain's pipes, the creaking of the ship's timbers, and the complaining of her masts; and then the gloom gradually rose, and in a few seconds she had totally disappeared!

"God in heaven!" exclaimed Mynheer Kloots.

Philip felt a hand upon his shoulder, and the cold darted through his whole frame. He turned round and met the one eye of Schriften, who screamed in his ear—

" *Philip Vanderdecken* —that's the *Flying Dutchman!*"

Chapter Ten

The sudden gloom which had succeeded to the pale light, had the effect of rendering every object still more indistinct to the astonished crew of the Ter Schilling. For a moment or more not a word was uttered by a soul on board. Some remained with their eyes still strained towards the point where the apparition had been seen, others turned away full of gloomy and foreboding thoughts. Hillebrant was the first who spoke: turning round to the eastern quarter, and observing a light on the horizon, he started, and seizing Philip by the arm, cried out, "What's that?"

"That is only the moon rising from the bank of clouds," replied Philip, mournfully.

"Well!" observed Mynheer Kloots wiping his forehead, which was damped with perspiration, "I *have* been told of this before, but I have mocked at the narration."

Philip made no reply. Aware of the reality of the vision, and how deeply it interested him, he felt as if he were a guilty person.

The moon had now risen above the clouds, and was pouring her mild pale light over the slumbering ocean. With a simultaneous impulse, every one directed his eyes to the spot where the strange vision had last been seen; and all was a dead, dead calm.

Since the apparition the pilot, Schriften, had remained on the poop; he now gradually approached Mynheer Kloots, and looking round, said—

"Mynheer Kloots, as pilot of this vessel, I tell you that you must prepare for very bad weather."

"Bad weather!" said Kloots, rousing himself from a deep reverie.

"Yes, bad weather, Mynheer Kloots. There never was a vessel which fell in with—what we have just seen but met with disaster soon afterwards. The very name of Vanderdecken is unlucky—He! he!"

Philip would have replied to this sarcasm, but he could not; his tongue was tied.

"What has the name of Vanderdecken to do with it?" observed Kloots.

"Have you not heard, then? The captain of that vessel we have just seen is a Mynheer Vanderdecken—he is the Flying Dutchman!"

"How know you that, pilot?" inquired Hillebrant.

"I know that, and much more, if I chose to tell," replied Schriften; "but never mind, I have warned you of bad weather, as is my duty;" and, with these words, Schriften went down the poop-ladder.

"God in heaven! I never was so puzzled and so frightened in my life," observed Kloots. "I don't know what to think or say.—What think you, Philip? was it not supernatural?"

"Yes," replied Philip, mournfully. "I have no doubt of it."

"I thought the days of miracles had passed," said the captain, "and that we were now left to our own exertions, and had no other warnings but those the appearance of the heavens gave us."

"And they warn us now," observed Hillebrant. "See how that bank of clouds has risen within these five minutes—the moon has escaped from it but it will soon catch her again—and see, there is a flash of lightning in the north-west."

"Well, my sons, I can brave the elements as well as any man, and do my best. I have cared little for gales or stress of weather; but I like not such a warning as we have had tonight. My heart's as heavy as lead, and that's the truth. Philip, send down for the bottle of schnapps, if it is only to clear my brain a little."

Philip was glad of an opportunity to quit the poop; he wished to have a few minutes to recover himself and collect his own thoughts. The appearance of the Phantom Ship had been to him a dreadful shock; not that he had not fully believed in its existence; but still, to have beheld, to have been so near that vessel—that vessel in which his father was fulfilling his awful doom— that vessel on board of which he felt sure that his own destiny was to be worked out—had given a whirl to his brain. When he had heard the sound of the boatswain's whistle on board of her, eagerly had he stretched his earing to catch the order given—and given, he was convinced, in his father's voice. Nor had his eyes been less called to aid in his attempt to discover the features and dress of those moving on her decks. As soon, then, as he had sent the boy up to Mynheer Kloots Philip hastened to his cabin and buried his face in the coverlid of his bed, and then he prayed—prayed until he had recovered his usual energy and courage, and brought his mind to that state of composure which could enable him to look forward calmly to danger and difficulty, and feel prepared to meet it with the heroism of a martyr.

Philip remained below not more than half an hour. On his return to the deck, what a change had taken place! He had left the vessel floating motionless on the still waters, with her lofty sails hanging down listlessly from the yards. The moon then soared aloft in her beauty, reflecting the masts and sails of the ship in extended lines upon the smooth sea. Now all was dark: the water rippled short and broke in foam; the smaller and lofty sails had been taken in, and the vessel was cleaving through the water; and the wind, in fitful gusts and angry moanings, proclaimed too surely that it had been awakened up to wrath, and was gathering its strength for destruction. The men were still busy reducing the sails, but they worked gloomily and discontentedly. What Schriften, the pilot, had said to them, Philip knew not; but that they avoided him and appeared to look upon him with feelings of ill-will, was evident. And each minute the gale increased.

"The wind is not steady," observed Hillebrant: "there is no saying from which quarter the storm may blow: it has already veered round five points. Philip, I don't much like the appearance of things, and I may say with the captain that my heart is heavy."

"And, indeed, so is mine," replied Philip; "but we are in the hands of a merciful Providence."

"Hard a-port! flatten in forward! brail up the trysail, my men! Be smart!" cried Kloots, as from the wind's chopping round to the northward and westward, the ship was taken aback, and careened low before it. The rain now came down in torrents, and it was so dark that it was with difficulty they could perceive each other on the deck.

"We must clew up the topsails while the men can get upon the yards. See to it forward, Mr Hillebrant."

The lightning now darted athwart the firmament, and the thunder pealed.

"Quick! quick, my men, let's furl all!"

The sailors shook the water from their streaming clothes, some worked, others took advantage of the night to hide themselves away, and commune with their own fears.

All canvass was now taken off the ship, except the fore-staysail, and she flew to the southward with the wind on her quarter. The sea had now risen, and roared as it curled in foam, the rain fell in torrents, the night was dark as Erebus, and the wet and frightened sailors sheltered themselves under the bulwarks. Although many had deserted from their duty, there was not one who ventured below that night. They did not collect together as usual—every man preferred solitude and his own thoughts. The Phantom Ship dwelt on their imaginations and oppressed their brains.

It was an interminably long and terrible night—they thought the day would never come. At last the darkness gradually changed to a settled sullen grey gloom—which was day. They looked at each other, but found no comfort in meeting each other's eyes. There was no one countenance in which a beam of hope could be found lurking. They were all doomed— they remained crouched where they had—sheltered themselves during the night, and said nothing.

The sea had now risen mountains high, and more than once had struck the ship abaft. Kloots was at the binnacle, Hillebrant and Philip at the helm, when a wave curled high over the quarter, and poured itself in resistless force upon the deck. The captain and his two mates were swept away, and dashed almost senseless against the bulwarks—the binnacle and compass were broken into fragments—no one ran to the helm—the vessel broached to—the seas broke clear over her, and the mainmast went by the board.

All was confusion. Captain Kloots was stunned, and it was with difficulty that Philip could persuade two of the men to assist him down below. Hillebrant had been more unfortunate—his right arm was broken, and he was otherwise severely bruised; Philip assisted him to his berth, and then went on deck again to try and restore order.

Philip Vanderdecken was not yet much of a seaman, but, at all events, he exercised that moral influence over the men which is ever possessed by resolution and courage. Obey willingly they did not, but they did obey, and in half an hour the vessel was clear of the wreck. Eased by the loss of her heavy mast, and steered by two of her best seamen, she again flew before the gale.

Where was Mynheer Von Stroom during all this work of destruction? In his bed-place, covered up with the clothes, trembling in every limb, and vowing that it ever again he put his foot on shore, not all the companies in the world should induce him to trust to salt-water again. It certainly was the best plan for the poor man.

But although for a time the men obeyed the orders of Philip, they were soon seen talking earnestly with the one-eyed pilot, and after a consultation of a quarter of an hour, they all left the deck, with the exception of the two at the helm. Their reasons for so doing were soon apparent—several returned with cans full of liquor, which they had obtained by forcing the hatches of the spirit-room. For about an hour Philip remained on deck, persuading the men not to intoxicate themselves, but in vain; the cans of grog offered to the men at the wheel were not refused, and, in a short time, the yawing of the vessel proved that the liquor had taken its effect. Philip then hastened down below to ascertain if Mynheer Kloots was sufficiently recovered to come on deck. He found him sunk into a deep sleep, and with difficulty it was that he roused him, and made him acquainted with the distressing intelligence. Mynheer Kloots followed Philip on deck; but he still suffered from his fail: his head was confused, and he reeled as he walked, as if he also had been making free with the liquor. When he had been on deck a few minutes, he sank down on one of the guns in a state of perfect helplessness; he had, in fact, received a severe concussion of the brain. Hillebrant was too severely injured to be able to move from his bed, and Philip was now aware of the helplessness of their situation. Daylight gradually disappeared, and as darkness came upon them, so did the scene become more appalling. The vessel still ran before the gale, but the men at the helm had evidently changed her course, as the wind that was on the starboard was now on the larboard quarter. But compass there was none on deck, and, even if there had been, the men in their drunken state would have refused to listen to Philip's orders or expostulations. "He," they said, "was no sailor, and was not to teach them how to steer the ship." The gale was now at its height. The rain had ceased, but the wind had increased, and it roared as it urged on the vessel, which, steered so wide by the drunken sailors, shipped seas over each gunnel; but the men laughed, and joined the chorus of their songs to the howling of the gale.

Schriften, the pilot, appeared to be the leader of the ship's company. With the can of liquor in his hand, he danced and sang, snapped his fingers, and, like a demon, peered with his one eye upon Philip; and then would he fall and roll with screams of laughter in the scuppers. More liquor was handed up as fast as it was called for. Oaths shrieks laughter, were mingled together; the men at the helm lashed it amid-ships, and hastened to join their companions and the Ter Schilling flew before the gale; the fore-staysail being the only sail set, checking her, as she yawed to starboard or to port. Philip remained on deck by the poop-ladder. Strange, thought he, that I should stand here, the only one left now capable of acting,—that I should be fated to look by myself upon this scene of horror and disgust—should here wait the severing of this vessel's timbers,—the loss of life which must accompany it—the only one calm and collected, or aware of what must soon take place. God forgive me, but I appear, useless and impotent as I am, to stand here like the master of the storm,—separated, as it were, from my brother mortals by my own peculiar destiny. It must be so. This wreck then must not be for me, I feel that it is not,—that I have a charmed life, or rather a protracted one, to fulfil the oath I registered in heaven. But the wind is not so loud, surely the water is not so rough: my forebodings may be wrong and all may yet be saved. Heaven grant it! For how melancholy, how lamentable is it to behold men created in God's own image, leaving the world, disgraced below the brute creation!

Philip was right in supposing that the wind was not so strong, nor the sea so high. The vessel, after running to the southward till past Table Bay, had, by the alteration made in her course, entered into False Bay, where, to a certain degree, she was sheltered from the violence of the winds and waves. But although the water was smoother, the waves were still more than sufficient to beat to pieces any vessel that might be driven on shore at the bottom of the bay, to which point the Ter Schilling was now running. The bay so far offered a fair chance of escape, as, instead of the rocky coast outside, against which, had the vessel run, a few seconds would have insured her destruction, there was a shelving beach of loose sand. But of this Philip could, of course, have no knowledge, for the land at the entrance of the bay had been passed unperceived in the darkness of the night. About twenty minutes more had elapsed, when Philip observed that the whole sea around them was one continued foam. He had hardly time for conjecture before the ship struck heavily on the sands, and the remaining masts fell by the board.

The crush of the falling masts, the heavy beating of the ship on the sands, which caused many of her timbers to part, with a whole sea which swept clean over the fated vessel, checked the songs and drunken revelry of the crew. Another minute, and the vessel was swung round on her broadside to the sea, and lay on her beam ends. Philip, who was to windward clung to the bulwark, while the intoxicated seamen floundered in the water to leeward, and attempted to gain the other side of the ship. Much to Philip's horror, he perceived the body of Mynheer Kloots sink down in the water (which now was several feet deep on the lee side of the deck), without any apparent effort on the part of the captain to save himself. He was then gone, and there were no hopes for him. Philip thought of Hillebrant, and hastened down below; he found him still in his bed-place, lying against the side. He lifted him out, and with difficulty climbed with him on deck, and laid him in the long-boat on the booms as the best chance of saving his life. To this boat the only one which could be made available, the crew had also repaired; but they repulsed Philip who would have got into her; and, as the sea made clean breakers over them, they cast loose the lashings which confined her. With the assistance of another heavy sea which lifted her from the chocks she was borne clear of the booms and dashed over the gunnel into the water, to leeward, which was comparatively smooth—not, however, without being filled nearly up to the thwarts. But this was little cared for by the intoxicated seamen, who, as soon as they were afloat, again raised their shouts and songs of revelry as they were borne away by the wind and sea towards the beach. Philip, who held on by the stump of the mainmast, watched them with an anxious eye, now perceiving them borne aloft on the foaming surf, now disappearing in the trough. More and more distant were the sounds of their mad voices, till, at last, he could hear them no more,—he beheld the boat balanced on an enormous rolling sea, and then he saw it not again.

Philip knew that now his only chance was to remain with the vessel, and attempt to save himself upon some fragment of the wreck. That the ship would long hold together he felt was impossible; already she had parted her upper decks, and each shock of the waves divided her more and more. At last, as he clung to the mast, he heard a noise abaft, and he then recollected that Mynheer Von Stroom was still in his cabin. Philip crawled aft, and found that the poop-ladder had been thrown against the cabin door, so as to prevent its being opened. He removed it and entered the cabin, where he found Mynheer Von Stroom clinging to windward with the grasp of death,—but it was not death, but the paralysis of fear. He spoke to him, but could obtain no reply, he attempted to move him, but it was impossible to make him let go the part of the bulk-head that he grasped. A loud noise and the rush of a mass of water told Philip that the vessel had parted amidships, and he unwillingly abandoned the poor supercargo to his fate, and went out of the cabin door. At the after-hatchway he observed something struggling,—it was Johannes the bear, who was swimming, but still fastened by a cord which prevented his escape. Philip took out his knife and released the poor animal, and hardly had he done this act of kindness, when a heavy sea turned over the after part of the vessel, which separated in many pieces, and Philip found himself struggling in the waves. He seized upon a part of the deck which supported him, and was borne away by the surf towards the beach. In a few minutes he was near to the land, and shortly afterwards the piece of planking to which he was clinging struck on the sand, and then, being turned over by the force of the running wave, Philip lost his hold, and was left to his own exertions. He struggled long, but, although so near to the shore, could not gain a footing; the returning wave dragged him back, and thus was he hurled to and fro until his strength was gone. He was sinking under the wave to rise no more when he felt something touch his hand. He seized it with the grasp of death. It was the shaggy hide of the bear Johannes, who was making for the shore, and who soon dragged him clear of the surf, so that he could gain a footing. Philip crawled up the beach above the reach of the waves, and, exhausted with fatigue, sank down in a swoon.

When Philip was recalled from his state of lethargy, his first feeling was intense pain in his still-closed eyes, arising from having been many hours exposed to the rays of an ardent sun. He opened them, but was obliged to close them immediately, for the light entered into them like the point of a knife. He turned over on his side, and covering them with his hand remained some time in that position, until, by degrees, he found that his eyesight was restored. He then rose, and, after a few seconds, could distinguish the scene around him. The sea was still rough, and tossed about in the surf fragments of the vessel; the whole sand was strewed with her cargo and contents. Near him was the body of Hillebrant, and the other bodies who were scattered on the beach told him that those who had taken to the boat had all perished.

It was, by the height of the sun, about three o'clock in the afternoon, as near as he could estimate; but Philip suffered such an oppression of mind, he felt so wearied, and in such pain, that he took but a slight survey. His brain was whirling, and all he demanded was repose. He walked away from the scene of destruction, and having found a sand-hill, behind which he was defended from the burning rays of the sun, he again lay down, and sank into a deep sleep, from which he did not wake until the ensuing morning.

Philip was roused a second time by the sensation of something pricking him on the chest. He started up, and beheld a figure standing over him. His eyes were still feeble, and his vision indistinct; he rubbed them for a time, for he first thought it was the bear Johannes, and again, that it was the supercargo Von Stroom, who had appeared before him; he looked again, and found that he was mistaken, although he had warrant for supposing it to be either, or both. A tall Hottentot, with an assaguay in his hand, stood by his side; over his shoulder he had thrown the fresh-severed skin of the poor bear, and on his head, with the curls descending to his waist, was one of the wigs of the supercargo Von Stroom. Such was the gravity of the black's appearance in this strange costume (for in every other respect he was naked), that, at any other time, Philip would have been induced to laugh heartily; but his feelings were now too acute. He rose upon his feet, and stood by the side of the Hottentot, who still continued immovable, but certainly without the slightest appearance of hostile intentions.

A sensation of overpowering thirst now seized upon Philip, and he made signs that he wished to drink. The Hottentot motioned to him to follow, and led over the sand-hills to the beach, where Philip discovered upwards of fifty men, who were busy selecting various articles from the scattered stores of the vessel. It was evident by the respect paid to Philip's conductor, that he was the chief of the kraal. A few words, uttered with the greatest solemnity, were sufficient to produce, though not exactly what Philip required, a small quantity of dirty water from a calabash, which, however, was to him delicious. His conductor then waved to him to take a seat on the sand.

It was a novel and appalling, and, nevertheless, a ludicrous scene: there was the white sand, rendered still more white by the strong glare of the sun, strewed with the fragments of the vessel, with casks, and bales of merchandise; there was the running surge with its foam, throwing about particles of the wreck: there were the bones of whales which had been driven on shore in some former gale and which, now half-buried in the sand, showed portions of huge skeletons; there were the mangled bodies of Philip's late companions, whose clothes, it appeared, had been untouched by the savages, with the exception of the buttons, which had been eagerly sought after; there were naked Hottentots (for it was summer time, and they wore not their sheepskin krosses) gravely stepping up and down the sand, picking up everything that was of no value, and leaving all that civilised people most coveted;—to crown all, there was the chief, sitting in the still bloody skin of Johannes, and the broad-bottomed wig of Mynheer Stroom, with all the gravity of a vice-chancellor in his countenance, and without the slightest idea that he was in any way ridiculous. The whole presented, perhaps, one of the most strange and chaotic tableaux that ever was witnessed.

Although, at that time, the Dutch had not very long formed their settlement at the Cape, a considerable traffic had been, for many years, carried on with the natives for skins and other African productions. The Hottentots were, therefore, no strangers to vessels, and, as hitherto they had been treated with kindness, were well-disposed towards Europeans. After a time, the Hottentots began to collect all the wood which appeared to have iron in it, made it up into several piles, and set them on fire. The chief then made a sign to Philip, to ask him if he was hungry; Philip replied in the affirmative, when his new acquaintance put his hand into a bag made of goat-skin, and pulled out a handful of very large beetles, and presented them to hum. Philip refused them with marks of disgust, upon which, the chief very sedately cracked and ate them; and having finished the whole handful, rose, and made a sign to Philip to follow him. As Philip rose, he perceived floating on the surf, his own chest; he hastened to it, and made signs that it was his, took the key out of his pocket and opened it, and then made up a bundle of articles most useful, not forgetting a bag of guilders. His conductor made no objection, but calling to one of the men near, pointed out the lock and hinges to him, and then set off, followed by Philip, across the sand-hills. In about an hour they arrived at the kraal, consisting of low huts covered with skins, and were met by the women and children, who appeared to be in high admiration at their chief's new attire: the showed every kindness to Philip, bringing him milk, which he drank eagerly. Philip surveyed these daughters of Eve, and, as he turned from their offensive, greasy attire, their strange forms, and hideous features, he sighed and thought of his charming Amine.

The sun was now setting, and Philip still felt fatigued. He made signs that he wished to repose. They led him into a hut, and, though surrounded as he was with filth and his nose assailed by every variety of bad smell attacked, moreover, by insects, he laid his head on his bundle, and uttering a short prayer of thanksgiving, was soon in a sound sleep.

The next morning he was awakened by the chief of the kraal, accompanied by another man who spoke a little Dutch. He stated his wish to be taken to the settlement where the ships came and anchored, and was fully understood; but the man said that there were no ships in the bay at the time. Philip, nevertheless, requested he might be taken there, as he felt that his best chance of getting on board of any vessel would be by remaining at the settlement, and, at all events, he would be in the company of Europeans, until a vessel arrived. The distance, he discovered, was but one day's march, or less. After some little conversation with the chief, the man who spoke Dutch desired Philip to follow him and that he would take him there. Philip drank plentifully from a bowl of milk brought him by one of the women, and again refusing a handful of beetles offered by the chief, he took up his bundle, and followed his new acquaintance.

Towards evening they arrived at the hills, from which Philip had a view of Table Bay and the few houses erected by the Dutch. To his delight, he perceived that there was a vessel under sail in the offing. On his arrival at the beach, to which he hastened, he found that she had sent a boat on shore for fresh provisions. He accosted the people, told them who he was, told them also of the fatal wreck of the Ter Schilling, and of his wish to embark.

The officer in charge of the boat willingly consented to take him on board, and informed Philip that they were homeward bound. Philip's heart leaped at the intelligence. Had she been outward bound, he would have joined her; but now he had a prospect of again seeing his dear Amine before he re-embarked to follow out his peculiar destiny. He felt that there was still some happiness in store for him, that his life was to be chequered with alternate privation and repose, and that his future prospect was not to be one continued chain of suffering until death.

He was kindly received by the captain of the vessel, who freely gave him a passage home; and in three months, without any events worth narrating, Philip Vanderdecken found himself once more at anchor before the town of Amsterdam.

Chapter Eleven

It need hardly be observed that Philip made all possible haste to his own little cottage, which contained all that he valued in this world. He promised to himself some months of happiness, for he had done his duty; and he felt that, however desirous of fulfilling his vow, he could not again leave home till the autumn, when the next fleet sailed, and it was now but the commencement of April. Much, too, as he regretted the loss of Mynheer Kloots and Hillebrant, as well as the deaths of the unfortunate crew, still there was some solace in the remembrance that he was for ever rid of the wretch Schriften, who had shared their fate; and besides he almost blessed the wreck, so fatal to others, which enabled him so soon to return to the arms of his Amine.

It was late in the evening; when Philip took a boat from Flushing, and went over to his cottage at Terneuse. It was a rough evening for the season of the year. The wind blew fresh, and the sky was covered with flaky clouds, fringed here and there with broad white edges, for the light of the moon was high in the heavens, and she was at her full. At times her light would be almost obscured by a dark cloud passing over her disk; at others, she would burst out in all her brightness. Philip landed, and, wrapping his cloak round him, hastened up to his cottage. As with a beating heart he approached, he perceived that the window of the parlour was open, and that there was a female figure leaning out. He knew that it could be no other than his Amine, and, after he crossed the little bridge, he proceeded to the window, instead of going to the door. Amine (for it was she who stood at the window) was so absorbed in contemplation of the heavens above her, and so deep in communion with her own thoughts, that she neither saw nor heard the approach of her husband. Philip perceived her abstraction, and paused when within four or five yards of her. He wished to gain the door without being observed, as he was afraid of alarming her by his too sudden appearance, for he remembered his promise, "that if dead he would, if permitted, visit her as his father had visited his mother." But while he thus stood in suspense, Amine's eyes were turned upon him: she beheld him; but a thick cloud now obscured the moon's disk, and the dim light gave to his form, indistinctly seen, an unearthly and shadowy appearance. She recognised her husband, but having no reason to expect his return, she recognised him as an inhabitant of the world of spirits. She started, parted the hair away from her forehead with both hands, and again earnestly gazed on him.

"It is I, Amine, do not be afraid," cried Philip, hastily.

"I am not afraid," replied Amine, pressing her hand to her heart. "It is over now. Spirit of my dear husband—for such I think thou art—I thank thee! Welcome, even in death, Philip—welcome!" and Amine waved her hand mournfully, inviting Philip to enter as she retired from the window.

"My God! she thinks me dead," thought Philip, and, hardly knowing how to act, he entered in at the window, and found her sitting on the sofa. Philip would have spoken; but Amine, whose eyes were fixed upon him as he entered, and who was fully convinced that he was but a supernatural appearance, exclaimed—

"So soon—so soon! O God! thy will be done: but it is hard to bear. Philip, beloved Philip, I feel that I soon shall follow you."

Philip was now more alarmed: he was fearful of any sudden reaction when Amine should discover that he was still alive.

"Amine, dear, hear me. I have appeared unexpectedly and at an unusual hour; but throw yourself into my arms, and you will find that your Philip is not dead."

"Not dead!" cried Amine, starting up.

"No, no, still warm in flesh and blood, Amine—still your fond and doting husband," replied Philip, catching her in his arms, and pressing her to his heart.

Amine sank from his embrace down upon the sofa, and fortunately was relieved by a burst of tears, while Philip, kneeling by her, supported her.

"O God! O God! I thank thee," relied Amine, at last. "I thought it was your spirit, Philip. O! I was glad to see even that," continued she, weeping on his shoulder.

"Can you listen to me, dearest?" said Philip, after a silence of a few moments.

"O speak—speak, love; I can listen for ever."

In a few words Philip then recounted what had taken place, and the occasion of his unexpected return, and felt himself more than repaid for all that he had suffered, by the fond endearments of his still agitated Amine.

"And your father, Amine?"

"He is well; we will talk of him to-morrow."

"Yes," thought Philip, as he awoke next morning, and dwelt upon the lovely features of his still slumbering wife; "yes, God is merciful. I feel that there is still happiness in store for me; nay, more, that that happiness also depends upon my due performance of my task, and that I should be punished if I were to forget my solemn vow. Be it so,—through danger and to death will I perform my duty, trusting to His mercy for a reward both here below and in heaven above. Am I not repaid for all that I have suffered? O yes more than repaid," thought Philip, as with a kiss he disturbed the slumber of his wife, and met her full dark eyes fixed upon him, beaming with love and joy.

Before Philip went down stairs, he inquired about Mynheer Poots.

"My father has indeed troubled me much," replied Amine. "I am obliged to lock the parlour when I leave it, for more than once I have found him attempting to force the locks of the buffets. His love of gold is insatiable: he dreams of nothing else, he has caused me much pain, insisting that I never should see you again, and that I should surrender to him all your wealth. But he fears me, and he fears your return much more."

"Is he well in health?"

"Not ill, but still evidently wasting away—like a candle burnt down to the socket, flitting and flaring alternately; at one time almost imbecile, at others, talking and planning as if he were in the vigour of his youth. O what a curse it must be—that love of money! I believe—I'm shocked to say so, Philip,—that that poor old man, now on the brink of a grave into which he can take nothing, would sacrifice your life and mine to have possession of those guilders, the whole of which I would barter for one kiss from thee."

"Indeed, Amine, has he then attempted anything in my absence?"

"I dare not speak my thoughts, Philip, nor will I venture upon surmises, which it were difficult to prove. I watch him carefully;—but talk no more about him. You will see him soon, and do not expect a hearty welcome, or believe that, if given, it is sincere, I will not tell him of your return, as I wish to mark the effect."

Amine then descended to prepare breakfast, and Philip walked out for a few minutes. On his return, he found Mynheer Poots sitting at the table with his daughter.

"Merciful Allah! am I right?" cried the old man: "is it you, Mynheer Vanderdecken?"

"Even so," replied Philip; "I returned last night."

"And you did not tell me, Amine."

"I wished that you should be surprised," replied Amine.

"I am surprised! When do you sail again, Mynheer Philip? very soon, I suppose? perhaps to-morrow?" said Mynheer Poots.

"Not for many months, I trust," replied Philip.

"Not for many months!—that is a long while to be idle. You must make money. Tell me, have you brought back plenty this time?"

"No," replied Philip; "I have been wrecked, and very nearly lost my life."

"But you will go again?"

"Yes, in good time I shall go again."

"Very well, we will take care of your house and your guilders."

"I shall perhaps save you the trouble of taking care of my guilders," replied Philip, to annoy the old man, "for I mean to take them with me."

"To take them with you! for what, pray?" replied Poots, in alarm.

"To purchase goods where I go, and make more money."

"But you may be wrecked again and then the money will be all lost. No, no; go yourself, Mynheer Philip; but you must not take your guilders."

"Indeed I will," replied Philip; "when I leave this, I shall take all my money with me."

During this conversation it occurred to Philip that, if Mynheer Poots could only be led to suppose that he took away his money with him, there would be more quiet for Amine who was now obliged, as she had informed him, to be constantly on the watch. He determined, therefore, when he next departed, to make the doctor believe that he had taken his wealth with him.

Mynheer Poots did not renew the conversation, but sank into gloomy thought. In a few minutes he left the parlour, and went up to his own room, when Philip stated to his wife what had induced him to make the old man believe that he should embark his property.

"It was thoughtful of you, Philip, and I thank you for your kind feeling towards me; but I wish you had said nothing on the subject. You do not know my father; I must now watch him as an enemy."

"We have little to fear from an infirm old man," replied Philip, laughing. But Amine thought otherwise, and was ever on her guard.

The spring and summer passed rapidly away, for they were happy. Many were the conversations between Philip and Amine, relative to what had passed—the supernatural appearance of his father's ship, and the fatal wreck.

Amine felt that more dangers and difficulty were preparing for her husband, but she never once attempted to dissuade him from renewing his attempts in fulfilment of his vow. Like him, she looked forward with hope and confidence, aware that, at some time, his fate must be accomplished, and trusting only that that hour would be long delayed.

At the close of the summer, Philip again went to Amsterdam, to procure for himself a berth in one of the vessels which were to sail at the approach of winter.

The wreck of the Ter Schilling was well known; and the circumstances attending it, with the exception of the appearance of the Phantom Ship, had been drawn up by Philip on his passage home, and communicated to the Court of Directors. Not only on account of the very creditable manner in which that report had been prepared, but in consideration of his peculiar sufferings and escape, he had been promised by the Company a berth, as second mate, on board of one of their vessels, should he be again inclined to sail to the East Indies.

Having called upon the Directors, he received his appointment to the Batavia, a fine vessel of about 400 tons burden. Having effected his purpose, Philip hastened back to Terneuse, and, in the presence of Mynheer Poots, informed Amine of what he had done.

"So you go to sea again?" observed Mynheer Poots.

"Yes, but not for two months, I expect," replied Philip.

"Ah!" replied Poots, "in two months!" and the old man muttered to himself.

How true it is that we can more easily bear up against a real evil than against suspense! Let it not be supposed that Amine fretted at the thought of her approaching separation from her husband; she lamented it, but feeling his departure to be an imperious duty, and having it ever in her mind, she bore up against her feelings, and submitted, without repining, to what could not be averted. There was, however, one circumstance, which caused her much uneasiness—that was the temper and conduct of her father. Amine, who knew his character well, perceived that he already secretly hated Philip, whom he regarded as an obstacle to his obtaining possession of the money in the house; for the old man was well aware that if Philip were dead, his daughter would care little who had possession of, or what became of it. The thought that Philip was about to take that money with him had almost turned the brain of the avaricious old man. He had been watched by

Amine, and she had seen him walk for hours muttering to himself, and not, as usual, attending to his profession.

A few evenings after his return from Amsterdam, Philip, who had taken cold, complained of not being well.

"Not well!" cried the old man, starting up; "let me see—yes, your pulse is very quick. Amine, your poor husband is very ill. He must go to bed, and I will give him something which will do him good. I shall charge you nothing, Philip—nothing at all."

"I do not feel so very unwell, Mynheer Poots," replied Philip; "I have a bad headache certainly."

"Yes, and you have fever also, Philip, and prevention is better than cure; so go to bed, and take what I send you, and you will be well to-morrow."

Philip went up stairs, accompanied by Amine; and Mynheer Poots went into his own room to prepare the medicine. So soon as Philip was in bed, Amine went down stairs, and was met by her father, who put a powder into her hands to give to her husband, and then left the parlour.

"God forgive me if I wrong my father," thought Amine, "but I have my doubts. Philip is ill, more so than he will acknowledge; and if he does not take some remedies, he may be worse—but my heart misgives me—I have a foreboding. Yet surely he cannot be so diabolically wicked."

Amine examined the contents of the paper: it was a very small quantity of dark-brown powder, and, by the directions of Mynheer Poots, to be given in a tumbler of warm wine. Mynheer Poots had offered to heat the wine. His return from the kitchen broke Amine's meditations.

"Here is the wine, my child; now give him a whole tumbler of wine, and the powder, and let him be covered up warm, for the perspiration will soon burst out and it must not be checked. Watch him, Amine, and keep the clothes on, and he will be well to-morrow morning." And Mynheer Poots quitted the room, saying, "Good night, my child."

Amine poured out the powder into one of the silver mugs on the table, and then proceeded to mix it up with the wine. Her suspicions had, for the time been removed by the kind tone of her father's voice. To do him justice as a medical practitioner, he appeared always to be most careful of his patients. When Amine mixed the powder, she examined and perceived that there was no sediment, and the wine was as clear as before. This was unusual, and her suspicions revived.

"I like it not," said she; "I fear my father—God help me!—I hardly know what to do—I will not give it to Philip. The warm wine may produce perspiration sufficient."

Amine paused, and again reflected. She had mixed the powder with so small a portion of wine that it did not fill a quarter of the cup; she put it on one side, filled another up to the brim with the warm wine, and then went up to the bedroom.

On the landing-place she was met by her father, whom she supposed to have retired to rest.

"Take care you do not spill it, Amine. That is right, let him have a whole cupful. Stop, give it to me; I will take it to him myself."

Mynheer Poots took the cup from Amine's hands, and went into Philip's room.

"Here, my son, drink this off, and you will be well," said Mynheer Poots, whose hand trembled so that he spilt the wine on the coverlid. Amine, who watched her father, was more than ever pleased that she had not put the powder into the cup. Philip rose on his elbow, drank off the wine, and Mynheer Poots then wished him good night.

"Do not leave him, Amine, I will see all right," said Mynheer Poots, as he left the room. And Amine, who had intended to go down for the candle left in the parlour, remained with her husband, to whom she confided her feelings and also the fact that she had not given him the powder.

"I trust that you are mistaken, Amine," replied Philip; "indeed I feel sure that you must be. No man could be so bad as you suppose your father."

"You have not lived with him as I have—you have not seen what I have seen," replied Amine. "You know not what gold will tempt people to do in this world—but, however, I may be wrong. At all events, you must go to sleep, and I shall watch you, dearest. Pray do not speak—I feel I cannot sleep just now—I wish to read a little—I will lie down by-and-by."

Philip made no further objections, and was soon in a sound sleep, and Amine watched him in silence till midnight long had passed.

"He breathes heavily," thought Amine; "but had I given him that powder, who knows if he had ever awoke again? My father is so deeply skilled in the Eastern knowledge, that I fear him. Too often has he, I well know, for a purse well filled with gold, prepared the sleep of death. Another would shudder at the thought; but he, who has dealt out death at the will of his employers, would scruple little to do so even to the husband of his own daughter; and I have watched him in his moods and know his thoughts and wishes. What a foreboding of mishap has come over me this evening!—what a fear of evil! Philip is ill, 'tis true, but not so very ill. No! no! Besides his time is not yet come; he has his dreadful task to finish. I would it were morning. How soundly he sleeps!—and the dew is on his brow. I must cover him up warm, and watch that he remains so. Some one knocks at the entrance-door. Now will they wake him. 'Tis a summons for my father."

Amine left the room, and hastened down stairs. It was as she supposed, a summons for Mynheer Poots to a woman taken in labour. "He shall follow you directly," said Amine; "I will now call him up." Amine went up stairs to the room where her father slept, and knocked; hearing no answer, as usual, she knocked again.

"My father is not used to sleep in this way," thought Amine, when she found no answer to her second call. She opened the door and went in. To her surprise, her father was not in bed. "Strange," thought she; "but I do not recollect having heard his footsteps coming up after he went down to take away the lights." And Amine hastened to the parlour, where, stretched on the sofa, she discovered her father apparently fast asleep; but to her call he gave no answer. "Merciful Heaven! is he dead?" thought she, approaching the light to her father's face. Yes, it was so!—his eyes were fixed and glazed—his lower jaw had fallen.

For some minutes, Amine leant against the wall in a state of bewilderment; her brain whirled; at last she recovered herself.

"'Tis to be proved at once," thought she, as she went up to the table, and looked into the silver cup in which she had mixed the powder—it was empty! "The God of Righteousness hath punished him!" exclaimed Amine; "but O! that this man should have been my father! Yes! it is plain. Frightened at his own wicked, damned intentions, he poured out more wine from the flagon, to blunt his feelings of remorse, and not knowing that the powder was still in the cup, he filled it up and drank himself—the death he meant for another! For another!—and for whom? one wedded to his own daughter!— Philip! my husband! Wert thou not my father," continued Amine, looking at the dead body, "I would spit upon thee? and curse thee!—but thou art punished, and may God forgive thee! thou poor, weak, wicked creature!"

Amine then left the room and went up stairs, where she found Philip still fast asleep, and in a profuse perspiration.

Most women would have awakened their husbands, but Amine thought not of herself; Philip was ill, and Amine would not arouse him to agitate him. She sat down by the side of the bed, and with her hands pressed upon her forehead, and her elbows resting on her knees, she remained in deep thought until the sun had risen and poured his bright beams through the casement.

She was roused from her reflections by another summons at the door of the cottage. She hastened down to the entrance, but did not open the door.

"Mynheer Poots is required immediately," said the girl, who was the messenger.

"My good Therese," replied Amine, "my father has more need of assistance than the poor woman; for his travail in this world I fear, is well over. I found him very ill when I went to call him, and he has not been able to quit his bed. I must now entreat you to do my message, and desire Father Seysen to come hither; for my poor father is, I fear, in extremity."

"Mercy on me!" replied Therese. "Is it so? Fear not but I will do your bidding, Mistress Amine."

The second knocking had awakened Philip, who felt that he was much better, and his headache had left him. He perceived that Amine had not taken any rest that night, and he was about to expostulate with her, when she at once told him what had occurred.

"You must dress yourself, Philip," continued she, "and must assist me to carry up his body, and place it in his bed, before the arrival of the priest. God of mercy! had I given you that powder, my dearest Philip—but let us not talk about it. Be quick, for Father Seysen will be here soon."

Philip was soon dressed, and followed Amine down into the parlour. The sun shone bright, and its rays were darted upon the haggard face of the old man, whose fists were clenched, and his tongue fixed between the teeth on one side of his mouth.

"Alas! this room appears to be fatal. How many more scenes of horror are to pass within it?"

"None, I trust," replied Amine; "this is not, to my mind, the scene of horror. It was when that old man (now called away—and a victim to his own treachery) stood by your bed-side, and with every mark of interest and kindness, offered you the cup—*that* was the scene of horror," said Amine, shuddering—"one which long will haunt me."

"God forgive him! as I do," replied Philip, lifting up the body, and carrying it up the stairs to the room which had been occupied by Mynheer Poots.

"Let it at least be supposed that he died in his bed, and that his death was natural," said Amine. "My pride cannot bear that this should be known, or that I should be pointed at as the daughter of a murderer! O Philip!"

Amine sat down, and burst into tears.

Her husband was attempting to console her, when Father Seysen knocked at the door. Philip hastened down to open it.

"Good morning, my son. How is the sufferer?"

"He has ceased to suffer, father."

"Indeed!" replied the good priest, with sorrow in his countenance; "am I then too late? yet have I not tarried."

"He went off suddenly, father, in a convulsion," replied Philip, leading the way up stairs.

Father Seysen looked at the body and perceived that his offices were needless, and then turned to Amine, who had not yet checked her tears.

"Weep, my child, weep! for you have cause," said the priest. "The loss of a father's love must be a severe trial to a dutiful and affectionate child. But yield not too much to your grief, Amine; you have other duties, other ties, my child—you have your husband."

"I know it, father," replied Amine; "still must I weep, for I was *his* daughter."

"Did he not go to bed last night then that his clothes are still upon him? When did he first complain?"

"The last time that I saw him, father," replied Philip; "he came into my room and gave me some medicine, and then he wished me good night. Upon on a summons to attend a sick bed, my wife went to call him, and found him speechless."

"It has been sudden," replied the priest; "but he was an old man, and old men sink at once. Were you with him when he died?"

"I was not, sir," replied Philip; "before my wife had summoned me and I had dressed myself, he had left this world."

"I trust, my children, for a better." Amine shuddered. "Tell me Amine," continued the priest, "did he show signs of grace before he died? for you know full well that he has long been looked on as doubtful in his creed and little attentive to the rites of our holy church."

"There are times, holy father," replied Amine, "when even a sincere Christian can be excused, even if he give no sign. Look at his clenched hands, witness the agony of death on his face, and could you, in that state expect a sign?"

"Alas! 'tis but too true, my child: we must then hope for the best. Kneel with me, my children, and let us offer up a prayer for the soul of the departed."

Philip and Amine knelt with the priest, who prayed fervently; and as they rose, they exchanged a glance which fully revealed what was passing in the mind of each.

"I will send the people to do their offices for the dead, and prepare the body for interment," said Father Seysen; "but it were as well not to say that he was dead before I arrived, or to let it be supposed that he was called away without receiving the consolations of our holy creed."

Philip motioned his head in assent as he stood at the foot of the bed, and the priest departed. There had always been a strong feeling against Mynheer Poots in the village;—his neglect of all religious duties—the doubt whether he was even a member of the church—his avarice and extortion—had created for him a host of enemies; but, at the same time, his great medical skill, which was fully acknowledged, rendered him of importance. Had it been known that his creed (if he had any) was Mahomedan, and that he had died in attempting to poison his son-in-law, it is certain that Christian burial would have been refused him, and the finger of scorn would have been pointed at his daughter. But as Father Seysen, when questioned, said, in a mild voice, that "he had departed in peace," it was presumed that Mynheer Poots had died a good Christian although he had acted little up to the tenets of Christianity during his life. The next day the remains of the old man were consigned to the earth with the usual rites; and Philip and Amine were not a little relieved in their minds at everything having passed off so quietly.

It was not until after the funeral had taken place that Philip, in company with Amine, examined the chamber of his father-in-law. The key of the iron chest was found in his pocket; but Philip had not yet looked into this darling repository of the old man. The room was full of bottles and boxes of drugs, all of which were either thrown away, or, if the utility of them was known to Amine, removed to a spare room. His table contained many drawers, which were now examined, and among the heterogeneous contents were many writings in Arabic—probably prescriptions. Boxes and papers were also found, with Arabic characters written upon them; and in the box which they first took up was a powder similar to that which Mynheer Poots had given to Amine. There were many articles and writings, which made it appear that the old man had dabbled in the occult sciences, as they were practised at that period, and those they hastened to commit to the flames.

"Had all these been seen by Father Seysen!" observed Amine, mournfully. "But here are some printed papers, Philip!"

Philip examined them, and found that they were acknowledgments of shares in the Dutch East-India Company.

"No, Amine, these are money, or what is as good—these are eight shares in the Company's capital, which will yield us a handsome income every year. I had no idea that the old man made such use of his money. I had some intention of doing the same with a part of mine before I went away, instead of allowing it to remain idle."

The iron chest was now to be examined. When Philip first opened it; he imagined that it contained but little; for it was large and deep, and appeared to be almost empty; but when he put his hands down to the bottom, he pulled out thirty or forty small bags, the contents of which, instead of being silver guilders, were all coins of gold; there was only one large bag of silver money. But this was not all; several small boxes and packets were also discovered, which, when opened, were found to contain diamonds and other precious stones. When everything was collected, the treasure appeared to be of great value.

"Amine, my love, you have indeed brought me an unexpected dower," said Philip.

"You may well say *unexpected*," replied Amine. "These diamonds and jewels my father must have brought with him from Egypt. And yet how penuriously were we living until we came to this cottage! And with all this treasure he would have poisoned my Philip for more! God forgive him!"

Having counted the gold, which amounted to nearly fifty thousand guilders, the whole was replaced, and they left the room.

"I am a rich man," thought Philip, after Amine had left him; "but of what use are riches to me? I might purchase a ship and be my own captain, but would not the ship be lost? That certainly does not follow; but the chances are against the vessel; therefore I will have no ship. But is it right to sail in the vessels of others with this feeling?—I know not; this, however, I know, that I have a duty to perform, and that all our lives are in the hands of a kind Providence, which calls us away when it thinks fit. I will place most of my money in the shares of the Company, and if I sail in their vessels, and they come to misfortune by meeting with my poor father, at least I shall be a common sufferer with the rest. And now to make my Amine more comfortable."

Philip immediately made a great alteration in their style of living. Two female servants were hired: the rooms were more comfortably furnished; and in everything in which his wife's comfort and convenience were concerned, he spared no expense. He wrote to Amsterdam and purchased several shares in the Company's stock. The diamonds and his own money he still left in the hands of Amine. In making these arrangements the two months passed rapidly away; and everything was complete when Philip again received his summons, by letter, to desire that he would join his vessel. Amine would have wished Philip to go out as a passenger instead of going as an officer, but Philip preferred the latter, as otherwise he could give no reason for his voyage to India.

"I know not why," observed Philip, the evening before his departure, "but I do not feel as I did when I last went away; I have no foreboding of evil this time."

"Nor have I," replied Amine; "but I feel as if you would be long away from me, Philip; and is not that an evil to a fond and anxious wife?"

"Yes, love, it is; but—"

"O, yes, I know it is your duty, and you must go," replied Amine, burying her face in his bosom.

The next day Philip parted from his wife, who behaved with more fortitude than on their first separation. "*All* were lost but *he* was saved," thought Amine. "I feel that he will return to me. God of Heaven, Thy will be done!"

Philip soon arrived at Amsterdam; and having purchased many things which he thought might be advantageous to him in case of accident, to which he now looked forward as almost certain, he embarked on board the Batavia, which was lying at single anchor, and ready for sea.

Chapter Twelve

Philip had not been long on board, ere he found that they were not likely to have a very comfortable passage; for the Batavia was chartered to convey a large detachment of troops to Ceylon and Java, for the purpose of recruiting and strengthening the Company's forces at those places. She was to quit the fleet off Madagascar, and run direct for the Island of Java; the number of soldiers on board being presumed sufficient to insure the ship against any attack or accidents from pirates or enemies' cruisers. The Batavia, moreover, mounted thirty guns, and had a crew of seventy-five men. Besides military stores, which formed the principal part of her cargo, she had on board a large quantity of specie for the Indian market. The detachment of soldiers was embarking when Philip went on board, and in a few minutes the decks were so crowded that it was hardly possible to move. Philip, who had not yet spoken to the captain, found out the first mate, and immediately entered upon his duty, with which, from his close application to it during his former voyage and passage home, he was much better acquainted than might have been imagined.

In a short time all traces of hurry and confusion began to disappear, the baggage of the troops was stowed away, and the soldiers having been told off in parties, and stationed with their messing utensils between the guns of the main deck, room was thus afforded for working the ship. Philip showed great activity as well as method in the arrangements proposed and the captain, during a pause in his own arduous duties, said to him—

"I thought you were taking it very easy, Mr Vanderdecken, in not joining the ship before, but, now you are on board, you are making up for lost time. You have done more during the forenoon than I could have expected. I am glad that you are come, though very sorry you were not here when we were stowing the hold, which, I am afraid, is not arranged quite so well as it might be. Mynheer Struys, the first mate, has had more to do than he could well give attention to."

"I am sorry that I should not have been here, sir," replied Philip; "but I came as soon as the Company sent me word."

"Yes, and as they know that you are a married man, and do not forget that you are a great shareholder, they would not trouble you too soon. I presume you will have the command of a vessel next voyage. In fact, you are certain of it, with the capital you have invested in their funds. I had a conversation with one of the senior accountants on the subject this very morning."

Philip was not very sorry that his money had been put out to such good interest, as to be the captain of a ship was what he earnestly desired. He replied, that "he certainly did hope to command a ship after the next voyage, when he trusted that he should feel himself quite competent to the charge."

"No doubt, no doubt, Mr Vanderdecken. I can see that clearly. You must be very fond of the sea."

"I am," replied Philip; "I doubt whether I shall ever give it up."

"*Never* give it up! You think so now. You are young, active, and full of hope; but you will tire of it by and bye, and be glad to lay by for the rest of your days."

"How many troops do we embark?" inquired Philip.

"Two hundred and forty-five rank and file, and six officers. Poor fellows! there are but few of them will ever return: nay, more than one-half will not see another birthday. It is a dreadful climate. I have landed three hundred men at that horrid hole, and in six months, even before I had sailed, there were not one hundred left alive."

"It is almost murder to send them there," observed Philip.

"Pshaw! they must die somewhere, and if they die a little sooner, what matter? Life is a commodity to be bought and sold like any other. We send out so much manufactured goods and so much money to barter for Indian commodities. We also send out so much life, and it gives a good return to the Company."

"But not to the poor soldiers, I am afraid."

"No; the Company buy it cheap and sell it dear," replied the captain, who walked forward.

True, thought Philip, they do purchase human life cheap, and make a rare profit of it, for without these poor fellows how could they hold their possessions in spite of native and foreign enemies? For what a paltry and cheap annuity do these men sell their lives? For what a miserable pittance do they dare all the horrors of a most deadly climate, without a chance, a hope of return to their native land, where they might haply repair their exhausted energies, and take a new lease of life! Good God! if these men may be thus heartlessly sacrificed to Mammon, why should I feel remorse if in the fulfilment of a sacred duty imposed on me by him who deals with us as He thinks meet, a few mortals perish? Not a sparrow fails to the ground without His knowledge, and it is for him to sacrifice or to save. I am but the creature of his will, and I but follow my duty,—but obey the commands of One whose ways are inscrutable. Still, if for my sake this ship be also doomed, I cannot but wish that I had been appointed to some other, in which the waste of human life might have been less.

It was not until a week after Philip arrived on board, that the Batavia and the remainder of the fleet were ready for sea.

It would be difficult to analyse the feelings of Philip Vanderdecken on this his second embarkation. His mind was so continually directed to the object of his voyage, that although he attended to his religious duty, yet the business of life passed before him as a dream. Assured of again meeting with the Phantom Ship, and almost equally assured that the meeting would be followed by some untoward event in all probability by the sacrifice of those who sailed with him, his thoughts preyed upon him, and wore him down to a shadow. He hardly ever spoke, except in the execution of his duty. He felt like a criminal; as one who, by embarking with them, had doomed all around him to death, disaster, and peril; and when *one* talked of his wife, and *another* of his children—when they would indulge in anticipations, and canvass happy projects, Philip would feel sick at heart, and would rise from the table and hasten to the solitude of the deck. At one time he would try to persuade himself that his senses had been worked upon in some moment of excitement, that he was the victim of an illusion; at another he would call to mind all the past—he would feel its terrible reality: and then the thought would suggest itself that with this supernatural vision Heaven had nothing to do; that it was but the work and jugglery of Satan. But then the relic—by such means the devil would not have worked. A few days after he had sailed, he bitterly repented that he had not stated the whole of his circumstances to Father Seysen, and taken his advice upon the propriety of following up his search; but it was now too late; already was the good ship Batavia more than a thousand miles from the port of Amsterdam, and his duty, whatever it might be, *must* be fulfilled.

As the fleet approached the Cape, his anxiety increased to such a degree that it was remarked by all who were on board. The captain and officers commanding the troops embarked, who all felt interested in him, vainly attempted to learn the cause of his anxiety. Philip would plead ill health; and his haggard countenance and sunken eyes silently proved that he was under acute suffering. The major part of the night he passed on deck, straining his eyes in every quarter, and watching each change in the horizon, in anticipation of the appearance of the Phantom Ship; and it was not till the day dawned that he sought a perturbed repose in his cabin. After a favourable passage, the fleet anchored to refresh at Table Bay, and Philip felt some small relief, that up to the present time the supernatural visitation had not again occurred.

As soon as the fleet had watered, they again made sail, and again did Philip's agitation become perceptible. With a favouring breeze, however, they rounded the Cape, passed by Madagascar, and arrived in the Indian Seas, when the Batavia parted company with the rest of the fleet, which steered to Cambroon and Ceylon. "And now," thought Philip, "will the Phantom Ship make her appearance? It has only waited till we should be left without a consort to assist us in distress." But the Batavia sailed in a smooth sea and under a cloudless sky, and nothing was seen. In a few weeks she arrived off Java, and previous to entering the splendid roads of Batavia, hove-to for the night. This was the last night they would be under sail, and Philip stirred not from the deck, but walked to and fro, anxiously waiting for the morning. The morning broke—the sun rose in splendour, and the Batavia steered into the roads. Before noon she was at anchor, and Philip, with his mind relieved, hastened down to his cabin, and took that repose which he so much required.

He awoke refreshed, for a great weight had been taken off his mind. "It does not follow, then," thought he, "that because I am on board the vessel that therefore the crew are doomed to perish; it does not follow that the Phantom Ship is to appear because I seek her. If so, I have no further weight upon my conscience. I seek her, it is true, and wish to meet with her; I stand, however, but the same chance as others; and it is no way certain, that, because I seek, I am sure to find. That she brings disaster upon all she meets, may be true, but not that I bring with me the disaster of meeting her. Heaven, I thank thee! Now can I prosecute my search without remorse."

Philip, restored to composure by these reflections, went on deck. The debarkation of the troops was already taking place, for they were as anxious to be relieved from their long confinement, as the seamen were to regain a little space and comfort. He surveyed the scene. The town of Batavia lay about one mile from them, low on the beach; from behind it rose a lofty chain of mountains, brilliant with verdure, and, here and there, peopled with country seats belonging to the residents, delightfully embosomed in forests of trees. The panorama was beautiful; the vegetation was luxuriant, and, from its vivid green, refreshing to the eye. Near to the town lay large and small vessels, a forest of masts; the water in the bay was of a bright blue, and rippled to a soft breeze; here and there small islets (like tufts of fresh verdure) broke the uniformity of the waterline; even the town itself was pleasing to the eye, the white colour of the houses being opposed to the dark foliage of the trees which grew in the gardens and lined the streets.

"Can it be possible," observed Philip to the captain of the Batavia, who stood by him, "that this beautiful spot can be so unhealthy? I should form a very different opinion from its appearance."

"Even," replied the captain, "as the venomous snakes of the country start up from among its flowers, so does Death stalk about in this beautiful and luxuriant landscape. Do you feel better, Mynheer Vanderdecken."

"Much better," replied Philip.

"Still, in your enfeebled state, I should recommend you to go on shore."

"I shall avail myself of your permission, with thanks. How long shall we stay here?"

"Not long, as we are ordered to run back. Our cargo is all ready for, us, and will be on board soon after we have discharged."

Philip took the advice of his captain; he had no difficulty in finding himself received by a hospitable merchant, who had a house at some distance from the town, and in a healthy situation. There he remained two months, during which he re-established his health, and then re-embarked a few days previous to the ship being ready for sea. The return voyage was fortunate, and in four months from the date of their quitting Batavia, they found themselves abreast of St. Helena; for vessels, at that period, generally made what is called the eastern passage, running down the coast of Africa, instead of keeping towards the American shores. Again they had passed the Cape without meeting with the Phantom Ship; and Philip was not only in excellent health, but in good spirits. As they lay becalmed, with the island in sight, they observed a boat pulling towards them, and in the course of three hours she arrived on board. The crew were much exhausted from having been two days in the boat, during which time they had never ceased pulling to gain the island. They stated themselves to be the crew of a small Dutch Indiaman, which had foundered, at sea two days before; she had started one of her planks, and filled so rapidly that the men had hardly time to save themselves. They consisted of the captain, mates, and twenty men belonging to the ship and an old Portuguese Catholic priest, who had been sent home by the Dutch governor, for having opposed the Dutch interests in the Island of Japan. He had lived with the natives, and been secreted by them for some time, as the Japanese government was equally desirous of capturing him with the intention of taking away his life. Eventually he found himself obliged to throw himself into the arms of the Dutch, as being the less cruel of his enemies.

The Dutch government decided that he should be sent away from the country; and he had, in consequence, been put on board of the Indiaman for a passage home. By the report of the captain and crew, one person only had been lost; but he was a person of consequence, having for many years held the situation of President in the Dutch factory in Japan. He was returning to Holland with the riches which he had amassed. By the evidence of the captain and crew, he had insisted, after he was put into the boat, upon going back to the ship to secure a casket of immense value, containing diamonds and other precious stones, which he had forgotten; they added, that while they were waiting for him the ship suddenly plunged her bowsprit under, and went down head foremost, and that it was with difficulty they had themselves escaped. They had waited for some time to ascertain if he would rise again to the surface, but he appeared no more.

"I knew that something would happen," observed the captain of the sunken vessel, after he had been sitting a short time in the cabin with Philip and the captain of the Batavia; "we saw the Fiend or Devil's Ship, as they call her, but three days before."

"What! the Flying Dutchman, as they name her?" asked Philip.

"Yes; that, I believe, is the name they give her," replied the captain. "I have often heard of her; but it never was my fate to fall in with her before, and I hope it never will be again, for I am a ruined man, and must begin the world afresh."

"I have heard of that vessel," observed the captain of the Batavia. "Pray, how did she appear to you?"

"Why, the fact is, I did not see anything but the loom of her hull," replied the other. "It was very strange; the night was fine, and the heavens clear; we were under top-gallant sails, for I do not carry on during the night, or else we might have put the royals on her; she would have carried them with the breeze. I had turned in, when about two o'clock in the morning, the mate called me to come on deck. I demanded what was the matter, and he replied he could hardly tell, but that the men were much frightened, and that there was a Ghost Ship, as the sailors termed it, in sight. I went on deck; all the horizon was clear, but on our quarter was a sort of fog, round as a ball, and not more than two cables' length from us. We were going about four knots and a half free, and yet we could not escape from this mist. 'Look there,' said the mate. 'Why, what the devil can it be?' said I, rubbing my eyes. 'No banks up to windward, and yet a fog in the middle of a clear sky, with a fresh breeze, and with water all around it;' for you see the fog did not cover more than half a dozen cables' length, as we could perceive by the horizon on each side of it. 'Hark, sir!' said the mate—'they are speaking again.' 'Speaking!' said I, and I listened; and from out this ball of fog I heard voices. At last, one cried out, 'Keep a sharp look out forward, d'ye hear?' 'Ay, ay, sir!' replied another voice. 'Ship on the starboard bow, sir.' 'Very well; strike the bell there forward.' And then we heard the bell toll. 'It must be a vessel,' said I to the mate. 'Not of this world, sir,' replied he. 'Hark!' 'A gun ready forward.' 'Ay, ay, sir!' was now heard out of the fog, which appeared to near us; 'all ready, sir.' 'Fire!' The report of the gun sounded in our ears like thunder, and then—"

"Well, and then?" said the captain of the Batavia, breathless.

"And then?" replied the other captain, solemnly, "the fog and all disappeared as if by magic, the whole horizon was clear and there was nothing to be seen."

"Is it possible?"

"There are twenty men on deck to tell the story," replied the captain, "and the old Catholic priest to boot, for he stood by me the whole time I was on deck. The men said that some accident would happen and in the morning watch, on sounding the well, we found four feet water. We took to the pumps, but it gained upon us, and we went down, as I have told you. The mate says that the vessel is well known—it is called the Flying Dutchman."

Philip made no remarks at the time, but he was much pleased at what he had heard. "If," thought he "the Phantom Ship of my poor father appears to others as well as to me, and they are sufferers, my being on board can make no difference. I do but take my chance of falling in with her, and do not risk the lives of those who sail in the same vessel with me. Now my mind is relieved, and I can prosecute my search with a quiet conscience."

The next day Philip took an opportunity of making the acquaintance of the Catholic priest, who spoke Dutch and other languages as well as he did Portuguese. He was a venerable old man, apparently about sixty years of age, with a white flowing beard, mild in his demeanour, and very pleasing in his conversation.

When Philip kept his watch that night, the old man walked with him, and it was then, after a long conversation, that Philip confided to him that he was of the Catholic persuasion.

"Indeed, my son, that is unusual in a Hollander."

"It is so," replied Philip; "nor is it known on board—not that I am ashamed of my religion, but I wish to avoid discussion."

"You are prudent, my son. Alas! if the reformed religion produces no better fruit than what I have witnessed in the East, it is little better than idolatry."

"Tell me, father," said Philip—"they talk of a miraculous vision—of a ship not manned by mortal men. Did you see it?"

"I saw what others saw," replied the priest; "and certainly, as far as my senses would enable me to judge, the appearance was most unusual—I may say supernatural; but I had heard of this Phantom Ship before, and moreover that its appearance was the precursor of disaster. So did it prove in our case, although, indeed, we had one on board, now no more, whose weight of guilt was more than sufficient to sink any vessel; one, the swallowing up of whom, with all that wealth from which he anticipated such enjoyment in his own country, has manifested that the Almighty will, even in this world, sometimes wreak just and awful retribution on those who have merited His vengeance."

"You refer to the Dutch President, who went down with the ship when it sank."

"I do; but the tale of that man's crime is long; to-morrow night, I will walk with you, and narrate the whole. Peace be with you, my son, and good night."

The weather continued fine, and the Batavia hove-to in the evening, with the intention of anchoring the next morning in the roadstead of St. Helena. Philip, when he went on deck to keep the middle watch, found the old priest at the gangway waiting for him. In the ship all was quiet; the men slumbered between the guns, and Philip, with his new acquaintance, went aft, and seating themselves on a hencoop, the priest commenced as follows:—

"You are not, perhaps, aware that the Portuguese, although anxious to secure for themselves a country discovered by their enterprise and courage, and the possession of which, I fear, has cost them many crimes, have still never lost sight of one point dear to all good Catholics—that of spreading wide the true faith, and planting the banner of Christ in the regions of idolatry. Some of our countrymen having been wrecked on the coast, we were made acquainted with the islands of Japan; and seven years afterwards, our holy and blessed St. Francis, now with God, landed on the Island of Ximo, where he remained for two years and five months, during which he preached our religion and made many converts. He afterwards embarked for China, his original destination, but was not permitted to arrive there; he died on his passage, and thus closed his pure and holy life. After his death, notwithstanding the many obstacles thrown in our way by the priests of idolatry, and the persecutions with which they occasionally visited the members of our faith, the converts to our holy religion increased greatly in the Japanese islands. The religion spread fast, and many thousands worshipped the true God.

"After a time, the Dutch formed a settlement at Japan, and when they found that the Japanese Christians around the factories would deal only with the Portuguese, in whom they had confidence, they became our enemies; and the man of whom we have spoken, and who at that period was the head of the Dutch Factory, determined, in his lust for gold, to make the Christian religion a source of suspicion to the emperor of the country, and thus to ruin the Portuguese and their adherents. Such, my son, was the conduct of one who professed to have embraced the reformed religion as being of greater purity than our own.

"There was a Japanese lord of great wealth and influence, who lived near us, and who, with two of his sons, had embraced Christianity, and had been baptised. He had two other sons, who lived at the emperor's court. This lord had made us a present of a house for a college and school of instruction: on his death, however, his two sons at court, who were idolaters, insisted upon our quitting this property. We refused, and thus afforded the Dutch principal an opportunity of inflaming these young noblemen against us: by this means he persuaded the Japanese emperor that the Portuguese and Christians had formed a conspiracy against his life and throne for, be it observed, that when a Dutchman was asked if he was a Christian, he would reply, 'No; I am a Hollander.'

"The emperor, believing in this conspiracy, gave an immediate order for the extirpation of the Portuguese, and then of all the Japanese who had embraced the Christian faith: he raised an army for this purpose and gave the command of it to the young nobleman I have mentioned, the sons of the lord who had given us the college. The Christians, aware that resistance was their only chance, flew to arms, and chose as their generals the other two sons of the Japanese lord, who, with their father, had embraced Christianity. Thus were the two armies commanded by four brothers, two on the one side and two on the other.

"The Christian army amounted to more than 40,000 men, but of this the emperor was not aware, and he sent a force, of about 25,000 to conquer and exterminate them. The armies met, and after an obstinate combat (for the Japanese are very brave) the victory was on the part of the Christians, and, with the exception of a few who saved themselves in the boats, the army of the emperor was cut to pieces.

"This victory was the occasion of making more converts, and our army was soon increased to upwards of 50,000 men. On the other hand, the emperor, perceiving that his troops had been destroyed, ordered new levies and raised a force of 150,000 men, giving directions to his generals to give no quarter to the Christians, with the exception of the two young lords who commanded them, whom he wished to secure alive, that he might put them to death by slow torture. All offers of accommodation were refused, and the emperor took the field in person. The armies again met, and on the first day's battle the victory was on the part of the Christians; still they had to lament the loss of one of their generals, who was wounded and taken prisoner, and, no quarter having been given, their loss was severe.

"The second day's combat was fatal to the Christians. Their general was killed; they were overpowered by numbers, and fell to a man. The emperor then attacked the camp in the rear, and put to the sword every old man, woman, and child. On the field of battle, in the camp, and by subsequent torture, more than 60,000 Christians perished. But this was not all; a rigorous search for Christians was made throughout the Islands for many years; and they were, when found, put to death by the most cruel torture. It was not until fifteen years ago, that Christianity was entirely rooted out of the Japanese empire, and during a persecution of somewhat more than sixteen years, it is supposed that upwards of 400,000 Christians were destroyed; and all this slaughter, my son, was occasioned by the falsehood and avarice of that man who met his just punishment but a few days ago. The Dutch Company, pleased with his conduct, which procured for them such advantages, continued him for many years as the president of their factory in Japan. He was a young man when he first went there, but his hair was grey when he thought of returning to his own country. He had amassed immense wealth—immense, indeed, must it have been to have satisfied avarice such as his! All has now perished with him, and he has been summoned to his account. Reflect a little, my son. Is it not better to follow up our path of duty; to eschew the riches and pleasures of this world, and, at our summons hence, to feel that we have hopes of bliss hereafter?"

"Most true, holy father," replied Philip, musing.

"I have but a few years to live," continued the old man, "and God knows I shall quit this world without reluctance."

"And so could I," replied Philip.

"*You*, my son!—no. You are young, and should be full of hopes. You have still to do your duty in that station to which it shall please God to call you."

"I know that I have a duty to perform," replied Philip. "Father, the night air is too keen for one so aged as you. Retire to your bed, and leave me to my watch and my own thoughts."

"I will, my son; may Heaven guard you! Take an old man's blessing. Good night."

"Good night," replied Philip, glad to be alone. "Shall I confess all to him?" thought Philip. "I feel I could confess to him—but no. I would not to Father Seysen—why to him? I should put myself in his power, and he might order me—No, no! my secret is my own. I need no advisers." And Philip pulled out the relic from his bosom, and put it reverently to his lips.

The Batavia waited a few days at St. Helena, and then continued her voyage. In six weeks Philip again found himself at anchor in the Zuyder Zee, and having the captain's permission, he immediately set off for his own home, taking with him the old Portuguese priest, *Mathias*, with whom he had formed a great intimacy, and to whom he had offered his protection for the time he might wish to remain in the Low Countries.

Chapter Thirteen

"Far be it from me to wish to annoy you, my son," said Father Mathias, as with difficulty he kept pace with the rapid strides of Philip, who was now within a quarter of a mile of his home; "but still, recollect that this is but a transitory world, and that much time has elapsed since you quitted this spot. For that reason, I would fain desire you, if possible, to check these bounding aspirations after happiness, these joyful anticipations in which you have indulged since we quitted the vessel. I hope and trust in the mercy of God, that all will be right, and that in a few minutes you will be in the arms of your much-loved wife; but still, in proportion as you allow your hopes to be raised, so will you inevitably have them crushed should disappointment cross your path. At Flushing we were told that there has been a dreadful visitation in this land, and death may not have spared even one so young and fair."

"Let us haste on father," replied Philip; "what you say is true, and suspense becomes most dreadful."

Philip increased his speed, leaving the old man to follow him: he arrived at the bridge with its wooden gate. It was then about seven o'clock in the morning, for they had crossed the Scheldt at the dawn of day.

Philip observed that the lower shutters were still closed.

"They might have been up and stirring before this," thought he, as he put his hand to the latch of the door. It was not fastened. Philip entered; there was a light burning in the kitchen; he pushed open the door, and beheld a maid-servant leaning back in her chair, in a profound sleep. Before he had time to go in and awaken her, he heard a voice at the top of the stairs, saying, "Marie, is that the doctor?"

Philip waited no longer; in three bounds he was on the landing-place above, and pushing by the person who had spoken, he opened the door of Amine's room.

A floating wick in a tumbler of oil gave but a faint and glimmering light; the curtains of the bed were drawn, and by the side of it was kneeling a figure which was well known to Philip—that of Father Seysen. Philip recoiled; the blood retreated to his heart; he could not speak: panting for breath, he supported himself against the wall, and at last vented his agony of feeling by a deep groan, which aroused the priest, who turned his head, and perceiving who it was, rose from his knees, and extended his hand in silence.

"She is dead, then!" at last exclaimed Philip.

"No! my son, not dead; there is yet hope. The crisis is at hand; in one more hour her fate will be decided: then, either will she be restored to your arms, or follow the many hundreds whom this fatal epidemic has consigned to the tomb."

Father Seysen then led Philip to the side of the bed, and withdrew the curtain. Amine lay insensible, but breathing heavily; her eyes were closed. Philip seized her burning hand, knelt down, pressed it to his lips, and burst into a paroxysm of tears. As soon as he had become somewhat composed, Father Seysen persuaded him to rise and sit with him by the side of the bed.

"This is a melancholy sight to witness at your return, Philip," said he; "and to you who are so ardent, so impetuous, it must be doubly so; but God's will be done. Remember, there is yet hope—not strong hope, I grant; but still, there is hope, for so told me the medical man who has attended her, and who will return, I expect, in a few minutes. Her disease is a typhus fever, which has swept off whole families within these last two months, and still rages violently; fortunate indeed, is the house which has to mourn but one victim. I would that you had not arrived just now, for it is a disease easily communicated. Many have fled from the country for security. To add to our misfortunes, we have suffered from the want of medical advice, for the physician and the patient have been swept away together."

The door was now slowly opened, and a tall, dark man, in a brown cloak, holding to his nose a sponge saturated with vinegar, entered the room. He bowed his head to Philip and the priest, and then went to the bedside. For a minute he held his fingers to the pulse of the sufferer, then laying down her arm, he put his hand to her forehead, and covered her up with the bedclothes. He handed to Philip the sponge and vinegar, making a sign that he should use it, and beckoned Father Seysen out of the room.

In a minute the priest returned. "I have received his directions, my son; he thinks that she may be saved. The clothes must be kept on her, and replaced if she should throw them off; but everything will depend upon quiet and calm after she recovers her senses."

"Surely, we can promise her that," replied Philip.

"It is not the knowledge of your return, or even the sight of you, which alarms me. Joy seldom kills, even when the shock is great, but there are other causes for uneasiness."

"What are they, holy Father?"

"Philip, it is now thirteen days that Amine has raved, and during that period I have seldom quitted her but to perform the duties of my office to others who required it. I have been afraid to leave her, Philip, for in her ravings she has told such a tale even unconnected as it has been, as has thrilled my soul with horror. It evidently has long lain heavily on her mind, and must retard her recovery. Philip Vanderdecken, you may remember that I would once have had the secret from you—the secret which forced your mother to her tomb, and which now may send your young wife to follow her, for it is evident that she knows all. Is it not true?"

"She does know all," replied Philip, mournfully.

"And she has in her delirium told all. Nay, I trust she has told more than all; but of that we will not speak now: watch her, Philip. I will return in half an hour, for by that time, the doctor tells me, the symptoms will decide whether she will return to reason, or be lost to you for ever."

Philip whispered to the priest that he had been accompanied by Father Mathias, who was to remain as his guest, and requested him to explain the circumstances of his present position to him, and see that he was attended to. Father Seysen then quitted the room, when Philip sat down by the bedside, and drew back the curtain.

Perhaps there is no situation in life so agonising to the feelings as that in which Philip was now placed. His joyful emotions, when expecting to embrace in health and beauty the object of his warmest affections, and of his continual thought during his long absence, suddenly checked by disappointment, anxiety and grief, at finding her lying emaciated, changed, corrupted with disease—her mind overthrown—her eyes unconscious of his presence—her existence hanging by a single hair—her frame prostrate before the king of terrors, who hovers over her with uplifted dart, and longs for the fiat which should permit him to pierce his unconscious victim.

"Alas!" thought Philip, "is it thus we meet, Amine? Truly did Father Mathias advise me, as I hurried so impetuously along, not (as I fondly thought) to happiness, but to misery. God of Heaven! be merciful, and forgive me. If I have loved this angelic creature of thy formation, even more than I have thee, spare her, good Heaven, spare her—or I am lost for ever."

Philip covered up his face, and remained for some time in prayer. He then bent over his Amine, and impressed a kiss upon her burning lips. They were burning hot; still there was moisture upon them, and Philip perceived that there was also moisture on her forehead. He felt her hand, and the palm of it was moist; and carefully covering her with the bedclothes, he watched her with anxiety and hope.

In a quarter of an hour he had the delight of perceiving that Amine was in a profuse perspiration; gradually her breathing became less heavy, and instead of the passive state in which she had remained, she moved, and became restless. Philip watched, and replaced the clothes as she threw them off, until she at last appeared to have fallen into a profound and sweet sleep. Shortly after, Father Seysen and the physician made their appearance. Philip stated, in few words, what had occurred. The doctor went to the bedside, and in half a minute returned.

"Your wife is spared to you, Mynheer, but it is not advisable that she should see you so unexpectedly; the shock may be too great in her weak state; she must be allowed to sleep as long as possible; on her waking she will have returned to reason. You must leave her then to Father Seysen."

"May I not remain in the room until she awakes? I will then hasten away unobserved."

"That will be useless; the disease is contagious, and you have been here too long already. Remain below; you must change your clothes, and see that they prepare a bed for her in another room, to which she must be transported as soon as you think she can bear it; and then let these windows be thrown open, that the room may be properly ventilated. It will not do to have a wife just rescued from the jaws of death run the risk of falling a sacrifice to the attentions necessary to a sick husband."

Philip perceived the prudence of this advice, and quitting the room with the medical man, he went and changed his clothes, and then joined Father Mathias, whom he found in the parlour below.

"You were right, Father," said Philip, throwing himself on the sofa.

"I am old and suspicious, you are young and buoyant, Philip; but I trust all may yet be well."

"I trust so too," replied Philip. He then remained silent and absorbed in thought, for now that the imminent danger was over, he was reflecting upon what Father Seysen had communicated to him, relative to Amine's having revealed the secret whilst in a state of mental aberration. The priest, perceiving that his mind was occupied, did not interrupt him. An hour had thus passed, when Father Seysen entered the room.

"Return thanks to Heaven, my son. Amine has awakened, and is perfectly sensible and collected. There is now little doubt of her recovery. She has taken the restorative ordered by the doctor though she was so anxious to repose once more, that she could hardly be persuaded to swallow it. She is now again fast asleep, and watched by one of the maidens, and in all probability will not move for many hours; but every moment of such sleep is precious, and she must not be disturbed. I will now see to some refreshment, which must be needful to us all. Philip, you have not introduced me to your companion, who, I perceive, is of my own calling."

"Forgive me, sir," replied Philip; "you will have great pleasure in making acquaintance with Father Mathias who has promised to reside with me, I trust, for some time. I will leave you together, and see to the breakfast being prepared; for the delay of which I trust Father Mathias will accept my apology."

Philip then left the room and went into the kitchen. Having ordered what was requisite to be taken into the parlour, he put on his hat and walked out of the house. He could not eat; his mind was in a state of confusion; the events of the morning had been too harassing and exciting, and he felt as if the fresh air was necessary to his existence.

As he proceeded, careless in which direction, he met many with whom he had been acquainted, and from whom he had received condolence at his supposed bereavement, and congratulations when they learnt from him that the danger was over; and from them he also learnt how fatal had been the pestilence.

Not one-third of the inhabitants of Terneuse and the surrounding country remained alive, and those who had recovered were in a state of exhaustion, which prevented them from returning to their accustomed occupations. They had combated disease, but remained the prey of misery and want; and Philip mentally vowed that he would appropriate all his savings to the relief of those around him. It was not until more than two hours had passed away that Philip returned to the cottage. On his arrival he found that Amine still slumbered, and the two priests were in conversation below.

"My son," said Father Seysen, "let us now have a little explanation. I have had a long conference with this good father, who hath much interested me with his account of the extension of our holy religion among the Pagans. He hath communicated to me much to rejoice at, and much to grieve for; but, among other questions put to him, I have (in consequence of what I have learnt during the mental alienation of your wife) interrogated him upon the point of a supernatural appearance of a vessel in the Eastern seas. You observe, Philip, that your secret is known to me, or I could not have put that question. To my surprise he hath stated a visitation of the kind to which he was eye-witness, and which cannot reasonably be accounted for, except by supernatural interposition. A strange and certainly most awful visitation! Philip, would it not be better (instead of leaving me in a maze of doubt) that you now confided to us both all the facts connected with this strange history, so that we may ponder on them, and give you the benefit of advice of those who are older than yourself, and who by their calling may be able to decide more correctly whether this supernatural power has been exercised by a good or evil intelligence?"

"The holy father speaks well, Philip Vanderdecken," observed Mathias.

"If it be the work of the Almighty, to whom should you confide, and by whom should you be guided, but by those who do his service on this earth? If of the evil one, to whom but to those whose duty and wish it is to counteract his baneful influence? And reflect, Philip, that this secret may sit heavily on the mind of your cherished wife, and may bow her to the grave, as it did your (I trust) sainted mother. With you, and supported by your presence, she may bear it well; but recollect how many are the lonely days and nights that she must pass during your absence, and how much she must require the consolation and help of others. A secret like this must be as a gnawing worm, and, strong as she may be in courage, must shorten her existence but for the support and the balm she may receive from the ministers of our faith. It was cruel and selfish of you, Philip, to leave her, a lone woman, to bear up against your absence, and at the same time oppressed with so fatal a knowledge."

"You have convinced me, holy father," replied Philip. "I feel that I should before this have made you acquainted with this strange history. I will now state the whole of the circumstances which have occurred, but with little hope your advice can help me in a case so difficult, and in a duty so peremptory, yet so perplexing."

Philip then entered into a minute detail of all that had passed, from the few days previous to his mother's death until the present time, and when he had concluded, he observed,—"You see father, that I have bound myself by a solemn vow—that that vow has been recorded and accepted, and it appears to me that I have nothing now to do but to follow my peculiar destiny."

"My son, you have told us strange and startling things—things not of this world—if you are not deceived. Leave us now. Father Mathias and I will consult upon this serious matter; and, when we are agreed, you shall know our decision."

Philip went upstairs to see Amine; she was still in a deep sleep. He dismissed the servant, and watched by the bedside. For nearly two hours did he remain there, when he was summoned down to meet the two priests.

"We have had a long conversation, my son," said Father Seysen, "upon this strange and perhaps supernatural occurrence. I say *perhaps*, for I would have rejected the frenzied communications of your mother as the imaginings of a heated brain; and for the same reason I should have been equally inclined to suppose that the high state of excitement that you were in at the time of her death may have disordered your intellect; but as Father Mathias positively asserts that a strange, if not supernatural, appearance of a vessel did take place, on his passage home, and which appearance tallies with and corroborates the legend—if so I may call it—to which you have given evidence, I say that it is not impossible but that it is supernatural."

"Recollect that the same appearance of the Phantom Ship has been permitted to me and to many others," replied Philip.

"Yes," replied Father Seysen; "but who is there alive of those who saw it but yourself? But that is of little importance. We will admit that the whole affair is not the work of man, but of a superior intelligence."

"Superior, indeed!" replied Philip. "It is the work of Heaven!"

"That is a point not so easily admitted; there is another power as well as that which is divine—that of the devil!—the arch-enemy of mankind! But as that power, inferior to the power of God, cannot act without his permission, we may indirectly admit that it is the will of Heaven that such sighs and portents should be allowed to be given on certain occasions."

"Then our opinions are the same, good Father."

"Nay, not exactly, my son. Elymas, the sorcerer, was permitted to practise his arts—gained from the devil—that it might be proved, by his overthrow and blindness, how inferior was his master to the Divine Ruler; but it does not therefore follow that sorcery generally was permitted. In this instance it may be true that the evil one has been permitted to exercise his power over the captain and crew of that ship, and, as a warning against such heavy offences, the supernatural appearance of the vessel may be permitted. So far we are justifiable in believing. But the great questions are, first, whether it be your father who is thus doomed? and, secondly, how far you are necessitated to follow up this mad pursuit, which, it appears to me—although it may end in your destruction—cannot possibly be the means of rescuing your father from his state of unhallowed abeyance? Do you understand me, Philip?"

"I certainly understand what you would say, Father; but—"

"Answer me not yet. It is the opinion of this holy Father as well as of myself, that, allowing the facts to be as you suppose, the revelations made to you are not from on high, but the suggestions of the devil to lead you into danger and ultimately to death; for if it were your task, as you suppose, why did not the vessel appear on this last voyage, and how can you (allowing that you met her fifty times) have communication with that, or with those which are but phantoms and shadows, things not of this world? Now, what we propose is, that you should spend a proportion of the money left by your father in masses for the repose of his soul, which your mother, in other circumstances, would certainly have done; and that, having so done, you should remain quietly on shore until some new sign should be given to you which may warrant our supposing that you are really chosen for this strange pursuit?"

"But my oath, Father—my recorded vow!"

"From that, my son, the holy Church hath power to absolve you; and that absolution you shall receive. You have put yourself into our hands, and by our decision you must be guided. If there be wrong, it is we, and not you, who are responsible; but, at present, let us say no more. I will now go up, and so soon as your wife awakens, prepare her for your meeting."

When Father Seysen had quitted the room, Father Mathias debated the matter with Philip. A long discussion ensued, in which similar arguments were made use of by the priest; and Philip, although not convinced, was at least doubtful and perplexed. He left the cottage.

"A new sign—a corroborative sign," thought Philip; "surely there have been signs and wonders enough. Still it may be true that masses for my father's soul may relieve him from his state of torture. At all events, if they decide for me I am not to blame. Well, then, let us wait for a new sign of the divine will—if so it must be;" and Philip walked on, occasionally thinking on the arguments of Father Seysen, and oftener thinking of Amine.

It was now evening, and the sun was fast descending. Philip wandered on, until at last he arrived at the very spot where he had knelt down and pronounced his solemn vow. He recognised it: he looked at the distant hills. The sun was just at the same height; the whole scene, the place, and the time were before him. Again Philip knelt down, took the relic from his bosom and kissed it. He watched the sun—he bowed himself to the earth. He waited for a sign, but the sun sank down, and the veil of night spread over the landscape. There was no sign; and Philip rose and walked home towards the cottage, more inclined than before to follow the suggestions of Father Seysen.

On his return, Philip went softly up stairs and entered the room of Amine, whom he found awake and in conversation with the priests. The curtain was closed, and he was not perceived. With a beating heart he remained near the wall at the head of the bed.

"Reason to believe that my husband has arrived!" said Amine, in a faint voice. "Oh tell me, why so?"

"His ship is arrived, we know; and one who had seen her said that all were well."

"And why is he not here, then? Who should bring the news of his return but himself? Father Seysen, either he has not arrived or he is here—I know he must be, if he is safe and well. I know my Philip too well. Say! is he not · here? Fear not, if you say yes; but if you say no, you kill me!"

"He is here, Amine," replied Father Seysen—"here and well."

"O God! I thank you; but where is he? If he is here, he must be in this room, or else you deceive me. Oh, this suspense is death!"

"I am here," cried Philip, opening the curtains.

Amine rose with a shriek, held out her arms, and then fell senseless back. In a few seconds, however, she was restored, and proved the truth of the good Father's assertion, "that joy does not kill."

We must now pass over the few days during which Philip watched the couch of his Amine, who rapidly regained her strength. As soon as she was well enough to enter upon the subject, Philip narrated all that had passed since his departure; the confession which he had made to Father Seysen, and the result. Amine, too glad that Philip should remain with her, added her persuasions to those of the priests, and, for some little time, Philip talked no more of going to sea.

Chapter Fourteen

Six weeks had flown away, and Amine, restored to health, wandered over the country, hanging on the arm of her adored Philip, or nestled by his side in their comfortable home. Father Mathias still remained their guest; the masses for the repose of the soul of Vanderdecken had been paid for, and more money had been confided to the care of Father Seysen to relieve the sufferings of the afflicted poor. It may be easily supposed that one of the chief topics of conversation between Philip and Amine, was the decision of the two priests, relative to the conduct of Philip. He had been absolved from his oath, but, at the same time that he submitted to his clerical advisers, he was by no means satisfied. His love for Amine, her wishes for his remaining at home, certainly added weight to the fiat of Father Seysen; but, although he in consequence obeyed it more willingly, his doubts of the propriety of his conduct remained the same. The arguments of Amine, who, now that she was supported by the opinion of the priests, had become opposed to Philip's departure; even her caresses, with which those arguments were mingled were effective but for the moment. No sooner was Philip left to himself no sooner was the question, for a time, dismissed, than he felt an inward accusation that he was neglecting a sacred duty. Amine perceived how often the cloud was upon his brow; she knew too well the cause, and constantly did she recommence her arguments and caresses, until Philip forgot that there was aught but Amine in the world.

One morning, as they were seated upon a green bank, picking the flowers that blossomed round them, and tossing them away in pure listlessness, Amine took the opportunity, that she had often waited for, to enter upon a subject hitherto unmentioned.

"Philip," said she, "do you believe in dreams? think you that we may have supernatural communications by such means?"

"Of course we may," replied Philip; "we have proof abundant of it in the holy writings."

"Why, then, do you not satisfy your scruples by a dream?"

"My dearest Amine, dreams come unbidden; we cannot command or prevent them."

"We can command them, Philip: say that you would dream upon the subject nearest to your heart, and you *shall*."

"I shall?"

"Yes! I have that power, Philip, although I have not spoken of it. I had it from my mother, with much more that of late I have never thought of. You know, Philip, I never say that which is not. I tell you, that, if you choose, you shall dream upon it."

"And to what good, Amine? If you have power to make me dream, that power must be from somewhere."

"It is, of course: there are agencies you little think of, which, in my country, are still called into use. I have a charm, Philip, which never fails."

"A charm, Amine! do you, then, deal in sorcery? for such powers cannot be from Heaven."

"I cannot tell. I only know the power is given."

"It must be from the devil, Amine."

"And why so, Philip? May I not use the argument of your own priests, who say, 'that the power of the devil is only permitted to be used by Divine intelligence, and that it cannot used without that permission?' Allow it then to be sorcery, or what you please, unless by Heaven permitted, it would fail. But I cannot see why we should suppose that it is from an evil source. We ask for a warning in a dream to guide our conduct in doubtful circumstances. Surely the evil one would rather lead us wrong than right!"

"Amine, we may be warned in a dream, as the patriarchs were of old; but to use mystic or unholy charms to procure a vision, is making a compact with the devil."

"Which compact the evil could not fulfil if not permitted by a higher power. Philip, your reasoning is false. We are told that, by certain means, duly observed, we may procure the dreams we wish. Our observance of these means is certainly the least we can attend to, to prove our sincerity. Forgive me, Philip, but are not observances as necessary in your religion— which I have embraced? Are we not told that the omission of the mere ceremony of water to the infant will turn all future chance of happiness to misery eternal."

Philip answered not for some time. "I am afraid, Amine," said he, at last, in a low tone; "I—"

"I fear nothing, Philip, when my intentions are good," replied Amine. "I follow certain means to obtain an end. What is that end? It is to find out (if possible) what may be the will of Heaven in this perplexing case. If it should be through the agency of the devil, what then? He becomes my servant, and not my master; he is permitted by Heaven to act against himself;" and Amine's eyes darted fire, as she thus boldly expressed herself.

"Did your mother often exercise her art?" inquired Philip, after a pause.

"Not to my knowledge; but it was said that she was most expert. She died young (as you know), or I should have known much more. Think you, Philip, that this world is solely peopled by such dross as we are?—things of clay—perishable and corruptible? Lords over beasts—and ourselves but little better. Have you not, from your own sacred writings, repeated acknowledgments and proofs of higher intelligences mixing up with mankind and acting here below? Why should what was then, not be now! and what more harm is there to apply for their aid now, than a few thousand years ago? Why should you suppose that they were permitted on the earth then—and not permitted now? What has become of them? Have they perished? have they been ordered back—to where—to heaven? If to heaven—the world and mankind have been left to the mercy of the devil and his agents. Do you suppose that we, poor mortals, have been thus abandoned? I tell you plainly, I think not. We no longer have the communications with those intelligences that we once had, because, as we become more enlightened, we become more proud, and seek them not: but that they still exist—a host of good against a host of evil, invisibly opposing each other—is my conviction. But, tell me, Philip, do you in your conscience believe that all that has been revealed to you is a mere dream of the imagination?"

"I do not believe so, Amine: you know well I wish I could."

"Then is my reasoning proved; for if such communications can be made to you, why cannot others? You cannot tell by what agency; your priests say it is that of the evil one; you think it is from on high. By the same rule who is to decide from whence the dream shall come?"

"'Tis true, Amine, but are you certain of your power?"

"Certain of this; but if it pleases superior intelligence to communicate with you, *that* communication may be relied upon. Either you will not dream, but pass away the hours in deep sleep, or what you dream will be connected with the question at issue."

"Then, Amine, I have made my mind up—I will dream: for at present my mind is racked by contending and perplexing doubts. I would know whether I am right or wrong. This night your art shall be employed."

"Not this night, nor yet to-morrow night, Philip. Think you one moment that, in proposing this, I serve you against my own wishes? I feel as if the dream will decide against me, and that you will be commanded to return to your duty; for I tell you honestly, I think not with the priests; but I am your wife, Philip, and it is my duty that you should not be deceived. Having the means, as I suppose, to decide your conduct, I offer them. Promise me that, if I do this, you will grant me a favour which I shall ask as my reward."

"It is promised, Amine, without its being known," replied Philip, rising from the turf; "and now let us go home."

We observed that Philip, previous to his sailing in the Batavia, had invested a large proportion of his funds in Dutch East India stock: the interest of the money was more than sufficient for the wants of Amine, and, on his return, he found that the funds left in her charge had accumulated. After paying to Father Seysen the sums for the masses, and for the relief of the poor, there was a considerable residue, and Philip had employed this in the purchase of more shares in the India Stock.

The subject of their conversation was not renewed. Philip was rather averse to Amine practising those mystical arts, which, if known to the priests, would have obtained for her in all probability the anathema of the Church. He could not but admire the boldness and power of Amine's reasonings, but still he was averse to reduce them into practice. The third day had passed away, and no more had been said upon the subject. Philip retired to bed, and was soon fast asleep; but Amine slept not. So soon as she was convinced that Philip would not be awakened, she slipped from the bed and dressed herself. She left the room, and in a quarter of an hour returned, bringing in her hand a small brazier of lighted charcoal, and two small pieces of parchment, rolled up and fixed by a knot to the centre of a narrow fillet. They exactly resembled the philacteries that were once worn by the Jewish nation, and were similarly applied. One of them she gently bound upon the forehead of her husband, and the other upon his left arm. She threw perfumes into the brazier, and as the form of her husband was becoming indistinct, from the smoke which filled the room, she muttered a few sentences, waved over him a small sprig of some shrub which she held in her white hand, and then closing the curtains and removing the brazier, she sat down by the side of the bed.

"If there be harm," thought Amine, "at least the deed is not his—'tis mine; they cannot say that he has practised arts that are unlawful and forbidden by his priests. On my head be it!" And there was a contemptuous curl on Amine's beautiful arched lip, which did not say much for her devotion to her new creed.

Morning dawned, and Philip still slumbered. "'Tis enough," said Amine, who had been watching the rising of the sun, as she beheld his upper limb a pear above the horizon. Again she waved her arm over Philip, holding the sprig in her hand, and cried, "Philip, awake!"

Philip started up, opened his eyes, and shut them again to avoid the glare of the broad daylight, rested upon his elbow, and appeared to be collecting his thoughts.

"Where am I?" exclaimed he. "In my own bed? Yes!" He passed his hand across his forehead, and felt the scroll.

"What is this," continued he, pulling it off and examining it. "And Amine, where is she? Good Heavens, what a dream! Another?" cried he, perceiving the scroll tied to his arm. "I see it now. Amine, this is your doing." And Philip threw himself down, and buried his face in the pillow.

Amine, in the mean time, had slipped into bed, and had taken her place by Philip's side. "Sleep, Philip, dear: sleep!" said she, putting her arms round him; "we will talk when we wake again."

"Are you there, Amine?" replied Philip, confused. "I thought I was alone; I have dreamed." And Philip again was fast asleep before he could complete his sentence. Amine, too, tired with watching, slumbered, and was happy.

Father Mathias had to wait a long while for his breakfast that morning; it was not till two hours later than usual that Philip and Amine made their appearance.

"Welcome my children," said he; "you are late."

"We are, Father," replied Amine; "for Philip slept, and I watched till break of day."

"He hath not been ill, I trust," replied the priest.

"No not ill; but I could not sleep," replied Amine.

"Then didst thou do well to pass the night—as I doubt not thou hast done, my child, in holy watchings."

Philip shuddered; he knew that the watching, had its cause been known, would have been, in the priest's opinion, anything but holy. Amine quickly replied—

"I have, indeed, communed with higher powers, as far as my poor intellect hath been able."

"The blessing of our holy Church upon thee, my child!" said the old man, putting his hand upon her head; "and on thee, too, Philip."

Philip, confused, sat down to the table; Amine was collected as ever. She spoke little, it is true, and appeared to commune with her own thoughts.

As soon as the repast was finished, the old priest took up his breviary, and Amine beckoning to Philip, they went out together. They walked in silence until they arrived at the green spot where Amine had first proposed to him that she should use her mystic power. She sat sown, an Philip, fully aware of her purpose, took his seat by her in silence.

"Philip," said Amine, taking his hand, and looking earnestly in his face, "last night you dreamed."

"I did indeed, Amine," replied Philip, gravely.

"Tell me your dream, for it will be for me to expound it."

"I fear it needs but little exposition, Amine. All I would know is, from what intelligence the dream has been received?"

"Tell me your dream," replied Amine, calmly.

"I thought," replied Philip, mournfully, "that I was sailing as captain of a vessel round the Cape; the sea was calm and the breeze light; I was abaft; the sun went down, and the stars were more than usually brilliant; the weather was warm, and I lay down on my cloak, with my face to the heavens, watching the gems twinkling in the sky and the occasionally falling meteors. I thought that I fell asleep, and awoke with a sensation as if sinking down. I looked around me; the masts; the rigging, the hull of the vessel—*all* had disappeared, and I was floating by myself upon a large, beautifully-shaped shell on the wide waste of waters. I was alarmed, and afraid to move, lest I should overturn my frail bark and perish. At last I perceived the fore-part of the shell pressed down, as if a weight were hanging to it; and soon afterwards, a small white hand, which grasped it. I remained motionless, and would have called out that my little bark would sink, but I could not. Gradually a figure raised itself from the waters and leaned with both arms over the fore-part of the shell, where I first had seen but the hand. It was a female, in form beautiful to excess; the skin was white as driven snow; her long loose hair covered her, and the ends floated in the water; her arms were rounded and like ivory; she said, in a soft sweet voice—

"'Philip Vanderdecken, what do you fear? Have you not a charmed life?'

"'I know not,' replied I, 'whether my life be charmed or not; but this I know, that it is in danger.'

"'In danger!' replied she; 'it might have been in danger when you were trusting to the frail works of men, which the waves love to rend to fragments—your *good* ships, as you call them, which but float about upon sufferance; but where can be the danger when in a mermaid's shell, which the mountain wave respects, and upon which the cresting surge dare not throw its spray? Philip Vanderdecken, you have come to seek your father!'

"'I have,' replied I; 'is it not the will of Heaven?'

"'It is your destiny—and destiny rules all above and below. Shall we seek him together? This shell is mine; you know not how to navigate it; shall I assist you?'

"'Will it bear us both?'

"'You will see,' replied she, laughing, as she sank down from the fore-part of the shell, and immediately afterwards appeared at the side, which was not more than three inches above the water. To my alarm, she raised herself up, and sat upon the edge, but her weight appeared to have no effect. As soon as she was seated in this way—for her feet still remained in the water—the shell moved rapidly along, and each moment increased its speed, with no other propelling power than that of her volition.

"'Do you fear now, Philip Vanderdecken?'

"'No!' replied I.

"She passed her hands across her forehead, threw aside the tresses which had partly concealed her face, and said—'Then look at me.'

"I looked, Amine, and I beheld you!"

"Me!" observed Amine, with a smile upon her lips.

"Yes, Amine, it was you. I called you by your name, and threw my arms round you. I felt that I could remain with you, and sail about the world for ever."

"Proceed, Philip," said Amine, calmly.

"I thought we ran thousands and thousands of miles—we passed by beautiful islands, set like gems on the ocean-bed; at one time bounding against the rippling current, at others close to the shore—skimming on the murmuring wave which rippled on the sand, whilst the cocoa-tree on the beach waved to the cooling breeze.

"'It is not in smooth seas that your father must be sought,' said she; 'we must try elsewhere.'

"By degrees the waves rose, until at last they were raging in their fury, and the shell was tossed by the tumultuous waters; but still not a drop entered, and we sailed in security over billows which would have swallowed up the proudest vessel.

"'Do you fear now, Philip?' said you to me.

"'No' replied I; 'with you, Amine, I fear nothing.'

"'We are now off the Cape again,' said she; 'and here you may find your father. Let us look well round us, for if we meet a ship it must be *his*. None but the Phantom Ship could swim in a gale like this.'

"Away we flew over the mountainous waves—skimming from crest to crest between them, our little bark sometimes wholly out of the water; now east, now west, north, south, in every quarter of the compass, changing our course each minute. We passed over hundreds of miles: at last we saw a vessel tossed by the furious gale.

"'There,' cried she, pointing with her finger, 'there is your father's vessel, Philip.'

"Rapidly did we approach—they saw us from on board, and brought the vessel to the wind. We were alongside—the gangway was clearing away—for though no boat could have boarded, our shell was safe. I looked up. I saw my father, Amine! Yes, saw him, and heard him as he gave his orders. I pulled the relic from my bosom, and held it out to him. He smiled as he stood on the gunnel, holding on by the main shrouds. I was just rising to mount on board, for they had handed to me the man-ropes, when there was a loud yell, and a man jumped from the gangway into the shell. You shrieked, slipped from the side and disappeared under the wave, and in a moment the shell, guided by the man who had taken your place, flew away from the vessel with the rapidity of thought. I felt a deadly chill pervade my frame. I turned round to look at my new companion—it was the pilot Schriften!—the one-eyed wretch who was drowned when we were wrecked in Table Bay!

"'No! no! not yet!' cried he.

"In an agony of despair and rage, I hurled him off his seat on the shell, and he floated on the wild waters.

"'Philip Vanderdecken,' said he, as he swam, 'we shall meet again!'

"I turned away my head in disgust, when a wave filled my bark, and down it sank. I was struggling under the water sinking still deeper and deeper, but without pain, when I awoke."

"Now, Amine," said Philip, after a pause, "what think you I of my dream?"

"Does it not point out that I am your friend, Philip, and that the pilot Schriften is your enemy?"

"I grant it; but he is dead."

"Is that so certain?"

"He hardly could have escaped without my knowledge."

"That is true, but the dream would imply otherwise. Philip, it is my opinion that the only way in which this dream is to be expounded is—that you remain on shore for the present. The advice is that of the priests. In either case you require some further intimation. In your dream *I* was your safe guide—be guided now by me again."

"Be it so, Amine. If your strange art be in opposition to our holy faith, you expound the dream in conformity with the advice of its ministers."

"I do. And now, Philip, let us dismiss the subject from our thoughts. Should the time come, your Amine will not persuade you from your duty; but recollect, you have promised to grant *one* favour when I ask it."

"I have: say, then, Amine what may be your wish?"

"O! nothing at present. I have no wish on earth but what is gratified. Have I not you, dear Philip?" replied Amine, fondly throwing herself on her husband's shoulder.

Chapter Fifteen

It was about three months after this conversation that Amine and Philip were again seated upon the mossy bank which we have mentioned, and which had become their favourite resort. Father Mathias had contracted a great intimacy with Father Seysen, and the two priests were almost as inseparable as were Philip and Amine. Having determined to wait a summons previous to Philip's again entering upon his strange and fearful task; and, happy in the possession of each other, the subject was seldom revived. Philip, who had, on his return, expressed his wish to the Directors of the Company for immediate employment, and, if possible, to have the command of a vessel, had, since that period, taken no further steps, nor had had any communication with Amsterdam.

"I am fond of this bank, Philip," said Amine; "I appear to have formed an intimacy with it. It was here, if you recollect, that we debated the subject of the lawfulness of inducing dreams; and it was here, dear Philip, that you told me your dream, and that I expounded it."

"You did so, Amine; but if you ask the opinion of Father Seysen, you will find that he would give rather a strong decision against you—he would call it heretical and damnable."

"Let him, if he pleases. I have no objection to tell him."

"I pray not, Amine; let the secret remain with ourselves only."

"Think you Father Mathias would blame me?"

"I certainly do."

"Well, I do not; there is a kindness and liberality about the old man that I admire. I should like to argue the question with him."

As Amine spoke, Philip felt something touch his shoulder, and a sudden chill ran through his frame. In a moment his ideas reverted to the probable cause: he turned round his head, and, to his amazement, beheld the (supposed to be drowned) mate of the Ter Schilling, the one-eyed Schriften, who stood behind him with a letter in his hand. The sudden appearance of this malignant wretch induced Philip to exclaim, "Merciful Heaven! is it possible?"

Amine, who had turned her head round at the exclamation of Philip, covered up her face, and burst into tears. It was not I fear that caused this unusual emotion on her part, but the conviction that her husband was never to be at rest but in the grave.

"Philip Vanderdecken," said Schriften, "he! he! I've a letter for you—it is from the Company."

Philip took the letter, but, previous to opening it, he fixed his eyes upon Schriften. "I thought," said he, "that you were drowned when the ship was wrecked in False Bay. How did you escape?"

"How did I escape?" replied Schriften. "Allow me to ask, how did you escape?"

"I was thrown up by the waves," replied Philip; "but—"

"But," interrupted Schriften, "he! he! the waves ought *not* to have thrown me up."

"And why not, pray? I did not say that."

"No! but I presume you wish it had been so; but, on the contrary, I escaped in the same way that you did—I was thrown up by the waves—he! he! but I can't wait here. I have done my bidding."

"Stop," replied Philip; "answer me one question. Do you sail in the same vessel with me this time?"

"I'd rather be excused," replied Schriften; "I am not looking for the Phantom Ship, Mynheer Vanderdecken;" and, with this reply, the little man turned round, and went away at a rapid pace.

"Is not this a summons, Amine?" said Philip, after a pause, still holding the letter in his hand, with the seal unbroken.

"I will not deny it, dearest Philip. It is most surely so; the hateful messenger appears to have risen from the grave that he might deliver it. Forgive me, Philip; but I was taken by surprise. I will not again annoy you with a woman's weakness."

"My poor Amine," replied Philip, mournfully. "Alas! why did I not perform my pilgrimage alone? It was selfish of me to link you with so much wretchedness, and join you with me in bearing the fardel of never-ending anxiety and suspense."

"And who should bear it with you, my dearest Philip, if it is not the wife of your bosom? You little know my heart if you think I shrink from the duty. No, Philip, it is a pleasure, even in its most acute pangs; for I consider that I am, by partaking with, relieving you of a portion of your sorrow, and I am proud that I am the wife of one who has been selected to be so peculiarly tried. But, dearest, no more of this. You must read the letter."

Philip did not answer. He broke the seal, and found that the letter intimated to him that he was appointed as first mate to the Vrow Katerina, a vessel which sailed with the next fleet; and requesting he would join as quickly as possible, as she would soon be ready to receive her cargo. The letter, which was from the secretary, further informed him that, after this voyage, he might be certain of having the command of a vessel as captain, upon conditions which would be explained when he called upon the Board.

"I thought, Philip, that you had requested the command of a vessel for this voyage," observed Amine, mournfully.

"I did," replied Philip; "but not having followed up my application, it appears not to have been attended to. It has been my own fault."

"And now it is too late."

"Yes, dearest, most assuredly so: but it matters not; I would as willingly, perhaps rather, sail this voyage as first mate."

"Philip, I may as well speak now. That I am disappointed, I must confess; I fully expected that you would have had the command of a vessel, and you may remember that I exacted a promise from you on this very bank upon which we now sit, at the time that you told me your dream. That promise I shall still exact, and I now tell you what I had intended to ask. It was, my dear Philip, permission to sail with you. With you, I care for nothing. I can be happy under every privation or danger; but to be left alone for so long, brooding over my painful thoughts, devoured by suspense, impatient, restless, and incapable of applying to any one thing—that, dear Philip, is the height of misery, and that is what I feel when you are absent. Recollect, I have your promise, Philip. As captain, you have the means of receiving your wife on board. I am bitterly disappointed in being left this time; do, therefore, to a certain degree, console me by promising that I shall sail with you next voyage, if Heaven permit your return."

"I promise it, Amine, since you are so earnest. I can refuse you nothing; but I have a foreboding that yours and my happiness will be wrecked for ever. I am not a visionary, but it does appear to me that, strangely mixed up as I am, at once with this world and the next, some little portion of futurity is opened to me. I have given my promise, Amine, but from it I would fain be released."

"And if ill *do* come, Philip, it is our destiny. Who can avert fate?"

"Amine, we are free agents, and to a certain extent are permitted to direct our own destinies."

"Ay, so would Father Seysen fain have made me believe; but what he said in support of his assertion was to me incomprehensible. And yet he said that it was a part of the Catholic faith. It may be so—I am unable to understand many other points. I wish your faith were made more simple. As yet the good man—for good he really is—has only led me into doubt."

"Passing through doubt, you will arrive at conviction, Amine."

"Perhaps so," replied Amine; "but it appears to me that I am as yet but on the outset of my journey. But come, Philip; let us return. You must to Amsterdam, and I will go with you. After your labours of the day, at least until you sail, your Amine's smiles must still enliven you. Is it not so?"

"Yes, dearest, I would have proposed it. I wonder much how Schriften could come here. I did not see his body it is certain, but his escape is to me miraculous. Why did he not appear when saved? where could he have been? What think you, Amine?"

"What I have long thought, Philip. He is a Ghoul with evil eye, permitted for some cause to walk the earth in human form; and is certainly, in some way, connected with your strange destiny. If it requires anything to convince me of the truth of all that has passed, it is his appearance— the wretched Afrit! Oh, that I had my mother's powers!—but I forget, it displeases you, Philip, that I ever talk of such things, and I am silent."

Philip replied not; and, absorbed in their own meditations, they walked back in silence to the cottage. Although Philip had made up his own mind, he immediately sent the Portuguese priest to summon Father Seysen, that he might communicate with them and take their opinion as to the summons he had received. Having entered into a fresh detail of the supposed death of Schriften, and his reappearance as a messenger, he then left the two priests to consult together, and went upstairs to Amine. It was more than two hours before Philip was called down, and Father Seysen appeared to be in a state of great perplexity.

"My son," said he, "we are much perplexed. We had hoped that our ideas upon this strange communication were correct, and that, allowing all that you have obtained from your mother and have seen yourself to have been no deception, still that it was the work of the evil one, and, if so, our prayers and masses would have destroyed this power. We advised you to wait another summons, and you have received it. The letter itself is of course nothing, but the reappearance of the bearer of the letter is the question to be considered. Tell me, Philip, what is your opinion on this point? It is possible he might have been saved—why not as well as yourself?"

"I acknowledge the possibility, Father," replied Philip; "he may have been cast on shore and have wandered in another direction. It is possible, although anything but probable; but since you ask me my opinion, I must say candidly that I consider he is no earthly messenger—nay, I am sure of it. That he is mysteriously connected with my destiny is certain. But who he is, and what he is, of course I cannot tell."

"Then, my son, we have come to the determination, in this instance not to advise. You must act now upon your own responsibility and your own judgment. In what way soever you may decide, we shall not blame you. Our prayers shall be, that Heaven may still have you in its holy keeping."

"My decision, holy Father is to obey the summons."

"Be it so, my son; something may occur which may assist to work out the mystery,—a mystery which I acknowledge to be beyond my comprehension, and of too painful a nature for me to dwell upon."

Philip said no more, for he perceived that the priest was not at all inclined to converse. Father Mathias took this opportunity of thanking Philip for his hospitality and kindness, and stated his intention of returning to Lisbon by the first opportunity that might offer.

In a few days Amine and Philip took leave of the priests and quitted for Amsterdam—Father Seysen taking charge of the cottage until Amine's return. On his arrival, Philip called upon, the Directors of the Company, who promised him a ship on his return from the voyage he was about to enter upon, making a condition that he should become part owner of the vessel. To this Philip consented, and then went down to visit the Vrow Katerina, the ship to which he had been appointed as first mate. She was still unrigged, and the fleet was not expected to sail for two months. Only part of the crew were on board, and the captain, who lived in Dort, had not yet arrived.

So far as Philip could judge, the Vrow Katerina was a very inferior vessel; she was larger than many of the others, but old, and badly constructed; nevertheless, as she had been several voyages to the Indies, and had returned in safety, it was to be presumed that she could not have been taken up by the Company if they had not been satisfied as to her seaworthiness. Having given a few directions to the men who were on board, Philip returned to the hostelrie where he had secured apartments for himself and Amine.

The next day, as Philip was superintending the fitting of the rigging, the captain of the Vrow Katerina arrived, and stepping on board of her by the plank which communicated with the quay, the first thing that he did was to run to the mainmast and embrace it with both arms, although there was no small portion of tallow on it to smear the cloth of his coat. "Oh! my dear Vrow, my Katerina!" cried he, as if he were speaking to a female. "How do you do? I'm glad to see you again—you have been quite well, I hope? You do not like being laid up in this way. Never mind, my dear creature! you shall soon be handsome again."

The name of this personage who thus made love to his vessel was Wilhelm Barentz. He was a young man, apparently not thirty years of age, of diminutive stature and delicate proportions. His face was handsome, but womanish. His movements were rapid and restless, and there was that appearance in his eye which would have warranted the supposition that he was a little flighty, even if his conduct had not fully proved the fact.

No sooner were the ecstasies of the captain over, than Philip introduced himself to him, and informed him of his appointment. "Oh! you are the first mate of the Vrow Katerina Sir, you are a very fortunate man. Next to being captain of her, first mate is the most enviable situation in the world."

"Certainly not on account of her beauty," observed Philip; "she may have many other good qualities."

"Not on account of her beauty! Why, sir, I say (as my father has said before me, and it was his Vrow before it was mine) that she is the handsomest vessel in the world. At present you cannot judge; and besides being the handsomest vessel, she has every good quality under the sun."

"I am glad to hear it, sir," replied Philip; "it proves that one should never judge by appearances. But is she not very old?"

"Old! not more than twenty-eight years—just in her prime. Stop, my dear sir, till you see her dancing on the waters, and then you will do nothing all day but discourse with me upon her excellence, and I have no doubt that we shall have a very happy time together."

"Provided the subject be not exhausted," replied Philip.

"That it never will be on my part: and allow me to observe, Mr Vanderdecken, that any officer who finds fault with the Vrow Katerina quarrels with me. I am her knight, and I have already fought three men in her defence,—I trust I shall not have to fight a fourth."

Philip smiled: he thought that she was not worth fighting for; but he acted upon the suggestion, and, from that time forward, he never ventured to express an opinion against the beautiful Vrow Katerina.

The crew were soon complete, the vessel rigged, her sails bent, and she was anchored in the stream, surrounded by the other ships composing the fleet about to be despatched. The cargo was then received on board, and, as soon as her hold was full, there came, to Philip's great vexation, an order to receive on board 150 soldiers and other passengers, many of whom were accompanied by their wives and families. Philip worked hard, for the captain did nothing but praise the vessel, and at last they had embarked everything, and the fleet was ready to sail.

It was now time to part with Amine, who had remained at the hostelrie, and to whom Philip had dedicated every spare moment that he could obtain. The fleet was expected to sail in two days, and it was decided that on the morrow they should part. Amine was cool and collected. She felt convinced that she should see her husband again, and with that feeling she embraced him as they separated on the beach, and he stepped into the boat in which he was to be pulled on board.

"Yes," thought Amine, as she watched the form of her husband, as the distance between them increased—"yes, I know that we shall meet again. It is not this voyage which is to be fatal to you or me; but I have a dark foreboding that the next, in which I shall join you, will separate us for ever—in which way I know not—but it is destined. The priests talk of free will. Is it free-will which takes him away from me? Would he not rather remain on shore with me? Yes. But he is not permitted, for he must fulfil his destiny. Free-will? Why, if it were not destiny it were tyranny. I feel, and have felt, as if these priests are my enemies; but why I know not: they are both good men, and the creed they teach is good. Goodwill and charity love to all, forgiveness of injuries, not judging others. All this is good; and yet my heart whispers to me that—but the boat is alongside, and Philip is climbing up the vessel. Farewell, farewell, my dearest husband. I would I were a man! No, no! 'tis better as it is."

Amine watched till she could no longer perceive Philip, and then walked slowly to the hostelrie. The next day, when she arose, she found that the fleet had sailed at daylight, and the channel, which had been so crowded with vessels, was now untenanted.

"He is gone," muttered Amine; "now, for many months of patient, calm enduring,—I cannot say of living, for I exist but in his presence."

Chapter Sixteen

We must leave Amine to her solitude, and follow the fortunes of Philip. The fleet had sailed with a flowing sheet, and bore gallantly down the Zuyder Zee; but they had not been under way an hour before the Vrow Katerina was left a mile or two astern. Mynheer Barentz found fault with the setting and trimming of the sails, and with the man at the helm, who was repeatedly changed; in short, with everything but his dear Vrow Katerina: but all would not do; she still dropped astern, and proved to be the worst-sailing vessel in the fleet.

"Mynheer Vanderdecken," said he, at last, "the Vrow, as my father used to say, is not so very *fast before* the wind. Vessels that are good on a wind seldom are; but this I will say, that, in every other point of sailing, there is no other vessel in the fleet equal to the Vrow Katerina."

"Besides," observed Philip, who perceived how anxious how captain was on the subject, "we are heavily laden, and have so many troops on deck."

The fleet cleared the sands and were then close-hauled, when the Vrow Katerina proved to sail even more slowly than before. "When we are so *very* close-hauled," observed Mynheer Barentz, "the Vrow does not do so well; but a point free, and then you will see how she will show her stern to the whole fleet. She is a fine vessel, Mynheer Vanderdecken, is she not?"

"A very fine, roomy vessel," replied Philip, which was all that in conscience, he could say.

The fleet sailed on, sometimes on a wind, sometimes free, but let the point of sailing be what it might, the Vrow Katerina was invariably astern, and the fleet had to heave-to at sunset to enable her to keep company; still, the captain continued to declare that the point of sailing on which they happened to be, was the only point in which the Vrow Katerina was deficient. Unfortunately, the vessel had other points quite as bad as her sailing; she was crank, leaky, and did not answer the helm well, but Mynheer Barentz was not to be convinced. He adored his ship and like all men desperately in love he could see no fault in his mistress. But others were not so blind, and the admiral, finding the voyage so much delayed by the bad sailing of one vessel, determined to leave her to find her way by herself so soon as they had passed the Cape. He was, however, spared the cruelty of deserting her, for a heavy gale came on which dispersed the whole fleet, and on the second day the good ship Vrow Katerina found herself alone, labouring heavily in the trough of the sea, leaking so much as to require hands constantly at the pumps, and drifting before the gale as fast to leeward almost as she usually sailed. For a week the gale continued, and each day did her situation become more alarming. Crowded with troops, encumbered with heavy stores she groaned and laboured, while whole seas washed over her, and the men could hardly stand at the pumps. Philip was active, and exerted himself to the utmost, encouraging the worn-out men, securing where aught had given way, and little interfered with by the captain, who was himself no sailor.

"Well," observed the captain to Philip, as they held on by the belaying-pins, "you'll acknowledge that she is a fine weatherly vessel in a gale—is she not? Softly, my beauty, softly," continued he, speaking to the vessel, as she plunged heavily into the waves, and every timber groaned. "Softly, my dear, softly. How those poor devils in the other ships must be knocking about now. Heh! Mynheer Vanderdecken, we have the start of them this time: they must be a terrible long way down to leeward. Don't you think so?"

"I really cannot pretend to say," replied Philip, smiling.

"Why, there's not one of them in sight. Yes! by Heavens, there is! Look on our lee-beam. I see one now. Well, she must be a capital sailer, at all events: look there, a point abaft the beam. Mercy on me! how stiff she must be to carry such a press of canvass!"

Philip had already seen her. It was a large ship on a wind, and on the same tack as they were. In a gale, in which no vessel could carry the topsails, the Vrow Katerina being under close-reefed foresails and staysails, the ship seen to leeward was standing under a press of sail—topgallant-sail, royals, flying jib, and every stitch of canvass which could be set in a light breeze. The waves were running mountains high, bearing each minute the Vrow Katerina down to the gunwale: and the ship seen appeared not to be affected by the tumultuous waters, but sailed steadily and smoothly on an even keel. At once Philip knew it must be the Phantom Ship, in which his father's doom was being fulfilled.

"Very odd, is it not?" observed Mynheer Barentz.

Philip felt such an oppression on his chest that he could not reply. As he held on with one hand, he covered up his eyes with the other.

But the seamen had now seen the vessel, and the legend was too well known. Many of the troops had climbed on deck when the report was circulated, and all eyes were now fixed upon the supernatural vessel; when a heavy squall burst over the Vrow Katerina, accompanied with peals of thunder and heavy rain, rendering it so thick that nothing could be seen. In a quarter of an hour it cleared away, and, when they looked to leeward the stranger was no longer in sight.

"Merciful Heaven! she must have been upset, and has gone down in the squall," said Mynheer Barentz. "I thought as much, carrying such a press of sail. There never was a ship that could carry more than the Vrow Katerina. It was madness on the part of the captain of that vessel; but I suppose he wished to keep up with us. Heh, Mynheer Vanderdecken?"

Philip did not reply to these remarks, which fully proved the madness of his captain. He felt that his ship was doomed, and when he thought of the numbers on board who might be sacrificed, he shuddered. After a pause, he said—

"Mynheer Barentz, this gale is likely to continue, and the best ship that ever was built cannot, in my opinion, stand such weather. I should advise that we bear up, and run back to Table Bay to refit. Depend upon it, we shall find the whole fleet there before us."

"Never fear for the good ship, Vrow Katerina," replied the captain; "see what weather she makes of it."

"Cursed bad," observed one of the seamen, for the seamen had gathered near to Philip to hear what his advice might be. "If I had known that she was such an old, crazy beast, I never would have trusted myself on board. Mynheer Vanderdecken is right; we must back to Table Bay ere worse befall us. That ship to leeward has given us warning—she is not seen for nothing,—ask Mr Vanderdecken, captain; he knows that well, for he *is* a sailor."

This appeal to Philip made him start; it was, however, made without any knowledge of Philip's interest in the Phantom Ship.

"I must say," replied Philip, "that, whenever I have fallen in with that vessel, mischief has ever followed."

"Vessel! why, what was there in that vessel to frighten you? She carried too much sail, and she has gone down."

"She never goes down," replied one of the seamen.

"No! no!" exclaimed many voices; "but we shall, if we do not run back."

"Pooh! nonsense! Mynheer Vanderdecken, what say you?"

"I have already stated my opinion," replied Philip, who was anxious, if possible, to see the ship once more in port, "that the best thing we can do, is to bear up for Table Bay."

"And, captain," continued the old seaman who had just spoken, "we are all determined that it shall be so, whether you like it or not; so up with the helm, my hearty, and Mynheer Vanderdecken will trim the sails."

"Why! what is this?" cried Captain Barentz. "A mutiny on board of the Vrow Katerina? impossible! The Vrow Katerina! the best ship, the fastest in the whole fleet!"

"The dullest old rotten tub," cried one of the seamen.

"What!" cried the captain, "what do I hear? Mynheer Vanderdecken, confine that lying rascal for mutiny."

"Pooh! nonsense! he's mad," replied the old seaman. "Never mind him; come, Mynheer Vanderdecken, we will obey you; but the helm must be up immediately."

The captain stormed, but Philip, by acknowledging the superiority of his vessel, at the same time that he blamed the seamen for their panic, pointed out to him the necessity of compliance, and Mynheer Barentz at last consented. The helm was put up, the sails trimmed, and the Vrow Katerina rolled heavily before the gale. Towards the evening the weather moderated, and the sky cleared up; both sea and wind subsided fast; the leaking decreased, and Philip was in hopes that in a day or two they would arrive safely in the Bay.

As they steered their course, so did the wind gradually decrease, until at last it fell calm; nothing remained of the tempest but a long heavy swell which set to the westward, and before which the Vrow Katerina was gradually drifting. This was respite to the worn-out seamen, and also to the troops and passengers, who had been cooped below or drenched on the main-deck.

The upper deck was crowded; mothers basked in the warm sun with their children in their arms; the rigging was filled with the wet clothes, which were hung up to dry on every part of the shrouds; and the seamen were busily employed in repairing the injuries of the gale. By their reckoning, they were not more than fifty miles from Table Bay, and each moment they expected to see the land to the southward of it. All was again mirth, and every one on board, except Philip, considered that danger was no more to be apprehended.

The second mate, whose name was Krantz, was an active, good seaman, and a great favourite with Philip, who knew that he could trust to him, and it was on the afternoon of this day that he and Philip were walking together on the deck.

"What think you, Vanderdecken, of that strange vessel we saw?"

"I have seen her before, Krantz; and—"

"And what?"

"Whatever vessel I have been in when I have seen her, that vessel has never returned into port—others tell the same tale."

"Is she, then, the ghost of a vessel?"

"I am told so; and there are various stories afloat concerning her: but of this, I assure you—that I am fully persuaded that some accident will happen before we reach port, although everything at this moment appears so calm, and our port is so near at hand."

"You are superstitious," replied Krantz; "and yet, I must say, that, to me, the appearance was not like a reality. No vessel could carry such sail in the gale; but yet, there are madmen afloat who will sometimes attempt the most absurd things. If it was a vessel, she must have gone down, for when it cleared up she was not to be seen. I am not very credulous, and nothing but the occurrence of the consequences which you anticipate will make me believe that there was anything supernatural in the affair."

"Well! I shall not be sorry if the event proves me wrong," replied Philip; "but I have my forebodings—we are not in port yet."

"No! but we are but a trifling distance from it, and there is every prospect of a continuance of fine weather."

"There is no saying from what quarter the danger may come," replied Philip; "we have other things to fear than the violence of the gale."

"True," replied Krantz; "but, nevertheless, don't let us croak. Notwithstanding all you say, I prophesy that in two days, at the farthest, we are safely anchored in Table Bay."

The conversation here dropped, and Philip was glad to be left alone. A melancholy had seized him—a depression of spirits, even greater than he had ever felt before. He leant over the gangway and watched the heaving of the sea.

"Merciful Heaven!" ejaculated he, "be pleased to spare this vessel; let not the wail of women, the shrieks of the poor children, now embarked, be heard; the numerous body of men, trusting to her planks,—let not them be sacrificed for my father's crimes." And Philip mused. "The ways of Heaven are indeed mysterious," thought he. "Why should others suffer because my father has sinned? And yet, is it not so everywhere? How many thousands fall on the field of battle in a war occasioned by the ambition of a king, or the influence of a woman! How many millions have been destroyed for holding a different creed of faith! *He* works in his own way, leaving us to wonder and to doubt!"

The sun had set before Philip had quitted the gangway and gone down below. Commending himself, and those embarked with him, to the care of Providence, he at last fell asleep; but, before the bell was struck eight times, to announce midnight, he was awakened by a rude shove of the shoulder, and perceived Krantz, who had the first watch, standing by him.

"By the Heaven above us! Vanderdecken, you have prophesied right. Up—quick! *The ship's on fire!*"

"On fire!" exclaimed Vanderdecken, jumping out of his berth— "where?"

"The main-hold."

"I will up immediately, Krantz. In the mean time, keep the hatches on and rig the pumps."

In less than a minute Philip was on deck, where he found Captain Barentz, who had also been informed of the case by the second mate. In a few words all was explained by Krantz: there was a strong smell of fire proceeding from the main-hold; and, on removing one of the hatches, which he had done without calling for any assistance, from a knowledge of the panic it would create, he found that the hold was full of smoke; he had put it on again immediately, and had only made it known to Philip and the captain.

"Thanks for your presence of mind," replied Philip; "we have now time to reflect quietly on what is to be done. If the troops and the poor women and children knew their danger, their alarm would have much impeded us: but how could she have taken fire in the main-hold?"

"I never heard of the Vrow Katerina talking fire before," observed the captain; "I think it is impossible. It must be some mistake—she is—"

"I now recollect that we have in our cargo several cases of vitriol in bottles," interrupted Philip. "In the gale, they must have been disturbed and broken. I kept them above all, in case of accident: this rolling, gunwale under, for so long a time must have occasioned one of them to fetch way."

"That's it, depend upon it," observed Krantz.

"I did object to receive them, stating that they ought to go out in some vessel which was not so encumbered with troops, so that they might remain on the main-deck; but they replied, that the invoices were made out and could not be altered. But now to act. My idea is, to keep the hatches on, so as to smother it if possible."

"Yes," replied Krantz; "and, at the same time, cut a hole in the deck just large enough to admit the hose, and pump as much water as we can down into the hold."

"You are right, Krantz; send for the carpenter, and set him to work. I will turn the hands up, and speak to the men. I smell the fire now very strong; there is no time to lose. If we can only keep the troops and the women quiet we may do something."

The hands were turned up, and soon made their appearance on deck, wondering why they were summoned. The men had not perceived the state of the vessel, for, the hatches having been kept on, the little smoke that issued ascended the hatchway, and did not fill the lower deck.

"My lads," said Philip, "I am sorry to say that we have reason to suspect that there is some danger of fire in the main-hold."

"I smell it!" cried one of the seamen.

"So do I," cried several others, with every show of alarm, and moving away as if to go below.

"Silence, and remain where you are, my men. Listen to what I say: if you frighten the troops and passengers we shall do nothing; we must trust to ourselves; there is no time to be lost. Mr Krantz and the carpenter are doing all that can be done at present; and now, my men, do me the favour to sit down on the deck, every one of you, while I tell you what we must do."

This order of Philip's was obeyed, and the effect was excellent: it gave the men time to compose themselves after the first shock; for, perhaps, of all shocks to the human frame, there is none which creates a greater panic than the first intimation of fire on board of a vessel—a situation, indeed, pitiable, when it is considered that you have to choose between the two elements seeking your destruction. Philip did not speak for a minute or two. He then pointed out to the men the danger of their situation, what were the measures which he and Krantz had decided upon taking; and how necessary it was that all should be cool and collected. He also reminded them that they had but little powder in the magazine, which was far from the site of the fire, and could easily be removed and thrown overboard; and that, if the fire could not be extinguished, they had a quantity of spars on deck to form a raft, which, with the boats, would receive all on board, and that they were but a short distance from land.

Philip's address had the most beneficial effects; the men rose up when he ordered them; one portion went down to the magazine, and handed up the powder, which was passed along and thrown overboard; another went to the pumps; and Krantz, coming up, reported the hole to have been cut in the planking of the deck above the main-hold: the hoses were fixed, and a quantity of water soon poured down, but it was impossible that the danger could be kept secret. The troops were sleeping on the deck and the very employment of the seamen pointed out what had occurred, even if the smoke, which now increased very much, and filled the lower deck, had not betrayed it. In a few minutes the alarm of *Fire!* was heard throughout the vessel, and men, women, and children, were seen, some hurrying on their clothes, some running frightened about the decks, some shrieking, some praying, and the confusion and terror were hardly to be described.

The judicious conduct of Philip was then made evident: had the sailors been awakened by the appalling cry, they would have been equally incapable of acting as were the troops and passengers. All subordination would have ceased: some would have seized the boats, and left the majority to perish: others would have hastened to the spirit-room, and, by their drunkenness added to the confusion and horror of the scene: nothing would have been effected, and almost all would in all probability have perished miserably. But this had been prevented by the presence of mind shown by Philip and the second-mate, for the Captain was a cipher:— not wanting in courage certainly, but without conduct or a knowledge of his profession. The seamen continued steady to their duty, pushing the soldiers out of the way as they performed their allotted tasks: and Philip perceiving this, went down below, leaving Krantz in charge; and by reasoning with the most collected, by degrees he brought the majority of the troops to a state of comparative coolness.

The powder had been thrown overboard, and another hole having been cut in the deck on the other side, the other pump was rigged, and double the quantity of water poured into the hold; but it was evident to Philip that the combustion increased. The smoke and steam now burst through the interstices of the hatchways and the holes cut in the deck with a violence that proved the extent of the fire which raged below, and Philip thought it advisable to remove all the women and children to the poop and quarter-deck of the ship, desiring the husbands of the women to stay with them. It was a melancholy sight, and the tears stood in Philip's eyes as he looked upon the group of females—some weeping and straining their children to their bosoms; some more quiet and more collected than the men: the elder children mute or crying because their mothers cried, and the younger ones, unconscious of danger playing with the first object which attracted their attention, or smiling at their parents. The officers commanding the troops were two ensigns newly entered, and very young men, ignorant of their duty and without any authority—for men in cases of extreme danger will not obey those who are more ignorant than themselves—and, at Philip's request, they remained with and superintended the women and children.

So soon as Philip had given his orders that the women and children should be properly clothed (which many of them were not), he went again forward to superintend the labour of the seamen, who already began to show symptoms of fatigue, from the excess of their exertions; but many of the soldiers now offered to work at the pumps, and their services were willingly accepted. Their efforts were in vain. In about half an hour more, the hatches were blown up with a loud noise, and a column of intense and searching flame darted up perpendicularly from the hold, high as the lower mast-head. Then was heard the loud shriek of the women, who pressed their children in agony to their breasts, as the seamen and soldiers who had been working the pumps, in their precipitate retreat from the scorching flames, rushed aft, and fell among the huddled crowd.

"Be steady, my lads—steady, my good fellows," exclaimed Philip; "there is no danger yet. Recollect we have our boats and raft, and although we cannot subdue the fire, and save the vessel, still we may, if you are cool and collected, not only save ourselves, but every one—even the poor infants who now appeal to you as men to exert yourselves in their behalf. Come, come, my lads, let us do our duty—we have the means of escape in our power if we lose no time. Carpenter, get your axes, and cut away the boom-lashings. Now, my men, let us get our boats out, and make a raft fur these poor women and children; we are not ten miles from the land. Krantz, see to the boats with the starboard watch: larboard watch with me, to launch over the booms. Gunners, take any of the cordage you can, ready for lashing. Come, my lads, there is no want of light—we can work without lanterns."

The men obeyed: as Philip, to encourage them, had almost jocularly remarked (for a joke is often well-timed, when apparently on the threshold of eternity) there was no want of light. The column of fire now ascended above the main-top—licking with its forky tongue the top-mast rigging—and embracing the main-mast in its folds: and the loud roar with which it ascended proved the violence and rapidity of the combustion below and how little time there was to be lost. The lower and main decks were now so filled with smoke that no one could remain there: some few poor fellows sick in their cots had long been smothered, for they had been forgotten. The swell had much subsided, and there was not a breath of wind: the smoke which rose from the hatchways ascended straight up in the air, which, as the vessel had lost all steerage way, was fortunate. The boats were soon in the water, and trusty men placed in them: the spars were launched over, arranged by the men in the boats and lashed together. All the gratings were then collected and firmly fixed upon the spars for the people to sit upon; and Philip's heart was glad at the prospect which he now had of saving the numbers which were embarked.

Chapter Seventeen

But their difficulties were not surmounted — the fire now had communicated to the main-deck and burst out of the port-holes amidships — and the raft which had been forming alongside was obliged to be drifted astern where it was more exposed to the swell. This retarded their labour, and, in the mean time the fire was making rapid progress; the main-mast which had long been burning, fell over the side with the lurching of the vessel, and the flames out of the main-deck ports soon showed their points above the bulwarks, while volumes of smoke were poured in upon the upper-deck almost suffocating the numbers which were crowded there; for all communication with the fore-part of the ship had been for some time cut off by the flames, and every one had retreated aft. The women and children were now carried on to the poop; not only to remove them farther from the suffocating smoke, but that they might be lowered down to the raft from the stern.

It was about four o'clock in the morning when all was ready, and by the exertions of Philip and the seamen, notwithstanding the swell, the women and children were safely placed on the raft where it was considered that they would be less in the way, as the men could relieve each other in pulling when they were tired.

After the women and children had been lowered down, the troops were next ordered to descend by the ladders; some few were lost in the attempt, falling under the boat's bottom and not re-appearing; but two-thirds of them were safely put on the berths they were ordered to take by Krantz, who had gone down to superintend this important arrangement. Such had been the vigilance of Philip, who had requested Captain Barentz to stand over the spirit-room hatch, with pistols, until the smoke on the main-deck rendered the precaution unnecessary, that not a single person was intoxicated, and to this might be ascribed the order and regularity which had prevailed during this trying scene. But before one-third of the soldiers had descended by the stern ladder, the fire burst out of the stern windows with a violence that nothing could withstand; spouts of vivid flame extended several feet from the vessel, roaring with the force of a blowpipe; at the same time the flames burst through all the after-ports of the main-deck, and those remaining on board found themselves encircled with fire, and suffocated with smoke and heat. The stern ladders were consumed in a minute and dropped into the sea the boats which had been receiving the men were obliged also to back astern from the intense heat of the flames; even those on the raft shrieked as they found themselves scorched by the ignited fragments which fell on them as they were enveloped in an opaque cloud of smoke, which hid from them those who still remained on the deck of the vessel. Philip attempted to speak to those on board, but he was not heard. A scene of confusion took place which ended in great loss of life. The only object appeared to be who should first escape; though, except by jumping overboard, there was no escape. Had they waited, and (as Philip would have pointed out to them) have one by one thrown themselves into the sea, the men in the boats were fully prepared to pick them up; or had they climbed out to the end of the latteen mizen-yard which was lowered down, they might have descended safely by a rope, but the scorching of the flames which surrounded them, and the suffocation from the smoke was overpowering, and most of the soldiers sprang over the taffrail at once, or as nearly so as possible. The consequence was, that there were thirty or forty in the water at the same time, and the scene was as heart-rending as it was appalling; the sailors in the boats dragging them in as fast as they could—the women on the raft, throwing to them loose garments to haul them in; at one time a wife shrieking as she saw her husband struggling and sinking into eternity; at another, curses and execrations from the swimmer who was grappled with by the drowning man, and dragged with him under the surface. Of eighty men who were left of the troops on board at the time of the bursting out of the flames from the stern windows, but twenty-five were saved. There were but few seamen left on board with Philip, the major part having been employed in making the raft or manning the three boats; those who were on board remained by his side, regulating their motions by his. After allowing full time for the soldiers to be picked up, Philip ordered the men to climb out to the end of the latteen yard which hung on the taffrail, and either to lower themselves down on the raft if it was under, or to give notice to the boats to receive them. The raft had been dropped farther astern by the seamen, that those on board of it might not suffer from the smoke and heat; and the sailors one after another lowered themselves down and were received by the boats. Philip desired Captain Barentz to go before him, but the captain refused. He was too much choked with smoke to say why, but no doubt but that it would have been something in praise of the Vrow Katerina. Philip then climbed out; he was followed by the captain, and they were both received into one of the boats.

The rope, which had hitherto held the raft to the ship, was now cast off, and it was taken in by the boats; and in a short time the Vrow Katerina was borne to leeward of them; and Philip and Krantz now made arrangements for the better disposal of the people. The sailors were almost all put into boats that they might relieve one another in pulling; the remainder were placed on the raft, along with the soldiers, the women, and the children. Notwithstanding that the boats were all as much loaded as they could well bear, the numbers on the raft were so great, that it sunk nearly a foot under water, when the swell of the sea poured upon it; but stanchions and ropes to support those on board had been fixed and the men remained at the sides, while the women and children were crowded together in the middle.

As soon as these arrangements were made, the boats took the raft in tow, and just as the dawn of day appeared, pulled in the direction of the land.

The Vrow Katerina was, by this time, one volume of flame: she had drifted about half a mile to leeward, and Captain Barentz, who was watching as he sat in the boat with Philip, exclaimed—"Well, there goes a lovely ship, a ship that could do everything but speak—I'm sure that not a ship in the fleet would have made such a bonfire as she has—does she not burn beautifully—nobly? My poor Vrow Katerina! perfect to the last, we never shall see such a ship as you again! Well, I'm glad my father did not live to see this sight, for it would have broken his heart, poor man."

Philip made no reply; he felt a respect even for Captain Barentz's misplaced regard for the vessel. They made but little way, for the swell was rather against them, and the raft was deep in the water. The day dawned, and the appearance of the weather was not favourable; it promised a return of the gale. Already a breeze ruffled the surface of the water, and the swell appeared to increase rather than go down. The sky was overcast and the horizon thick. Philip looked out for the land, but could not perceive it, for there was a haze on the horizon, so that he could not see more than five miles. He felt that to gain the shore before the coming night was necessary for the preservation of so many individuals of whom more than sixty were women and children, who without any nourishment, were sitting on a frail raft, immersed in the water. No land in sight—a gale coming on, and in all probability, a heavy sea and dark night. The chance was indeed desperate, and Philip was miserable—most miserable—when he reflected that so many innocent beings might, before the next morning, be consigned to a watery tomb,—and why?—yes, there was the feeling—that although Philip could reason against—he never could conquer; for his own life he cared nothing—even the idea of his beloved Amine was nothing in the balance at these moments. The only point which sustained him, was the knowledge that he had his duty to perform, and, in the full exercise of his duty, he recovered himself.

"Land ahead!" was now cried out by Krantz, who was in the headmost boat, and the news was received with a shout of joy from the raft and the boats. The anticipation and the hope the news gave was like manna in the wilderness—and the poor women on the raft, drenched sometimes above the waist by the swell of the sea, clasped the children in their arms still closer, and cried—"My darling, you shall be saved."

Philip stood upon the stern-sheets to survey the land, and he had the satisfaction of finding that it was not five miles distant and a ray of hope warmed his heart. The breeze now had gradually increased, and rippled the water. The quarter from which the wind came was neither favourable nor adverse, being on the beam. Had they had sails for the boats, it would have been otherwise, but they had been stowed away, and could not be procured. The sight of land naturally rejoiced them all, and the seamen in the boat cheered, and double-banked the oars, to increase their way; but the towing of a large raft sunk under water was no easy task; and they could not, with all their exertions, advance more than half a mile an hour.

Until noon they continued their exertions not without success; they were not three miles from the land; but, as the sun passed the meridian a change took place; the breeze blew strong; the swell of the sea rose rapidly; and the raft was often so deeply immersed in the waves as to alarm them for the safety of those upon her. Their way was proportionably retarded, and by three o'clock they had not gained half a mile from where they had been at noon. The men not having had refreshment of any kind during the labour and excitement of so many hours, began to flag in their exertions. The wish for water was expressed by all—from the child who appealed to its mother, to the seaman who strained at the oar. Philip did all he could to encourage the men but finding themselves so near to the land, and so overcome with fatigue, and that the raft in tow would not allow them to approach their haven they murmured, and talked of the necessity of casting loose the raft and looking out for themselves. A feeling of self prevailed, and they were mutinous; but Philip expostulated with them, and out of respect for him, they continued their exertions for another hour, when a circumstance occurred which decided the question, upon which they had recommenced a debate.

The increased swell and the fresh breeze had so beat about and tossed the raft, that it was with difficulty, for some time, that its occupants could hold themselves on it. A loud shout, mingled with screams, attracted the attention of those in the boats, and Philip looking back, perceived that the lashings of the raft had yielded to the force of the waves, and that it had separated amidship. The scene was agonising; husbands were separated from their wives and children—each floating away from each other—for the part of the raft which was still towed by the boats had already left the other far astern. The women rose up and screamed, and held up their children; some, more frantic, dashed into the water between them, and attempted to gain the floating wreck upon which their husbands stood, and sank before they could be assisted. But the horror increased—one lashing having given way, all the rest soon followed; and, before the boats could turn and give assistance, the sea was strewed with the spars which composed the raft, with men, women, and children clinging to them. Loud were the yells of despair, and the shrieks of the women, as they embraced their offspring, and in attempting to save them were lost themselves. The spars of the raft still close together, were hurled one upon the other by the swell, and many found death by being jammed between them. Although all the boats hastened to their assistance, there was so much difficulty and danger in forcing them between the spars, that but few were saved, and even those few were more than the boats could well take in. The seamen and a few soldiers were picked up, but all the females and the children had sunk beneath the waves.

The effect of this catastrophe may be imagined, but hardly described. The seamen who had debated as to casting them adrift to perish, wept as they pulled towards the shore. Philip was overcome, he covered his face, and remained for some time without giving directions, and heedless of what passed.

It was now five o'clock in the evening; the boats had cast off the tow-lines and vied with each other in their exertions. Before the sun had set, they all had arrived at the beach, and were safely landed in the little sand bay into which they had steered; for the wind was off the shore and there was no surf. The boats were hauled up, and the exhausted men lay down on the sands, till warm with the heat of the sun, and forgetting that they had neither eaten nor drunk for so long a time, they were soon fast asleep. Captain Barentz, Philip, and Krantz; as soon as they had seen the boats secured, held a short consultation, and were then glad to follow the example of the seamen; harassed and worn out with the fatigue of the last twenty-four hours, their senses were soon drowned in oblivion.

For many hours they all slept soundly, dreamt of water, and awoke to the sad reality that they were tormented with thirst, and were on a sandy heath with the salt waves mocking them; but they reflected how many of their late companions had been swallowed up, and felt thankful that they had been spared. It was early dawn when they all rose from the forms which they had impressed on the yielding sand; and by the directions of Philip, they separated in every direction, to look for the means of quenching their agony of thirst. As they proceeded over sand-hills, they found growing in the sand a low spongy-leaf sort of shrub, something like what in our greenhouses is termed the ice-plant; the thick leaves of which were covered with large drops of dew. They sank down on their knees, and proceeded from one to the other licking off the moisture which was abundant, and soon felt a temporary relief. They continued their search till noon without success, and hunger was now added to their thirst; they then returned to the beach to ascertain if their companions had been more successful. They had also quenched their thirst with the dew of heaven but had found no water or means of subsistence; but some of them had eaten the leaves of the plant which had contained the dew in the morning, and had found them, although acid, full of watery sap and grateful to the palate. The plant in question is the one provided by bounteous Providence for the support of the camel and other beasts in the arid desert, only to be found there, and devoured by all ruminating animals with avidity. By the advice of Philip they collected a quantity of this plant and put it into the boats, and then launched.

They were not more than fifty miles from Table Bay; and although they had no sails, the wind was in their favour. Philip pointed out to them how useless it was to remain, when before morning they would, in all probability arrive at where they would obtain all they required. The advice was approved of and acted upon; the boats were shoved off and the oars resumed. So tired and exhausted were the men, that their oars dipped mechanically into the water, for there was no strength left to be applied; it was not until the next morning at daylight, that they had arrived opposite False Bay, and they had still many miles to pull. The wind in their favour had done almost all—the men could do little or nothing.

Encouraged, however, by the sight of land which they knew, they rallied; and about noon they pulled, exhausted, to the beach at the bottom of Table Bay, near to which were the houses, and the fort protecting the settlers, who had for some few years resided there. They landed close to where a broad rivulet at that season (but a torrent in the winter) poured its stream into the bay. At the sight of fresh water, some of the men dropped their oars, threw themselves into the sea when out of their depth—others when the water was above their waists—yet they did not arrive so soon as those who waited till the boat struck the beach and jumped out upon dry land. And then they threw themselves into the rivulet, which coursed over the shingle, about five or six inches in depth allowing the refreshing stream to pour into their mouths till they could receive no more, immersing their hot hands, and rolling in it with delight.

Despots and fanatics have exerted their ingenuity to invent torments for their victims—how useless—the rack, the boot, tire,—all that they have imagined are not to be compared to the torture of extreme thirst. In the extremity of agony the sufferers cry for water, and it is not refused: they might have spared themselves their refined ingenuity of torment, and the disgusting exhibition of it, had they only confined the prisoner in his cell, and refused him *water*.

As soon as they satisfied the most pressing of all wants, they rose dripping from the stream, and walked up to the houses of the factory; the inhabitants of which, perceiving that boats had landed when there was no vessel in the bay, naturally concluded that some disaster had happened, and were walking down to meet them. Their tragical history was soon told. The thirty-six men that stood before them were all that were left of nearly three hundred souls embarked, and they had been more than two days without food. At this intimation no further questions were asked by the considerate settlers, until the hunger of the sufferers had been appeased when the narrative of their sufferings was fully detailed by Philip and Krantz.

"I have an idea that I have seen you before," observed one of the settlers. "Did you come on shore when the fleet anchored?"

"I did not," replied Philip; "but I have been here."

"I recollect now," replied the man; "you were the only survivor of the Ter Schilling, which was lost in False Bay."

"Not the only survivor," replied Philip; "I thought so myself; but I afterwards met the pilot, a one-eyed man, of the name of Schriften, who was my shipmate: he must have arrived here after me. You saw him, of course?"

"No, I did not. No one belonging to the Ter Schilling ever came here after you; for I have been a settler here ever since, and it is not likely that I should forget such a circumstance."

"He must, then, have returned to Holland by some other means."

"I know not how. Our ships never go near the coast after they leave the bay; it is too dangerous."

"Nevertheless, I saw him," replied Philip, musing.

"If you saw him, that is sufficient; perhaps some vessel had been blown down to the eastern side, and picked him up; but the natives in that part are not likely to have spared the life of a European. The Caffres are a cruel people."

The information that Schriften had not been seen at the Cape was a subject of meditation to Philip. He had always had an idea as the reader knows, that there was something supernatural about the man; and this opinion was corroborated by the report of the settler.

We must pass over the space of two months during which the wrecked seamen were treated with kindness by the settlers, and at the expiration of which a small brig arrived at the bay, and took in refreshments: she was homeward bound, with a full cargo, and being chartered by the Company, could not refuse to receive on board the crew of the Vrow Katerina. Philip, Krantz, and the seamen embarked; but Captain Barentz remained behind to settle at the Cape.

"Should I go home," said he to Philip, who argued with him, "I have nothing in the world to return for. I have no wife—no children. I had but one dear object, my Vrow Katerina, who was my wife, my child, my everything;—she is gone, and I never shall find another vessel like her; and if I could, I should not love it as I did her. No, my affections are buried with her,—are entombed in the deep sea. How beautifully she burnt!—she went out of the world like a phoenix, as she was. No! no! I will be faithful to her—I will send for what little money I have, and live as near to her tomb as I can—I never shall forget her as long as I live. I shall mourn over her, and 'Vrow Katerina,' when I die, will be found engraven on my heart."

Philip could not help wishing that his affections had been fixed upon a more deserving object, as then, probably, the tragical loss had not taken place; but he changed the subject, feeling that, being no sailor, Captain Barentz was much better on shore than in the command of a vessel. They shook hands and parted—Philip promising to execute Barentz's commission, which was to turn his money into articles most useful to a settler, and have them sent out by the first fleet which should sail from the Zuyder Zee. But this commission it was not Philip's good fortune to execute. The brig, named the Wilhelmina sailed and soon arrived at St. Helena. After watering she proceeded on her voyage. They had made the Western Isles, and Philip was consoling himself with the anticipation of soon joining his Amine, when to the northward of the islands, they met with a furious gale before which they were obliged to scud for many days, with the vessel's head to the south-east; and as the wind abated, and they were able to haul to it, they fell in with a Dutch fleet of five vessels, commanded by an admiral, which had left Amsterdam more than two months, and had been buffeted about by contrary gales for the major part of that period. Cold, fatigue, and bad provisions, had brought on the scurvy; and the ships were so weakly manned, that they could hardly navigate them. When the captain of the Wilhelmina reported to the admiral that he had part of the crew of the Vrow Katerina on board, he was ordered to send them immediately to assist in navigating his crippled fleet. Remonstrance was useless. Philip had but time to write to Amine, acquainting her with his misfortunes and disappointment; and, confiding the letter to his wife, as well as his narrative of the loss of the Vrow Katerina for the directors, to the charge of the captain of the Wilhelmina, he hastened to pack up his effects, and repaired on board of the admiral's ship with Krantz and the crew. To them were added six of the men belonging to to Wilhelmina, whom the admiral insisted on retaining; and the brig, having received the admiral's despatches, was then permitted to continue her voyage.

Perhaps there is nothing more trying to the seaman's feelings than being unexpectedly forced to recommence another series of trials, at the very time when they anticipate repose from their former; yet how often does this happen! Philip was melancholy. "It is my destiny," thought he, using the words of Amine, "and why should I not submit?" Krantz was furious, and the seamen discontented and mutinous; but it was useless. Might is right on the vast ocean, where there is no appeal—no trial or injunction to be obtained.

But hard as their case appeared to them, the admiral was fully justified in his proceeding. His ships were almost unmanageable with the few hands who could still perform their duty; and this small increase of physical power might be the means of saving hundreds who lay helpless in their hammocks. In his own vessel, the Lion which was manned with two hundred and fifty men when she sailed from Amsterdam, there were not more than seventy capable of doing duty; and the other ships had suffered in proportion.

The first captain of the Lion was dead, the second captain in his hammock, and the admiral had no one to assist him but the mates of the vessel, some of whom crawled up to their duty more dead than alive. The ship of the second in command, the Dort, was even in a more deplorable plight. The commodore was dead; the first captain was still doing his duty; but he had but one more officer capable of remaining on deck.

The admiral sent for Philip into his cabin, and having heard his narrative of the loss of the Vrow Katerina, he ordered him to go on board the commodore's ship as captain, giving the rank of commodore to the captain at present on board of her; Krantz was retained on board his own vessel, as second captain; for by Philip's narrative, the admiral perceived at once that they were both good officers and brave men.

Chapter Eighteen

The fleet under Admiral Rymelandt's command was ordered to proceed to the East Indies by the western route, through the Straits of Magellan into the Pacific Ocean—it being still imagined, notwithstanding previous failures, that this route offered facilities which might shorten the passage to the Spice Islands.

The vessels composing the fleet were the Lion of forty-four guns, bearing the admiral's flag; the Dort of thirty-six guns, with the commodore's pendant—to which Philip was appointed; the Zuyder Zee of twenty; the Young Frau of twelve, and a ketch of four guns, called the Schevelling.

The crew of the Vrow Katerina were divided between the two larger vessels; the others, being smaller, were easier worked with fewer hands. Every arrangement having been made, the boats were hoisted up, and the ships made sail. For ten days they were baffled by light winds, and the victims to the scurvy increased considerably on board of Philip's vessel. Many died and were thrown overboard, and others were carried down to their hammocks.

The newly-appointed commodore, whose name was Avenhorn, went on board of the admiral, to report the state of the vessel and to suggest, as Philip had proposed to him, that they should make the coast of South America, and endeavour by bribery or by force to obtain supplies either from the Spanish inhabitants or the natives. But to this the admiral would not listen. He was an imperious, bold, and obstinate man, not to be persuaded or convinced, and with little feeling for the sufferings of others. Tenacious of being advised, he immediately rejected a proposition which, had it originated with himself, would probably have been immediately acted upon; and the commodore returned on board his vessel, not only disappointed, but irritated by the language used towards him.

"What are we do, Captain Vanderdecken? you know too well our situation—it is impossible we can continue long at sea; if we do, the vessel will be drifting at the mercy of the waves, while the crew die a wretched death in their hammocks. At present we have forty men left; in ten days more we shall probably have but twenty; for as the labour becomes more severe, so do they drop down the faster. Is it not better to risk our lives in combat with the Spaniards, than die here like rotten sheep?"

"I perfectly agree with you, commodore," replied Philip;—"but still we must obey orders. The admiral is an inflexible man."

"And a cruel one. I have a great mind to part company in the night, and if he finds fault, I will justify myself to the Directors on my return."

"Do nothing rashly—perhaps, when day by day he finds his own ship's company more weakened, he will see the necessity, of following your advice."

A week had passed away after this conversation, and the fleet had made little progress. In each ship the ravages of the fatal disease became more serious, and, as the commodore had predicted, he had but twenty men really able to do duty. Nor had the admiral's ship and the other vessels suffered less. The commodore again went on board to reiterate his proposition.

Admiral Rymelandt was not only a stern, but a vindictive man. He was aware of the propriety of the suggestion made by his second in command, but having refused it, he would not acquiesce; and he felt revengeful against the commodore, whose counsel he must now either adopt, or by refusing it be prevented from taking the steps so necessary for the preservation of his crew, and the success of his voyage. Too proud to acknowledge himself in error, again did he decidedly refuse, and the commodore went back to his own ship. The fleet was then within three days of the coast, steering to the southward for the Straits of Magellan, and that night, after Philip had returned to his cot, the commodore went on deck and ordered the course of the vessel to be altered some points more to the westward. The night was very dark, and the Lion was the only ship which carried a poop-lantern, so that the parting company of the Dort was not perceived by the admiral and the other ships of the fleet. When Philip went on deck next morning, he found that their consorts were not in sight. He looked at the compass, and perceiving that the course was altered, inquired at what hour and by whose directions. Finding that it was by his superior officer, he of course said nothing. When the commodore came on deck, he stated to Philip that he felt himself warranted in not complying with the admiral's orders, as it would have been sacrificing the whole ship's company. This was, indeed, true.

In two days they made the land, and running into the shore, perceived a large town and Spaniards on the beach. Then anchored at the mouth of the river, and hoisted English colours, when a boat came on board to ask them who they were and what they required? The commodore replied that the vessel was English, for he knew that the hatred of the Spanish to the Dutch was so great that, if known to belong to that nation, he would have had no chance of procuring any supplies, except by force. He stated that he had fallen in with a Spanish vessel, a complete wreck, from the whole of the crew being afflicted with the scurvy; that he had taken the men out, who were now in their hammocks below, as he considered it cruel to leave so many of his fellow-creatures to perish, and that he had come out of his course to land them at the first Spanish fort he could reach. He requested that they would immediately send on board vegetables and fresh provisions for the sick men, whom it would be death to remove, until after a few days, when they would be a little restored; and added, that in return for their assisting the Spaniards, he trusted the governor would also send supplies for his own people.

This well made-up story was confirmed by the officer sent on board by the Spanish governor. Being requested to go down below and see the patients, the sight of so many poor fellows in the last stage of that horrid disease—their teeth fallen out, gums ulcerated, bodies full of tumours and sores—was quite sufficient; and hurrying up from the lower deck, as he would have done from a charnel-house, the officer hastened on shore and made his report.

In two hours a large boat was sent off with fresh beef and vegetables sufficient for three days' supply for the ship's company, and these were immediately distributed among the men. A letter of thanks was returned by the commodore, stating that his health was so indifferent as to prevent his coming on shore in person to thank the governor, and forwarding a pretended list of the Spaniards on board, in which he mentioned some officers and people of distinction, whom he imagined might be connected with the family of the governor, whose name and titles he had received from the messenger sent on board; for the Dutch knew full well the majority of the noble Spanish families—indeed, alliances had continually taken place between them, previous to their assertion of their independence. The commodore concluded his letter by expressing a hope that, in a day or two, he should be able to pay his respects, and make arrangements for the landing of the sick, as he was anxious to proceed on his voyage of discovery.

On the third day, a fresh supply of provisions was sent on board, and so soon as they were received the commodore, in an English uniform went on shore and called upon the governor, gave a long detail of the sufferings of the people he had rescued, and agreed that they should be sent on shore in two days, as they would by that time be well enough to be moved. After many compliments, he went on board, the governor having stated his intention to return his visit on the following day, if the weather were not too rough. Fortunately, the weather was rough for the next two days, and it was not until the third that the governor made his appearance. This was precisely what the commodore wished.

There is no disease, perhaps, so dreadful or so rapid in its effects upon the human frame, and at the same time so instantaneously checked, as the scurvy, if the remedy can be procured. A few days were sufficient to restore those, who were not able to turn in their hammocks, to their former vigour. In the course of the six days nearly all the crew of the Dort were convalescent, and able to go on deck; but still they were not cured. The commodore waited for the arrival of the governor, received him with all due honours, and then, so soon as he was in the cabin, told him very politely that he and all his officers with him were prisoners. That the vessel was a Dutch man-of-war, and that it was his own people, and not Spaniards, who had been dying of the scurvy. He consoled him, however, by pointing out that he had thought it preferable to obtain provisions by this *ruse*, than to sacrifice lives on both sides by taking them by force, and that his Excellency's captivity would endure no longer than until he had received on board a sufficient number of live bullocks and fresh vegetables to insure the recovery of the ship's company; and, in the mean time, not the least insult would be offered to him. Whereupon the Spanish governor first looked at the commodore and then at the file of armed men at the cabin-door, and then to his distance from the town; and then called to mind the possibility of his being taken out to sea. Weighing all these points in his mind, and the very moderate ransom demanded (for bullocks were not worth a dollar a piece in that country), he resolved, as he could not help himself, to comply with the commodore's terms. He called for pen and ink, and wrote an order to send on board immediately all that was demanded. Before sunset the bullocks and vegetables were brought off, and, so soon as they were alongside, the commodore, with many bows and many thanks, escorted the governor to the gangway, complimenting him with a salvo of great guns, as he had done before, on his arrival. The people on shore thought that his Excellency had paid a long visit, but, as he did not like to acknowledge that he had been deceived, nothing was said about it, at least in his hearing, although the facts were soon well known. As soon as the boats were cleared, the commodore weighed anchor and made sail well satisfied with having preserved his ship's company and as the Falkland Islands, in case of parting company, had been named as the rendezvous, he steered for them. In a fortnight he arrived, and found that his admiral was not yet there. His crew were now all recovered, and his fresh beef was not yet expended, when he perceived the admiral and the three other vessels in the offing.

It appeared that so soon as the Dort had parted company, the admiral had immediately acted upon the advice that the commodore had given him, and had run for the coast. Not being so fortunate in a *ruse* as his second in command, he had landed an armed force from the four vessels, and had succeeded in obtaining several head of cattle, at the expense of an equal number of men killed and wounded. But at the same time they had collected a large quantity of vegetables of one sort or another, which they had carried on board and distributed with great success to the sick, who were gradually recovering.

Immediately that the admiral had anchored, he made the signal for the commodore to repair on board, and taxed him with disobedience of orders in having left the fleet. The commodore did not deny that he had so done, but excused himself upon the plea of necessity, offering to lay the whole matter before the Court of Directors so soon as they returned; but the admiral was vested with most extensive powers, not only of the trial, but the *condemnation* and punishment of any person guilty of mutiny and insubordination in his fleet. In reply, he told the commodore that he was a prisoner, and to prove it, he confined him in irons under the half-deck.

A signal was then made for all the captains: they went on board, and of course Philip was of the number. On their arrival, the admiral held a summary court-martial, proving to them by his instructions that he was so warranted to do. The result of the court-martial could be but one—condemnation for a breach of discipline, to which Philip was obliged reluctantly to sign his name. The admiral then gave Philip the appointment of second in command, and the commodore's pendant, much to the annoyance of the captains commanding the other vessels; but in this the admiral proved his judgment, as there was no one of them so fit for the task as Philip. Having so done, he dismissed them. Philip would have spoken to the late commodore, but the sentry opposed it, as against his orders; and with a friendly nod, Philip was obliged to leave him without the desired communication.

The fleet remained three weeks at the Falkland Islands, to recruit the ships' companies. Although there was no fresh beef, there was plenty of scurvy-grass and penguins. These birds were in myriads on some parts of the island, which, from the propinquity of their nests, built of mud, went by the name of *towns*. There they sat close together (the whole area which they covered being bare of grass) hatching their eggs and rearing their young. The men had but to select as many eggs and birds as they pleased and so numerous were they, that when they had supplied themselves, there was no apparent diminution of the numbers. This food, although in a short time not very palatable to the seamen, had the effect of restoring them to health, and before the fleet sailed, there was not a man who was afflicted with the scurvy. In the mean time the commodore remained in irons, and many were the conjectures concerning his ultimate fate. The power of life and death was known to be in the admiral's hands, but no one thought that such power would be exerted up on a delinquent of so high a grade. The other captains kept aloof from Philip, and he knew little of what was the general idea. Occasionally when on board of the admiral's ship, he ventured to bring up the question, but was immediately silenced; and feeling that he might injure the late commodore (for whom he had a regard), he would risk nothing by importunity; and the fleet sailed for the Straits of Magellan without anybody being aware of what might be the result of the court-martial.

It was about a fortnight after they had left the Falkland Islands, that they entered the Straits. At first they had a leading wind which carried them half through, but this did not last, and they then had to contend not only against the wind, but against the current, and they daily lost ground. The crews of the ships also began to sicken from fatigue and cold. Whether the admiral had before made up his mind, or whether irritated by his fruitless endeavours to continue his voyage, it is impossible to say; but after three weeks' useless struggle against the wind and currents, he hove to and ordered the captains on board, when he proposed that the prisoner should receive his punishment—and that punishment was—*to be deserted*; that is, to be sent on shore with a day's food, where there was no means of obtaining support, so as to die miserably of hunger. This was a punishment frequently resorted to by the Dutch at that period, as will be seen by reading an account of their voyages; but at the same time seldom, if ever, awarded to one of so high a rank as that of commodore.

Philip immediately protested against it, and so did Krantz, although they were both aware, that by so doing, they would make the admiral their enemy; but the other captains, who viewed both of them with a jealous eye, and considered them as interlopers and interfering with their advancement, sided with the admiral. Notwithstanding this majority, Philip thought it his duty to expostulate.

"You know well, admiral," said he, "that I joined in his condemnation for a breach of discipline: but at the same time there was much in extenuation. He committed a breach of discipline to save his ship's company, but not an error in judgment, as you yourself proved, by taking the same measure to save your own men. Do not, therefore, visit an offence of so doubtful a nature with such cruelty. Let the Company decide the point when you send him home, which you can do so soon as you arrive in India. He is sufficiently punished by losing his command: to do what you propose will be ascribed to feelings of revenge more than to those of justice. What success can we deserve if we commit an act of such cruelty; and how can we expect a merciful Providence to protect us from the winds and waves, when we are thus barbarous towards each other?"

Philip's arguments were of no avail. The admiral ordered him to return on board his ship, and had he been able to find an excuse, he would have deprived him of his command. This he could not well do; but Philip was aware that the admiral was now his inveterate enemy. The commodore was taken out of irons and brought into the cabin, and his sentence was made known to him.

"Be it so, admiral," replied Avenhorn; "for to attempt to turn you from your purpose, I know would be unavailing. I am not punished for disobedience of orders, but for having, by my disobedience, pointed out to you your duty—a duty which you were forced to perform afterwards by necessity. Then be it so; let me perish on these black rocks, as I shall, and my bones be whitened by the chilly blasts which howl over their desolation. But mark me, cruel and vindictive man! I shall not be the only one whose bones will bleach there. I prophesy that many others will share my fate, and even you, admiral, *may* be of the number,—if I mistake not, we shall lie side by side."

The admiral made no reply, but gave a sign for the prisoner to be removed. He then had a conference with the captains of the three smaller vessels; and, as they had been all along retarded by the heavier sailing of his own ship, and the Dort commanded by Philip, he decided that they should part company, and proceed on as fast as they could to the Indies—sending on board of the two larger vessels all the provisions they could spare, as they already began to run short.

Philip had left the cabin with Krantz after the prisoner had been removed. He then wrote a few lines upon a slip of paper—"Do not leave the beach when you are put on shore, until the vessels are out of sight;" and requesting Krantz to find an opportunity to deliver this to the commodore, he returned on board of his own ship.

When the crew of the Dort heard of the punishment about to be inflicted upon their old commander, they were much excited. They felt that he had sacrificed himself to save them, and they murmured much at the cruelty of the admiral.

About an hour after Philip's return to his ship, the prisons was sent on shore and landed on the desolate and rocky coast, with a supply of provisions for two days. Not a single article of extra clothing, or the means of striking a light, was permitted him. When the boat's keel grazed the beach, ha was ordered out. The boat shoved off, and the men were not permitted even to bid him farewell.

The fleet, as Philip had expected, remained hove to shifting the provisions, and it was not till after dark that everything was arranged. This opportunity was not lost. Philip was aware that it would be considered a breach of discipline, but to that he was indifferent; neither did he think it likely that it would come to the ears of the admiral, as the crew of the Dort were partial both to the commodore and to him. He had desired a seaman whom he could trust, to put into one of the boats a couple of muskets, and a quantity of ammunition, several blankets, and various other articles, besides provisions for two or three months for one person; and as soon as it was dark the men pulled on shore with the boat, found the commodore on the beach waiting for them, and supplied him with all these necessaries. They then rejoined their ship, without the admiral's having the least suspicion of what had been done, and shortly after the fleet made sail on a wind, with their heads off shore. The next morning, the three smaller vessels parted company, and by sunset had gained many miles to windward, after which they were not again seen.

The admiral had sent for Philip to give him his instructions, which were very severe, and evidently framed so as to be able to afford him hereafter some excuse for depriving him of his command. Among others, his orders were, as the Dort drew much less water than the admiral's ship, to sail ahead of him during the night, that if they approached too near the land as they beat across the Channel, timely notice might be given to the admiral, if in too shallow water. This responsibility was the occasion of Philip's being always on deck when they approached the land on either side of the Straits. It was the second night after the fleet had separated that Philip had been summoned on deck as they were nearing the land of Terra del Fuego: he was watching the man in the chains heaving the head, when the officer of the watch reported to him that the admiral's ship was ahead of them instead of astern. Philip made inquiry as to when he passed, but could not discover; he went forward, and saw the admiral's ship with her poop-light, which, when the admiral was astern, was not visible. "What can be the admiral's reason for this?" thought Philip; "has he run ahead for purpose to make a charge against me of neglect of duty? It must be so. Well, let him do as he pleases; he must wait now till we arrive in India, for I shall not allow him to *desert* me; and with the Company, I have as much, and I rather think, as a large proprietor, more interest than he has. Well as he has thought proper to go ahead, I have nothing to do but to follow. 'You may come out of the chains there.'"

Philip went forward: they were now, as he imagined, very near to the land, but the night was dark and they could not distinguish it. For half an hour they continued their course, much to Philip's surprise, for he now thought he could make out the loom of the land, dark as it was. His eyes were constantly fixed upon the ship ahead, expecting every minute that she would go about; but no, she continued her course, and Philip followed with his own vessel.

"We are very close to the land, sir," observed Vander Hagen, the lieutenant, who was the officer of the watch.

"So it appears to me: but the admiral is closer and draws much more water than we do," replied Philip.

"I think I see the rocks on the beam to leeward, sir."

"I believe you are right," replied Philip: "I cannot understand this. Ready about, and get a gun ready—they must suppose us to be ahead of them, depend up on it."

Hardly had Philip given the order, when the vessel struck heavily on the rocks. Philip hastened aft; he found that the rudder had been unshipped, and the vessel was immovably fixed. His thoughts then reverted to the admiral. "Was he on shore?" He ran forward, and the admiral was still sailing on with his poop-light about two cables' length ahead of him.

"Fire the gun, there," cried Philip, perplexed beyond measure.

The gun was fired, and immediately followed up by the flash and report of another gun close astern of them. Philip looked with astonishment over the quarter, and perceived the admiral's ship close astern to him, and evidently on shore as well as his own.

"Merciful Heaven!" exclaimed Philip, rushing forward, "what can this be?" He beheld the other vessel, with her light ahead, still sailing on and leaving them. The day was now dawning, and there was sufficient light to make out the land. The Dort was on shore not fifty yards from the beach, and surrounded by the high and barren rocks; yet the vessel ahead was apparently sailing on over the land. The seamen crowded on the forecastle, watching this strange phenomenon; at last it vanished from their sight.

"That's the Flying Dutchman, by all that's holy!" cried one of the seamen, jumping off the gun.

Hardly had the man uttered these words when the vessel disappeared.

Philip felt convinced that it was so, and he walked away aft in a very perturbed state. It must have been his father's fatal ship which had decoyed them to probable destruction. He hardly knew how to act. The admiral's wrath he did not wish, just at that moment, to encounter. He sent for the officer of the watch, and having desired him to select a crew for the boat, out of those men who had been on deck, and could substantiate his assertions, ordered him to go on board of the admiral, and state what had happened.

As soon as the boat had shoved off, Philip turned his attention to the state of his own vessel. The daylight had increased and Philip perceived that they were surrounded by rocks, and had run on shore between two reefs, which extended half a mile from the mainland. He sounded round his vessel, and discovered that she was fixed from forward to aft, and that without lightening her, there was no chance of getting her off. He then turned to where the admiral's ship lay aground and found that, to all appearance, she was in even a worse plight, as the rocks to leeward of her were above the water, and she was much more exposed, should bad weather come on. Never, perhaps, was there a scene more cheerless and appalling: a dark wintry sea—a sky loaded with heavy clouds—the wind cold and piercing—the whole line of the coast one mass of barren rocks, without the slightest appearance of vegetation; the inland part of the country presented an equally sombre appearance, and the higher points were capped with snow, although it was not yet the winter season. Sweeping the coast with his eye, Philip perceived, not four miles to leeward of them (so little progress had they made), the spot where they had *deserted* the commodore.

"Surely this has been a judgment on him for his cruelty," thought Philip, "and the prophecy of poor Avenhorn will come true—more bones than his will bleach on those rocks." Philip, turned round again to where the admiral's ship was on shore, and started back, as he beheld a sight even more dreadful than all that he had viewed—the body of Vander Hagen, the officer sent on board of the admiral hanging at the main-yard-arm. "My God! is it possible?" exclaimed Philip, stamping with sorrow and indignation.

His boat was returning on board, and Philip awaited it with impatience. The men hastened up the side, and breathlessly informed Philip that the admiral, as soon as he had heard the lieutenant's report, and his acknowledgment that he was officer of the watch, had ordered him to be hung, and that he had sent them back with a summons for him to repair on board immediately, and that they had seen another rope preparing at the other yardarm.

"But not for you, sir," cried the men—"that shall never be—you shall not go on board—and we will defend you with our lives."

The whole ship's company joined in this resolution, and expressed their determination to resist the admiral. Philip thanked them kindly—stated his intention of not going on board, and requested that they would remain quiet, until it was ascertained what steps the admiral might take. He then went down to his cabin, to reflect upon what plan he should proceed. As he looked out of the stern windows, and perceived the body of the young man still swinging in the wind, he almost wished that he was in his place, for then there would be an end to his wayward fate: but he thought of Amine, and felt, that for her he wished to live. That the Phantom Ship should have decoyed him to destruction was also a source of much painful feeling, and Philip meditated, with his hands pressed to his temples. "It is my destiny," thought he at last, "and the will of Heaven must be done: we could not have been so deceived if Heaven had not permitted it." And then his thoughts reverted to his present situation.

That the admiral had exceeded his powers in taking the life of the officer was undeniable, as although his instructions gave him power of life and death, still it was only to be decided by the sentence of the court-martial held by the captains commanding the vessels of the fleet; he therefore felt himself justified in resistance. But Philip was troubled with the idea that such resistance might lead to much bloodshed; and he was still debating how to act, when they reported to him that there was a boat coming from the admiral's ship. Philip went upon deck to receive the officer, who stated that it was the admiral's order that he should immediately come on board, and that he must consider himself now under arrest and deliver up his sword.

"No! no!" exclaimed the ship's company of the Dort. "He shall not go on board. We will stand by our captain to the last."

"Silence, men! silence!" cried Philip. "You must be aware, sir," said he to the officer, "that in the cruel punishment of that innocent young man the admiral has exceeded his powers: and, much as I regret to see any symptoms of mutiny and insubordination, it must be remembered, that if those in command disobey the orders they have received, by exceeding them, they not only set the example, but give an excuse for those who otherwise would be bound to obey them, to do the same. Tell the admiral that his murder of that innocent man has determined me no longer to consider myself under his authority, and that I will hold myself as well as him answerable to the

Company whom we serve, for our conduct. I do not intend to go on board and put myself in his power, that he might gratify his resentment by my ignominious death. It is a duty that I owe these men under my command to preserve my life, that I may, if possible, preserve theirs in this strait; and you may also add, that a little reflection must point out to him that this is no time for us to war with, but to assist each other with all our energies. We are here, shipwrecked on a barren coast, with provisions insufficient for any lengthened stay, no prospect of succour, and little of escape. As the commodore truly prophesied, many more are likely to perish as well as him—and even the admiral himself may be of the number. I shall wait his answer; if he choose to lay aside all animosity, and refer our conduct to a higher tribunal, I am willing to join with him in rendering that assistance to each other which our situation requires—if not, you must perceive, and of course will tell him, that I have those with me who will defend me against any attempt at force. You have my answer, sir, and may return on board."

The officer went to the gangway, but found that none of his crew, except the bowman were in the boat; they had gone up to gain from the men of the Dort the true history of what they but imperfectly heard: and before they were summoned to return, had received full intelligence. They coincided with the seamen of the Dort, that the appearance of the Phantom Ship, which had occasioned their present disaster, was a judgment upon the admiral, for his conduct in having so cruelly *deserted* the poor commodore.

Upon the return of the officer with Philip's answer, the rage of the admiral was beyond all bounds. He ordered the guns aft which would bear upon the Dort to be double-shotted, and fired into her; but Krantz pointed out to him that they could not bring more guns to bear upon the Dort, in their present situation, than the Dort could bring to bear upon them; that their superior force was thus neutralised, and that no advantage could result from taking such a step. The admiral immediately put Krantz under arrest, and proceeded to put into execution his insane intentions. In this he was, however, prevented by the seamen of the Lion, who neither wished to fire upon their consort, or to be fired at in return. The report of the boat's crew had been circulated through the ship, and the men felt too much ill-will against the admiral, an perceived at the same time the extreme difficulty of their situation, to wish to make it worse. They did not proceed to open mutiny, but they went down below, and when the officers ordered them up, they refused to go upon deck; and the officers, who were equally disgusted with the admiral's conduct, merely informed him of the state of the ship's company, without naming individuals so as to excite his resentment against any one in particular. Such was the state of affairs when the sun went down.

Nothing had been done on board the admiral's ship, for Krantz was under arrest, and the admiral had retired in a state of fury to his cabin.

In the mean time, Philip and the ship's company had not been idle— they had laid an anchor out astern, and hove taut: they had started all the water, and were pumping it out, when a boat pulled alongside, and Krantz made his appearance on deck.

"Captain Vanderdecken, I have come to put myself under your orders, if you will receive me—if not, render me your protection; for, as sure as fate, I should have been hanged to-morrow morning, if I had remained in my own ship. The men in the boat have come with the same intention—that of joining you, if you will permit them."

Although Philip would have wished it had been otherwise, he could not well refuse to receive Krantz, under the circumstances of the case. He was very partial to him, and to save his life, which certainly was in danger, he would have done much more. He desired that the boat's crew should return; but when Krantz had stated to him what had occurred on board the Lion, and the crew earnestly begged him not to send them back to almost certain death, which their having effected the escape of Krantz would have assured, Philip reluctantly allowed them to remain.

The night was tempestuous, but the wind being now off shore, the water was not rough. The crew of the Dort, under the directions of Philip and Krantz, succeeded in lightening the vessel so much during the night, that the next morning they were able to haul her off, and found that her bottom had received no serious injury. It was fortunate for them that they had not discontinued their exertions, for the wind shifted a few hours before sunrise, and by the time that they had shipped their rudder, it came on to blow fresh down the Straits, the wind being accompanied with a heavy swell.

The admiral's ship still lay aground, and apparently no exertions were used to get her off. Philip was much puzzled how to act: leave the crew of the Lion he could not; nor indeed could he refuse, or did he wish to refuse the admiral, if he proposed coming on board; but he now made up his mind that it should only be as a passenger, and that he would himself retain the command. At present he contented himself with dropping his anchor outside, clear of the reef, where he was sheltered by a bluff cape, under which the water was smooth, about a mile distant from where the admiral's ship lay on shore; and he employed his crew in replenishing his water-casks from a rivulet close to where the ship was anchored. He waited to see if the other vessel got off, being convinced that if she did not, some communication must soon take place. As soon as the water was complete, he sent one of his boats to the place where the commodore had been landed, having resolved to take him on board, if they could find him; but the boat returned without having seen anything of him, although the men had clambered over the hills to a considerable distance.

On the second morning after Philip had hauled his vessel off, they observed that the boats of the admiral's ship were passing and repassing from the shore, landing her stores and provisions; and the next day, from the tents pitched on shore, it was evident that she was abandoned, although the boats were still employed in taking articles out of her. That night it blew fresh, and the sea was heavy; the next morning her masts were gone, and she turned on her broadside: she was evidently a wreck, and Philip now consulted with Krantz how to act. To leave the crew of the Lion on shore was impossible: they must all perish when the winter set in upon such a desolate coast. On the whole, it was considered advisable that the first communication should come from the other party, and Philip resolved to remain quietly at anchor.

It was very plain that there was no longer any subordination among the crew of the Lion, who were to be seen, in the day time, climbing over the rocks in every direction, and at night, when their large fires were lighted, carousing and drinking. This waste of provisions was a subject of much vexation to Philip. He had not more than sufficient for his own crew, and he took it for granted that, so soon as what they had taken on shore should be expended, the crew of the Lion would ask to be received on board of the Dort.

For more than a week did affairs continue in this state when one morning a boat was seen pulling towards the ship and in the stern-sheets Philip recognised the officer who had been sent on board to put him under arrest. When the officer came on deck he took off his hat to Philip.

"You do, then, acknowledge me as in command," observed Philip.

"Yes, sir, most certainly; you were second in command, but now you are first—for the admiral is dead."

"Dead!" exclaimed Philip—"and how?"

"He was found dead on the beach, under a high cliff, and the body of the commodore was in his arms; indeed, they were both grappled together. It is supposed, that in his walk up to the top of the hill, which he used to take every day, to see if any vessels might be in the Straits, he fell in with the commodore—that they had come to contention, and had both fallen over the precipice together. No one saw the meeting, but they must have fallen over the rocks, as the bodies are dreadfully mangled."

On inquiry, Philip ascertained that all chance of saving the Lion had been lost after the second night, when she had beat in her larboard streak, and six feet water in the hold; that the crew had been very insubordinate, and had consumed almost all the spirits; and that not only all the sick had already perished, but also many others who had either fallen over the rocks, when they were intoxicated, or had been found dead in the morning from their exposure during the night.

"Then the poor commodore's prophecy has been fulfilled!" observed Philip to Krantz. "Many others, and even the admiral himself, have perished with him—peace be with them! And now let us get away from this horrible place as soon as possible."

Philip then gave orders to the officer to collect his men, and the provisions that remained, for immediate embarkation. Krantz followed soon after with all the boats, and before night everything was on board. The bodies of the admiral and commodore were buried where they lay, and the next morning the Dort was under weigh, and with a slanting wind was laying a fair course through the Straits.

Chapter Nineteen

It appeared as if their misfortunes were to cease, after the tragical death of the two commanders. In a few days, the Dort had passed through the Straits of Magellan, and was sailing in the Pacific Ocean with a blue sky and quiet sea. The ship's company recovered their health and spirits, and the vessel being now well manned, the duty was carried on with cheerfulness.

In about a fortnight, they had gained well up on the Spanish coast, but although they had seen many of the inhabitants on the beach, they had not fallen in with any vessels belonging to the Spaniards. Aware that if he met with a Spanish ship of superior force it would attack him, Philip had made every preparation, and had trained his men to the guns. He had now, with the joint crews of the vessels, a well-manned ship, and the anticipation of prize-money had made his men very eager to fall in with some Spaniard, which they knew that Philip would capture if he could. Light winds and calms detained them for a month on the coast, when Philip determined upon running for the Isle St. Marie, where, though he knew it was in possession of the Spaniards, he yet hoped to be able to procure refreshments for the ship's Company, either by fair means or by force. The Dort was, by their reckoning, about thirty miles from the island, and having run in until after dark, they had hove to till the next morning. Krantz was on deck; he leant over the side, and as the sails flapped to the masts, he attempted to define the line of the horizon. It was very dark, but as he watched, he thought that he perceived a light for a moment, and which then disappeared. Fixing his eyes on the spot, he soon made out a vessel, hove to, and not two cables' length distant. He hastened down to apprise Philip and procure a glass. By the time Philip was on deck the vessel had been distinctly made out to be a three-masted xebeque, very low in the water. After a short consultation it was agreed that the boats on the quarter should be lowered down, and manned and armed without noise, and that they should steal gently alongside and surprise her. The men were called up, silence enjoined, and in a few minutes the boat's crew had possession of the vessel; having boarded her and secured the hatches before the alarm could be given by the few who were on deck. More men were then taken on board by Krantz, who, as agreed upon, lay to under the lee of the Dort until the daylight made its appearance. The hatches were then taken off, and the prisoners sent on board of the Dort. There were sixty people on board,—a large number for a vessel of that description.

On being interrogated, two of the prisoners, who were well-dressed and gentlemanlike persons, stepped forward and stated that the vessel was from St. Mary's, bound to Lima, with a cargo of flour and passengers; that the crew and captain consisted of twenty-five men, and all the rest who were on board had taken that opportunity of going to Lima. That they themselves were among the passengers, and trusted that the vessel and cargo would be immediately released, as the two nations were not at war.

"Not at war at home, I grant," replied Philip, "but in these seas, the constant aggressions of your armed ships compel me to retaliate, and I shall therefore make a prize of your vessel and cargo. At the same time, as I have no wish to molest private individuals, I will land all the passengers and crew at St. Mary's, to which place I am bound in order to obtain refreshments, which now I shall expect will be given cheerfully as your ransom, so as to relieve me from resorting to force." The prisoners protested strongly against this, but without avail. They then requested leave to ransom the vessel and cargo, offering a larger sum than they both appeared to be worth: but Philip, being short of provisions refused to part with the cargo, and the Spaniards appeared much disappointed at the unsuccessful issue of their request. Finding that nothing would induce him to part with the provisions, they then begged hard to ransom the vessel; and to this, after a consultation with Krantz, Philip gave his assent. The two vessels then made sail, and steered on for the island, then about four leagues distant. Although Philip had not wished to retain the vessel, yet, as they stood in together, her superior speed became so manifest, that he almost repented that he had agreed to ransom her.

At noon, the Dort was anchored in the roads, out of gunshot, and a portion of the passengers allowed to go on shore and make arrangements for the ransom of the remainder, while the prize was hauled alongside, and her cargo hoisted into the ship. Towards evening, three large boats with livestock and vegetables, and the sum agreed upon for the ransom of the xebeque, came alongside; and as soon as one of the boats was cleared, the prisoners were permitted to go on shore in it, with the exception of the Spanish pilot, who, at the suggestion of Krantz, was retained, with a promise of being released directly the Dort was clear of the Spanish seas. A negro slave was also, at his own request, allowed to remain on board, much to the annoyance of the two passengers before mentioned, who claimed the man as their property, and insisted that it was an infraction of the agreement which had been entered into. "You prove my right by your own words," replied Philip; "I agreed to deliver up all the passengers, but no *property*; the slave will remain on board."

Finding their endeavours ineffectual, the Spaniards took a haughty leave. The Dort remained at anchor that night to examine her rigging, and the next morning they discovered that the xebeque had disappeared, having sailed unperceived by them during the night.

As soon as the anchor was up and sail made on the ship, Philip went down to his cabin with Krantz, to consult as to their best course. They were followed by the negro slave, who, shutting the door and looking watchfully round, said that he wished to speak with them. His information was most important, but given rather too late. The vessel which had been ransomed, was a government advice-boat, the fastest sailer the Spaniards possessed. The pretended two passengers were officers of the Spanish navy, and the others were the crew of the vessel. She had been sent down to collect the bullion and take it to Lima, and at the same time to watch for the arrival of the Dutch fleet, intelligence of whose sailing had been some time before received overland. When the Dutch fleet made its appearance, she was to return to Lima with the news, and a Spanish force would be detached against it. They further learnt that some of the supposed casks of flour contained 2,000 gold doubloons each, others bars of silver; this precaution having been taken in case of capture. That the vessel had now sailed for Lima there was no doubt. The reason why the Spaniards were so anxious not to leave the negro on board of the Dort, was, that they knew that he would disclose what he now had done. As for the pilot, he was a man whom the Spaniards knew they could trust, and for that reason they had better be careful of him, or he would lead the Dort into some difficulty.

Philip now repented that he had ransomed the vessel, as he would, in all probability, have to meet and cope with a superior force, before he could make his way clear out of these seas; but there was no help for it. He consulted with Krantz, and it was agreed that they should send for the ship's company and make them acquainted with these facts; arguing that a knowledge of the valuable capture which they had made, would induce the men to fight well, and stimulate them with the hopes of further success. The ship's company heard the intelligence with delight, professed themselves ready to meet double their force, and then by the directions of Philip, the casks were brought up on the quarter-deck, opened, and the bullion taken out. The whole, when collected, amounted to about half a million of dollars, as near as they could estimate it, and a distribution of the coined money was made from the capstan the very next day; the bars of metal being reserved until they could be sold, and their value ascertained.

For six weeks Philip worked his vessel up the coast, without falling in with any vessel under sail. Notice had been given by the advice-boat, as it appeared, and every craft large and small, was at anchor under the batteries.

They had nearly run up the whole coast, and Philip had determined that the next day he would stretch across to Batavia, when a ship was seen inshore under a press of sail, running towards Lima. Chase was immediately given, but the water shoaled, and the pilot was asked if they could stand on. He replied in the affirmative, stating that they were now in the shallowest water, and that it was deeper within. The leadsman was ordered into the chains, but at the first heave, the lead-line broke; another was sent for, and the Dort still carried on under a heavy press of sail. Just then, the negro slave went up to Philip, and told him that he had seen the pilot with his knife in the chains, and that he thought he must have cut the lead-line so far through, as to occasion its being carried away, and told Philip not to trust him. The helm was immediately put down; but as the ship went round she touched on the bank, dragged, and was again clear.—"Scoundrel!" cried Philip. "So you cut the lead-line? The negro saw you, and has saved us."

The Spaniard leaped down from off the gun, and, before he could be prevented, had buried his knife in the heart of the negro. "Maldetto! take that for your pains," cried he in a fury, grinding his teeth and flourishing his knife.

The negro fell dead. The pilot was seized and disarmed by the crew of the Dort, who were partial to the negro, as it was from his information that they had become rich.

"Let them do with him as they please," said Krantz to Philip.

"Yes," replied Philip, "summary justice."

The crew debated a few minutes, and then lashed the pilot to the negro, and carried him off to the taffrail. There was a heavy plunge, and he disappeared under the eddying waters in the wake of the vessel.

Philip now determined to shape his course for Batavia. He was within a few days' sail of Lima, and had every reason to believe that vessels had been sent out to intercept him. With a favourable wind he now stood away from the coast, and for three days made a rapid passage. On the fourth, at daylight, two vessels appeared to windward, bearing down upon him. That they were large armed vessels was evident; and the display of Spanish ensigns and pennants, as they rounded to, about a mile to windward, soon showed that they were enemies. They proved to be a frigate of a larger size than the Dort and a corvette of twenty-two guns.

The crew of the Dort showed no alarm at this disparity of force; they clinked their doubloons in their pockets, vowed not to return them to their lawful owners, if they could help it, and flew with alacrity to their guns. The Dutch ensign was displayed in defiance, and the two Spanish vessels again putting their heads towards the Dort, that they might lessen their distance, received some raking shot, which somewhat discomposed them, but they rounded to at a cable's length, and commenced the action with great spirit, the frigate lying on the beam, and the corvette on the bow of Philip's vessel. After half an hour's determined exchange of broadsides, the fore-mast of the Spanish frigate fell, carrying away with it the maintop-mast; and this accident impeded her firing. The Dort immediately made sail, stood on to the corvette, which she crippled with three or four broadsides, then tacked, and fetched alongside of the frigate, whose lee guns were still impeded with the wreck of the foremast. The two vessels now lay head and stern, within ten feet of each other, and the action recommenced to the disadvantage of the Spaniard. In a quarter of an hour the canvass, hanging overside, caught fire from the discharge of the guns, and very soon communicated to the ship, the Dort still pouring in a most destructive broadside, which could not be effectually returned. After every attempt to extinguish the flames, the captain of the Spanish vessel resolved that both vessels should share the same fate. He put his helm up, and running her on to the Dort, grappled with her, and attempted to secure the two vessels together. Then raged the conflict; the Spaniards attempting to pass their grappling-chains so as to prevent the escape of their enemy, and the Dutch endeavouring to frustrate their attempt. The chains and sides of hot vessels were crowded with men fighting desperately; those struck down falling between the two vessels, which the wreck of the foremast still prevented from coming into actual collision. During this conflict, Philip and Krantz were not idle. By squaring the after-yards, and putting all sail on forward they contrived that the Dort should pay off before the wind with her antagonist, and by this manoeuvre they cleared themselves of the smoke which so incommoded them; and having good way on the two vessels, they then rounded to so as to get on the other tack, and bring the Spaniard to leeward. This gave them a manifest advantage and soon terminated the conflict. The smoke and flames were beat back on the Spanish vessel—the fire which had communicated to the Dort was extinguished—the Spaniards were no longer able to prosecute their endeavours to fasten the two vessels together, and retreated to within the bulwarks of their own vessel; and after great exertions, the Dort was disengaged, and forged ahead of her opponent, who was soon enveloped in a sheet of flame. The corvette remained a few cables' length to windward, occasionally firing a gun. Philip poured in a broadside, and she hauled down her colours. The action might now be considered at an end, and the object was to save the crew of the burning frigate. The boats of the Dort were hoisted out, but only two of them would swim. One of them was immediately despatched to the corvette, with orders for her to send all her boats to the assistance of the frigate, which was done, and the major part of the surviving crew were saved. For two hours the guns of the frigate, as they were heated by the flames, discharged themselves; and then, the fire having communicated to the magazine she blew up, and the remainder of her hull sank slowly and disappeared. Among the prisoners, in the uniform of the Spanish service, Philip perceived the two pretended passengers; this proving the correctness of the negro's statement. The two men-of-war had been sent out of Lima on purpose to intercept him, anticipating, with such a preponderating force, an easy victory. After some consultation with Krantz, Philip agreed, that as the corvette was in such a crippled state, and the nations were not actually at war, it would be advisable to release her with all the prisoners. This was done, and the Dort again made sail for Batavia, and anchored in the roads three weeks after the combat had taken the place. He found the remainder of the fleet, which had been despatched before them, and had arrived there some weeks, had taken in their cargoes, and were ready to sail for Holland. Philip wrote his despatches in which he communicated to the Directors the events of the voyage; and then went on shore, to reside at the house of the merchant who had formerly received him, until the Dort could be freighted for her voyage home.

Chapter Twenty

We must return to Amine, who is seated on the mossy bank where she and Philip conversed when they were interrupted by Schriften, the pilot. She is in deep thought, with her eyes cast down, as if trying to recall the past. "Alas! for my mother's power," exclaimed she; "but it is gone—gone for ever! This torment and suspense I cannot bear—those foolish priests too!" And Amine rose from the bank and walked towards her cottage.

Father Mathias had not returned to Lisbon. At first he had not found an opportunity, and afterwards, his debt of gratitude towards Philip induced him to remain by Amine, who appeared each day to hold more in aversion the tenets of the Christian faith. Many and many were the consultations with Father Seysen, many were the exhortations of both the good old men to Amine, who, at times, would listen without reply, and at others, argue boldly against them. It appeared to them, that she rejected their religion with an obstinacy as unpardonable as it was incomprehensible. But, to her, the case was more simple: she refused to believe, she said, that which she could not understand. She went so far as to acknowledge the beauty of the principles, the purity of the doctrine; but when the good priests would enter into the articles of their faith, Amine would either shake her head, or attempt to turn the conversation. This only increased the anxiety of the good Father Mathias to convert and save the soul of one so young and beautiful; and he now no longer thought of returning to Lisbon, but devoted his whole time to the instruction of Amine, who, wearied by his incessant importunities, almost loathed his presence.

Upon reflection, it will not appear surprising that Amine rejected a creed so dissonant to her wishes and intentions. The human mind is of that proud nature, that it requires all its humility to be called into action before it will bow, even to the Deity.

Amine knew that her mother had possessed superior knowledge, and an intimacy with unearthly intelligences. She had seen her practise her art with success, although so young at the time, that she could not now recall to mind the mystic preparations by which her mother had succeeded in her wishes; and it was now that her thoughts were wholly bent upon recovering what she had forgotten, that Father Mathias was exhorting her to a creed which positively forbade even the attempt. The peculiar and awful mission of her husband strengthened her opinion in the lawfulness of calling in the aid of supernatural agencies; and the arguments brought forward by these worthy, but not over-talented, professors of the Christian creed, had but little effect upon a mind so strong, and so decided, as that of Amine—a mind which, bent as it was upon one object, rejected with scorn tenets, in roof of which, they could offer no visible manifestation, and which would have bound her blindly to believe what appeared to her contrary to common sense. That her mother's art could bring evidence of *its* truth she had already shown, and satisfied herself in the effect of the dream which she had proved upon Philip;—but what proof could they bring forward?—Records—*which they would not permit her to read!*

"Oh! that I had my mother's art," repeated Amine once more as she entered the cottage; "then would I know where I was at this moment. Oh! for the black mirror, in which I used to peer at her command, and tell her what passed in array before me. How well do I remember that time—the time of my father's absence, when I looked into the liquid on the palm of my hand, and told her of the Bedouin camp—of the skirmish—the horse without a rider—and the turban on the sand!" And again Amine fell into deep thought. "Yes," cried she, after a time, "thou canst assist me, mother! Give me in a dream thy knowledge; thy daughter begs it as a boon. Let me think again. The word—what was the word? what was the name of the spirit—Turshoon? Yes, methinks it was Turshoon. Mother! mother! help your daughter."

"Dost thou call upon the Blessed Virgin, my child?" said Father Mathias, who had entered the room as she pronounced the last words. "If so, thou dost well, for she may appear to thee in thy dreams, and strengthen thee in the true faith."

"I called upon my own mother, who is in the land of spirits, good father," replied Amine.

"Yes; but as an infidel, not, I fear, in the land of the blessed spirits, my child."

"She hardly will be punished for following the creed of her fathers, living where she did, where no other creed was known?" replied Amine indignantly. "If the good on earth are blessed in the next world—if she had, as you assert she had, a soul to be saved—an immortal spirit—He who made that spirit will not destroy it because she worshipped as her fathers did. Her life was good: why should she be punished for ignorance of that creed which she never had an opportunity of rejecting?"

"Who shall dispute the will of Heaven, my child? Be thankful that you are permitted to be instructed, and to be received into the bosom of the holy church."

"I am thankful for many things, father; but I am weary, and must wish you a good night."

Amine retired to her room—but not to sleep. Once more did she attempt the ceremonies used by her mother, changing them each time, as doubtful of her success. Again the censer was lighted—the charms essayed; again the room was filled with smoke as she threw in the various herbs which she had knowledge of, for all the papers thrown aside at her father's death had been carefully collected, and on many were directions found as to the use of those herbs. "The word! the word! I have the first—the second word! Help me, mother!" cried Amine, as she sat by the side of the bed, in the room, which was now so full of smoke that nothing could be distinguished. "It is of no use," thought she, at last, letting her hands fall at her side; "I have forgotten the art. Mother! mother! help me in my dreams this night."

The smoke gradually cleared away, and, when Amine lifted up her eyes, she perceived a figure standing before her. At first she thought she had been successful in her charm; but, as the figure became more distinct, she perceived that it was Father Mathias, who was looking at her with a severe frown and contracted brow, his arms folded before him.

"Unholy child! what dost thou?"

Amine had roused the suspicions of the priests, not only by her conversation, but by several attempts which she had before made to recover her lost art; and on one occasion, in which she had defended it, both Father Mathias and Father Seysen had poured out the bitterest anathemas upon her, or any one who had resort to such practices. The smell of the fragrant herbs thrown into the censer, and the smoke, which afterwards had escaped through the door and ascended the stairs, had awakened the suspicious of Father Mathias, and he had crept up silently, and entered the room without her perceiving it. Amine at once perceived her danger. Had she been single, she would have dared the priest; but, for Philip's sake, she determined to mislead him.

"I do no wrong, father," replied she calmly, "but it appears to me not seemly that you should enter the chamber of a young woman during her husband's absence. I might have been in my bed. It is a strange intrusion."

"Thou canst not mean this, woman! My age—my profession—are a sufficient warranty," replied Father Mathias, somewhat confused at this unexpected attack.

"Not always, father, if what I have been told of monks and priests be true," replied Amine. "I ask again, why comest thou here into an unprotected woman's chamber?"

"Because I felt convinced that she was practising unholy arts."

"Unholy arts!—what mean you? Is the leech's skill unholy? Is it unholy to administer relief to those who suffer?—to charm the fever and the ague, which rack the limbs of those who live in this unwholesome climate?"

"All charms are most unholy."

"When I said charms, father, I meant not what you mean; I simply would have said a remedy. If a knowledge of certain powerful herbs, which, properly combined, will form a specific to ease the suffering wretch—an art well known unto my mother, and which I now would fain recall—if that knowledge, or a wish to regain that knowledge, be unholy, then are you correct."

"I heard thee call upon thy mother for her help."

"I did, for she well knew the ingredients; but I, I fear, have not the knowledge that she had. Is that sinful, good father?"

"'Tis, then, a remedy that you would find?" replied the priest; "I thought that thou didst practise that which is most unlawful."

"Can the burning of a few weeds be then unlawful? What did you expect to find? Look you, father, at these ashes—they may, with oil, be rubbed into the pores and give relief—but can they do more? What do you expect from them—a ghost?—a spirit?—like the prophet raised for the King of Israel?" And Amine laughed aloud.

"I am perplexed, but not convinced," replied the priest.

"I, too, am perplexed and not convinced," responded Amine, scornfully. "I cannot satisfy myself that a man of your discretion could really suppose that there was mischief in burning weeds; nor am I convinced that such was the occasion of your visit at this hour of the night to a lone woman's chamber. There may be natural charms more powerful than those you call supernatural. I pray you, father, leave this chamber. It is not seemly. Should you again presume, you leave the house. I thought better of you. In future, I will not be left at any time alone."

This attack of Amine's upon the reputation of the old priest was too severe. Father Mathias immediately quitted the room, saying, as he went out, "May God forgive you for your false suspicions and great injustice! I came here for the cause I have stated, and no more."

"Yes!" soliloquised Amine, as the door closed, "I know you did; but I must rid myself of your unwelcome company. I will have no spy upon my actions—no meddler to thwart me in my will. In your zeal you have committed yourself, and I will take the advantage you have given me. Is not the privacy of a woman's chamber to be held sacred by you sacred men! In return for assistance in distress—for food and shelter—you would become a spy. How grateful, and how worthy of the creed which you profess!" Amine opened her door as soon as she had removed the censer, and summoned one of the women of the house to stay that night in her room, stating that the priest had entered her chamber, and she did not like the intrusion.

"Holy father! is it possible?" replied the woman. Amine made no reply, but went to bed; but Father Mathias heard all that passed as he paced the room below. The next day he called upon Father Seysen, and communicated to him what had occurred and the false suspicions of Amine.

"You have acted hastily," replied Father Seysen, "to visit a woman's chamber at such an hour of the night."

"I had my suspicions, good Father Seysen."

"And she will have hers. She is young and beautiful."

"Now, by the blessed Virgin—"

"I absolve you, good Mathias," replied Father Seysen, "but still, if known, it would occasion much scandal to our church."

And known it soon was; for the woman who had been summoned by Amine did not fail to mention the circumstance and Father Mathias found himself everywhere so coldly received, and, besides, so ill at ease with himself, that he very soon afterwards quitted the country, and returned to Lisbon, angry with himself for his imprudence, but still more angry with Amine for her unjust suspicions.

Chapter Twenty One

The cargo of the Dort was soon ready, and Philip sailed and arrived at Amsterdam without any further adventure. That he reached his cottage, and was received with delight by Amine need hardly be said. She had been expecting him; for the two ships of the squadron, which had sailed on his arrival at Batavia, and which had charge of his despatches, had, of course, carried letters to her from Philip, the first letters she had ever received from him during his voyages. Six weeks after the letters Philip himself made his appearance, and Amine was happy. The Directors were, of course, highly satisfied with Philip's conduct, and he was appointed to the command of a large armed ship, which was to proceed to India in the spring, one-third of which, according to agreement, was purchased by Philip out of the funds which he had in the hands of the Company. He had now five months of quiet and repose to pass away, previous to his once more trusting to the elements and this time, as it was agreed, he had to make arrangements on board for the reception of Amine.

Amine narrated to Philip what had occurred between her and the priest Mathias, and by what means she had rid herself of his unwished for surveillance.

"And were you practising your mother's arts, Amine?"

"Nay, not practising them, for I could not recall them, but I was trying to recover them."

"Why so, Amine? this must not be. It is, as the good father said, 'unholy.' Promise me you will abandon them now and for ever."

"If that act be unholy, Philip, so is your mission. You would deal and co-operate with the spirits of another world—I would do no more. Abandon your terrific mission—abandon your seeking after disembodied spirits, stay at home with you Amine, and she will cheerfully comply with your request."

"Mine is an awful summons from the Most High."

"Then the Most High permits your communion with those who are not of this world?"

"He does; you know even the priests do not gainsay it although they shudder at the very thought."

"If then He permits to one, He will to another; nay, ought that I can do is but with His permission."

"Yes, Amine, so does He permit evil to stalk on the earth but He countenances it not."

"He countenances your seeking after your doomed father, your attempts to meet him; nay, more He commands it. If you are thus permitted, why may not I be? I am your wife, a portion of yourself; and when I am left over a desolate hearth while you pursue your course of danger, may not I appeal also to the immaterial world to give me that intelligence which will soothe my sorrow, lighten my burden, and which, at the same time, can hurt no living creature? Did I attempt to practise these arts for evil purposes, it were just to deny them me, am wrong to continue them; but I would but follow in the step of my husband, and seek, as he seeks, with a good intent."

"But it is contrary to our faith."

"Have the priests declared your mission contrary to their faith? or, if they have, have they not been convinced to the contrary, and been awed to silence? But why argue, my dear Philip? Shall I not now be with you? and while with you I will attempt no more. You have my promise; but if separated I will not say but I shall then require of the invisible a knowledge of my husband's motions, when in search of the invisible also."

The winter passed rapidly away, for it was passed by Philip in quiet and happiness; the spring came on, the vessel was to be fitted out, and Philip and Amine repaired to Amsterdam.

The Utrecht was the name of the vessel to which he had been appointed, a ship of 400 tons, newly launched, and pierced for twenty-four guns. Two more months passed away, during which Philip superintended the fitting and loading of the vessel, assisted by his favourite Krantz, who served in her as first mate. Every convenience and comfort that Philip could think of was prepared for Amine; and in the month of May he started with orders to stop at Gambroon and Ceylon, run down the Straits of Sumatra, and from thence to force his way into the China seas, the Company having every reason to expect from the Portuguese the most determined opposition to the attempt. His ship's company was numerous, and he had a small detachment of soldiers on board to assist the supercargo, who carried out many thousand dollars to make purchases at ports in China, where their goods might not be appreciated. Every care had been taken in the equipment of the vessel, which was perhaps the finest, the best manned, and freighted with the most valuable cargo, which had ever been sent out by the India Company.

The Utrecht sailed with a flowing sheet, and was soon clear the English Channel; the voyage promised to be auspicious, favouring gales bore them without accident to within a few hundred miles of the Cape of Good Hope, when, for the first time, they were becalmed. Amine was delighted: in the evenings she would pace the deck with Philip; then all was silent, except the splash of the wave as it washed against the side of the vessel—all was in repose and beauty, as the bright southern constellations sparkled over their heads.

"Whose destinies can be in these stars, which appear not to those who inhabit the northern regions?" said Amine, as she cast her eyes above, and watched them in their brightness; "and what does that falling meteor portend? what causes its rapid descent from heaven?"

"Do you then put faith in stars, Amine?"

"In Araby we do; and why not? They were not spread over the sky to give light—for what then?"

"To beautify the world. They have their uses, too."

"Then you agree with me—they have their uses, and the destinies of men are there concealed. My mother was one of those who could read them well. Alas! for me they are a sealed book."

"Is it not better so, Amine?"

"Better!—say better to grovel on this earth with our selfish, humbled race, wandering in mystery and awe, and doubt, when we can communicate with the intelligences above! Does not the soul leap at her admission to confer with superior powers? Does not the proud heart bound at the feeling that its owner is one of those more gifted than the usual race of mortals? Is it not a noble ambition?"

"A dangerous one—most dangerous."

"And therefore most noble. They seem as if they would speak to me: look at you bright star—it beckons to me."

For some time, Amine's eyes were raised aloft; she spoke not, and Philip remained at her side. She walked to the gangway of the vessel, and looked down upon the placid wave, pierced by the moonbeams far below the surface.

"And does your imagination, Amine, conjure up a race of beings gifted to live beneath that deep blue wave, who sport amidst the coral rocks, and braid their hair with pearls?" said Philip, smiling.

"I know not, but it appears to me that it would be sweet to live there. You may call to mind your dream, Philip; I was then, according to your description, one of those same beings."

"You were," replied Philip, thoughtfully.

"And yet I feel as if water would reject me, even if the vessel were to sink. In what manner this mortal frame of mine may be resolved into its elements, I know not; but this I do feel, that it never will become the sport of, or be tossed by, the mocking waves. But come in, Philip, dearest; it is late, and the decks are wet with dew."

When the day dawned, the look-out man at the masthead reported that he perceived something floating on the still surface of the water, on the beam of the vessel. Krantz went up with his glass to examine, and made it out to be a small boat, probably cut adrift from some vessel. As there was no appearance of wind, Philip permitted a boat to be sent to examine it and after a long pull, the seamen returned on board, towing the small boat astern.

"There is a body of a man in it, sir," said the second mate to Krantz, as he gained the gangway; "but whether he is quite dead or not, I cannot tell."

Krantz reported this to Philip, who was, at that time sitting at breakfast with Amine, in the cabin, and then proceeded to the gangway, to where the body of the man had been already handed up by the seamen. The surgeon, who had been summoned, declared that life was not yet extinct, and was ordering him to be taken below, for recovery, when, to their astonishment, the man turned as he lay, sat up, and ultimately rose upon his feet and staggered to a gun, when, after a time, he appeared to be fully recovered. In reply to questions put to him, he said that he was in a vessel which had been upset in a squall, that he had time to cut away the small boat astern, and that all the rest of the crew had perished. He had hardly made this answer, when Philip, with Amine, came out of the cabin, and walked up to where the seamen were crowded round the man; the seamen retreated so as to make an opening, when Philip and Amine, to their astonishment and horror, recognised their old acquaintance, one-eyed pilot Schriften.

"He! he! Captain Vanderdecken I believe—glad to see you in command, and you too, fair lady."

Philip turned away with a chill at his heart; Amine's eye flashed as she surveyed the wasted form of the wretched creature. After a few seconds she turned round and followed Philip into the cabin, where she found him with his face buried in his hands.

"Courage, Philip, courage!" said Amine; "it was indeed a heavy shock, and I fear me, forebodes evil; but what then? it is our destiny."

"It is! it ought perhaps to be mine," replied Philip, raising his head; "but you, Amine, why should you be a partner—"

"I am your partner, Philip, in life and in death. I would not die first, Philip, because it would grieve you; but your death will be the signal for mine, and I will join you quickly."

"Surely, Amine, you would not hasten your own?"

"Yes! and require but one moment for this little steel to do its duty."

"Nay! Amine, that is not lawful—our religion forbids it."

"It may do so, but I cannot tell why. I came into this world without my own consent; surely I may leave it without asking the leave of priests! But let that pass for the present what will you do with that Schriften?"

"Put him on shore at the Cape—I cannot bear the odious wretch's presence. Did you not feel the chill, as before, when you approached him?"

"I did—I knew that he was there before I saw him; but still I know not why, I feel as if I would not send him away."

"Why not?"

"I believe it is because I am inclined to brave destiny, not to quail at it. The wretch can do no harm."

"Yes, he can—much: he can render the ship's company mutinous and disaffected; besides, he attempted to deprive me of my relic."

"I almost wish he had done so; then must you have discontinued this wild search."

"Nay, Amine, say not so; it is my duty, and I have taken my solemn oath—"

"But this Schriften—you cannot well put him ashore at the Cape; being a Company's officer, you might send him home if you found a ship there homeward bound; still were I you I would let destiny work. He is woven in with ours, that is certain. Courage, Philip, and let him remain."

"Perhaps you are right, Amine: I may retard, but cannot escape, whatever may be my intended fate."

"Let him remain, then, and let him do his worst. Treat him with kindness—who knows what we may gain from him?"

"True, true, Amine; he has been my enemy without cause. Who can tell?—perhaps he may become my friend."

"And if not, you will have done your duty. Send for him now."

"No, not now—to-morrow; in the mean time, I will order him every comfort."

"We are talking as if he were one of us, which I feel that he is not," replied Amine; "but still, mundane or not we cannot but offer mundane kindness, and what this world, or rather what this ship, affords. I long now to talk with him to see if I can produce any effect upon his ice-like frame. Shall I make love to the ghoul?" And Amine burst into a bitter laugh.

Here the conversation dropped, but its substance was not disregarded. The next morning, the surgeon having reported that Schriften was apparently quite recovered, he was summoned into the cabin. His frame was wasted away to a skeleton, but his motions and his language were as sharp and petulant as ever.

"I have sent for you, Schriften, to know if there is anything that I can do to make you more comfortable. Is there anything that you want?"

"Want?" replied Schriften, eyeing first Philip and then Amine. "He! he I think I want filling out a little."

"That you will, I trust, in good time; my steward has my orders to take care of you."

"Poor man," said Amine, with a look of pity, "how much he must have suffered! Is not this the man who brought you the letter from the Company, Philip?"

"He! he! yes! Not very welcome, was it, lady?"

"No, my good fellow; it's never a welcome message to a wife, that sends her husband away from her. But that was not your fault."

"If a husband will go to sea and leave a handsome wife when he has, as they say, plenty of money to live upon on shore, he! he!"

"Yes, indeed, you may well say that," replied Amine.

"Better give it up. All folly, all madness—eh, captain?"

"I must finish this voyage, at all events," replied Philip to Amine, "whatever I may do afterwards. I have suffered much, and so have you, Schriften. You have been twice wrecked; now tell me, what do you wish to do? Go home in the first ship, or go ashore at the Cape, or—"

"Or do anything, so I get out of this ship—he! he!"

"Not so. If you prefer sailing with me, as I know you are a good seaman, you shall have your rating and pay of pilot—that is, if you choose to follow my fortunes."

"Follow?—Must follow. Yes! I'll sail with you, Mynheer Vanderdecken, I wish to be always near you—he! he!"

"Be it so, then: as soon as you are strong again, you will go to your duty; till then, I will see that you want for nothing."

"Nor I, my good fellow. Come to me if you do, and I will be your help," said Amine. "You have suffered much; but we will do what we can to make you forget it."

"Very good!—very kind!" replied Schriften, surveying the lovely face and figure of Amine. After a times shrugging up his shoulders, he added— "A pity! Yes, it is! Must be, though."

"Farewell!" continued Amine, holding out her hand to Schriften.

The man took it, and a cold shudder went to her heart; but she, expecting such a result, would not appear to feel it. Schriften held her hand for a second or two in his own, looking at it earnestly, and then at Amine's face. "So fair—so good! Mynheer Vanderdecken, I thank you. Lady, may Heaven preserve you!" Then squeezing the hand of Amine, which he had not released, Schriften hastened out of the cabin.

So great was the sudden icy shock which passed through Amine's frame when Schriften pressed her hand, that when with difficulty she gained the sofa, she fell upon it. After remaining with her hand pressed against her heart for some time, during which Philip bent over her, she said, in a breathless voice, "That creature must be supernatural—I am sure of it—I am now convinced. Well," continued she, after a pause of some little while, "all the better, if we can make him a friend; and if I can I will."

"But think you, Amine, that those who are not of this world have feelings of kindness, gratitude, and ill-will, as we have? Can they be made subservient?"

"Most surely so. If they have ill-will—as we know they have—they must also be endowed with the better feelings. Why are there good and evil intelligences? They may have disencumbered themselves of their mortal clay, but the soul must be the same. A soul without feeling were no soul at all. The soul is active in this world, and must be so in the next. If angels can pity, they must feel like us. If demons can vex, they must feel like us. Our feelings change, then why not theirs? Without feelings, there were no heaven, no hell. Here our souls are confined, cribbed, and overladen—

borne down by the heavy flesh by which they are, for the time, polluted; but the soul that has winged its flight from clay is, I think, not one jot more pure, more bright, or more perfect, than those within ourselves. Can they be made subservient, say you! Yes, they can; they can be forced, when mortals possess the means and power. The evil-inclined may be forced to good, as well as to evil. It is not the good and perfect spirits that we subject by art, but those that are inclined to wrong. It is over them that mortals have the power. Our arts have no power over the perfect spirits, but over those which are ever working evil, and which are bound to obey and do good, if those who master them require it."

"You still resort to forbidden arts, Amine. Is that right?"

"Right! If we have power given to us, it is right to use it."

"Yes, most certainly, for good; but not for evil."

"Mortals in power, possessing nothing but what is mundane, are answerable for the use of that power; so those gifted by superior means are answerable as they employ those means. Does the God above make a flower to grow, intending that it should not be gathered! No! neither does he allow supernatural aid to be given, if he did not intend that mortals should avail themselves of it."

As Amine's eyes beamed upon Philip's, he could not for the moment subdue the idea rising in his mind, that she was not like other mortals; and he calmly observed, "Am I sure, Amine, that I am wedded to one mortal as myself?"

"Yes! yes! Philip, compose yourself, I am but mortal; would to Heaven I were not. Would to Heaven I were one of those who could hover over you, watch you in all your perils, save and protect you in this your mad career but I am but a poor weak woman, whose heart beats fondly, devotedly for you—who for you would dare all and everything—who, changed in her nature, has become courageous and daring from her love—and who rejects all creeds which would prevent her from calling upon heaven, or earth, or hell, to assist her in retaining with her her soul's existence!"

"Nay! nay! Amine,—say not you reject the creed. Does not this,"— and Philip pulled from his bosom the holy relic,—"does not this, and the message sent by it, prove our creed is true?"

"I have thought much of it, Philip. At first it startled me almost into a belief; but even your own priests helped to undeceive me. They would not answer you; they would have left you to guide yourself; the message and the holy word, and the wonderful signs given, were not in unison with their creed, and they halted. May I not halt, if they did? The relic may be as mystic, as powerful as you describe; but the agencies may be false and wicked—the power given to it may have fallen into wrong hands; the power remains the same, but it is applied to uses not intended."

"The power, Amine, can only be exercised by those who are friends to Him who died upon it."

"Then is it no power at all or if a power, not half so great as that of the arch-fiend; for his can work for good and evil both. But on this point, dear Philip, we do not well agree, nor can we convince each other. You have been taught in one way, I another. That which our childhood has imbibed— which has grown up with our growth, and strengthened with our years—is not to be eradicated. I have seen my mother work great charms and succeed. You have knelt to priests. I blame not you!—blame not, then, your Amine. We both mean well—I trust do well."

"If a life of innocence and purity were all that were required, my Amine would be sure of future bliss."

"I think it is; and thinking so, it is my creed. There are many creeds: who shall say which is the true one? And what matters it?—they all have the same end in view—a future Heaven."

"True Amine, true," replied Philip, pacing the cabin thoughtfully; "and yet our priests say otherwise."

"What is the basis of their creed, Philip?"

"Charity and good-will."

"Does charity condemn to eternal misery those who have never heard this creed—who have lived and died worshipping the Great Being after their best endeavours, and little knowledge?"

"No, surely."

Amine made no further observations; and Philip, after pacing for a few minutes in deep thought, walked out of the cabin.

The Utrecht arrived at the Cape, watered, and proceeded on her voyage, and, after two months of difficult navigation, cast anchor off Gambroon. During this time Amine had been unceasing in her attempts to gain the good-will of Schriften. She had often conversed with him on deck, and had done him every kindness, and had overcome that fear which his near approach had generally occasioned. Schriften gradually appeared mindful of this kindness, and at last to be pleased with Amine's company. To Philip he was at times civil and courteous, but not always; but to Amine he was always deferent. His language was mystical,—she could not prevent his chuckling laugh, his occasional "He! he!" from breaking forth. But when they anchored at Gambroon, he was on such terms with her, that he would occasionally come into the cabin; and, although he would not sit down, would talk to Amine for a few minutes, and then depart. While the vessel lay at anchor at Gambroon, Schriften one evening walked up to Amine, who was sitting on the poop. "Lady," said he, after a pause, "yon ship sails for your own country in a few days."

"So I am told," replied Amine.

"Will you take the advice of one who wishes you well? Return in that vessel—go back to your own cottage, and stay there till your husband comes to you once more."

"Why is this advice given?"

"Because I forebode danger—nay, perhaps death, a cruel death—to one I would not harm."

"To me!" replied Amine, fixing her eyes upon Schriften, and meeting his piercing gaze.

"Yes, to you. Some people can see into futurity further than others."

"Not if they are mortal," replied Amine.

"Yes, if they are mortal. But, mortal or not, I do see that which I would avert. Tempt not destiny further."

"Who can avert it? If I take your counsel, still was it my destiny to take your counsel. If I take it not, still it was my destiny."

"Well, then, avoid what threatens you."

"I fear not, yet do I thank you. Tell me, Schriften, hast thou not thy fate some way interwoven with that of my husband? I feel that thou hast."

"Why think you so, lady?"

"For many reasons: twice you have summoned him—twice have you been wrecked, and miraculously reappeared and recovered. You know, too, of his mission—that is evident."

"But proves nothing."

"Yes! it proves much; for it proves that you knew what was supposed to be known but to him alone."

"It was known to you, and holy men debated on it," replied Schriften, with a sneer.

"How knew you that, again?"

"He! he!" replied Schriften. "Forgive me, lady; I meant not to affront you."

"You cannot deny that you are connected mysteriously and incomprehensibly with this mission of my husband's. Tell me, is it, as he believes, true and holy?"

"If he thinks that it is true and holy, it becomes so."

"Why, then, do you appear his enemy?"

"I am not *his* enemy, fair lady."

"You are not his enemy?—why, then, did you once attempt to deprive him of the mystic relic by which the mission is to be accomplished?"

"I would prevent his further search, for reasons which must not be told. Does that prove that I am his enemy? Would it not be better that he should remain on shore with competence and you, than be crossing the wild seas on this mad search? Without the relic it is not to be accomplished. It were a kindness, then, to take it from him."

Amine answered not, for she was lost in thought.

"Lady," continued Schriften, after a time, "I wish you well. For your husband I care not, yet do I wish him no harm. Now, hear me; if you wish for your future life to be one of ease and peace—if you wish to remain long in this world with the husband of your choice, of your first and warmest love—if you wish that he should die in his bed at a good old age, and that you should close his eyes, with children's tears lamenting, and their smiles reserved to cheer their mother—all this I see, and can promise is in futurity, if you will take that relic from his bosom and give it up to me. But if you would that he should suffer more than man has ever suffered, pass his whole life in doubt anxiety, and pain, until the deep wave receive his corpse, then let him keep it. If you would that your own days be shortened, and yet those remaining be long in human suffering—if you would be separated from him, and die a cruel death—then let him keep it. I can read futurity and such must be the destiny of both. Lady, consider well; I must leave you now. To-morrow I will have your answer."

Schriften walked away and left Amine to her own reflections. For a long while she repeated to herself the conversation and denunciations of the man, whom she was now convinced was not of this world, and was in some way or another deeply connected with her husband's fate. "To me he wishes well, no harm to my husband, and would prevent his search. Why would he?—that he will not tell. He has tempted me tempted me most strangely. How easy 'twere to take the relic whilst Philip sleeps upon my bosom—but how treacherous! And yet a life of competence and ease, a smiling family, a good old age; what offers to a fond and doting wife! And if not, toil, anxiety, and a watery grave; and for me! Pshaw! that's nothing. And yet to die separated from Philip, is that nothing? Oh, no, the thought is dreadful.—I do believe him. Yes he has foretold the future, and told it truly. Could I persuade Philip? No! I know him well; he has vowed, and is not to be changed. And yet, if the relic were taken without his knowledge, he would not have to blame himself. Who then would he blame? Could I deceive him? I, the wife of his bosom, tell a lie? No! no! it must not be. Come what will, it is our destiny, and I am resigned. I would that Schriften had not spoken! Alas! we search into futurity, and then would fain retrace our steps, and wish we had remained in ignorance."

"What makes you so pensive, Amine?" said Philip, who some time afterwards walked up to where she was seated.

Amine replied not at first. "Shall I tell him all?" thought she. "It is my only chance—I will." Amine repeated the conversation between her and Schriften. Philip made no reply; he sat down by Amine and took her hand. Amine dropped her head upon her husband's shoulder. "What think you, Amine?" said Philip, after a time.

"I could not steal your relic, Philip; perhaps you'll give it to me."

"And my father, Amine, my poor father—his dreadful doom to be eternal! He who appealed, was permitted to appeal to his son, that that dreadful doom might be averted. Does not the conversation of this man prove to you that my mission is not false? Does not his knowledge of it strengthen all? Yet, why would he prevent it?" continued Philip, musing.

"Why I cannot tell, Philip, but I would fain prevent it. I feel that he has power to read the future, and has read aright."

"Be it so; he has spoken, but not plainly. He has promised me what I have long been prepared for—what I vowed to Heaven to suffer. Already have I suffered much, and am prepared to suffer more. I have long looked upon this world as a pilgrimage, and (selected as I have been) trust that my reward will be in the other. But, Amine, you are not bound by oath to Heaven, you have made no compact. He advised you to go home. He talked of a cruel death. Follow his advice and avoid it."

"I am not bound by oath, Philip; but hear me; as I hope for future bliss, I now bind myself."

"Hold, Amine!"

"Nay, Philip, you cannot prevent me; for if you do now, I will repeat it when you are absent. A cruel death were a charity to me, for I shall not see you suffer. Then may I never expect future bliss, may eternal misery be my portion, if I leave you as long as fate permits us to be together. I am yours—your wife; my fortunes, my present, my future, my all, are embarked with you, and destiny may do its worst, for Amine will not quail. I have no recreant heart to turn aside from danger or from suffering. In that one point, Philip, at least, you chose, you wedded well."

Philip raised her hand to his lips in silence, and the conversation was not resumed. The next evening, Schriften came up again to Amine. "Well, lady?" said he.

"Schriften, it cannot be," replied Amine; "yet do I thank you much."

"Lady, if he must follow up his mission, why should you?"

"Schriften, I am his wife—as for ever, in this world, and the next. You cannot blame me."

"No," replied Schriften, "I do not blame, I admire you. I feel sorry. But, after all, what is death? Nothing. He! he!" and Schriften hastened away, and left Amine to herself.

Chapter Twenty Two

The Utrecht sailed from Gambroon, touched at Ceylon, and proceeded on her voyage in the Eastern seas. Schriften still remained on board; but since his last conversation with Amine he had kept aloof, and appeared to avoid both her and Philip; still there was not, as before, any attempt to make the ship's company disaffected, nor did he indulge in his usual taunts and sneers. The communication he had made to Amine had also its effect upon her and Philip; they were more pensive and thoughtful; each attempted to conceal their gloom from the other; and when they embraced, it was with the mournful feeling that perhaps it was an indulgence they would soon be deprived of: at the same time, they steeled their hearts to endurance and prepared to meet the worst. Krantz wondered at the change, but of course could not account for it. The Utrecht was not far from the Andaman Isles, when Krantz, who had watched the barometer, came in early one morning and called Philip.

"We have every prospect of a typhoon, sir," said Krantz; "the glass and the weather are both threatening."

"Then we must make all snug. Send down top-gallant yards and small sails directly. We will strike top-gallant masts. I will be out in a minute."

Philip hastened on deck. The sea was smooth, but already the moaning of the wind gave notice of the approaching storm. The vacuum in the air was about to be filled up, and the convulsion would be terrible; a white haze gathered fast, thicker and thicker; the men were turned up, everything of weight was sent below, and the guns were secured. Now came a blast of wind which careened the ship, passed over, and in a minute she righted as before; then another and another, fiercer and fiercer still. The sea, although smooth, at last appeared white as a sheet with foam, as the typhoon swept along in its impetuous career; it burst upon the vessel, which bowed down to her gunnel and there remained; in a quarter of an hour the hurricane had passed over, and the vessel was relieved, but the sea had risen, and the wind was strong. In another hour the blast again came, more wild, more furious than the first, the waves were dashed into their faces, torrents of rain descended, the ship was thrown on her beam ends, and thus remained till the wild blast had passed away, to sweep destruction far beyond them, leaving behind it a tumultuous angry sea.

"It is nearly over, I believe, sir," said Krantz. "It is clearing up a little to windward."

"We have had the worst of it, I believe," said Philip.

"No! there is worse to come," said a low voice near to Philip. It was Schriften who spoke.

"A vessel to windward scudding before the gale," cried Krantz.

Philip looked to windward, and in the spot where the horizon was clearest, he saw a vessel under topsails and foresail, standing right down. "She is a large vessel; bring me my glass." The telescope was brought from the cabin, but before Philip could use it, a haze had again gathered up to windward, and the vessel was not to be seen.

"Thick again," observed Philip, as he shut in his telescope; "we must look out for that vessel, that she does not run too close to us."

"She has seen us, no doubt, sir," said Krantz.

After a few minutes the typhoon again raged, and the atmosphere was of a murky gloom. It seemed as if some heavy fog had been hurled along by the furious wind; nothing was to be distinguished except the white foam of the sea, and that not the distance of half a cable's length, where it was lost in one dark grey mist. The storm-stay-sail, yielding to the force of the wind, was rent into strips and flogged and cracked with a noise even louder than the gale. The furious blast again blew over, and the mist cleared up a little.

"Ship on the weather beam close aboard of us," cried one of the men.

Krantz and Philip sprang upon the gunwale, and beheld the large ship bearing right down upon them, not three cables' length distant.

"Helm up! she does not see us, and she will be aboard of us!" cried Philip. "Helm up, I say, hard up, quick!"

The helm was put up, as the men, perceiving their imminent danger, climbed upon the guns to look if the vessel altered her course; but no— down she came, and the head-sails of the Utrecht having been carried away, to their horror they perceived that she would not answer her helm, and pay off as they required.

"Ship ahoy!" roared Philip through his trumpet—but the gale drove the sound back.

"Ship ahoy!" cried Krantz on the gunwale, waving his hat. It was useless—down she came, with the waters foaming under her bows, and was now within pistol-shot of the Utrecht.

"Ship ahoy!" roared all the sailors, with a shout that must have been heard: it was not attended to: down came the vessel upon them, and now her cutwater was within ten yards of the Utrecht. The men of the Utrecht, who expected that their vessel would be severed in half by the concussion, climbed upon the weather gunwale, all ready to catch at the ropes of the other vessel, and climb on board of her. Amine, who had been surprised at the noise on deck, had come out, and had taken Philip by the arm.

"Trust to me—the shock—," said Philip. He said no more; the cutwater of the stranger touched their sides; one general cry was raised by the sailors of the Utrecht,—they sprang to catch at the rigging of the other vessel's bowsprit, which was now pointed between their masts—they caught at nothing—nothing—there was no shock—no concussion of the two vessels—the stranger appeared to cleave through them—her hull passed along in silence—no cracking of timbers—no falling of masts—the foreyard passed through their mainsail, yet the canvas was unrent—the whole vessel appeared to cut through the Utrecht, yet left no trace of injury—not fast, but slowly, as if she were really sawing through her by the heaving and tossing of the sea with her sharp prow. The stranger's forechains had passed their gunwale before Philip could recover himself. "Amine," cried he at last, "the Phantom Ship!—my father!"

The seamen of the Utrecht, more astounded by the marvellous result than by their former danger, threw themselves down upon deck; some hastened below, some prayed, others were dumb with astonishment and fear. Amine appeared more calm than any, not excepting Philip; she surveyed the vessel as it slowly forced its way through; she beheld the seamen on board of her coolly leaning over the gunwale, as if deriding the destruction they had occasioned; she looked for Vanderdecken himself, and on the poop of the vessel, with his trumpet under his arm she beheld the image of her Philip—the same hardy, strong build—the same features—about the same age apparently—there could be no doubt it was the *doomed* Vanderdecken.

"See, Philip," said she, "see your father!"

"Even so—Merciful Heaven! It is—it is!" and Philip, overpowered by his feelings, sank upon deck.

The vessel had now passed over the Utrecht; the form of the elder Vanderdecken was seen to walk aft and look over the taffrail; Amine perceived it to start and turn away suddenly—she looked down, and saw Schriften shaking his fist in defiance at the supernatural being! Again the Phantom Ship flew to leeward before the gale, and was soon lost in the mist but, before that, Amine had turned and perceived the situation of Philip. No one but herself and Schriften appeared able to act or move. She caught the pilot's eye, beckoned to him, and with his assistance Philip was led into the cabin.

Chapter Twenty Three

"I have then seen him," said Philip, after he had lain down on the sofa in the cabin for some minutes to recover himself while Amine bent over him. "I have at last seen him, Amine! Can you doubt now?"

"No, Philip, I have now no doubt," replied Amine, mournfully; "but take courage, Philip."

"For myself, I want not courage—but for you, Amine—you know that his appearance portends a mischief that will surely come."

"Let it come," replied Amine, calmly; "I have long been prepared for it, and so have you."

"Yes, for my self; but not for you."

"You have been wrecked often, and have been saved—then why should not I?"

"But the sufferings!"

"Those suffer least who have most courage to bear up against them. I am but a woman weak and frail in body, but I trust I have that within me which will not make you feel ashamed of Amine. No, Philip, you will have no wailing; no expression of despair from Amine's lips; if she can console you she will; if she can assist you she will; but come what may, if she cannot serve you, at least she will prove no burden to you."

"Your presence in misfortune would unnerve me, Amine."

"It shall not; it shall add to your resolution. Let fate do its worst."

"Depend upon it, Amine, that will be ere long."

"Be it so," replied Amine; "but Philip, it were as well you showed yourself on deck; the men are frightened, and your absence will be observed."

"You are right," said Philip; and rising and embracing her, he left the cabin.

"It is but too true, then," thought Amine. "Now to prepare for disaster and death; the warning has come. I would I could know more. Oh! mother, mother, look down upon thy child, and in a dream reveal the mystic arts which I have forgotten,—then should I know more; but I have promised

Philip, that unless separated—yes, that idea is worse than death, and I have a sad foreboding; my courage fails me only when I think of that!"

Philip, on his return to the deck, found the crew of the vessel in great consternation. Krantz himself appeared bewildered—he had not forgotten the appearance of the Phantom Ship off Desolation Harbour, and the vessels following her their destruction. This second appearance, more awful than the former, quite unmanned him; and when Philip came out of the cabin he was leaning in gloomy silence against the weather-bulkhead.

"We shall never reach port again, sir," said he to Philip, as he came up to him.

"Silence, silence; the men may hear you."

"It matters not; they think the same," replied Krantz.

"But they are wrong," replied Philip, turning to the seamen. "My lads! that some disaster may happen to us, after the appearance of this vessel is most probable; I have seen her before more than once, and disasters did then happen; but here I am, alive and well, therefore it does not prove that we cannot escape as I have before done. We must do our best, and trust in Heaven. The gale is breaking fast, and in a few hours we shall have fine weather. I have met this Phantom Ship before, and care not how often I meet it again. Mr Krantz, get up the spirits—the men have had hard work, and must be fatigued."

The very prospect of obtaining liquor appeared to give courage to the men; they hastened to obey the order, and the quantity served out was sufficient to give courage to the most tearful, and induce others to defy old Vanderdecken and his whole crew of imps. The next morning the weather was fine, the sea smooth, and the Utrecht went gaily on her voyage.

Many days of gentle breezes and favouring winds gradually wore off the panic occasioned by the supernatural appearance; and, if not forgotten, it was referred to either in jest or with indifference, he now had run through the straits of Malacca, and entered the Polynesian archipelago. Philip's orders were to refresh and call for instructions at the small island of Boton, then in possession of the Dutch. They arrived there in safety, and after remaining two days, again sailed on their voyage, intending to make their passage between the Celebes and the island of Galago. The weather was still clear and the wind light; they proceeded cautiously, on account of the reefs and currents, and with a careful watch for the piratical vessels, which have for centuries infested those seas; but they were not molested, and had gained well up among the islands to the north of Galago, when it fell calm, and the vessel was borne to the eastward of it by the current. The calm lasted several days, and they could procure no anchorage; at last they found themselves among the cluster of islands near to the northern coast of New Guinea.

The anchor was dropped, and the sails furled for the night; a drizzling small rain came on, the weather was thick, and watches were stationed in every part of the ship, that they might not be surprised by the pirate proas, for the current ran past the ship at the rate of eight or nine miles per hour, and these vessels, if hid among the islands, might sweep down upon them unperceived.

It was twelve o'clock at night, when Philip, who was in bed, was awakened by a shock; he thought it might be a proa running alongside, and he started from his bed and ran out. He found Krantz, who had been awakened by the same cause, running up undressed. Another shock succeeded, and the ship careened to port. Philip then knew that the ship was on shore.

The thickness of the night prevented them from ascertaining where the were, but the lead was thrown over the side, and they found that they were lying on shore on a sandbank, with not more than fourteen feet water on the deepest side, and that they were broadside on with a strong current pressing them further up on the bank; indeed the current ran like a mill-race, and each minute they were swept into shallow water.

On examination they found that the ship had dragged her anchor which, with the cable, was still taut from the starboard bow, but this did not appear to prevent the vessel from being swept further up on the bank. It was supposed that the anchor had parted at the shank, and another anchor was let go.

Nothing more could be done till daybreak, and impatiently did they wait till the next morning. As the sun rose, the mist cleared away, and they discovered that they were on shore on a sandbank, a small portion of which was above water, and round which the current ran with great impetuosity. About three miles from them was a cluster of small islands with cocoa-trees growing on them, but with no appearance of inhabitants.

"I fear we have little chance," observed Krantz to Philip. "If we lighten the vessel the anchor may not hold, and we shall be swept further on, and it is impossible to lay out an anchor against the force of this current."

"At all events we must try; but I grant that our situation is anything but satisfactory. Send all the hands aft."

The men came aft, gloomy and dispirited.

"My lads!" said Philip, "why are you disheartened?"

"We are doomed, sir; we knew it would be so."

"I thought it probable that the ship would be lost—I told you so; but the loss of the ship does not involve that of the ship's company—nay, it does not follow that the ship is to be lost, although she may be in great difficulty, as she is at present. What fear is there for us, my men?—the water is smooth—we have plenty of time before us—we can make a raft and take to our boats—it never blows among these islands, and we have land close under our lee. Let us first try what we can do with the ship; if we fail we must then take care of ourselves."

The men caught at the idea and went to work willingly; the water-casks were started, the pumps set going, and everything that could be spared was thrown over to lighten the ship; but the anchor still dragged, from the strength of the current and bad holding-ground; and Philip and Krantz perceived that they were swept further on the bank.

Night came on before they quitted their toil, and then a fresh breeze sprung up and created a swell, which occasioned the vessel to heat on the hard sand; thus did they continue until the next morning. At daylight the men resumed their labours, and the pumps were again manned to clear the vessel of the water which had been started, but after a time they pumped up sand. This told them that a plank had started and that their labours were useless; the men left their work, but Philip again encouraged them and pointed out that they could easily save themselves, and all that they had to do was to construct a raft which would hold provisions for them, and receive that portion of the crew who could not be taken into the boats.

After some repose the men again set to work; the top-sails were struck, the yards lowered down, and the raft was commenced under the lee of the vessel, where the strong current was checked. Philip, recollecting his former disaster took great pains in the construction of this raft, and aware that as the water and provisions were expended there would be no occasion to tow so heavy a mass, he constructed it in two parts, which might easily be severed, and thus the boats would have less to tow, as soon as circumstances would enable them to part with one of them.

Night again terminated their labours, and the men retired to rest the weather continuing fine, with very little wind. By noon the next day the raft was complete; water and provisions were safely stowed on board; a secure and dry place was fitted up for Amine in the centre of one portion; spare robes, sails, and everything which could prove useful in case of their being forced on shore, were put in. Muskets and ammunition were also provided, and everything was ready, when the men came aft and pointed out to Philip that there was plenty of money on board, which it was folly to leave, and that they wished to carry as much as they could away with them. As this intimation was given in a way that made it evident they intended that it should be complied with, Philip did not refuse; but resolved, in his own mind, that when they arrived at a place where he could exercise his authority, the money should be reclaimed for the Company to whom it belonged. The men went down below, and while Philip was making arrangements with Amine, handed the casks of dollars out of the hold, broke them open and helped themselves—quarrelling with each other for the first possession, as each cask was opened. At last every man had obtained as much as he could carry, and had placed his spoil on the raft with his baggage, or in the boat to which he had been appointed. All was now ready—Amine was lowered down, and took her station—the boats took in tow the raft which was cast off from the vessel, and away they went with the current, pulling with all their strength to avoid being stranded upon that part of the sandbank which appeared above water. This was the great danger which they had to encounter, and which they very narrowly escaped.

They numbered eighty-six souls in all: in the boats there were thirty-two; the rest were on the raft, which, being well-built and full of timber, floated high out of the water, now that the sea was so smooth. It had been agreed upon by Philip and Krantz, that one of them should remain on the raft and the other in one of the boats; but at the time the raft quitted the ship, they were both on the raft, as they wished to consult, as soon as they discovered the direction of the current, which would be the most advisable course for them to pursue. It appeared, that as soon as the current had passed the bank, it took a more southerly direction towards New Guinea. It was then debated between them whether they should or should not land on that island, the natives of which were known to be pusillanimous, yet treacherous. A long debate ensued, which ended, however, in their resolve not to decide as yet, but wait and see what might occur. In the mean time, the boats pulled to the westward, while the current set them fast down in a southerly direction.

Night came on and the boats dropped the grapnels with which they had been provided; and Philip was glad to find that the current was not near so strong, and the grapnels held both boats and raft. Covering themselves up with the spare sails with which they had provided themselves, and setting a watch, the tired seamen were soon fast asleep.

"Had I not better remain in one of the boats?" observed Krantz. "Suppose, to save themselves, the boats were to leave the raft."

"I have thought of that," replied Philip, "and have, therefore, not allowed any provisions or water in the boats; they will not leave us for that reason."

"True, I had forgotten that."

Krantz remained on watch, and Philip retired to the repose which he so much needed. Amine met him with open arms.

"I have no fear, Philip," said she; "I rather like this wild, adventurous change. We will go on shore and build our hut beneath the cocoa-trees, and I shall repine when the day comes which brings succour, and releases us from our desert isle. What do I require but you?"

"We are in the hands of One above, dear, who will act with us as He pleases. We have to be thankful that it is no worse," replied Philip. "But now to rest, for I shall soon be obliged to watch."

The morning dawned with a smooth sea and a bright blue sky; the raft had been borne to leeward of the cluster of uninhabited islands of which we spoke, and was now without hopes of reaching them; but to the westward were to be seen on the horizon the refracted heads and trunks of cocoa-nut trees, and in that direction it was resolved that they should tow the raft. The breakfast had been served out, and the men had taken to the oars, when they discovered a proa, full of men, sweeping after them from one of the islands to windward. That it was a pirate vessel there could be no doubt; but Philip and Krantz considered that their force was more than sufficient to repel them, should an attack be made. This was pointed out to the men; arms were distributed to all in the boats, as well as to those on the raft; and that the seamen might not be fatigued, they were ordered to lie on their oars, and await the coming up of the vessel.

As soon as the pirate was within range, having reconnoitred her antagonists, she ceased pulling, and commenced firing from a small piece of cannon, which was mounted on her bows. The grape and langridge which she poured upon, them wounded several of the men, although Philip had ordered them to lie down flat on the raft and in the boats. The pirate advanced nearer, and her fire became more destructive, without any opportunity of returning it by the Utrecht's people. At last it was proposed, as the only chance of escape, that the boats should attack the pirate. This was agreed to by Philip; more men were sent in the boats; Krantz took the command; the raft was cast off, and the boats pulled away. But scarcely had they cleared the raft, when, as by one sudden thought, they turned round, and pulled away in the opposite direction. Krantz's voice was heard by Philip, and his sword was seen to sash through the air; a moment afterwards he lunged into the sea, and swam to the raft. It appeared that the people in the boats, anxious to preserve the money which they had possession of, had agreed among themselves to pull away and leave the raft to its fate. The proposal for attacking the pirate had been suggested with that view, and as soon as they were clear of the raft, they put their intentions into execution. In vain had Krantz expostulated and threatened; they would have taken his life; and when he found that his efforts were of no avail he leaped from the boat. "Then are we lost, I fear," said Philip. "Our numbers are so reduced, that we cannot hope to hold out long. What think you, Schriften?" ventured Philip addressing the pilot who stood near to him.

"Lost—but not lost by the pirates—no harm there! He! he!"

The remark of Schriften was correct. The pirates, imagining that in taking to their boats the people had carried with them everything that was valuable, instead of firing at the raft immediately gave chase to the boats. The sweeps were now out and the proa flew over the smooth water, like a sea-bird, passed the raft, and was at first evidently gaining on the boats but their speed soon slackened, and as the day passed, the boats and then the pirate vessel disappeared in the southward; the distance between them being apparently much the same as at the commencement of the chase.

The raft being now at the mercy of the wind and waves Philip and Krantz collected the carpenter's tools which had been brought from the ship, and selecting two spars from the raft, they made every preparation for stepping a mast and setting sail by the next morning.

The morning dawned, and the first objects that met their view were the boats pulling back towards the raft, followed closely by the pirate. The men had pulled the whole night, and were worn out with fatigue It was presumed that a consultation had been held, in which it was agreed that they should make a sweep, so as to return to the raft, as, if they gained it, they would be able to defend themselves, and moreover obtain provisions and water, which they had not on board at the time of their desertion. But it was fated otherwise; gradually the men dropped from their oars, exhausted, into the bottom of the boat and the pirate vessel followed them with renewed ardour. The boats were captured one by one; the booty found was more than the pirates anticipated, and it hardly need be said that not one man was spared. All this took place within three miles of the raft, and Philip anticipated that the next movement of the vessel would be towards them, but he was mistaken. Satisfied with their booty, and imagining that there could be no more on the raft, the pirate pulled away to the eastward, towards the islands from amongst which she had first made her appearance. Thus were those who expected to escape, and who had deserted their companions, deservedly punished; whilst those who anticipated every disaster from this desertion discovered that it was the cause of their being saved.

The remaining people on board the raft amounted to about forty-five; Philip, Krantz, Schriften, Amine, the two mates, sixteen seamen, and twenty-four soldiers, who had been embarked at Amsterdam. Of provisions they had sufficient for three or four weeks; but of water they were very short, already not having sufficient for more than three days at the usual allowance. As soon as the mast had been stepped and rigged, and the sails set (although there was hardly a breath of wind), Philip explained to the men the necessity of reducing the quantity of water, and it was agreed that it should be served out so as to extend the supply to twelve days, the allowance being reduced to half a pint per day.

There was a debate at this time, as the raft was in two parts, whether it would not be better to cast off the smaller one and put all the people on board the other; but this proposal was overruled, as, in the first place, although the boats had deserted them, the number on the raft had not much diminished, and moreover, the raft would steer much better under sail, now that it had length, than it would do if they reduced its dimensions and altered its shape to a square mass of floating wood.

For three days it was a calm, the sun poured down his hot beams upon them, and the want of water was severely felt; those who continued to drink spirits suffered the most.

On the fourth day the breeze sprung up favourably, and the sail was filled; it was a relief to their burning brows and blistered backs; and as the raft sailed on at the rate of four miles an hour, the men were gay and full of hope. The land below the cocoa-nut trees was now distinguishable, and they anticipated that the next day they could land and procure the water which they now so craved for. All night they carried sail, but the next morning they discovered that the current was strong against them, and that what they gained when the breeze was fresh, they lost from the adverse current as soon as it went down; the breeze was always fresh in Use morning, but it fell calm in the evening. Thus did they continue for four days more, every noon being not ten miles from the land, but the next morning swept away to a distance, and having their ground to retrace. Eight days had now passed, and the men, worn out with the exposure to the burning sun, became discontented and mutinous. At one time they insisted that the raft should be divided, that they might gain the land with the other half; at another, that the provisions which they could no longer eat should be thrown overboard to lighten the raft. The difficulty under which they lay was the having no anchor or grapnel to the raft, the boats having carried away with them all that had been taken from the ship. Philip then proposed to the men that, as everyone of them had such a quantity of dollars, the money should be sewed up in canvas bags, each man's property separate; and that with this weight to the ropes they would probably be enabled to hold the raft against the current for one night, when they would be able the next day to gain shore; but this was refused—they would not risk their money. No, no—fools! they would sooner part with their lives by the most miserable of all deaths. Again and again was this proposed to them by Philip and Krantz, but without success.

In the mean time Amine had kept up her courage and her spirits, proving to Philip a valuable adviser and a comforter in his misfortunes. "Cheer up, Philip," would she say; "we shall yet build our cottage under the shade of those cocoa-nut trees, and pass a portion, if not the remainder of our lives in peace; for who indeed is there who would think to find us in these desolate and untrodden regions?"

Schriften was quiet and well-behaved; talked much with Amine, but with nobody else. Indeed, he appeared to have a stronger feeling in favour of Amine than he had ever shown before. He watched over her and attended her; and Amine would often look up after being silent and perceive Schriften's face wear an air of pity and melancholy which she had believed it impossible that he could have exhibited.

Another day passed; again they neared the land, and again did the breeze die away, and they were swept back by the current. The men now arose, and in spite of the endeavours of Philip and Krantz, they rolled into the sea all the provisions and stores, everything but one cask of spirits and the remaining stock of water; they then sat down at the upper end of the raft with gloomy, threatening looks and in close consultation.

Another night closed in; Philip was full of anxiety. Again he urged them to anchor with their money, but in vain; they ordered him away, and he returned to the after part of the raft, upon which Amine's secure retreat had been erected; he leant on it in deep thought and melancholy, for he imagined that Amine was asleep.

"What disturbs you, Philip?"

"What disturbs me? The avarice and folly of these men. They will die, rather than risk their hateful money. They have the means of saving themselves and us, and they will not. There is weight enough in bullion on the fore part of the raft to hold a dozen floating masses such as this, yet they will not risk it. Cursed love of gold, it makes men fools, madmen, villains! We have now but two days' water—doled out as it is drop by drop. Look at their emaciated, broken-down, wasted forms, and yet see how they cling to money, which probably they will never have occasion for, even if they gain the land. I am distracted!"

"You suffer, Philip, you suffer from privation, but I have been careful; I thought that this would come; I have saved both water and biscuit—I have here four bottles;—drink, Philip, and it will relieve you."

Philip drank; it did relieve him, for the excitement of the day had pressed heavily on him.

"Thanks, Amine—thanks, dearest! I feel better now.—Good Heaven! are they such fools as to value the dross of metal above one drop of water in a time of suffering and privation such as this?"

The night closed in as before; the stars shone bright, but there was no moon. Philip had risen at midnight to relieve Krantz from the steerage of the raft. Usually the men had lain about in every part of the raft, but this night the majority of them remained forward. Philip was communing with his own bitter thoughts, when he heard a scuffle forward? and the voice of Krantz crying out to him for help, he quitted the helm, and seizing his cutlass ran forward, where he found Krantz down, and the men securing him. He fought his way to him, but was himself seized and disarmed. "Cut away—cut away," was called out by those who held him; and, in a few seconds, Philip had the misery to behold the after part of the raft, with Amine upon it, drifted apart from the one on which he stood.

"For mercy's sake! my wife—my Amine—for Heaven's sake, save her!" cried Philip, struggling in vain to disengage himself. Amine also, who had run to the side of the raft held out her arms—it was in vain—they were separated more than a cable's length. Philip made one more desperate struggle, and then fell down deprived of sense and motion.

Chapter Twenty Four

It was not until the day had dawned that Philip opened his eyes, and discovered Krantz kneeling at his side; at first his thoughts were scattered and confused; he felt that some dreadful calamity had happened to him, but he could not recall to mind what it was. At last it rushed upon him, and he buried his face in his hands.

"Take comfort," said Krantz; "we shall probably gain the shore to-day, and we will go in search of her as soon as we can."

"This, then, is the separation and the cruel death to her which that wretch Schriften prophesied to us," thought Philip; "cruel indeed to waste away to a skeleton, under a burning sun, without one drop of water left to cool her parched tongue; at the mercy of the winds and waves; drifting about—alone—all alone—separated from her husband, in whose arms she would have died without regret; maddened with suspense and with the thoughts of what I may be suffering, or what may have been my fate. Pilot, you are right; there can be no more cruel death to a fond and doting wife. Oh! my head reels! What has Philip Vanderdecken to live for now?"

Krantz offered such consolation as his friendship could suggest, but in vain. He then talked of revenge, and Philip raised his head. After a few minutes' thought, he rose us. "Yes," replied he, "revenge!—revenge upon these dastards and traitors! Tell me, Krantz how many can we trust?"

"Half of the men, I should think, at least. It was a surprise." A spar had been fitted as a rudder, and the raft had now gained nearer the shore than it ever had done before. The men were in high spirits at the prospect, and every man was sitting on his own store of dollars which in their eyes, increased in value in proportion as did their prospect of escape.

Philip discovered from Krantz, that it was the soldiers and the most indifferent seamen who had mutinied on the night before, and cut away the other raft; and that all the best men had remained neuter.

"And so they will be now, I imagine," continued Krantz; "the prospect of gaining the shore has, in a manner, reconciled them to the treachery of their companions."

"Probably," replied Philip, with a bitter laugh; "but I know what will rouse them. Send them here to me."

Philip talked to the seamen whom Krantz had sent over to him. He pointed out to them that the other men were traitors not to be relied upon; that they would sacrifice everything and everybody for their own gain; that they had already done so for money, and that they themselves would have no security, either on the raft or on shore, with such people; that they dare not sleep for fear of having their throats cut, and that it were better at once to get rid of those who could not be true to each other; that it would facilitate their escape, and that they could divide between themselves the money which the others had secured, and by which they would double their own shares. That it had been his intention, although he had said nothing to enforce the restoration of the money for the benefit of the Company, as soon as they had gained a civilised port, where the authorities could interfere; but that, if they consented to join and aid him, he would now give them the whole of it for their own use.

What will not the desire of gain effect? Is it therefore to be wondered at, that these men, who were indeed but little better than those who were thus in his desire of retaliation, denounced by Philip, consented to his proposal? It was agreed, that if they did not gain the shore, the others should be attacked that very night, and tossed into the sea.

But the consultation with Philip had put the other party on the alert; they too held council, and kept their arms by their sides. As the breeze died away, they were not two miles from the land, and once more they drifted back into the ocean. Philip's mind was borne down with grief at the loss of Amine; but it recovered to a certain degree when he thought of revenge: that feeling stayed him up, and he often felt the edge of his cutlass, impatient for the moment of retribution.

It was a lovely night; the sea was now smooth as glass, and not a breath of air moved in the heavens; the sail of the raft hung listless down the mast, and was reflected upon the calm surface by the brilliancy of the starry night alone. It was a night for contemplation—for examination of oneself, and adoration of the Deity; and here, on's frail raft, were huddled together more than forty beings, ready for combat, for murder, and for spoil. Each party pretended to repose; yet each were quietly watching the motions of the other, with their hands upon their weapons. The signal was to be given by Philip: it was, to let go the halyards of the yard, so that the sail should fall down upon a portion of the other party, and entangle them. By Philip's directions, Schriften had taken the helm, and Krantz remained by his side.

The yard and sail fell clattering down, and then the work of death commenced; there was no parley, no suspense; each man started upon his feet and raised his sword. The voices of Philip and of Krantz alone were heard, and Philip's sword did its work. He was nerved to his revenge, and never could be satiated as long as one remained who had sacrificed his Amine. As Philip had expected, many had been covered up and entangled by the falling of the sail, and their work was thereby made easier.

Some fell where they stood: others reeled back, and sunk down under the smooth water; others were pierced as they floundered under the canvas. In a few minutes the work of carnage was complete. Schriften meanwhile looked on, and ever and anon gave vent to his chuckling laugh—his demoniacal "he! he!"

The strife was over, and Philip stood against the mast to recover his breath. "So far art thou revenged, my Amine," thought he; "but, oh! what are these paltry lives compared to thine?" And now that his revenge was satiated, and he could do no more, be covered his face up in his hands, and wept bitterly, while those who had assisted him were already collecting the money of the slain for distribution. These men, when they found that three only of their side had fallen lamented that there had not been more, as their own shares of the dollars would have been increased.

There were now but thirteen men besides Philip, Krantz, and Schriften, left upon the raft. As the day dawned, the breeze again sprung up, and they shared out the portions of water, which would have been the allowance of their companions who had fallen. Hunger they felt not; but the water revived their spirits.

Although Philip had had little to say to Schriften since the separation from Amine, it was very evident to him and to Krantz that all the pilot's former bitter feelings had returned. His chuckle, his sarcasms, his "He! he!" were incessant; and his eye was now as maliciously directed to Philip as it was when they first met. It was evident that Amine alone had for the time conquered his disposition; and that with her disappearance had vanished all the good will of Schriften towards her husband. For this Philip cared little; he had a much more serious weight on his heart—the loss of his dear Amine; and he felt reckless and indifferent concerning anything else.

The breeze now freshened, and they expected that in two hours, they would run on the beach, but they were disappointed; the step of the mast gave way from the force of the wind, and the sail fell upon the raft. This occasioned great delay; and before they could repair the mischief, the wind again subsided, and they were left about a mile from the beach. Tired and worn out with his feelings, Philip at last fell asleep by the side of Krantz, leaving Schriften at the helm. He slept soundly—he dreamt of Amine— he thought she was under a grove of cocoa-nuts, in a sweet sleep; that he stood by and watched her, and that she smiled in her sleep and murmured

"Philip," when suddenly he was awakened by some unusual movement. Half dreaming still, he thought that Schriften, the pilot, had in his sleep been attempting to gain his relic, had passed the chain over his head, and was removing quietly from underneath his neck the portion of the chain which, in his reclining posture, he lay upon. Startled at the idea, he threw up his hand to seize the arm of the wretch, and found that he had really seized hold of Schriften, who was kneeling by him, and in possession of the chain and relic. The struggle was short, the relic was recovered, and the pilot lay at the mercy of Philip, who held him down with his knee on his chest. Philip replaced the relic on his bosom, and, excited to madness, rose from the body of the now breathless Schriften, caught it in his arms, and hurled it into the sea.

"Man or devil! I care not which," exclaimed Philip, breathless; "escape now, if you can!"

The struggle had already roused up Krantz and others, but not in time to prevent Philip from wreaking his vengeance upon Schriften. In few words, he told Krantz what had passed; as for the men, they cared not; they laid their heads down again, and, satisfied that their money was safe, inquired no further.

Philip watched to see if Schriften would rise up again, and try to regain the raft; but he did not make his appearance above water, and Philip felt satisfied.

Chapter Twenty Five

What pen could portray the feelings of the fond and doting Amine, when she first discovered that she was separated from her husband? In a state of bewilderment, she watched the other raft as the distance between them increased. At last the shades of night hid it from her aching eyes, and she dropped down in mute despair.

Gradually she recovered herself, and turning round, she exclaimed, "Who's here?"

No answer.

"Who's here!" cried she in a louder voice; "alone—alone—and Philip gone. Mother, mother, look down upon your unhappy child!" and Amine frantically threw herself down so near to the edge of the raft, that her long hair, which had fallen down, floated on the wave.

"Ah me! where am I?" cried Amine, after remaining in a state of torpor for some hours. The sun glared fiercely upon her, and dazzled her eyes as she opened them—she cast them on the blue wave close by her, and beheld a large shark motionless by the side of the raft, waiting for his prey. Recoiling from the edge, she started up. She turned round and beheld the raft vacant, and the truth flashed on her. "Oh! Philip, Philip!" cried she, "then it is true and you are gone for ever! I thought it was only a dream: I recollect all now. Yes—all—all!" And Amine sank down again upon her cot which had been placed in the centre of the raft, and remained motionless for some time.

But the demand for water became imperious; she seized one of the bottles, and drank. "Yet why should I drink or eat? why should I wish to preserve life?" She rose, and looked round the horizon. "Sky and water, nothing more. Is this the death I am to die—the cruel death prophesied by Schriften—a lingering death under a burning sun, while my vitals are parched within? Be it so! Fate, I dare thee to thy worst—we can die but once—and without him, what care I to live? But yet I may see him again," continued Amine, hurriedly, after a pause. "Yes, I may—who knows? then welcome life; I'll nurse thee for that bare hope—bare indeed, with naught to feed on. Let me see—is it here still?" Amine looked at her zone, and perceived her dagger was still in it. "Well, then, I will live since death is at my command, and be guardful of life for my dear husband's sake." And

Amine threw herself on her resting-place that she might forget every thing. She did: from that morning till the noon of the next day she remained in a state of torpor.

When she again rose, she was faint; again she looked round her—there was but sky and water to be seen.

"Oh! this solitude—it is horrible! death would be a release—but no, I must not die—I must live for Philip." She refreshed herself with water and a few pieces of biscuit, and folded her arms across her breast. "A few more days without relief, and all must be over. Was ever woman situated as I am, and yet I dare to indulge hope? Why, 'tis madness! And why am I thus singled out: because I have wedded with Philip? It may be so; if so, I welcome it. Wretches! who thus severed me from my husband; who to save their own lives, sacrificed a helpless woman! Nay! they might have saved me, if they had had the least pity;—but no, they never felt it. And these are Christians! The creed that the old priests would have had me—yes! that Philip would have had me embrace. Charity and good-will! They talk of it, but I have never seen them practise it! Loving one another!—forgiving one another!—say rather hating and preying upon one another! A creed never practised: why, if not practised of what value is it? Any creed were better—I abjure it, and if I be saved, will abjure it still for ever. Shade of my mother! is it that I have listened to these men—that I have to win my husband's love, tried to forget that which thou taughtest, even when a child at thy feet—that faith which our forefathers for thousands of years lived and died in—that creed proved by works, and obedience to the prophet's will is it for this that I am punished? Tell me, mother—oh! tell me in my dreams."

The night closed in, and with the gloom rose heavy clouds; the lightning darted through the firmament, ever and anon lighting up the raft. At last, the flashes were so rapid, not following each other—but darting down from every quarter at once, that the whole firmament appeared as if on fire, and the thunder rolled along the heavens, now near and loud, then rumbling in the distance. The breeze rose up fresh, and the waves tossed the raft, and washed occasionally even to Amine's feet, as she stood in the centre of it.

"I like this—this is far better than that calm and withering heat—this rouses me," said Amine as she cast her eyes up, and watched the forked lightning till her vision became obscured. "Yes, this is as it should be. Lightning, strike me if you please—waves, wash me off and bury me in a briny tomb—pour the wrath of the whole elements upon this devoted head—I care not, I laugh at, I defy it all. Thou canst but kill, this little steel can do as much. Let those who hoard up wealth—those who live in splendour— those that are happy—those who have husbands, children, aught to love—

let them tremble; I have nothing. Elements! be ye fire, or water, or earth, or air, Amine defies you! And yet—no no, deceive not thyself. Amine, there is no hope; thus will I mount my funeral bier, and wait the will of destiny." And Amine regained the secure place which Philip had fitted up for her in the centre of the raft, threw herself down upon her bed and shut her eyes.

The thunder and lightning was followed up by torrents of heavy rain, which fell till daylight; the wind still continued fresh, but the sky cleared, and the sun shone out. Amine remained shivering in her wet garments: the heat of the sun proved too powerful for her exhausted state, and her brain wandered. She rose up in a sitting posture, looked around her, saw verdant fields in every direction, the cocoa-nuts waving to the wind—imagined even that she saw her own Philip in the distance hastening to her; she held out her arms strove to get up, and run to meet him, but her limbs refused their office; she called to him, she screamed, and sank back exhausted on her resting-place.

Chapter Twenty Six

We must for a time return to Philip, and follow his strange destiny. A few hours after he had thrown the pilot into the sea they gained the shore, so long looked at with anxiety and suspense. The spars of the raft, jerked by the running swell undulated and rubbed against each other, as they rose and fell to the waves breaking on the beach. The breeze was fresh, but the surf was trifling, and the landing was without difficulty. The beach was shelving, of firm white sand, interspersed and strewed with various brilliant-coloured shells; and here and there, the bleached fragments and bones of some animal which had been forced out of its element to die. The island was, like all the others, covered with a thick wood of cocoa-nut trees, whose tops waved to the breeze, or bowed to the blast, producing a shade and a freshness which would have been duly appreciated by any other party than the present, with the exception only of Krantz; for Philip thought of nothing but his lost wife, and the seamen thought of nothing but of their sudden wealth. Krantz supported Philip to the beach, and led him to the shade; but after a minute he rose, and running down to the nearest point, looked anxiously for the portion of the raft which held Amine, which was now far, far away. Krantz had followed, aware that, now the first paroxysms were past, there was no fear of Philip's throwing away his life.

"Gone, gone for ever!" exclaimed Philip, pressing his hands to the balls of his eyes.

"Not so, Philip, the same providence which has preserved us, will certainly assist her. It is impossible that she can perish among so many islands many of which are inhabited; and a woman will be certain of kind treatment."

"If I could only think so," replied Philip.

"A little reflection may induce you to think that it is rather an advantage than otherwise, that she is thus separated—not from you, but from so many lawless companions whose united force we could not resist. Do you think that, after any lengthened sojourn on this island, these people with us would permit you to remain in quiet possession of your wife? No!—they would respect no laws; and Amine has, in my opinion, been miraculously preserved from shame and ill treatment, if not from death."

"They durst not, surely! Well, but Krantz, we must make a raft and follow her; we must not remain here—I will seek her through the wide world."

"Be it so, if you wish, Philip, and I will follow your fortunes," replied Krantz, glad to find that there was something, however wild the idea, for his mind to feed on. "But now let us return to the raft, seek the refreshment we so much require, and after that we will consider what may be the best plan to pursue."

To this, Philip, who was much exhausted, tacitly consented, and he followed Krantz to where the raft had been beached. The men had left it, and were each of them sitting apart from one another under the shade of his own chosen cocoa-nut tree. The articles which had been saved on the raft had not been landed, and Krantz called upon them to come and carry the things on shore—but no one would answer or obey. They each sat watching their money, and afraid to leave it, lest they should be dispossessed of it by the others. Now that their lives were, comparatively speaking, safe, the demon of avarice had taken full possession of their souls; there they sat, exhausted, pining for water, longing for sleep, and yet they dared not move,—they were fixed as if by the wand of the enchanter.

"It is the cursed dollars which have turned their brains," observed Krantz to Philip; "let us try if we cannot manage to remove what we most stand in need of, and then we will search for water."

Philip and Krantz collected the carpenter's tools, the best arms, and all the ammunition, as the possession of the latter would give them an advantage in case of necessity; they then dragged on shore the sail and some small spars, all of which they carried up to a clump of cocoa-nut trees, about a hundred yards from the beach.

In half an hour they had erected an humble tent, and put into it what they had brought with them, with the exception of the major part of the ammunition, which, as soon as he was screened by the tent, Krantz buried in a heap of dry sand behind it; he then, for their immediate wants, cut down with an axe a small cocoa-nut tree in full bearing. It must be for those who have suffered the agony of prolonged thirst, to know the extreme pleasure with which the milk of the nuts were one after the other poured down the parched throats of Krantz and Philip. The men witnessed their enjoyment in silence, and with gloating eyes. Every time that a fresh cocoa-nut was seized and its contents quaffed by their officers, more sharp and agonising was their own devouring thirst—still closer did their dry lips glue themselves together—yet they moved not, although they felt the tortures of the condemned.

Evening closed in; Philip had thrown himself down on the spare sails, and had fallen asleep, when Krantz set off to explore the island upon which they had been thrown. It was small, not exceeding three miles in length, and at no one part more than five hundred yards across. Water there was none, unless it were to be obtained by digging; fortunately, the young cocoa-nuts prevented the absolute necessity for it. On his return, Krantz passed the men in their respective stations. Each was awake, and raised himself on his elbow to ascertain if it were an assailant; but, perceiving Krantz, they again dropped down. Krantz passed the raft—the water was now quite smooth, for the wind had shifted off shore, and the spars which composed the raft hardly jostled each other. He stepped upon it, and, as the moon was bright in the heavens he took the precaution of collecting all the arms which had been left, and throwing them as far as he could into the sea. He then walked to the tent, where he found Philip still sleeping soundly, and in a few minutes he was reposing by his side. And Philip's dreams were of Amine; he thought that he saw the hated Schriften rise again from the waters, and, climbing up to the raft, seat himself by her side. He thought that he again heard his unearthly chuckle and his scornful laugh, as his unwelcome words fell upon her distracted ears. He thought that she fled into the sea to avoid Schriften, and that the waters appeared to reject her—she floated on the surface. The storm rose, and once more he beheld her in the sea-shell skimming over the waves. Again, she was in a furious surf on the beach, and her shell sank, and she was buried in the waves: and then he saw her walking on shore without fear and without harm, for the water which spared no one, appeared to spare her. Philip tried to join her, but was prevented by some unknown power, and Amine waved her hand and said, "We shall meet again, Philip; yes, once more on this earth shall we meet again."

The sun was high in the heavens and scorching in his heat, when Krantz first opened his eyes, and awakened Philip. The axe again procured for them their morning's meal. Philip was silent; he was ruminating upon his dreams, which had afforded him consolation. "We shall meet again!" thought he. "Yes, once more at least we shall meet again. Providence! I thank thee."

Krantz then stepped out to ascertain the condition of the men. He found them faint, and so exhausted, that they could not possibly survive much longer, yet still watching over their darling treasure. It was melancholy to witness such perversion of intellect, and Krantz thought of a plan which might save their lives. He proposed to them each separately, that they should bury their money so deep, that it was not to be recovered without time: this would prevent any one from attacking the treasure of the other, without its being perceived and the attempt frustrated, and would enable them to obtain their necessary food and refreshment without danger of being robbed.

To this plan they acceded. Krantz brought out of the tent the only shovel in their possession, and they, one by one, buried their dollars many feet deep in the yielding sand. When they had all secured their wealth, he brought them one of the axes, and the cocoa-nut trees fell, and they were restored to new life and vigour. Having satiated themselves, they then lay down upon the several spots under which they had buried their dollars, and were soon enjoying that repose which they all so much needed.

Philip and Krantz had now many serious consultations as to the means which should be taken for quitting the island, and going in search of Amine; for although Krantz thought the latter part of Philip's proposal useless, he did not venture to say so. To quit this island was necessary; and provided they gained one of those which were inhabited, it was all that they could expect. As for Amine, he considered that she was dead before this, either having been washed off the raft, or that her body was lying on it exposed to the decomposing heat of a torrid sun.

To cheer Philip, he expressed himself otherwise; and whenever they talked about leaving the island, it was not to save their own lives, but invariably to search after Philip's lost wife. The plan which they proposed and acted upon was, to construct a light raft, the centre to be composed of three water-casks, sawed in half, in a row behind each other, firmly fixed by cross pieces to two long spars on each side. This, under sail, would move quickly through the water, and be manageable so as to enable them to steer a course. The outside spars had been selected and hauled on shore, and the work was already in progress; but they were left alone in their work, for the seamen appeared to have no idea at present of quitting the island. Restored by food and repose, they were now not content with the money which they had—they were anxious for more. A portion of each party's wealth had been dug up, and they now gambled all day with pebbles, which they had collected on the beach, and with which they had invented a game. Another evil had crept among them: they had cut steps in the largest cocoa-nut trees, and with the activity of seamen had mounted them, and by tapping the top of the trees, and fixing empty cocoa-nuts underneath, had obtained the liquor, which in its first fermentation is termed toddy, and is afterwards distilled into arrack. But as toddy, it is quite sufficient to intoxicate; and every day the scenes of violence and intoxication, accompanied with oaths and execrations, became more and more dreadful. The losers tore their hair, and rushed like madmen upon those who had gained their dollars; but Krantz had fortunately thrown their weapons into the sea, and those he had saved, as well as the ammunition, he had secreted.

Blows and bloodshed, therefore, were continual, but loss of life there was none, as the contending parties were separated by the others, who were anxious that the play should not be interrupted. Such had been the state of affairs for now nearly a fortnight while the work of the raft had slowly proceeded. Some of the men had lost their all, and had, by the general consent of those who had won their wealth, been banished to a certain distance that they might not pilfer from them. These walked gloomily round the island, or on the beach, seeking some instrument by which they might avenge themselves, and obtain repossession of their money. Krantz and Philip had proposed to these men to join them and leave the island, but they had sullenly refused.

The axe was now never parted with by Krantz. He cut down what cocoa-nut trees they required for subsistence, and prevented the men from notching more trees to procure the means of inebriation. On the sixteenth day all the money had passed into the hands of three men, who had been more fortunate than the rest. The losers were now by far the more numerous party, and the consequence was, that the next morning these three men were found lying strangled on the beach; the money had been re-divided, and the gambling had re-commenced with more vigour than ever.

"How can this end?" exclaimed Philip to Krantz, as he looked upon the blackened countenances of the murdered men.

"In the death of all," replied Krantz. "We cannot prevent it. It is a judgment."

The raft was now ready; the sand had been dug from beneath it, so as to allow the water to flow in and float it, and it was now made fast to a stake and riding on the peaceful waters. A large store of cocoa-nuts, old and young, had been procured and put on board of her, and it was the intention of Philip and Krantz to have quitted the island the next day.

Unfortunately, one of the men, when bathing, had perceived the arms lying in the shallow water. He had dived down and procured a cutlass: others had followed his example, and all had armed themselves. This induced Philip and Krantz to sleep on board of the raft and keep watch; and that night, as the play was going on, a heavy loss on one side ended in a general fray. The combat was furious for all were more or less excited by intoxication. The result was melancholy, for only three were left alive. Philip, with Krantz watched the issue; every man who fell wounded was put to the sword, and the three left, who had been fighting on the same side, rested panting on their weapons. After a pause two of them communicated with each other, and the result was an attack upon the third man, who fell dead beneath their blows.

"Merciful Father! are these thy creatures?" exclaimed Philip.

"No," replied Krantz, "they worshipped the devil as Mammon. Do you imagine that those two, who could now divide more wealth than they could well spend if they return to their country—will consent to a division? Never—they must have all—yes, all!"

Krantz had hardly expressed his opinion, when one of the men, taking advantage of the other turning round a moment from him, passed his sword through his back. The man fell with a groan, and the sword was again passed through his body.

"Said I not so? But the treacherous villain shall not reap his reward," continued Krantz, levelling the musket which he held in his hand, and shooting him dead.

"You have done wrong, Krantz; you have saved him from the punishment he deserved. Left alone on the island, without the means of obtaining his subsistence, he must have perished miserably and by inches, with all his money round him; that would have been torture indeed!"

"Perhaps I was wrong. If so, may Providence forgive me, I could not help it. Let us go ashore, for we are now on this island alone. We must collect the treasure and bury it, so that it may be recovered; and, at the same time, take a portion with us; for who knows but that we may have occasion for it. Tomorrow we had better remain here, for we shall have enough to do in burying the bodies of these infatuated men, and the wealth which has caused their destruction."

Philip agreed to the propriety of the suggestion; the next day they buried the bodies where they lay; and the treasure was all collected in a deep trench, under a cocoa-nut tree, which they carefully marked with their axe. About five hundred pieces of gold were selected and taken on board of the raft with the intention of secreting them about their persons, and resorting to them in case of need.

The following morning they hoisted their sail and quitted the island. Need it be said in what direction they steered? As may be well imagined, in that quarter where they had last seen the raft with the isolated Amine.

Chapter Twenty Seven

The raft was found to answer well, and although her progress through the water was not very rapid, she obeyed the helm and was under command. Both Philip and Krantz were very careful in taking such marks and observations of the island as should enable them, if necessary, to find it again. With the current to assist them they now proceeded rapidly to the southward, in order that they might examine a large island which lay in that direction. Their object, after seeking for Amine was to find out the direction of Ternate; the king of which they knew to be at variance with the Portuguese, who had a fort and factory at Tidore, not very far distant from it; and from thence to obtain a passage in one of the Chinese junks, which, on their way to Bantam, called at that island.

Towards evening they had neared the large island, and they soon ran down it close to the beach. Philip's eyes wandered in every direction to ascertain whether anything on the shore indicated the presence of Amine's raft, but he could perceive nothing of the kind, nor did he see any inhabitants.

That they might not pass the object of their search during the night, they ran their raft on shore, in a small cove where the waters were quite smooth, and remained there until the next morning, when they again made sail and prosecuted their voyage. Krantz was steering with the long sweep they had fitted for the purpose, when he observed Philip, who had been for some time silent, take from his breast the relic which he wore, and gaze attentively upon it.

"Is that your picture, Philip?" observed Krantz.

"Alas! no, it is my destiny," replied Philip, answering without reflection.

"Your destiny! What mean you?"

"Did I say my destiny? I hardly know what I said," replied Philip, replacing the relic in his bosom.

"I rather think you said more than you intended," replied Krantz; "but at the same time something near the truth. I have often perceived you with that trinket in your hand, and I have not forgotten how anxious Schriften was to obtain it and the consequences of his attempt upon it. Is there not some secret—some mystery attached to it? Surely, if so, you must now sufficiently know me as your friend to feel me worthy of your confidence."

"That you are my friend, Krantz, I feel; my sincere and much-valued friend, for we have shared much danger together and that is sufficient to make us friends; that I could trust you, I believe, but I feel as if I dare not trust any one. There is a mystery attached to this relic (for a relic it is), which as yet has been confided to my wife and holy men alone."

"And if trusted to holy men, surely it may be trusted to sincere friendship, than which nothing is more holy."

"But I have a presentiment that the knowledge of my secret would prove fatal to you. Why I feel such a presentiment I know not; but I feel it, Krantz; and I cannot afford to lose you, my valued friend."

"You will not then make use of my friendship, it appears," replied Krantz. "I have risked my life with you before now and I am not to be deterred from the duties of friendship by a childish foreboding on your part, the result of an agitated mind and a weakened body. Can anything be more absurd than to suppose that a secret confided to me can be pregnant with danger, unless it be, indeed, that my zeal to assist you may lead me into difficulties. I am not of a prying disposition; but we have been so long connected together, and are now so isolated from the rest of the world, that it appears to me it would be a solace to you, were you to confide in one whom you can trust, what evidently has long preyed upon your mind. The consolation and advice of a friend, Philip, are not to be despised, and you will feel relieved if able to talk over with him a subject which evidently oppresses you. If, therefore, you value my friendship, let me share with you in your sorrows."

There are few who have passed through life so quietly, as not to recollect how much grief has been assuaged by confiding its cause to, and listening to the counsels and consolations of some dear friend. It must not, therefore appear surprising that, situated as he was, and oppressed with the loss of Amine, Philip should regard Krantz as one to whom he might venture to confide his important secret. He commenced his narrative with no injunctions, for he felt that if Krantz could not respect his secret for his secret's sake, or from good will towards him, he was not likely to be bound by any promise; and as, during the day, the raft passed by the various small capes and headlands of the island, he poured into Krantz's ear the history which the reader is acquainted with. "Now you know all," said Philip, with a deep sigh, as the narrative was concluded. "What think you? Do you credit my strange tale, or do you imagine as some well would, that it is a mere phantom of a disordered brain?"

"That it is not so, Philip, I believe," replied Krantz; "for I too have had ocular proof of the correctness of a part of your history. Remember how often I have seen this Phantom Ship—and if your father is permitted to range over the seas, why should you not be selected and permitted to reverse his doom? I fully believe every word that you have told me, and since you have told me this, I can comprehend much that in your behaviour at times appeared unaccountable; there are many who would pity you, Philip, but I envy you."

"Envy me?" cried Philip.

"Yes! envy you: and gladly would I take the burden of your doom on my own shoulders, were it only possible. Is it not a splendid thought that you are summoned to so great a purpose,—that instead of roaming through the world as we all do in pursuit of wealth, which possibly we may lose after years of cost and hardship, by the venture of a day, and which, at all events, we must leave behind us,—you are selected to fulfil a great and glorious work—the work of angels, I may say—that of redeeming the soul of a father, *suffering* indeed for his human frailties, but not doomed to perish for eternity; you have, indeed, an object of pursuit worthy of all the hardships and dangers of a maritime life. If it ends in your death, what then? Where else ends our futile cravings, our continual toil, after nothing? We all must die—but how few—who, indeed, besides yourself—was ever permitted before his death to ransom the soul of the author of his existence! Yes, Philip, I envy you!"

"You think and speak like Amine. She, too, is of a wild and ardent soul, that would mingle with the beings of the other world, and hold intelligence with disembodied spirits."

"She is right," replied Krantz; "there are events in my life, or rather connected with my family, which have often fully convinced me that this is not only possible but permitted. Your story has only corroborated what I already believed."

"Indeed! Krantz?"

"Indeed, yes; but of that hereafter: the night is closing in we must again put our little bark in safety for the night, and there is a cove which I think appears suited for the purpose."

Before morning a strong breeze, right on shore, had sprung up, and the surf became so high as to endanger the raft; to continue their course was impossible; they could only haul up their raft, to prevent its being dashed to pieces by the force of the waves, as the seas broke on the shore. Philip's thoughts were, as usual, upon Amine; and as he watched the tossing waters, as the sunbeams lightened up their crests, he exclaimed, "Ocean, hast thou my Amine? If so, give up thy dead! What is that?" continued he, pointing to a speck on the horizon.

"The sail of a small craft of some description or another," replied Krantz; "and apparently coming down before the wind to shelter herself in the very nook we have selected."

"You are right; it is the sail of a vessel—of one of those peroquas which skim over these seas; how she rises on the swell! She is full of men apparently."

The peroqua rapidly approached, and was soon close to the beach; the sail was lowered, and she was backed in through the surf.

"Resistance is useless should they prove enemies," observed Philip. "We shall soon know our fate."

The people in the peroqua took no notice of them until the craft had been hauled up and secured; three of them then advanced towards Philip and Krantz, with spears in their hands, but evidently with no hostile intentions. One addressed them in Portuguese asking them who they were.

"We are Hollanders," replied Philip.

"A part of the crew of the vessel which was wrecked?" inquired he.

"Yes!"

"You have nothing to fear—you are enemies to the Portuguese, and so are we. We belong to the island of Ternate—our king is at war with the Portuguese, who are villains. Where are your companions? on which island?"

"They are all dead," replied Philip. "May I ask you whether you have fallen in with a woman, who was adrift on a part of the raft by herself: or have you heard of her?"

"We have heard that a woman was picked up on the beach to the southward, and carried away by the Tidore people to the Portuguese settlement, on the supposition that she was a Portuguese."

"Then God be thanked, she is saved," cried Philip. "Merciful Heaven! accept my thanks.—To Tidore you said?"

"Yes; we are at war with the Portuguese, we cannot take you there."

"No! but we shall meet again."

The person who accosted them was evidently of consequence. His dress was to a certain degree Mahometan, but mixed up with Malay; he carried arms in his girdle and a spear in his hand; his turban was of printed chintz;

and his deportment like most persons of rank in that country, was courteous and dignified.

"We are now returning to Ternate, and will take you with us. Our king will be pleased to receive any Hollanders, especially as you are enemies to the Portuguese dogs. I forgot to tell you that we have one of your companions with us in the boat; we picked him up at sea much exhausted, but he is now doing well."

"Who can it be?" observed Krantz; "it must be some one belonging to some other vessel."

"No," replied Philip, shuddering, "it must be Schriften."

"Then my eyes must behold him before I believe it," replied Krantz.

"Then believe your eyes," replied Philip, pointing to the form of Schriften, who was now walking towards them.

"Mynheer Vanderdecken, glad to see you. Mynheer Krantz, I hope you are well. How lucky that we should all be saved. He! he!"

"The ocean has then, indeed, given up its dead, as I requested," thought Philip.

In the mean time, Schriften, without making any reference to the way in which they had so unceremoniously parted company, addressed Krantz with apparent good-humour, and some slight tinge of sarcasm. It was some time before Krantz could rid himself of him.

"What think you of him, Krantz?"

"That he is a part of the whole, and has his destiny to fulfil as well as you. He has his part to play in this wondrous mystery, and will remain until it is finished. Think not of him. Recollect, your Amine is safe."

"True," replied Philip, "the wretch is not worth a thought; we have now nothing to do but to embark with these people; hereafter we may rid ourselves of him, and strive then to rejoin my dearest Amine."

Chapter Twenty Eight

When Amine again came to her senses, she found herself lying on the leaves of the palmetto, in a small hut. A hideous black child sat by her, brushing off the flies. Where was she?

The raft had been tossed about for two days, during which Amine remained in a state of alternate delirium and stupor. Driven by the current and the gale, it had been thrown on shore on the eastern end of the coast of New Guinea. She had been discovered by some of the natives, who happened to be on the beach trafficking with some of the Tidore people. At first they hastened to rid her of her garments, although they perceived that she was not dead; but before they had left her as naked as themselves, a diamond of great value, which had been given to her by Philip, attracted the attention of one of the savages; failing in his attempt to pull it off, he pulled out a rusty, blunt knife, and was busily sawing at the finger, when an old woman of authority interfered and bade him desist. The Tidore people also, who were friends with the Portuguese, pointed out that to save one of that nation would insure a reward; they stated moreover, that they would, on their return, inform the people of the Factory establishment that one of their countrywomen had been thrown on shore on a raft. To this Amine owed the care and attention that was paid to her; that part of New Guinea being somewhat civilised by occasional intercourse with the Tidore people, who came there to exchange European finery and trash for the more useful productions of the island.

The Papoose woman carried Amine into her hut, and there she lay for many days, wavering between life and death, carefully attended, but requiring little except the moistening of her parched lips with water, and the brushing off of the mosquitoes and flies.

When Amine opened her eyes, the little Papoose ran out to acquaint the woman, who followed her into the hut. She was of large size, very corpulent and unwieldy, with little covering on her body; her hair, which was woolly in its texture, was partly plaited, partly frizzled, a cloth round her waist, and a piece of faded yellow silk on her shoulders, was all her dress. A few silver rings, on her fat fingers, and a necklace of mother-of-pearl, were her ornaments. Her teeth were jet black, from the use of the betel-nut, and her whole appearance was such as to excite disgust in the breast of Amine.

She addressed Amine, but her words were unintelligible: and the sufferer, exhausted with the slight effort she had made, fell back into her former position, and closed her eyes. But if the woman was disgusting, she was kind, and by her attention and care Amine was able in the course of three weeks, to crawl out of the hut and enjoy the evening breeze. The natives of the island would at times surround her, but they treated her with respect, from fear of the old woman. Their woolly hair was frizzled or plaited, sometimes powdered white with chunam. A few palmetto-leaves round the waist and descending to the knee was their only attire; rings through the nose and ears, and feathers of birds, particularly the bird of paradise, were their ornaments; but their language was wholly unintelligible. Amine felt grateful for life; she sat under the shade of the trees, and watched the swift peroquas as they skimmed the blue sea which was expanded before her; but her thoughts were elsewhere—they were on Philip.

One morning Amine came out of the hut with joy on her countenance, and took her usual seat under the trees. "Yes, mother, dearest mother, I thank thee; thou hast appeared to me; thou hast recalled to me thy arts, which I had forgotten, and had I but the means of conversing with these people, even now would I know where my Philip might be."

For two months did Amine remain under the care of the Papoose woman. When the Tidore people returned, they had an order to bring the white woman, who had been cast on shore, to the Factory, and repay those who had taken charge of her. They made signs to Amine, who had now quite recovered her beauty, that she was to go with them. Any change was preferable to staying where she was, and Amine followed them down to a peroqua, on which she was securely fixed, and was soon darting through the water with her new companions; and, as they flew along the smooth seas, Amine thought of Philip's dream and the mermaid's shell.

By the evening they had arrived at the southern point of Galolo, where they landed for the night: the next day they gained the place of their destination, and Amine was led up to the Portuguese factory.

That the curiosity of those who were stationed there was roused, is not to be wondered at—the history given by the natives of Amine's escape appeared so miraculous. From the commandant to the lowest servant, every one was waiting to receive her. The beauty of Amine, her perfect form, astonished them. The commandant addressed a long compliment to her in

Portuguese, and was astonished that she did not make a suitable reply—but as Amine did not understand a word that he said, it would have been more surprising if she had.

As Amine made signs that she could not understand the language, it was presumed that she was either English or Dutch, and an interpreter was sent for. She then explained that she was the wife of a Dutch captain, whose vessel had been wrecked, and that she did not know whether the crew had been saved or not. The Portuguese were very glad to hear that a Dutch vessel had been wrecked, and very glad that so lovely a creature as Amine had been saved. She was informed by the commandant that she was welcome, and that during her stay there everything should be done to make her comfortable; that in three months they expected a vessel from the Chinese seas, proceeding to Goa, and that, if inclined, she should have a passage to Goa in that vessel, and from that city she would easily find other vessels to take her wherever she might please to go; she was then conducted to an apartment, and left with a little negress to attend upon her.

The Portuguese commandant was a small, meagre, little man dried up to a chip, from long sojourning under a tropical sun. He had very large whiskers, and a very long sword: these were the two most remarkable features in his person and dress.

His attentions could not be misinterpreted; and Amine would have laughed at him, had she not been fearful that she might be detained. In a few weeks, by due attention, she gained the Portuguese language so far as to ask for what she required; and before she quitted the island of Tidore she could converse fluently. But her anxiety to leave, and to ascertain what had become of Philip, became greater every day; and at the expiration of the three months her eyes were continually bent to seaward, to catch the first glimpse of the vessel which was expected. At last it appeared; and as Amine watched the approach of the canvas from the west, the commandant fell on his knees, and declaring his passion, requested her not to think I of departure, but to unite her fate with his.

Amine was cautious in her reply, for she knew that she was in his power. "She must first receive intelligence of her husband's death, which was not yet certain; she would proceed to Goa, and if she discovered that she was single, she would write to him."

This answer, as it will be discovered, was the cause of great suffering to Philip. The commandant, fully assured that he could compass Philip's death, was satisfied—declared that, as soon as he had any positive intelligence, he would bring it to Goa himself, and made a thousand protestations of truth and fidelity.

"Fool!" thought Amine, as she watched the ship, which was now close to the anchorage.

In half an hour the vessel had anchored, and the people had landed. Amine observed a priest with them as they walked up to the fort. She shuddered—she knew not why. When they arrived, she found herself in the presence of Father Mathias.

Chapter Twenty Nine

Both Amine and Father Mathias started, and drew back with surprise, at this unexpected meeting. Amine was the first to extend her hand; she had almost forgotten at the moment how they had parted, in the pleasure she experienced in meeting with a well-known face.

Father Mathias coldly took her hand, and laying his own upon her head, said; "May God bless thee, and forgive thee, my daughter, as I have long done." Then the recollection of what had passed rushed into Amine's mind, and she coloured deeply.

Had Father Mathias forgiven her? The event would show; but this is certain, he now treated her as an old friend, listened with interest to her history of the wreck, and agreed with her upon the propriety of her accompanying him to Goa.

In a few days the vessel sailed, and Amine quitted the factory and its enamoured commandant. They ran through the Archipelago in safety, and were crossing the mouth of the Bay of Bengal, without having had any interruption to fine weather.

Father Mathias had returned to Lisbon when he quitted Ternicore, and, tired of idleness, had again volunteered to proceed as a missionary to India. He had arrived at Formosa, and, shortly after his arrival, had received directions from his superior to return, on important business, to Goa; and thus it was that he fell in with Amine at Tidore.

It would be difficult to analyse the feelings of Father Mathias towards Amine—they varied so often. At one moment he would call to mind the kindness shown to him by her and Philip, the regard he had for the husband, and the many good qualities which he acknowledged that she possessed; and *now* he would recollect the disgrace, the unmerited disgrace, he had suffered through her means and he would then canvass whether she really did believe him an intruder in her chamber for other motives than those which actuated him or whether she had taken advantage of his indiscretion. These accounts were nearly balanced in his mind: he could have forgiven all if he had thought that Amine was a sincere convert to the Church; but his strong conviction that she was not only an unbeliever, but that she practised forbidden arts, turned the scale against her. He watched her narrowly and when in her conversation she showed any religious feeling, his heart warmed towards her: but when, on the contrary, any words escaped her lips which seemed to show that she thought lightly of his creed, then the full tide of indignation and vengeance poured into his bosom.

It was in crossing the Bay of Bengal, to pass round the southern cape of Ceylon, that they first met with bad weather; and when the storm increased, the superstitious seamen lighted candles before the small image of the saint which was shrined on deck. Amine observed it, and smiled with scorn; and as she did so, almost unwittingly, she perceived that the eye of Father Mathias was earnestly fixed upon her.

"The Papooses I have just left do no worse than worship their idols, and are termed idolaters," muttered Amine. "What, then, are these Christians?"

"Would you not be better below?" said Father Mathias, coming over to Amine. "This is no time for women to be on deck; they would be better employed in offering up prayers for safety."

"Nay, father, I can pray better here. I like this conflict of the elements; and as I view, I bow down in admiration of the Deity who rules the storm — who sends the winds forth in their wrath, or soothes them into peace."

"It is well said, my child," replied Father Mathias; "but the Almighty is not only to be worshipped in his works, but in the closet, with meditation, self-examination and faith. Hast thou followed up the precepts which thou hast been taught? — hast thou reverenced the sublime mysteries which have been unfolded to thee?"

"I have done my best, father," replied Amine, turning away her head, and watching the rolling wave.

"Hast thou called upon the Holy Virgin, and upon the saints — those intercessors for mortals erring like thyself?"

Amine made no answer; she did not wish to irritate the priest, neither would she tell an untruth.

"Answer me, child," continued the priest with severity.

"Father," replied Amine, "I have appealed to God alone — the God of the Christians — the God of the whole universe!"

"Who believes not everything, believes nothing, young woman. I thought as much! I saw thee smile with scorn just now. Why didst thou smile?"

"At my own thoughts, good father."

"Say rather at the true faith shown by others."

Amine made no answer.

"Thou art still an unbeliever and a heretic. Beware, young woman!—beware!"

"Beware of what, good father? Why should I beware? Are there not millions in these climes more unbelieving and more heretic, perhaps, than I? How many have you converted to your faith? What trouble, what toil, what dangers have you not undergone to propagate that creed; and why do you succeed so ill? Shall I tell you, father? It is because the people have already had a creed of their own—a creed taught to them from their infancy, and acknowledged by all who live about them. Am I not in the same position? I was brought up in another creed; and can you expect that that can be dismissed, and the prejudices of early years at once eradicated? I have thought much of what you have told me—have felt that much is true—that the tenets of your creed are godlike: is not that much? and yet you are not content. You would have blind acknowledgment, blind obedience: I were then an unworthy convert. We shall soon be in port: then teach me, and convince me, if you will. I am ready to examine and confess, but on conviction only. Have patience, good father, and the time may come when I *may* feel what now I *do not*—that yon bit of painted wood is a thing to bow down to and adore."

Notwithstanding this taunt at the close of this speech, there was so much truth in the observations of Amine, that Father Mathias felt their power. As the wife of a Catholic he had been accustomed to view Amine as one who had backslided from the Church of Rome—not as one who had been brought up in another creed. He now recalled to mind that she had never yet been received into the Church, for Father Seysen had not considered her as in a proper state to be admitted, and had deferred her baptism until he was satisfied of her full belief.

"You speak boldly; but you speak as you feel, my child," replied Father Mathias, after a pause. "We will, when we arrive at Goa, talk over these things, and, with the blessing of God, the new faith shall be made manifest to you."

"So be it," replied Amine.

Little did the priest imagine that Amine's thoughts were at that moment upon a dream she had had at New Guinea, in which her mother appeared, and revealed to her her magic arts, and that Amine was longing to arrive at Goa that she might practise them.

Every hour the gale increased, and the vessel laboured and leaked. The Portuguese sailors were frightened, and invoked their saints. Father Mathias and the other passengers gave themselves up for lost, for the pumps could not keep the vessel free; and their cheeks blanched as the waves washed furiously over the vessel: they prayed and trembled. Father Mathias gave them absolution. Some cried like children, some tore their hair, some cursed, and cursed the saints they had but the day before invoked. But Amine stood unmoved; and as she heard them curse, she smiled in scorn.

"My child," said Father Mathias, checking his tremulous voice, that he might not appear agitated before one whom he saw so calm and unmoved amidst the roaring of the elements—"my child, let not this hour of peril pass away. Before thou art summoned, let me receive thee into the bosom of our Church—give thee pardon for thy sins, and certainty of bliss hereafter."

"Good father, Amine is not to be frightened into belief, even if she feared the storm," replied she; "nor will she credit your power to forgive her sins merely because she says in fear that which in her calm reason she might reject. If ever fear could have subjected me, it was when I was alone upon the raft—that was, indeed a trial of my strength of mind, the bare recollection of which is, at this moment, more dreadful than the storm now raging, and the death which may await us. There is a God on high in whose mercy I trust—in whose love I confide—to whose will I bow. Let him do his will."

"Die not, my child, in unbelief."

"Father," replied Amine, pointing to the passengers and seamen, who were on the deck crying and wailing, "these are Christians—these men have been promised by you, but now, the inheritance of perfect bliss. What is their faith, that it does not give them strength to die like men? Why is it that a woman quails not, while they lie grovelling on the deck?"

"Life is sweet, my child—they leave their wives, their children, and they dread hereafter. Who is prepared to die?"

"I am," replied Amine. "I have no husband—at least, I fear I have no husband. For me life has no sweets; yet, one little hope remains—a straw to the sinking wretch. I fear not death, for I have nought to live for. Were Philip here, why, then indeed—but he is gone before me, and now, to follow him is all I ask."

"He died in the faith, my child—if you would meet him, do the same."

"He never died like these," replied Amine, looking with scorn at the passengers.

"Perhaps he lived not as they have lived," replied Father Mathias. "A good man dies in peace, and hath no fear."

"So die the good men of all creeds, father," replied Amine; "and in all creeds death is equally terrible to the wicked."

"I will pray for thee, my child," said Father Mathias, sinking on his knees.

"Many thanks—thy prayers will be heard, even though offered for one like me," replied Amine, who, clinging to the man-ropes, made her way up to the ladder, and gained the deck.

"Lost! signora, lost!" exclaimed the captain, wringing his hands as he crouched under the bulwark.

"No!" replied Amine, who had gained the weather side, and held on by a rope; "not lost this time."

"How say you, signora?" replied the captain, looking with admiration at Amine's calm and composed countenance. "How say you, signora?"

"Something tells me, good captain, that you will not be lost if you exert yourselves—something tells it to me here," and Amine laid her hand to her heart. Amine had a conviction that the vessel would not be lost, for it had not escaped her observation that the storm was less violent, although, in their terror, this had been unnoticed by the sailors.

The coolness of Amine, her beauty, perhaps, the unusual sight of a woman so young, calm and confiding, when all others were in despair, had its due effect upon the captain and sea men. Supposing her to be a Catholic, they imagined that she had had some warrant for her assertion, for credulity and superstition are close friends. They looked upon Amine with admiration and respect, recovered their energies, and applied to their duties. The pumps were again worked; the storm abated during the night, and the vessel was, as Amine had predicted, saved.

The crew and passengers looked upon her almost as a saint, and talked of her to Father Mathias, who was sadly perplexed. The courage which she had displayed was extraordinary; even when he trembled, she showed no sign of fear. He made no reply, but communed with his own mind, and the result was unfavourable to Amine. What had given her such coolness? What had given her the spirit of prophecy? Not the God of the Christians, for she was no believer. Who then? and Father Mathias thought of her chamber at Terneuse, and shook his head.

Chapter Thirty

We must now again return to Philip and Krantz, who had a long conversation upon the strange reappearance of Schriften. All that they could agree upon was, that he should be carefully watched, and that they should dispense with his company as soon as possible. Krantz had interrogated him as to his escape, and Schriften had informed him, in his usual sneering manner, that one of the sweeps of the raft had been allowed to get adrift during the scuffle, and that he had floated on it, until he had gained a small island; that on seeing the peroqua he had once more launched it, and supported himself by it, until he was perceived and picked up. As there was nothing impossible, although much of the improbable, in this account, Krantz asked no more questions. The next morning, the wind having abated, they launched the peroqua, and made sail for the island of Ternate.

It was four days before they arrived, as every night they landed and hauled up their craft on the sandy beach. Philip's heart was relieved at the knowledge of Amine's safety, and he could have been happy at the prospect of again meeting her, had he not been so constantly fretted by the company of Schriften.

There was something so strange, so contrary to human nature, that the little man, though diabolical as he appeared to be in his disposition, should never hint at, or complain of, Philip's attempts upon his life. Had he complained—had he accused Philip of murder—had he vowed vengeance, and demanded justice on his return to the authorities, it had been different—but no—there he was, making his uncalled-for and impertinent observations with his eternal chuckle and sarcasm, as if he had not the least cause of anger or ill-will.

As soon as they arrived at the principal port and town of Ternate, they were conducted to a large cabin, built of palmetto leaves and bamboo, and requested not to leave it until their arrival had been announced to the king. The peculiar courtesy and good breeding of these islanders was the constant theme of remark of Philip and Krantz; their religion, as well as their dress, appeared to be a compound of the Mahometan and Malayan.

After a few hours, they were summoned to attend the audience of the king, held in the open air. The king was seated under a portico, attended by a numerous concourse of priests and soldiers. There was much company but little splendour. All who were about the king were robed in white, with white turbans, but he himself was without ornament. The first thing that struck Philip and Krantz, when they were ushered into the presence of the king, was the beautiful cleanliness which everywhere prevailed: every dress was spotless and white as the sun could bleach it.

Having followed the example of those who introduced them, and saluted the king after the Mahometan custom, they were requested to be seated; and through the Portuguese interpreters—for the former communication of the islanders with the Portuguese, who had been driven from the place, made the Portuguese language well known by many—a few questions were put by the king, who bade them welcome, and then requested to know how they had been wrecked.

Philip entered into a short detail, in which he stated that his wife had been separated from him, and was, he understood, in the hands of the Portuguese factory at Tidore. He requested to know if his majesty could assist him in obtaining her release, or in going to join her.

"It is well said," replied the king. "Let refreshments be brought in for the strangers, and the audience be broken up."

In a few minutes there remained of all the court but two or three of the king's confidential friends and advisers; and a collation of curries, fish, and a variety of other dishes, was served up. After it was over, the king then said, "The Portuguese are dogs, they are our enemies—will you assist us to fight them? We have large guns, but do not understand the use of them as well as you do. I will send a fleet against the Portuguese at Tidore, if you will assist me. Say, Hollanders, will you fight? You," addressing Philip, "will then recover your wife."

"I will give an answer to you to-morrow," replied Philip, "I must consult with my friend. As I told you before, I was the captain of the ship, and this was my second in command—we will consult together." Schriften, whom Philip had represented as a common seaman, had not been brought up into the presence of the king.

"It is good," replied the king; "to-morrow we will expect your reply."

Philip and Krantz took their leave, and, on their return to the cabin, found that the king had sent them, as a present, two complete Mahometan dresses, with turbans. These were welcome, for their own garments were sadly tattered, and very unfit for exposure to the burning sun of those climes. Their peaked hats, too, collected the rays of heat, which were intolerable; and they gladly exchanged them for the white turban. Secreting their money in the Malayan sash, which formed a part of the attire, they soon robed themselves in the native garments, the comfort of which was immediately acknowledged. After a long consultation, it was decided that they should accept the terms offered by the king, as this was the only feasible way by which Philip could hope to re-obtain possession of Amine. Their consent was communicated to the king on the following day, and every preparation was made for the expedition.

And now was to be beheld a scene of bustle and activity. Hundreds and hundreds of peroquas, of every dimension, floating close to the beach, side by side, formed a raft extending nearly half a mile on the smooth water of the bay, teeming with men, who were equipping them for the service: some were fitting the sails; others were carpentering where required; the major portion were sharpening their swords, and preparing the deadly poison of the pine-apple for their creeses. The beach was a scene of confusion: water in jars, bags of rice, vegetables, salt-fish, fowls in coops, were everywhere strewed about among the armed natives, who were obeying the orders of the chiefs, who themselves walked up and down, dressed in their gayest apparel, and glittering in their arms and ornaments. The king had six long brass four-pounders, a present from an Indian captain; these, with a proportionate quantity of shot and cartridges, were (under the direction of Philip and Krantz) fitted on some of the largest peroquas, and some of the natives were instructed how to use them. At first, the king, who fully expected the reduction of the Portuguese fort, stated his determination to go in person, but in this he was overruled by his confidential advisers, and by the request of Philip, who could not allow him to expose his valuable life. In ten days all was ready, and the fleet, manned by seven thousand men, made sail for the island of Tidore.

It was a beautiful sight, to behold the blue rippling sea, covered with nearly six hundred of these picturesque craft, all under sail, and darting through the water like dolphins in pursuit of prey; all crowded with natives, whose white dresses formed a lively contrast with the deep blue of the water. The large peroquas, in which were Philip and Krantz, with the native commanders, were gaily decorated with streamers and pennons of all colours, that flowed out and snapped with the fresh breeze. It appeared rather to be an expedition of mirth and merriment, than one which was proceeding to bloodshed and slaughter.

On the evening of the second day they had made the island of Tidore, and run down to within a few miles of the Portuguese factory and fort. The natives of the country, who disliked, though they feared to disobey, the Portuguese, had quitted their huts near the beach and retired into the woods. The fleet, therefore, anchored and lay near the beach, without molestation, during the night. The next morning, Philip and Krantz proceeded to reconnoitre.

The port and factory of Tidore were built upon the same principle as almost all the Portuguese defences in those seas. An outer fortification, consisting of a ditch, with strong palisades embedded in masonry, surrounded the factory and all the houses of the establishment. The gates of the outer wall were open all day for ingress and egress, and closed only at night. On the seaward side of this enclosure was what may be termed the citadel, or real fortification; it was built of solid masonry, with parapets, was surrounded by a deep ditch, and was only accessible by a drawbridge, mounted with cannon on every side. Its real strength, however, could not well be perceived, as it was hidden by the high palisading which surrounded the whole establishment. After a careful survey, Philip recommended that the large peroquas with the cannon should attack by sea, while the men of the small vessels should land and surround the fort, taking advantage of every shelter which was afforded them to cover themselves while they harassed the enemy with their matchlocks, arrows, and spears. This plan having been approved of, one hundred and fifty peroquas made sail; the others were hauled on the beach, and the men belonging to them proceeded by land.

But the Portuguese had been warned of their approach, and were fully prepared to receive them; the guns mounted to the seaward were of heavy calibre and well served. The guns of the peroquas, though rendered as effectual as they could be, under the direction of Philip, were small, and did little damage to the thick stone front of the fort. After an engagement of four hours, during which the Ternate people lost a great number of men, the peroquas, by the advice of Philip and Krantz, hauled off, and returned to where the remainder of the fleet was stationed; and another council of war was held. The force, which had surrounded the fort, on the land side, was, however, not withdrawn, as it cut off any supplies or assistance; and, at the same time, occasionally brought down any of the Portuguese who might expose themselves—a point of no small importance, as Philip well knew, with a garrison so small as that in the fort.

That they could not take the fort by means of their cannon was evident; on the sea side it was for them impregnable: their efforts must now be directed to the land. Krantz, after the native chiefs had done speaking, advised that they should wait until dark, and then proceed to the attack in the following way. When the breeze set along shore, which it would do in the evening, he proposed that the men should prepare large bundles of dry palmetto and cocoa-nut leaves; that they should carry their bundles and stack them against the palisades to windward, and then set fire to them. They would thus burn down the palisades, and gain an entrance into the outer fortification; after which they could ascertain in what manner they should next proceed. This advice was too judicious not to be followed. All the men who had not matchlocks were set to collect fagots; a large quantity of dry wood was soon got together, and before night they were ready for the second attack.

The white dresses of the Ternates were laid aside: with nothing on them but their belts, and scimitars, and creeses, and blue under-drawers, they silently crept up to the palisades, there deposited their fagots, and then again returned, again to perform the same journey. As the breastwork of fagots increased, so did they more boldly walk up, until the pile was completed; they then, with a loud shout, fired it in several places. The flames mounted, the cannon of the fort roared, and many fell under the discharges of grape and hand-grenade. But stifled by the smoke, which poured in volumes upon them, the people in the fort were soon compelled to quit the ramparts to avoid suffocation. The palisades were on fire, and the flames mounting in the air, swept over, and began to attack the factory and houses. No resistance was now offered, and the Ternates tore down the burning palisades, and forced their way into the intrenchment, and with their scimitars and creeses put to death all who had been so unfortunate as not to take refuge in the citadel. These were chiefly native servants, whom the attack had surprised, and for whose lives the Portuguese seemed to care but little, for they paid no attention to their cries to lower the drawbridge, and admit them into the fort.

The factory, built of stone, and all the other houses, were on fire, and the island was lighted up for miles. The smoke had cleared away, and the defences of the fort were now plainly visible in the broad glare of the flames. "If we had scaling-ladders," cried Philip, "the fort would be ours; there is not a soul on the ramparts."

"True, true," replied Krantz, "but even as it is, the factory walls will prove an advantageous post for us after the fire is extinguished; if we occupy it, we can prevent them showing themselves while the ladders are constructing. To-morrow night we may have them ready, and having first smoked the fort with a few more fagots, we may afterwards mount the walls, and carry the place."

"That will do," replied Philip, as he walked away. He then joined the native chiefs, who were collected together outside of the intrenchment, and communicated to them his plans. When he had made known his views, and the chiefs had assented to them, Schriften, who had come with the expedition unknown to Philip, made his appearance.

"That won't do; you'll never take that fort, Philip Vanderdecken. He! he!" cried Schriften.

Hardly had he said the words when a tremendous explosion took place, and the air was filled with large stones, which flew and fell in every direction, killing and maiming hundreds. It was the factory which had blown up, for in its vaults there was a large quantity of gunpowder, to which the fire had communicated.

"So ends that scheme, Mynheer Vanderdecken. He! he!" screamed Schriften; "you'll never take that fort."

The loss of life and the confusion caused by this unexpected result occasioned a panic, and all the Ternate people fled down to the beach where their peroquas were lying.

It was in vain that Philip and their chiefs attempted to rally them. Unaccustomed to the terrible effects of gunpowder in any large quantities, they believed that something supernatural had occurred, and many of them jumped into the peroquas and made sail, while the remainder were confused, trembling, and panting, all huddled together, on the beach.

"You'll never take that fort, Mynheer Vanderdecken," screamed the well-known voice.

Philip raised his sword to cleave the little man in two, but he let it fall again. "I fear he tells an unwelcome truth," thought Philip; "but why should I take his life for that?"

Some few of the Ternate chiefs still kept up their courage, but the major part were as much alarmed as their people. After some consultation, it was agreed that the army should remain where it was till the next morning, when they should finally decide what to do.

When the day dawned, now that the Portuguese fort was no longer surrounded by the other buildings, they perceived that it was more formidable than they had at first supposed. The ramparts were filled with men, and they were bringing cannon to bear on the Ternate forces. Philip had a consultation with Krantz, and both acknowledged, that, with the present panic, nothing more could be done. The chiefs were of the same opinion, and orders were given for the return of the expedition, indeed, the Ternate chiefs were fully satisfied with their success; they had destroyed the large fort, the factory, and all the Portuguese buildings; a small fortification only was uninjured; that was built of stone, and inaccessible, and they knew that the report of what had been done would be taken and acknowledged by the king as a great victory. The order was therefore given for embarkation, and in two hours the whole fleet, after a loss of about seven hundred men, was again on its way to Ternate. Krantz and Philip this time embarked in the same peroqua, that they might have the pleasure of each other's conversation. They had not, however, sailed above three hours when it fell calm, and, towards the evening, there was every prospect of bad weather. When the breeze again sprung up, it was from an adverse quarter, but these vessels steer so close to the wind, that this was disregarded: by midnight however the wind had increased to a gale, and before they were clear of the N.E. headland of Tidore, it blew a hurricane and many were washed off into the sea from the different craft, and those who could not swim, sank, and were drowned. The sails were lowered, and the vessels lay at the mercy of the wind and waves, every sea washing over them. The fleet was drifting fast on the shore, and before morning dawned, the vessel in which were Philip and Krantz was among the rollers on the beach off the northern end of the island. In a short time she was dashed to pieces, and every one had to look out for himself. Philip and Krantz laid hold of one fragment, and were supported by it till they gained the shore; here they found about thirty more companions, who had suffered the same fate as themselves. When the day dawned, they perceived that the major part of the fleet had weathered the point, and that those who had not, would in all probability escape, as the wind had moderated.

The Ternate people proposed, that as they were well armed, they should, as soon as the weather moderated, launch some of the craft belonging to the islanders, and join the fleet but Philip, who had been consulting with Krantz, considered this a good opportunity for ascertaining the fate of Amine. As the Portuguese could prove nothing against them, they could either deny that they had been among the assailants, or might plead that they had been forced to join them. At all risks, Philip was determined to remain, and Krantz agreed to share his fate; and seeming to agree with them, they allowed the Ternate people to walk to the Tidore peroquas, and while they were launching them, Philip and Krantz fell back into the jungle and disappeared. The Portuguese had perceived the wreck of their enemies, and, irritated by the loss they had sustained, they had ordered the people of the island to go out and capture all who were driven on shore. Now that they were no longer assailed, the Tidore people obeyed them, and very soon fell in with Philip and Krantz, who had quietly sat down under the shade of a large tree, waiting the issue. They were led away to the fort, where they arrived by nightfall. They were ushered into the presence of the Commandant, the same little man who had made love to Amine, and as they were dressed in Mussulman's attire, he was about to order them to be hung, when Philip told him that they were Dutchmen, who had been wrecked, and forced by the king of Ternate to join his expedition; that they had taken the earliest opportunity of escaping, as was very evident, since those who had been thrown on shore with them had got off in the island boats, while they chose to remain. Whereupon the little Portuguese Commandant struck his sword firm down on the pavement of the ramparts, *looked* very big, and then ordered them to prison for further examination.

Chapter Thirty One

As every one descants upon the want of comfort in a prison, it is to be presumed that there are no very comfortable ones. Certainly that to which Philip and Krantz were ushered, had anything rather than the air of an agreeable residence. It was under the fort, with a very small aperture looking towards the sea, for light and air. It was very hot and moreover destitute of all those little conveniences which add so much to one's happiness in modern houses and hotels. In fact, it consisted of four bare walls, and a stone floor, and that was all.

Philip, who wished to make some inquiries relative to Amine, addressed, in Portuguese, the soldier who brought them down.

"My good friend, I beg your pardon—"

"I beg yours," replied the soldier, going out of the door, and locking them in.

Philip leant gloomily against the wall; Krantz, more mercurial, walked up and down three steps each way and turn.

"Do you know what I am thinking of?" observed Krantz, after a pause in his walk. "It is very fortunate that (lowering his voice) we have all our doubloons about us; if they don't search us, we may yet get away by bribing."

"And I was thinking," rejoined Philip, "that I would sooner be here than in company with that wretch Schriften, whose sight is poison to me."

"I did not much admire the appearance of the Commandant; but I suppose we shall know more to-morrow."

Here they were interrupted by the turning of the key, and the entrance of a soldier with a chatty of water, and a large dish of boiled rice. He was not the man who had brought them to the dungeon, and Philip accosted him.

"You have had hard work within these last two days?"

"Yes, indeed! signor."

"The natives forced us to join the expedition, and we escaped."

"So I heard you say, signor."

"They lost nearly a thousand men," said Krantz.

"Holy St. Francis! I am glad of it."

"They will be careful how they attack Portuguese in a hurry, I expect," rejoined Krantz.

"I think so," replied the soldier.

"Did you lose many men?" ventured Philip, perceiving that the man was loquacious.

"Not ten of our own people. In the factory there were about a hundred of the natives, with some women and children; but that is of no consequence."

"You had a young European woman here, I understand," said Philip with anxiety; "one who was wrecked in a vessel—was she among those who were lost?"

"Young woman!—Holy St. Francis. Yes, now I recollect. Why the fact is—"

"Pedro!" called a voice from above; the man stopped, put his fingers to his lips, went out, and locked the door.

"God of Heaven! give me patience," cried Philip; "but this is too trying."

"He will be down here again to-morrow morning," observed Krantz.

"Yes! to-morrow morning but what an endless time will suspense make of the intervening hours."

"I feel for you," replied Krantz; "but what can be done? The hours must pass, though suspense draws them out into interminable years; but I hear footsteps."

Again the door was unlocked, and the first soldier made his appearance. "Follow me—the Commandant would speak with you."

This unexpected summons was cheerfully complied with by Philip and his companion. They walked up the narrow stone steps, and at last found themselves in a small room in presence of the Commandant, with whom our readers have been already made acquainted. He was lolling on a small sofa, his long sword lay on the table before him, and two young native women were fanning him, one at his head, and the other at his feet.

"Where did you get those dresses?" was the first interrogatory.

"The natives, when they brought us prisoners from the island on which we had saved ourselves, took away our clothes, and gave us these as a present from their king."

"And engaged you to serve in their fleet, in the attack of this fort?"

"They forced us," replied Krantz; "for, as there was no war between our nations, we objected to this service: notwithstanding which, they put us on board, to make the common people believe that they were assisted by Europeans."

"How am I to know the truth of this?"

"You have our word in the first place, and our escape from them in the second."

"You belonged to a Dutch East-Indiaman. Are you officers or common seamen?"

Krantz, who considered that they were less likely to be detained if they concealed their rank on board, gave Philip a slight touch with his finger as he replied, "We are inferior officers. I was third mate, and this man was pilot."

"And your captain, where is he?"

"I—I cannot say whether he is alive or dead."

"Had you no woman on board?"

"Yes! the captain had his wife."

"What has become of her?"

"She is supposed to have perished on a portion of the raft which broke a drift."

"Ha!" replied the Commandant, who remained silent for some time.

Philip looked at Krantz, as much as to say, "Why all this subterfuge;" but Krantz gave him a sign to leave him to speak.

"You say you don't know whether your captain is alive or dead?"

"I do."

"Now, suppose I was to give you your liberty, would you have any objection to sign a paper, stating his death, and swearing to the truth of it?"

Philip stared at the Commandant, and then at Krantz.

"I see no objection, exactly; except that if it were sent home to Holland we might get into trouble. May I ask, Signor Commandant, why you wish for such a paper?"

"No!" roared the little man, in a voice like thunder. "I will give no reason, but that I wish it; that is enough; take your choice—the dungeon, or liberty and a passage by the first vessel which calls."

"I don't doubt—in fact—I'm sure, he must be dead by this time," replied Krantz, drawling out the words in a musing manner. "Commandant, will you give us till to-morrow morning to make our calculations?"

"Yes, you may go."

"But not to the dungeon, Commandant," replied Krantz; "we are not prisoners certainly; and, if you wish us to do you a favour, surely you will not ill-treat us?"

"By your own acknowledgment you have taken up arms against the most Christian King; however, you may remain at liberty for the night—to-morrow morning will decide whether or no you are prisoners."

Philip and Krantz thanked the little Commandant for his kindness, and then hastened away to the ramparts. It was now dark, and the moon had not yet made her appearance. They sat there on the parapet enjoying the breeze, and feeling the delight of liberty even after their short incarceration; but, near to them, soldiers were either standing or lying, and they spoke but in whispers.

"What could he mean by requiring us to give a certificate of the captain's death; and why did you answer as you did?"

"Philip Vanderdecken, that I have often thought of the fate of your beautiful wife, you may imagine; and when I heard that she was brought here, I then trembled for her. What must she appear, lovely as she is, when placed in comparison with the women of this country? And that little Commandant—is he not the very person who would be taken with her charms? I denied our condition, because I thought he would be more likely to allow us our liberty as humble individuals, than as captain and first-mate; particularly as he suspects that we led on the Ternate people to the attack; and when he asked for a certificate of your death, I immediately imagined that he wanted it in order to induce Amine to marry him. But where is she? is the question. If we could only find out that soldier, we might gain some information."

"Depend upon it, she is here," replied Philip, clenching his hands.

"I am inclined to think so," said Krantz; "that she is alive, I feel assured."

The conversation was continued until the moon rose, and threw her beams over the tumbling waters. Philip and Krantz turned their faces toward the sea, and leant over the battlements in silence; after some time their reveries were disturbed by a person coming up to them with a "Buenos noctes, signor."

Krantz immediately recognised the Portuguese soldier, whose conversation with him had been interrupted.

"Good night, my friend! We thank Heaven that you have no longer to turn the key upon us."

"Yes, I'm surprised!" replied the soldier, in a low tone.—"Our Commandant is fond of exercising his power; he rules here without appeal, that I can tell you."

"He is not within hearing of us now," replied Krantz. "It is a lovely spot this to live in! How long have you been in this country?"

"Now thirteen years, signor, and I'm tired of it. I have a wife and children in Oporto—that is, I *had*—but whether they are alive or not, who can tell?"

"Do you not expect to return and see them?"

"Return—signor! no Portuguese soldier like me ever returns. We are enlisted for five years, and we lay our bones here."

"That is hard indeed."

"Hard, signor," replied the soldier in a low whisper; "it is cruel and treacherous. I have often thought of putting the muzzle of my arquebuse to my head; but while there's life there's hope."

"I pity you, my good fellow," rejoined Krantz; "look you, I have two gold pieces left—take one; you may be able to send it home to your poor wife."

"And here is one of mine, too, my good fellow," added Philip, putting another in his hand.

"Now may all the saints preserve you, signors," replied the soldier, "for it is the first act of kindness shown to me for many years—not that my wife and children have much chance of ever receiving it."

"You were speaking about a young European woman when we were in the dungeon," observed Krantz, after a pause.

"Yes, signor, she was a very beautiful creature. Our commandant was very much in love with her."

"Where is she now?"

"She went away to Goa, in company with a priest who knew her, Father Mathias, a good old man; he gave me absolution when he was here."

"Father Mathias!" exclaimed Philip; but a touch from Krantz checked him.

"You say the commandant loved her?"

"Oh yes: the little man was quite mad about her; and had it not been for the arrival of Father Mathias, he would never have let her go, that I'm sure of, although she was another man's wife."

"Sailed for Goa, you said?"

"Yes, in a ship which called here. She must have been very glad to have got away, for our little commandant persecuted her all day long, and she evidently was grieving for her husband. Do you know, signors, if her husband is alive?"

"No, we do not; we have heard nothing of him."

"Well, if he is, I hope he will not come here; for should the commandant have him in his power, it would go hard with him. He is a man who sticks at nothing. He is a brave little fellow, *that* cannot be denied; but to get possession of that lady, he would remove all obstacles at any risk—and a husband is a very serious one, signors. Well, signors," continued the soldier, after a pause, "I had better not be seen here too long—you may command me if you want anything; recollect, my name is Pedro—good night to you, and a thousand thanks," and the soldier walked away.

"We have made one friend, at all events," said Krantz, "and we have gained information of no little importance."

"Most important," replied Philip. "Amine then has sailed for Goa with Father Mathias! I feel that she is safe, and in good hands. He is an excellent man, that Father Mathias—my mind is relieved."

"Yes; but recollect you are in the power of your enemy. We must leave this place as quick as we can—to-morrow we must sign the paper. It is of little consequence, as we shall probably be at Goa before it arrives; and even if we are not, the news of your death would not occasion Amine to marry this withered piece of mortality."

"That I feel assured of; but it may cause her great suffering."

"Not worse than her present suspense, believe me, Philip; but it is useless canvassing the past—it must be done. I shall sign as Cornelius Richter, our third mate; you, as Jacob Vantreat—recollect that."

"Agreed," replied Philip, who then turned away, as if willing to be left to his own thoughts. Krantz perceived it, and lay down under the embrasure, and was soon fast asleep.

Chapter Thirty Two

Tired out with the fatigue of the day before, Philip had laid himself down by Krantz and fallen asleep; early the next morning he was awakened by the sound of the commandant's voice, and his long sword rattling as usual upon the pavement. He rose, and found the little man rating the soldiers—threatening some with the dungeons, others with extra duty. Krantz was also on his feet before the commandant had finished his morning's lecture. At last, perceiving them, in a stern voice he ordered them to follow him into his apartment. They did so, and the commandant, throwing himself upon his sofa, inquired whether they were ready to sign the required paper, or go back to the dungeon. Krantz replied that they had been calculating chances and that they were in consequence so perfectly convinced of the death of the captain, that they were willing to sign any paper to that effect; at which reply, the commandant immediately became very gracious, and having called for materials, he wrote out the document, which was duly subscribed to by Krantz and Philip. As soon as they had signed it, and he had it in his possession, the little man was so pleased, that he requested them to partake of his breakfast.

During the repast, he promised that they should leave the island by the first opportunity. Although Philip was taciturn, yet, as Krantz made himself very agreeable, the commandant invited them to dinner. Krantz, as they became more familiar, informed him that they had each a few pieces of gold, and wished to be allowed a room where they could keep their table. Whether it was the want of society or the desire of obtaining the gold, probably both, the commandant offered that they should join his table, and pay their proportion of the expenses; a proposal which was gladly acceded to. The terms were arranged, and Krantz insisted upon putting down the first week's payment in advance. From that moment the commandant was the best of friends with them, and did nothing but caress them whom he had so politely shoved into a dungeon below water. It was on the evening of the third day, as they were smoking their Manilla cheroots that Krantz, perceiving the commandant in a peculiarly good humour, ventured to ask him why he was so anxious for a certificate of the captain's death; and in reply was informed, much to the astonishment of Philip, that Amine had agreed to marry him upon his producing such a document.

"Impossible!" cried Philip, starting from his seat.

"Impossible, signor,—and why impossible?" replied the commandant, curling his mustachios with his fingers, with a surprised and angry air.

"I should have said impossible too," interrupted Krantz, who perceived the consequences of Philip's indiscretion, "for had you seen, commandant, how that woman doated upon her husband, how she fondled him, you would with us have said, it was impossible that she could have transferred her affections so soon; but women are women, and soldiers have a great advantage over other people; perhaps she has some excuse, commandant.— Here's your health, and success to you."

"It is exactly what I would have said," added Philip, acting upon Krantz's plan: "but she has a great excuse, commandant, when I recollect her husband, and have you in my presence."

Soothed with the flattery, the commandant replied, "Why, yes, they say military men are very successful with the fair sex.—I presume it is because they look up to us for protections and where can they be better assured of it, than with a man who wears a sword at his thigh?—Come, signors we will drink her health. Here's to the beautiful Amine Vanderdecken."

"To the beautiful Amine Vanderdecken!" cried Krantz, tossing off his wine.

"To the beautiful Amine Vanderdecken," followed Philip. "But, commandant, are you not afraid to trust her at Goa, where there are so many enticements for a woman, so many allurements held out for her sex?"

"No, not in the least—I am convinced that she loves me—nay, between ourselves, that she doats upon me."

"Liar!" exclaimed Philip.

"How, signor! is that addressed to me?" cried the commandant, seizing his sword, which lay on the table.

"No, no," replied Philip, recovering himself; "it was addressed to her. I have heard her swear to her husband, that she would exist for no other but him."

"Ha! ha! Is that all?" replied the commandant; "my friend, you do not know women."

"No, nor is he very partial to them either," replied Krantz, who then leant over to the commandant and whispered, "He is always so when you talk of women. He was cruelly jilted once, and hates the whole sex."

"Then we must be merciful to him," replied the little officer: "suppose we change the subject."

When they repaired to their own room, Krantz pointed out to Philip the necessity for his commanding his feelings, as otherwise they would again be immured in the dungeon. Philip acknowledged his rashness, but pointed out to Krantz, that the circumstance of Amine having promised to marry the commandant, if he procured certain intelligence of his death, was the cause of his irritation. "Can it be so? Is it possible that she can have been so false?" exclaimed Philip; "yet his anxiety to procure that document seems to warrant the truth of his assertion."

"I think, Philip, that in all probability it is true," replied Krantz, carelessly; "but of this you may be assured, that she has been placed in a situation of great peril, and has only done so to save herself for your sake. When you meet, depend upon it she will fully prove to you that necessity had compelled her to deceive him in that way and that if she had not done so, she would, by this time, have fallen a prey to his violence."

"It may be so," replied Philip, gravely.

"It is so, Philip, my life upon it. Do not for a moment harbour a thought so injurious to one who lives but in your love. Suspect that fond and devoted creature! I blush for you, Philip Vanderdecken."

"You are right, and I beg her pardon for allowing such feelings or thoughts to have for one moment overpowered me," responded Philip; "but it is a hard case for a husband who loves as I do, to hear his wife's name bandied about, and her character assailed by a contemptible wretch like this commandant."

"It is, I grant; but still I prefer even that to a dungeon," replied Krantz, "and so, good night."

For three weeks they remained in the fort, every day becoming more intimate with the commandant, who often communicated with Krantz, when Philip was not present, turning the conversation upon his love for Amine and entering into a minute detail of all that had passed. Krantz perceived that he was right in his opinion, and that Amine had only been cajoling the commandant, that she might escape. But the time passed heavily away with Philip and Krantz, for no vessel made its appearance.

"When shall I see her again?" soliloquised Philip one morning, as he lolled over the parapet, in company with Krantz.

"See who?" said the commandant, who happened to be at his elbow.

Philip turned round and stammered something unintelligible.

"We were talking of his sister, commandant," said Krantz, taking his arm, and leading him away. — "Do not mention the subject to my friend, for it is a very painful one, and forms one reason why he is so inimical to the sex. She was married to his intimate friend and ran away from her husband: it was his only sister; and the disgrace broke his mother's heart, and has made him miserable. Take no notice of it, I beg."

"No, no, certainly not; I don't wonder at it: the honour of one's family is a serious affair," replied the commandant. — "Poor young man, what with his sister's conduct, and the falsehood of his own intended, I don't wonder at his being so grave and silent. Is he of good family, signor?"

"One of the noblest in all Holland," replied Krantz; — "he is heir to a large property, and independent by the fortune of his mother; but these two unfortunate events induced him to quit the States secretly, and he embarked for these countries that he might forget his grief."

"One of the noblest families?" replied the commandant; — "then he is under an assumed name — Jacob Vancheat is not his true name, of course."

"Oh, no," replied Krantz; — "that it is not, I assure you; but my lips are sealed on that point."

"Of course, except to a friend who can keep a secret. I will not ask it now. So he is really noble?"

"One of the highest families in the country, possessing great wealth and influence — allied to the Spanish nobility by marriage."

"Indeed!" rejoined the commandant, musing — "I dare say he knows many of the Portuguese as well."

"No doubt of it, they are all more or less connected."

"He must prove to you a most valuable friend, Signor Richter."

"I consider myself provided for for life as soon as we return home. He is of a very grateful, generous disposition, as he would prove to you, should you ever fall in with him."

"I have no doubt of it; and I can assure you that I am heartily tired of staying in this country. Here I shall remain probably for two years more before I am relieved, and then shall have to join my regiment at Goa, and not be able to obtain leave to return home without resigning my commission. But he is coming this way."

After this conversation with Krantz, the alteration in the manner of the Portuguese commandant, who had the highest respect for nobility, was most marked. He treated Philip with a respect which was observable to all in the fort; and which was, until Krantz had explained the cause, a source of astonishment to Philip himself. The commandant often introduced the subject to Krantz, and sounded him as to whether his conduct towards Philip had been such as to have made a favourable impression; for the little man now hoped, that through such an influential channel, he might reap some benefit.

Some days after this conversation, as they were all three seated at table, a corporal entered, and saluting the commandant, informed him that a Dutch sailor had arrived at fort, and wished to know whether he should be admitted. Both Philip and Krantz turned pale at this communication—they had a presentiment of evil but they said nothing. The sailor was ordered in, and in a few minutes, who should make his appearance but their tormentor, the one-eyed Schriften. On perceiving Philip and Krantz seated at the table, he immediately exclaimed, "Oh! Captain Philip Vanderdecken, and my good friend Mynheer Krantz, first mate of the good ship Utrecht, I am glad to meet you again."

"Captain Philip Vanderdecken!" roared the commandant, as he sprung from his chair.

"Yes, that is my captain, Mynheer Philip Vanderdecken and that is my first mate, Mynheer Krantz; both of the good ship Utrecht: we were wrecked together, were we not. Mynheer? He! he!"

"Sangue de—Vanderdecken! the husband! Corpo del diavolo—is it possible!" cried the commandant, panting for breath, as he seized his long sword with both hands and clenched it with fury.—"What, then, I have been deceived, cajoled, laughed at!" Then, after a pause—the veins of his forehead distending so as almost to burst—he continued, with a suppressed voice, "Most noble sir, I thank you; but now it is my turn.—What, ho! there! Corporal—men, here, instantly—quick!"

Philip and Krantz felt convinced that all denial was useless. Philip folded his arms and made no reply. Krantz merely observed, "A little reflection will prove to you, sir, that this indignation is not warranted."

"Not warranted!" rejoined the commandant with a sneer, "you have deceived me; but you are caught in your own trap. I have the paper signed, which I shall not fail to make use of. *You* are dead, you know, Captain; I have your own hand to it, and your wife will be glad to believe it."

"She has deceived you, commandant, to get out of your power, nothing more," said Vanderdecken. "She would spurn a contemptible withered wretch like yourself, were she as free as the wind."

"Go on, go on; it will be my turn soon. Corporal, throw these two men into the dungeon: a sentry at the door till further orders. Away with them! Most noble sir, perhaps your influential friends in Holland and Spain will enable you to get out again."

Philip and Krantz were led away by the soldiers, who were very much surprised at this change of treatment. Schriften followed them; and as they walked across the rampart to the stairs which led to their prison, Krantz, in his fury, burst from the soldiers, and bestowed a kick upon Schriften, which sent him several feet forward on his face.

"That was a good one—he! he!" cried Schriften, smiling and looking at Krantz as he regained his legs.

There was an eye, however, which met theirs with an intelligent glance, as they descended the stairs to the dungeon. It was that of the soldier Pedro. It told them that there was one friend upon whom they could rely, and who would spare no endeavour to assist them in their new difficulty. It was a consolation to them both; a ray of hope which cheered them as they once more descended the narrow steps, and heard the heavy key turned which again secured them in their dungeon.

Chapter Thirty Three

"Thus are all our hopes wrecked," said Philip, mournfully; "what chance have we now of escaping from this little tyrant?"

"Chances turn up," replied Krantz; "at present, the prospect is not very cheering. Let us hope for the best. I have an idea in my head which may probably be turned to some account," continued Krantz, "as soon as the little man's fury is over."

"Which is?"

"That, much as he likes your wife, there is something which he likes quite as well—money. Now, as we know where all the treasure is concealed, I think he may be tempted to offer us our liberty, if we were to promise to put it into his possession."

"That is not impossible. Confound that little malignant wretch Schriften; he certainly is not, as you say, of this world. He has been my persecutor through life, and appears to act from an impulse not his own."

"Then must he be part and portion of your destiny. I'm thinking whether our noble commandant intends to leave us without anything to eat or drink."

"I should not be surprised; that he will attempt my life I am convinced, but not that he can take it; he may, however, add to its sufferings."

As soon as the commandant had recovered from his fury, he ordered Schriften in, to be examined more particularly; but, after every search made for him, Schriften was nowhere to be found. The sentry at the gate declared that he had not passed: and a new search was ordered, but in vain. Even the dungeons and galleries below were examined, but without success.

"Can he be locked up with the other prisoners?" thought the commandant: "impossible—but I will go and see."

He descended and opened the door of the dungeon, looked in, and was about to return without speaking, when Krantz said, "Well, signor, this is kind treatment, after having lived so long and so amicably together; to throw us into prison merely because a fellow declares that we are not what we represented ourselves to be; perhaps you will allow us a little water to drink?"

The commandant, confused by the extraordinary disappearance of Schriften hardly knew how to reply. He at last said in a milder tone than was to be anticipated, "I will order them to bring some, signor."

He then closed the door of the dungeon and disappeared.

"Strange," observed Philip, "he appears more pacified already." In a few minutes the door was again opened, and Pedro came in with a chatty of water.

"He has disappeared like magic, signors, and is nowhere to be found. We have searched everywhere, but in vain."

"Who?—the little old seaman?"

"Yes, he whom you kicked as you were led to prison. The people all say, that it must have been a ghost. The sentry declares that he never left the fort, nor came near him; so how he has got away is a riddle, which I perceive has frightened our commandant not a little."

Krantz gave a long whistle as he looked at Philip.

"Are you to have charge of us, Pedro?"

"I hope so."

"Well, tell the commandant that when he is ready to listen to me, I have something of importance to communicate."

Pedro went out.

"Now, Philip, I can frighten this little man into allowing us to go free, if you will consent to say that you are not the husband of Amine."

"That I cannot do, Krantz. I will not utter such a falsehood."

"I was afraid so, and yet it appears to me that we may avail ourselves of duplicity to meet cruelty and injustice. Unless you do as I propose, I hardly know how I can manage it; however, I will try what I can do."

"I will assist you in every way, except disclaiming my wife: that I never will do."

"Well, then, I will see if I can make up a story that will suit all parties: let me think."

Krantz continued musing as he walked up and down, and was still occupied with his own thoughts, when the door opened, and the commandant made his appearance.

"You have something to impart to me, I understand—what is it?"

"First, sir, bring that little wretch down here and confront him with us."

"I see no occasion for that," replied the commandant; "what, sir, may you have to say?"

"Do you know who you have in your company when you speak to that one-eyed deformity?"

"A Dutch sailor, I presume."

"No—a spirit—a demon—who occasioned the loss of the vessel; and who brings misfortune wherever he appears."

"Holy Virgin! what do you tell me, signor?"

"The fact, Signor Commandant. We are obliged to you for confining us here, while he is in the fort; but beware for yourself."

"You are laughing at me."

"I am not; bring him down here. This noble gentleman has power over him. I wonder, indeed, at his daring to stay while he is so near; he has on his heart that which will send him trembling away. Bring him down here, and you shall at once see him vanish with curses and screams."

"Heaven defend us!" cried the commandant, terrified.

"Send for him now, signor."

"He is gone—vanished—not to be found!"

"I thought as much," replied Philip, significantly.

"He is gone—vanished—you say. Then, commandant, you will probably apologise to this noble gentleman for your treatment of him, and permit us to return to our former apartments. I will there explain to you this most strange and interesting history."

The commandant, more confused than ever, hardly knew how to act. At last he bowed to Philip, and begged that he would consider himself at liberty; "and," continued he to Krantz, "I shall be most happy at an immediate explanation of this affair, for everything appears so contradictory."

"And must, until it is explained. I will follow you into your own room; a courtesy you must not expect from my noble friend, who is not a little indignant at your treatment of him."

The commandant went out, leaving the door open. Philip and Krantz followed: the former retiring to his own apartment; the latter, bending his steps after the commandant to his sitting-room. The confusion which whirled in the brain of the commandant made him appear most ridiculous. He hardly knew whether to be imperative or civil; whether he was really speaking to the first mate of the vessel, or to another party; or whether he had insulted a noble, or been cajoled by a captain of a vessel: he threw himself down on his sofa, and Krantz, taking his seat in a chair, stated as follows:—

"You have been partly deceived and partly not, commandant. When we first came here, not knowing what treatment we might receive, we concealed our rank; afterwards I made known to you the rank of my friend on shore; but did not think it worth while to say anything about his situation on board of the vessel. The fact is, as you may well suppose of a person of his dignity, he was owner of the fine ship which was lost through the intervention of that one-eyed wretch; but of that by-and-by. Now for the story. About ten years ago there was a great miser in Amsterdam; he lived in the most miserable way that a man could live in; wore nothing but rags; and having been formerly a seaman, his attire was generally of the description common to his class. He had one son, to whom he denied the necessaries of life, and whom he treated most cruelly. After vain attempts to possess a portion of his father's wealth, the devil instigated the son to murder the old man, who was one day found dead in his bed; but as there were no marks of violence which could be sworn to, although suspicion fell upon the son, the affair was hushed up, and the young man took possession of his father's wealth. It was fully expected that there would now be rioting and squandering on the part of the heir, as is usually the case; but, on the contrary, he never spent anything, but appeared to be as poor—even poorer—than he ever was. Instead of being gay and merry, he was, in appearance, the most miserable, downcast person in the world; and he wandered about, seeking a crust of bread wherever he could find it. Some said that he had been inoculated by his father, and was as great a miser as his father had been; others shook their heads, and said that all was not right. At last, after pining away for six or seven years, the young man died at an early age, without confession or absolution; in fact, he was found dead in his bed. Beside the bed there was a paper addressed to the authorities, in which he acknowledged that he had murdered his father for the sake of his wealth; and that when he went to take some of it for his expenses on the day afterwards, he found his father's spirit sitting on the bags of money, and menacing him with instant death, if he touched one piece. He returned again and again, and found his father a sentinel as before. At last, he gave up attempting to obtain it: his crime made him miserable, and he continued in possession, without daring to expend one sixpence of all the money. He requested that, as his end was approaching, the money should be given to the church of his patron saint, wherever that church might be found; if there was not one, then that a church might be built and endowed. Upon investigation, it appeared that there was no such church in either Holland or the Low Countries (for you know that there are not many Catholics there); and they applied to the Catholic countries, Lisbon and Spain, but there again they were at fault; and it was discovered, that the only church dedicated to that saint was one which had been erected by a Portuguese nobleman in the city of Goa, in the East Indies. The Catholic bishop determined that the money should be sent to Goa and, in consequence it was embarked on board of my patron's vessel, to be delivered up to the first Portuguese authorities he might fall in with.

"Well, signor, the money, for better security was put down into the captain's cabin, which, of course, was occupied by my noble friend, and when he went to bed the first night he was surprised to perceive a little one-eyed old man sitting on the boxes."

"Merciful Saviour!" exclaimed the commandant, "what, the very same little man who appeared here this day?"

"The very same," replied Krantz.

The commandant crossed himself, and Krantz proceeded:—

"My noble patron was, as you may imagine, rather alarmed; but he is very courageous in disposition, and he inquired of the old man who he was, and how he had come on board.

"'I came on board with my own money,' replied the spectre. 'It is all my own, and I shall keep it. The Church shall never have one stiver of it if I can help it.'

"Whereupon, my patron pulled out a famous relic, which he wears on his bosom, and held it towards him; at which the old man howled and screamed, and then most unwillingly disappeared. For two more nights the spectre was obstinate, but at the sight of the relic, he invariably went off howling, as if in great pain; every time that he went away, invariably crying out 'Lost—lost!'—and during the remainder of the voyage he did not trouble us any more.

"We thought, when our patron told us this, that he referred to the money being lost to him, but it appears he referred to the ship; indeed it was very inconsiderate to have taken the wealth of a parricide on board; we could not expect any good fortune with such a freight, and so it proved. When the ship was lost, our patron was very anxious to save the money; it was put on the raft, and when we landed, it was taken on shore and buried, that it might be restored and given to the church to which it had been bequeathed; but the men who buried it are all dead, and there is no one but my friend here, the patron, who knows the spot.—I forgot to say that as soon as the money was landed on the island and buried, the spectre appeared as before, and seated itself over the spot where the money was interred. I think, if this had not been the case, the seamen would have taken possession of it. But, by its appearance here this day, I presume it is tired, and has deserted its charge, or else has come here that the money might be sent for, though I cannot understand why."

"Strange—very strange! So there is a large treasure buried in the sand?"

"There is."

"I should think, by the spectre's coming here, that it has abandoned it."

"Of course it has, or it would not be here."

"What can you imagine to have been the cause of its coming?"

"Probably to announce its intention, and request my friend to have the treasure sent for; but you know it was interrupted."

"Very true; but it called your friend Vanderdecken."

"It was the name which he took on board of the ship."

"And it was the name of the lady."

"Very true. He fell in with her at the Cape of Good Hope, and brought her away with him."

"Then she is his wife?"

"I must not answer that question. It is quite sufficient that he treats her as his wife."

"Ah! indeed. But about this treasure. You say that no one knows where it is buried but the patron, as you call him?"

"No one."

"Will you express my regret at what has passed, and tell him I will have the pleasure of seeing him to-morrow."

"Certainly, signor," replied Krantz, rising from his chair, and wishing the commandant a good evening as he retired.

"I was after one thing, and have found another. A spectre that must have been; but he must be a bold spectre that can frighten me from doubloons; besides, I can call in the priests. Now, let me see: if I let this man go on condition that he reveals the site of the treasure to the authorities—that is to me—why then I need not lose the fair young woman. If I forward this paper to her, why then I gain her; but I must first get rid of him. Of the two, I prefer—yes!—the gold! But I cannot obtain both. At all events, let me obtain the money first. I want it more than the Church does; but if I do get the money, these two men can expose me. I must get rid of them—silence them for ever—and then perhaps I may obtain the fair Amine also. Yes, their death will be necessary to secure either; that is, after I have the first in my possession. Let me think."

For some minutes the commandant walked up and down the room, reflecting upon the best method of proceeding. "He says it was a spectre, and he has told a plausible story," thought he; "but I don't know—I have my doubts; they may be tricking me. Well, be it so. If the money is there, I will have it; and if not, I will have my revenge. Yes! I have it: not only must they be removed, but by degrees all the others too who assist in bringing the treasure away. Then—but—who's there, Pedro?"

"Yes, signor."

"How long have you been here?"

"But as you spoke, signor; I thought I heard you call."

"You may go—I want nothing."

Pedro departed; but he had been some time in the room, and had overheard the whole of the commandant's soliloquy.

Chapter Thirty Four

It was a bright morning when the Portuguese vessel on which Amine was on board entered into the bay and roadstead of Goa. Goa was then at its zenith,—a proud, luxurious, superb, wealthy city—the capital of the East—a city of palaces whose viceroy reigned supreme. As they approached the river, the two mouths of which form the island upon which Goa is built, the passengers were all on deck; and the Portuguese captain, who had often been there, pointed out to Amine the most remarkable buildings. When they had passed the forts, they entered the river, the whole line of whose banks were covered with the country seats of the nobility and hidalgos—splendid buildings embosomed in groves of orange-trees, whose perfume scented the air.

"There, signora, is the country palace of the viceroy," said the captain, pointing to a building which covered nearly three acres of ground.

The ship sailed on until they arrived nearly abreast of the town, when Amine's eyes were directed to the lofty spires of the churches, and other public edifices; for Amine had seen but little of cities during her life, as may be perceived when her history is recollected.

"That is the Jesuits' church, with their establishment," said the captain, pointing to a magnificent pile. "In the church now opening upon us lie the canonised bones of the celebrated Saint Francisco, who sacrificed his life in his zeal for the propagation of the Gospel in these countries."

"I have heard of him from Father Mathias," replied Amine; "but what building is that?"

"The Augustine convent; and the other, to the right, is the Dominican."

"Splendid, indeed!" observed Amine.

"The building you see now, on the water-side, is the viceroy's palace; that to the right again, is the convent of the barefooted Carmelites; yon lofty spire is the cathedral of St. Catherine; and that beautiful and light piece of architecture is the church of our Lady of Pity. You observe there a building with a dome, rising behind the viceroy's palace?"

"I do," replied Amine.

"That is the Holy Inquisition."

Although Amine had heard Philip speak of the Inquisition, she knew little about its properties; but a sudden tremor passed through her frame as the name was mentioned, which she could not herself account for.

"Now we open upon the viceroy's palace, and you perceive what a beautiful building it is," continued the captain. "That large pile, a little above it, is the Custom-house, abreast of which we shall come to an anchor. I must leave you now, signora."

A few minutes afterwards the ship anchored opposite the Custom-house. The captain and passengers went on shore with the exception of Amine, who remained in the vessel while Father Mathias went in search of an eligible place of abode.

The next morning the priest returned on board the ship, with the intelligence that he had obtained a reception for Amine in the Ursuline convent, the abbess of which establishment he was acquainted with; and before Amine went on shore, he cautioned her that the lady-abbess was a strict woman, and would be pleased if she conformed as much as possible to the rules of the convent; that this convent only received young persons of the highest and most wealthy families, and he trusted that she would be happy there. He also promised to call upon her, and talk upon those subjects so dear to his heart, and so necessary to her salvation. The earnestness and kindness with which the old man spoke melted Amine to tears; and the holy father quitted her side to go down and collect her baggage with a warmth of feeling towards her which he had seldom felt before, and with greater hopes than ever that his endeavours to convert her would not ultimately be thrown away.

"He is a good man," thought Amine, as she descended—and Amine was right. Father Mathias was a good man; but, like all men, he was not perfect. A zealot in the cause of his religion, he would have cheerfully sacrificed his life as a martyr; but if opposed or thwarted in his views, he could then be cruel and unjust.

Father Mathias had many reasons for placing Amine in the Ursuline convent. He felt bound to offer her that protection which he had so long received under her roof; he wished her to be under the surveillance of the abbess, for he could not help imagining, although he had no proof, that she was still essaying or practising forbidden arts. He did not state this to the abbess, as he felt it would be unjust to raise suspicions; but he represented Amine as one who would do honour to their faith to which she was not yet quite converted. The very idea of effecting a conversion is to the tenants of a convent an object of surpassing interest, and the abbess was much better pleased to receive one who required her counsels and persuasions, than a really pious Christian, who would give her no trouble. Amine went on shore with Father Mathias; she refused the palanquin which had been prepared for her, and walked up to the convent. They landed between the Custom-house and the viceroy's palace, passed through the large square behind it, and then went up the Strada Diretta, or straight street, which led up to the Church of Pity, near to which the convent is situated. This street is the finest in Goa, and is called Strada Diretta from the singular fact that almost all the streets in Goa are quadrants or segments of circles. Amine was astonished. The houses were of stone, lofty and massive; at each story was thrown out a balcony of marble, elaborately carved; and over each door were the arms of the nobility, or hidalgos, to whom the houses belonged. The square behind the palace and the wide streets were filled with living beings; elephants with gorgeous trappings; led or mounted horses in superb housings; palanquins, carried by natives in splendid liveries; running footmen; syces; every variety of nation, from the proud Portuguese to the half-covered native; Mussulmans, Arabs, Hindoos, Armenians; officers and soldiers in their uniforms, all crowded and thronged together,—all was bustle and motion. Such was the wealth, the splendour, and luxury of the proud city of Goa—the Empress of the East at the time we are now describing.

In half an hour they forced their way through the crowd, and arrived at the convent, where Amine was well received by the abbess; and, after a few minutes' conversation, Father Mathias took his leave; upon which the abbess immediately set about her task of conversion. The first thing she did was to order some dried sweetmeats—not a bad beginning, as they were palatable; but as she happened to be very ignorant, and unaccustomed to theological disputes, her subsequent arguments did not go down as well as the fruit. After a rambling discourse of about an hour, the old lady felt tired, and felt as if she had done wonders. Amine was then introduced to the nuns, most of whom were young, and all of good family. Her dormitory was shown to her; and expressing a wish to be alone, she was followed into her chamber by only sixteen of them, which was about as many as the chamber could well hold.

We must pass over the two months during which Amine remained in the convent. Father Mathias had taken every step to ascertain if her husband had been saved upon any of the islands which were under the Portuguese dominions, but could gain no information. Amine was soon weary of the convent; she was persecuted by the harangues of the old abbess, but more disgusted at the conduct and conversation of the nuns. They all had secrets to confide to her—secrets which had been confided to the whole convent before: such secrets, such stories, so different from Amine's chaste ideas—such impurity of thought—that Amine was disgusted at them. But how could it be otherwise? The poor creatures had been taken from the world in the full bloom of youth, under a ripening sun, and had been immured in this unnatural manner to gratify the avarice and pride of their families. Its inmates being wholly composed of the best families, the rules of this convent were not so strict as others; licences were given—greater licences were taken—and Amine, to her surprise, found that in this society, devoted to Heaven, there were exhibited more of the bad passions of human nature than she had before met with. Constantly watched, never allowed a moment to herself, her existence became unbearable; and, after three months, she requested Father Mathias would find her some other place of refuge, telling him frankly that her residence in that place was not very likely to assist her conversion to the tenets of his faith. Father Mathias fully comprehended her, but replied, "I have no means."

"Here are means," replied Amine, taking the diamond ring from her finger. "This is worth eight hundred ducats in our country; here, I know not how much."

Father Mathias took the ring. "I will call upon you to-morrow morning, and let you know what I have done. I shall acquaint the lady abbess that you are going to your husband, for it would not be safe to let her suppose that you have reasons for quitting the convent. I have heard what you state mentioned before, but have treated it as scandal: but you, I know, are incapable of falsehood."

The next day Father Mathias returned, and had an interview with the abbess, who after a time sent for Amine, and told her that it was necessary that she should leave the convent. She consoled her as well as she could at leaving such a happy place, sent for some sweetmeats to make the parting less trying, gave her a blessing, and made her over to Father Mathias; who, when they were alone, informed Amine "that he had disposed of the ring for eighteen hundred dollars, and had procured apartments for her in the house of a widow lady, with whom she was to board."

Taking leave of the nuns, Amine quitted the convent with Father Mathias, and was soon installed in her new apartments, in a house which formed part of a spacious square called the Terra di Sabaio. After the introduction to her hostess, Father Mathias left her. Amine found her apartments fronting the square, airy and commodious. The landlady, who had escorted her to view them, not having left her, she inquired "what large church that was on the other side of the square?"

"It is the Ascension," replied the lady; "the music is very fine there; we will go and hear it to-morrow, if you please."

"And that massive building in face of us?"

"That is the Holy Inquisition," said the widow, crossing herself.

Amine again started, she knew not why. "Is that your child?" said Amine, as a boy of about twelve years old entered the room.

"Yes," replied the widow, "the only one that is left me. May God preserve him." The boy was handsome and intelligent, and Amine, for her own reasons, did everything she could to make friends with him, and was successful.

Chapter Thirty Five

Amine had just returned from an afternoon's walk through the streets of Goa: she had made some purchases at different shops in the bazaar, and had brought them home under her mantilla. "Here, at last, thank Heaven, I am alone and not watched," thought Amine, as she threw herself on the couch. "Philip, Philip, where are you?" exclaimed she. "I have now the means, and I soon will know." Little Pedro, the son of the widow, entered the room, ran up to Amine and kissed her. "Tell me, Pedro, where is your mother."

"She is gone out to see her friends this evening, and we are alone. I will stay with you."

"Do so, dearest. Tell me, Pedro, can you keep a secret?"

"Yes, I will—tell it me."

"Nay, I have nothing to tell, but I wish to do something: I wish to make a play, and you shall see things in your hand."

"Oh! yes, show me, do show me."

"If you promise not to tell."

"No, by the Holy Virgin, I will not."

"Then you shall see."

Amine lighted some charcoal in a chafing-dish, and put it at her feet; she then took a reed pen, some ink from a small bottle, and a pair of scissors, and wrote down several characters on a paper singing, or rather chanting, words which were not intelligible to her young companion. Amine then threw frankincense and coriander seed into the chafing-dish, which threw out a strong aromatic smoke; and desiring Pedro to sit down by her on a small stool, she took the boy's right hand and held it in her own. She then drew upon the palm of his hand a square figure with characters on each side of it, and in the centre poured a small quantity of the ink, so as to form a black mirror of the size of half a crown.

"Now all is ready," said Amine; "look, Pedro, what see you in the ink?"

"My own face," replied the boy.

She threw more frankincense upon the chafing-dish, until the room was full of smoke, and then chaunted:—

"Turshoon, turyo-shoon—come down, come down.

"Be present, ye servants of these names.

"Remove the veil, and be correct."

The characters she had drawn upon the paper, she had divided with the scissors, and now taking one of the pieces, she dropped it into the chafing-dish still holding the boy's hand.

"Tell me now, Pedro, what do you see?"

"I see a man sweeping," replied Pedro, alarmed.

"Fear not, Pedro, you shall see more. Has he done sweeping?"

"Yes, he has."

And Amine muttered words, which were unintelligible, and threw into the chafing-dish the other half of the paper with the characters she had written down. "Say now, Pedro, 'Philip Vanderdecken, appear.'"

"Philip Vanderdecken appear!" responded the boy, trembling.

"Tell me what thou seest, Pedro—tell me true?" said Amine anxiously.

"I see a man lying down on the white sand—(I don't like this play)."

"Be not alarmed, Pedro, you shall have sweetmeats directly. Tell me what thou seest, how the man is dressed?"

"He has a short coat—he has white trowsers—he looks about him—he takes something out of his breast and kisses it."

"'Tis he, 'tis he! and he lives! Heaven, I thank thee. Look again, boy."

"He gets up—(I don't like this play; I am frightened; indeed I am)."

"Fear not."

"Oh, yes, I am—I cannot," replied Pedro, falling on his knees; "pray let me go."

Pedro had turned his hand, and spilt the ink, the charm was broken, and Amine could learn no more. She soothed the boy with presents, made him repeat his promise that he would not tell, and postponed further search into fate until the boy should appear to have recovered from his terror, and be willing to resume the ceremonies.

"My Philip lives—mother, dear mother, I thank you."

Amine did not allow Pedro to leave the room until he appeared to have quite recovered from his fright; for some days she did not say anything to him, except to remind him of his promise not to tell his mother, or any one else, and she loaded him with presents.

One afternoon when his mother was gone out Pedro came in and asked Amine "whether they should not have the play ever again!"

Amine, who was anxious to know more, was glad of the boy's request, and soon had everything prepared. Again was her chamber filled with the smoke of the frankincense: again was she muttering her incantations: the magic mirror was on the boy's hand, and once more had Pedro cried out, "Philip Vanderdecken, appear!" when the door burst open, and Father Mathias, the widow, and several other people made their appearance. Amine started up—Pedro screamed and ran to his mother.

"Then I was not mistaken at what I saw in the cottage at Terneuse," cried Father Mathias, with his arms folded over his breast, and with looks of indignation; "accursed sorceress! you are detected."

Amine returned his gaze with scorn, and coolly replied, "I am not of your creed—you know it. Eaves-dropping appears to be a portion of your religion. This is my chamber—it is not the first time I have had to request you to leave it—I do so now—you—and those who have come in with you."

"Take up all those implements of sorcery first," said Father Mathias to his companions. The chafing-dish, and other articles used by Amine, were taken away; and Father Mathias and the others quitting the room: Amine was left alone.

Amine had a foreboding that she was lost; she knew that magic was a crime of the highest degree in Catholic countries, and that she had been detected in the very act. "Well, well," thought Amine: "it is my destiny, and I can brave the worst."

To account for the appearance of Father Mathias and the witnesses, it must be observed, that the little boy Pedro had, the day after Amine's first attempt, forgotten his promise, and narrated to his mother all that had passed. The widow, frightened at what the boy had told her, thought it right to go to Father Mathias, and confide to him what her son had told her, as it was, in her opinion, sorcery. Father Mathias questioned Pedro closely, and, convinced that such was the case, determined to have witnesses to confront Amine. He, therefore, proposed that the boy should appear to be willing to try again, and had instructed him for the purpose, having previously arranged that they should break in upon Amine, as we have described.

About half an hour afterwards, two men dressed in black gowns came into Amine's room, and requested that she would follow them, or that force would be used. Amine made no resistance: they crossed the square: the gate of a large building was opened, they desired her to walk in, and, in a few seconds, Amine found herself in one of the dungeons of the Inquisition.

Chapter Thirty Six

Previous to continuing our narrative, it may be as well to give our readers some little insight into the nature, ceremonies, and regulations of the Inquisition, and in describing that of Goa, we may be said to describe all others, with very trifling, if any, variation.

The Santa Casa, or Inquisition of Goa, is situated on one side of a large square, called the Terra di Sabaio. It is a massy handsome pile of stone buildings, with three doors in the front: the centre one is larger than the two lateral, and it is through the centre door that you go into the Hall of Judgment. The side-doors lead to spacious and handsome apartments for the Inquisitors, and officers attached to the establishment.

Behind these apartments are the cells and dungeons of the Inquisition; they are in two long galleries, with double doors to each, and are about ten feet square. There are about two hundred of them; some are much more comfortable than the others, as light and air are admitted into them: the others are wholly dark. In the galleries the keepers watch, and not a word or a sound can proceed from any cell without their being able to overhear it. The treatment of those confined is, as far as respects their food, very good: great care is taken that the nourishment is of that nature that the prisoners may not suffer from the indigestion arising from want of exercise. Surgical attendance is also permitted them; but unless on very particular occasions no priests are allowed to enter. Any consolation to be derived from religion, even the office of confessor and extreme unction, in case of dissolution, are denied them. Should they die during their confinement, whether proved guilty or not of the crime of which they are accused, they are buried without any funeral ceremony, and tried afterwards; if then found guilty, their bones are disinterred, and the execution of their sentence is passed upon their remains.

There are two Inquisitors at Goa: one the Grand Inquisitor, and the other his second, who are invariably chosen from the order of St. Dominique; these two are assisted in their judgment and examinations by a large number selected from the religious orders, who are termed deputies of the Holy Office, but who only attend when summoned: they have other officers, whose duty it is to examine all published books, and ascertain if there is anything in their pages contrary to the holy religion. There is also a public accuser, a procureur of the Inquisition, and lawyers, who are permitted to plead the case of the prisoners, but whose chief business and interest it is to obtain their secrets and betray them. What are termed *Familiars* of the Inquisition, are in fact, nothing but this description of people: but this disgraceful office is taken upon themselves by the highest nobility, who think it an honour, as well as a security, to be enrolled among the Familiars of the Inquisition, who are thus to be found dispersed throughout society; and every careless word, or expression, is certain to be repeated to the Holy Office. A summons to attend at the Inquisition is never opposed; if it were, the whole populace would rise and enforce it. Those who are confined in the dungeons of the Inquisition are kept separate; it is a very uncommon thing to put two together: it is only done when it is considered that the prolonged solitude of the dungeon has created such a depression of spirits as to endanger the life of the party. Perpetual silence is enjoined and strictly kept. Those who wail or weep, or even pray, in their utter darkness, are forced by blows to be quiet. The cries and shrieks of those who suffer from this chastisement, or from the torture, are carried along the whole length of the corridors, terrifying those who, in solitude and darkness, are anticipating the same fate.

The first question put to a person arrested by the Inquisition, is a demand, "What is his property?" He is desired to make an exact declaration of everything that he is worth, and swear to the truth of his assertions; being informed that, if there is any reservation on his part, (although he may be at that time innocent of the charges produced against him) he will, by his concealment, have incurred the wrath of the Inquisition; and that, if discharged for the crime he is accused of, he will again be arrested for having taken a false oath to the Inquisition; that, if innocent, his property will be safe, and not interfered with. It is not without reason that this demand is made. If a person accused confesses his crime, he is, in most cases, eventually allowed to go free, but all his property becomes confiscated.

By the rules of the Inquisition it is made to appear as if those condemned have the show of justice; for, although two witnesses are sufficient to warrant the apprehension of any individual, seven are necessary to convict him; but as the witnesses are never confronted with the prisoners, and torture is often applied to the witnesses, it is not difficult to obtain the number required. Many a life is falsely sworn away by the witness, that he may save his own. The chief crimes which are noticed by the Inquisition are those of sorcery, heresy, blasphemy, and what is called *Judaism*.

To comprehend the meaning of this last crime, for which more people have suffered from the Inquisition than for any other, the reader must be informed, that when Ferdinand and Isabella of Castile drove all the Jews out of Spain, they fled to Portugal, where they were received on the sole condition that they should embrace Christianity: this they consented, or appeared to consent, to do; but these converts were despised by the Portuguese people, who did not believe them to be sincere. They obtained the title of *New* Christians, in contradistinction to that of *Old* Christians. After a time the two were occasionally intermingled in marriage; but when so, it was always a reproach to the old families; and descendants from these alliances were long termed, by way of reproach, as having a portion of the New Christians in them.

The descendants of the old families thus intermingled, not only lost *caste*, but, as the genealogy of every family was well known, they were looked upon with suspicion, and were always at the mercy of the Holy Office, when denounced for Judaism, — that is, for returning to the old Jewish practices of keeping the Passover, and the other ceremonies enforced by Moses.

Let us see how an accusation of this kind works in the hands of the Inquisition. A really sincere Catholic, descended from one of these unhappy families, is accused and arrested by the orders of the Inquisition; he is ordered to declare his property, which, — convinced of his innocence, and expecting soon to be released, he does without reservation. But hardly has the key of the dungeon turned upon him, when all his effects are seized and sold by public auction, it being well understood that they never will be restored to him. After some months' confinement, he is called into the Hall of Justice, and asked if he knows why he is in prison; they advise him earnestly to confess and to conceal nothing, as it is the only way by which he can obtain his liberty. He declares his ignorance and being sent for several times, persists in it. The period of the *auto-da-fé*, or act of faith, which takes place every two or three years, (that is, the public execution of those who have been found guilty by the Inquisition,) approaches. The public accuser then comes forward, stating that the prisoner has been accused by a number of witnesses of Judaism. They persuade him to acknowledge his guilt. He persists in his innocence; they then pass a sentence on him, which they term *Convicte Invotivo*, which means "found guilty, but will not confess his crime;" and he is sentenced to be burnt at the approaching celebration. After this they follow him to his cell, and exhort him to confess his guilt, and promise that if he does confess he shall be pardoned; and these appeals are continued until the evening of the day before his execution. Terrified at the idea of a painful death, the wretch, at last, to save his life, consents. He is called into the Hall of Judgment, confesses the crime that he has not committed, and imagines that he is now saved. — Alas! now he has entangled himself, and cannot escape.

"You acknowledge that you have been guilty of observing the laws of Moses. These ceremonies cannot be performed alone; you cannot have eaten the Paschal lamb *alone*; tell us immediately, who were those who assisted at those ceremonies, or your life is still forfeited, and the stake is prepared for you."

Thus has he accused himself without gaining anything, and if he wishes to save his life, he must accuse others; and who can be accused but his own friends and acquaintances? nay, in all probability, his own relations—his brothers, sisters, wife, sons, or daughters—for it is natural to suppose that, in all such practices, a man will trust only his own family. Whether a man confesses his guilt, or dies asserting his innocence, his worldly property is in either case confiscated; but it is of great consequence to the Inquisition that he should confess, as his act of confession, with his signature annexed, is publicly read, and serves to prove to the world that the Inquisition is impartial and just; nay, more, even merciful, as it pardons those who have been proved to be guilty.

At Goa the accusations of sorcery and magic were much more frequent than at the Inquisitions at other places, arising from the customs and ceremonies of the Hindoos being very much mixed up with absurd superstitions. These people, and the slaves from other parts, very often embraced Christianity to please their masters; but since, if they had been baptised and were afterwards convicted of any crime, they were sentenced to the punishment by fire; whereas if they had not been baptised, they were only punished by whipping, imprisonment, or the galleys; upon this ground alone many refused to embrace Christianity.

We have now detailed all that we consider, up to the present, necessary for the information of the reader; all that is omitted he will gather as we proceed with our history.

Chapter Thirty Seven

A few hours after Amine had been in the dungeon, the jailors entered: without speaking to her they let down her soft silky hair, and cut it close off. Amine, with her lip curled in contempt, and without resistance and expostulation, allowed them to do their work. They finished, and she was again left to her solitude.

The next day the jailors entered her cell, and ordered her to bare her feet, and follow them. She looked at them, and they at her. "If you do not, we must," observed one of the men, who was moved by her youth and beauty. Amine did as she was desired, and was led into the Hall of Justice, where she found only the Grand Inquisitor and the Secretary.

The Hall of Justice was a long room with lofty windows on each side, and also at the end opposite to the door through which she had been led in. In the centre, on a raised daïs, was a long table covered with a cloth of alternate blue and fawn coloured stripes; and at the end opposite to where Amine was brought in, was raised an enormous crucifix, with a carved image of our Saviour. The jailor pointed to a small bench, and intimated to Amine that she was to sit down.

After a scrutiny of some moments, the secretary spoke:—

"What is your name?"

"Amine Vanderdecken."

"Of what country?"

"My husband is of the Low Countries; I am from the East."

"What is your husband?"

"The captain of a Dutch Indiaman."

"How came you here?"

"His vessel was wrecked, and we were separated."

"Whom do you know here?"

"Father Mathias."

"What property have you?"

"None; it is my husband's."

"Where is it?"

"In the custody of Father Mathias."

"Are you aware why you are brought here?"

"How should I be?" replied Amine, evasively; "tell me what I am accused of?"

"You must know whether you have done wrong or not. You had better confess all your conscience accuses you of."

"My conscience does not accuse me of doing anything."

"Then you will confess nothing?"

"By your own showing, I have nothing to confess."

"You say you are from the East: are you a Christian?"

"I reject your creed."

"You are married to a Catholic?"

"Yes a true Catholic."

"Who married you?"

"Father Seysen, a Catholic, priest."

"Did you enter into the bosom of the Church?—did he venture to marry you without your being baptised?"

"Some ceremony did take place which I consented to."

"It was baptism, was it not?"

"I believe it was so termed."

"And now you say that you reject the creed?"

"Since I have witnessed the conduct of those who profess it, I do. At the time of my marriage I was disposed towards it."

"What is the amount of your property in the Father Mathias's hands."

"Some hundreds of dollars—he knows exactly."

The Grand Inquisitor rang a bell; the jailors entered, and Amine was led back to her dungeon.

"Why should they ask so often about my money?" mused Amine; "if they require it, they may take it. What is their power? What would they do with me? Well, well, a few days will decide." A few days;—no, no, Amine; years, perhaps would have passed without decision, but that in our months from the date of your incarceration, the *auto-da-fé*, which had not been celebrated for upwards of three years, was to take place, and there was not a sufficient number of those who were to undergo the last punishment to render the ceremony imposing. A few more were required for the stake, or you would not have escaped from those dungeons so soon. As it was, a month of anxiety and suspense, almost insupportable, had to be passed away before Amine was again summoned to the Hall of Justice.

Amine, at the time we have specified, was again introduced to the Hall of Justice, and was again asked if she would confess. Irritated at her long confinement and the injustice of the proceedings, she replied, "I have told you once for all, that I have nothing to confess; do with me as you will, but be quick."

"Will torture oblige you to confess?"

"Try me," replied Amine, firmly, "try me, cruel men, and if you gain but one word from me, then call me craven. I am but a woman, but I dare you—I defy you."

It was seldom that such expressions fell upon the ears of her judges, and still more seldom that a countenance was lighted up with such determination. But the torture was never applied until after the accusation had been made and answered.

"We shall see," said the Grand Inquisitor; "take her away."

Amine was led back to her cell. In the mean time, Father Mathias had had several conferences with the Inquisitor. Although in his wrath he had accused Amine, and had procured the necessary witnesses against her, he now felt uneasy and perplexed. His long residence with her—her invariable kindness till the time of his dismissal—his knowledge that she had never embraced the faith—her boldness and courage—nay, her beauty and youth—all worked strongly in her favour. His only object now was to persuade her to confess that she was wrong, induce her to embrace the faiths, and save her. With this view he had obtained permission from the Holy Office to enter her dungeon and reason with her,—a special favour which, for many reasons, they could not well refuse him. It was on the third day after her second examination, that the bolts were removed at an unusual hour, and Father Mathias entered the cell, which was again barred, and he was left alone with Amine. "My child! my child!" exclaimed Father Mathias, with sorrow in his countenance.

"Nay, father, this is mockery. It is you who brought me here—leave me."

"I brought you here, 'tis true; but I would now remove you, if you will permit me, Amine."

"Most willingly; I'll follow you."

"Nay, nay; there is much to talk over, much to be done. This is not a dungeon from which people can escape so easily."

"Then tell me what have you to say; and what is it must be done?"

"I will."

"But stop; before you say one word, answer me one question as you hope for bliss. Have you heard aught of Philip?"

"Yes, I have. He is well."

"And where is he?"

"He will soon be here."

"God, I thank thee! shall I see him, father?"

"That must depend upon yourself."

"Upon myself? Then tell me, quickly, what would they have me do?"

"Confess your sins—your crimes."

"What sins?—what crimes?"

"Have you not dealt with evil beings, invoked the spirits, and gained the assistance of those who are not of this world?"

Amine made no reply.

"Answer me. Do you not confess?"

"I do not confess to have done anything wrong."

"This is useless. You were seen by me and others. What will avail your denial? Are you aware of the punishment which most surely awaits you, if you do not confess, and become a member of our Church?"

"Why am I to become a member of your Church? Do you then punish those who refuse?"

"No; had you not already consented to receive baptism, you would not have been asked to become so; but, having been baptised, you must now become a member, or be supposed to fall back into heresy."

"I knew not the nature of your baptism at that time."

"Granted; but you consented to it."

"Be it so. But pray, what may be the punishment, if I refuse?"

"You will be burnt alive at the stake; nothing can save you. Hear me, Amine Vanderdecken: when next summoned, you must confess all; and, asking pardon, request to be received into the Church; then will you be saved, and you will—"

"What?"

"Again be clasped in Philip's arms."

"My Philip—my Philip!—you indeed press me hard; but, father, if I confess I am wrong, when I feel that I am not—"

"Feel that you are not!"

"Yes. I invoked my mother's assistance; she gave it me in a dream. Would a mother have assisted her daughter if it were wrong?"

"It was not your mother, but a fiend who took the likeness."

"It was my mother. Again you ask me to say that I believe that which I cannot."

"That which you cannot! Amine Vanderdecken, be not obstinate."

"I am not obstinate, good father. Have you not offered me what is to me beyond all price, that I should again be in the arms of my husband? Can I degrade myself to a lie?—not for life, or liberty, or even for my Philip."

"Amine Vanderdecken, if you will confess your crime before you are accused, you will have done much; after your accusation has been made, it will be of little avail."

"It will not be done, either before or after, father. What I have done I have done, but a crime it is not to me and mine—with you it may be, but I am not of yours."

"Recollect also that you peril your husband, for having wedded with a sorceress. Forget not; to-morrow I will see you again."

"My mind is troubled," replied Amine. "Leave me, father, it will be a kindness."

Father Mathias quitted the cell, pleased with the last words of Amine. The idea of her husband's danger seemed to have startled her.

Amine threw herself down on the mattress in the corner of the cell, and hid her face.

"Burnt alive!" exclaimed she after a time, sitting up and passing her hands over her forehead. "Burnt alive! and these are Christians. This, then was the cruel death foretold by that creature, Schriften—foretold—yes, and therefore must be—it is my destiny—I cannot save myself. If I confess then, I confess that Philip is wedded to a sorceress, and he will be punished too. No, never—never; I can suffer; 'tis cruel—'tis horrible to think of,—but 'twill soon be over. God of my fathers, give me strength against these wicked men, and enable me to hear all, for my dear Philip's sake."

The next evening, Father Mathias again made his appearance. He found Amine calm and collected: she refused to listen to his advice or follow his injunctions. His last observation, that "her husband would be in peril if she was found guilty of sorcery," had steeled her heart, and she had determined that neither torture nor the stake should make her confess the act. The priest left the cell, sick at heart; he now felt miserable at the idea of Amine's perishing by so dreadful a death; accused himself of precipitation, and wished that he had never seen Amine, whose constancy and courage, although in error, excited his admiration and his pity. And then he thought of Philip, who had treated him so kindly—how could he meet him? And if he asked for his wife, what answer could he give?

Another fortnight passed, when Amine was again summoned to the Hall of Judgment, and again asked if she confessed her crimes. Upon her refusal, the accusations against her were read. She was accused by Father Mathias with practising forbidden arts, and the depositions of the boy Pedro and the other witnesses were read. In his zeal, Father Mathias also stated that he had found her guilty of the same practices at Terneuse; and, moreover, that in the violent storm, when all expected to perish, she had remained calm and courageous and told the captain that they would be saved; which could only have been known by an undue spirit of prophecy, given by evil spirits. Amine's lip curled in derision when she heard the last accusation. She was asked if she had any defence to make.

"What defence can be offered," replied she, "to such accusations as these? Witness the last—because I was not so craven as the Christians, I am accused of sorcery. The old dotard! but I will expose him. Tell me, if one knows that sorcery is used, and conceals or allows it, is he not a participator and equally guilty?"

"He is," replied the Inquisitor, anxiously awaiting the result.

"Then I denounce—" and Amine was about to reveal that Philip's mission was known, and not forbidden by Fathers Mathias and Seysen; when, recollecting that Philip would be implicated, she stopped.

"Denounce whom?" inquired the Inquisitor.

"No one," replied Amine, folding her arms and dropping her head.

"Speak, woman!"

Amine made no answer.

"The torture will make you speak."

"Never!" replied Amine. "Never! Torture me to death, if you choose; I prefer it to a public execution!"

The Inquisitor and the secretary consulted a short time. Convinced that Amine would adhere to her resolution and requiring her for public execution, they abandoned the idea of the torture.

"Do you confess?" inquired the Inquisitor.

"No," replied Amine, firmly.

"Then take her away."

The night before the *auto-da-fé*, Father Mathias again entered the cell of Amine, but all his endeavours to convert her were useless.

"To-morrow will end it all, father," replied Amine; "leave me—I would be alone."

Chapter Thirty Eight

We must now return to Philip and Krantz. When the latter retired from the presence of the Portuguese Commandant, he communicated to Philip what had taken place, and the fabulous tale which he had invented to deceive the Commandant. "I said that you alone knew where the treasure was concealed," continued Krantz, "that you might be sent for, for in all probability he will keep me as a hostage: but never mind that, I must take my chance. Do you contrive to escape somehow or other, and rejoin Amine."

"Not so," rejoined Philip; "you must go with me, my friend: I feel that, should I part with you, happiness would no longer be in store for me."

"Nonsense—that is but an idle feeling: besides, I will evade him somehow or another."

"I will not show the treasure unless you go with me."

"Well, you may try it at all events."

A low tap at the door was heard. Philip rose and opened it (for they had retired to rest), and Pedro came in. Looking carefully round him, and then shutting the door softly, he put his finger on his lips, to enjoin them to silence. He then in a whisper told them what he had overheard. "Contrive, if possible, that I go with you," continued he; "I must leave you now; he still paces his room." And Pedro slipped out of the door, and crawled stealthily away along the ramparts.

"The treacherous little rascal! But we will circumvent him if possible," said Krantz, in a low tone. "Yes, Philip, you are right, we must both go, for you will require my assistance. I must persuade him to go himself. I'll think of it—so, Philip, good night."

The next morning Philip and Krantz were summoned to breakfast; the Commandant received them with smiles and urbanity. To Philip he was peculiarly courteous. As soon as the repast was over, he thus communicated to him his intentions and wishes:—

"Signor, I have been reflecting upon what your friend told me, and the appearance of the spectre yesterday, which created such confusion; it induced me to behave with a rashness for which I must now offer my most sincere apologies. The reflections which I have made, joined with the feelings of devotion which must be in the heart of every true Catholic, have determined me, with your assistance, to obtain this treasure dedicated to the holy church. It is my proposal that you should take a party of soldiers under your orders, proceed to the island on which it is deposited, and having obtained it, return here. I will detain any vessel which may in the mean time put into the roadstead, and you shall then be the bearers of the treasure and of my letters to Goa. This will give you an honourable introduction to the authorities, and enable you to pass away your time there in the most agreeable manner. You will, also, signor, be restored to your wife, whose charms had such an effect upon me; and for mention of whose name in the very unceremonious manner which I did, I must excuse myself upon the ground of total ignorance of who she was, or of her being in any way connected with your honourable person. If these measures suit you, signor, I shall be most happy to give orders to that effect."

"As a good Catholic myself," replied Philip, "I shall be most happy to point out the spot where the treasure is concealed, and restore it to the church. Your apologies relative to my wife I accept with pleasure, being aware that your conduct proceeded from ignorance of her situation and rank; but I do not exactly see my way clear. You propose a party of soldiers. Will they obey me? Are they to be trusted? I shall have only myself and friend against them, and will they be obedient?"

"No fear of that, signor, they are well disciplined; there is not even occasion for your friend to go with you. I wish to retain him with me, to keep me company during your absence."

"Nay! that I must object to," replied Philip; "I will not trust myself alone."

"Perhaps I may be allowed to give an opinion on this subject?" observed Krantz. "I see no reason, if my friend goes accompanied within a party of soldiers only, why I should not go with him; but I consider it would be unadvisable that he proceed in the way the commandant proposes, either with or without me. You must recollect, commandant, that it is no trifling sum which is to be carried away; that it will be open to view, and will meet the eyes of your men; that these men have been detained many years in this country, and are anxious to return home. When, therefore, they find themselves with only two strangers with them—away from your authority, and in possession of a large sum of money—will not the temptation be too strong? They will only have to run down the southern channel, gain the port of Bantam and they will be safe; having obtained both freedom and wealth. To send, therefore, my friend and me, would be to send us to almost certain death; but if you were to go, commandant, then the danger would no longer exist. Your presence and your authority would control them; and; whatever their wishes or thoughts might be, they would quail before the flash of your eye."

"Very true—very true," replied Philip—"all this did not occur to me."

Nor had it occurred to the commandant, but when pointed out, the force of these suggestions immediately struck him, and long before Krantz had finished speaking, he had resolved to go himself.

"Well, signors," replied he; "I am always ready to accede to your wishes; and since you consider my presence necessary and as I do not think there is any chance of another attack from the Ternate people just now, I will take upon myself the responsibility of leaving the fort for a few days under the charge of my lieutenant, while we do this service to holy Mother Church. I have already sent for one of the native vessels, which are large and commodious, and will, with your permission, embark to-morrow."

"Two vessels will be better," observed Krantz; "in the first place, in case of an accident; and next, because we can embark all the treasure in one with ourselves, and put a portion of the soldiers in the other; so that we may be in greater force, in case of the sight of so much wealth stimulating them to insubordination."

"True, signor," we will have two vessels; "your advice is good."

Everything was thus satisfactorily arranged, with the exception of their wish that Pedro should accompany them on their expedition. They were debating how this should be brought on the tapis, when the soldier came to them, and stated that the commandant had ordered him to be of the party, and that he was to offer his services to the two strangers.

On the ensuing day everything was prepared. Ten soldiers and a corporal had been selected by the commandant; and it required but little time to put into the vessels the provisions and other articles which were required. At daylight they embarked—the Commandant and Philip in one boat; Krantz, with the corporal and Pedro, in the other. The men, who had been kept in ignorance of the object of the expedition, were now made acquainted with it by Pedro, and a long whispering took place between them, much to the satisfaction of Krantz, who was aware that the mutiny would soon be excited, when it was understood that those who composed the expedition were to be sacrificed to the avarice of the commandant. The weather being fine they sailed on during the night; passed the island of Ternate at ten leagues' distance; and before morning were among the cluster of isles, the southernmost of which was the one on which the treasure had been buried. On the second night the vessels were beached upon a small island; and then, for the first time, a communication took place between the soldiers who had been in the boat with Pedro and Krantz, and those who had been embarked with the commandant. Philip and Krantz had also an opportunity of communicating apart for a short time.

When they made sail the next morning, Pedro spoke openly; he told Krantz that the soldiers in the boat had made up their minds, and that he had no doubt that the others would do so before night; although they had not decidedly agreed upon joining them in the morning when they had re-embarked. That they would despatch the commandant, and then proceed to Batavia, and from thence obtain a passage home to Europe.

"Cannot you accomplish your end without murder?"

"Yes, we could; but not our revenge. You do not know the treatment which we have received from his hands; and sweet as the money will be to us, his death will be even sweeter. Besides, has he not determined to murder us all in some way or another? It is but justice. No, no; if there was no other knife ready—mine is."

"And so are all ours!" cried the other soldiers, putting their hands to their weapons.

One more day's sail brought them within twenty miles of the island; for Philip knew his landmarks well. Again they handed, and all retired to rest, the commandant dreaming of wealth and revenge; while it was arranging that the digging up of the treasure which he coveted should be the signal for his death.

Once more did they embark, and the commandant heeded not the dark and lowering faces with which he was surrounded. He was all gaiety and politeness. Swiftly did they skim over the dark-blue sea, between the beautiful islands with which it was studded; and before the sun was three hours high, Philip recognised the one sought after, and pointed out to the commandant the notched cocoa-nut tree, which served as a guide to the spot where the money had been concealed. They landed on the sandy beach, and the shovels were ordered to be brought on shore by the impatient little officer; who little thought that every moment of time gained was but so much *time* lost to him, and that while he was smiling and meditating treachery, that others could do the same.

The party arrived under the tree—the shovels soon removed the light sand, and in a few minutes, the treasure was exposed to view. Bag after bag was handed up, and the loose dollars collected into heaps. Two of the soldiers had been sent to the vessels for sacks to put the loose dollars in, and the men had desisted from their labour; they laid aside their spades, looks were exchanged, and all were ready.

The commandant turned round to call to and hasten the movements of the men who had been sent for the sacks, when three or four knives simultaneously pierced him through the back; he fell, and was expostulating, when they were again buried in his bosom, and he lay a corpse. Philip and Krantz remained silent spectators — the knives were drawn out, wiped, and replaced in their sheaths.

"He has met his reward," said Krantz.

"Yes," exclaimed the Portuguese soldiers — "justice, nothing but justice."

"Signors, you shall have your share," observed Pedro; "shall they not, my men?"

"Yes! yes!"

"Not one dollar, my good friends," replied Philip; "take all the money, and may you be happy; all we ask, is your assistance to proceed on our way to where we are about to go. And now, before you divide your money, oblige me by burying the body of that unfortunate man."

The soldiers obeyed. Resuming their shovels, they soon scooped out a shallow grave: the commandant's body was thrown in, and covered up from sight.

Chapter Thirty Nine

Scarcely had the soldiers performed their task, and thrown down their shovels, when they commenced an altercation. It appeared that this money was to be again the cause of slaughter and bloodshed. Philip and Krantz determined to sail immediately in one of the peroquas, and leave them to settle their disputes as they pleased. He asked permission of the soldiers to take from the provisions and water, of which there was ample supply, a larger proportion than was their share; stating, that he and Krantz had a long voyage and would require it, and pointing out to them that there were plenty of cocoa-nuts for their support. The soldiers, who thought of nothing but their newly-acquired wealth allowed him to do as he pleased; and, having hastily collected as many cocoa-nuts as they could, to add to their stock of provisions, before noon, Philip and Krantz had embarked and made sail in the peroqua, leaving the soldiers with their knives again drawn, and so busy in their angry altercation as to be heedless of their departure.

"There will be the same scene over again, I expect," observed Krantz, as the vessel parted swiftly from the shore.

"I have little doubt of it; observe, even now they are at blows and stabs."

"If I were to name that spot, it should be the '*Accursed Isle.*'"

"Would not any other be the same, with so much to inflame the passions of men?"

"Assuredly: what a curse is gold!"

"And what a blessing!" replied Krantz. "I am sorry Pedro is left with them."

"It is their destiny," replied Philip; "so let's think no more of them. Now what do you propose? With this vessel, small as she is, we may sail over these seas in safety, and we have, I imagine, provisions sufficient for more than a month."

"My idea is, to run into the track of the vessels going to the westward, and obtain a passage to Goa."

"And if we do not meet with any, we can, at all events, proceed up the Straits, as far as Pulo Penang without risk. There we may safely remain until a vessel passes."

"I agree with you; it is our best, nay our only, place; unless, indeed, we were to proceed to Cochin, where junks are always leaving for Goa."

"But that would be out of our way, and the junks cannot well pass us in the Straits, without their being seen by us."

They had no difficulty in steering their course; the islands by day, and the clear stars by night, were their compass. It is true that they did not follow the more direct track, but they followed the more secure, working up the smooth waters, and gaining to the northward more than to the west. Many times they were chased by the Malay proas which infested the islands, but the swiftness of their little peroqua was their security; indeed, the chase was, generally speaking, abandoned as soon as the smallness of the vessel was made out by the pirates, who expected that little or no booty was to be gained.

That Amine and Philip's mission was the constant theme of their discourse, may easily be imagined. One morning, as they were sailing between the isles, with less wind than usual, Philip observed:

"Krantz, you said that there were events in your own life, or connected with it, which would corroborate the mysterious tale I confided to you. Will you now tell me to what you referred?"

"Certainly," replied Krantz; "I've often thought of doing so, but one circumstance or another has hitherto prevented me; this is, however, a fitting opportunity. Prepare, therefore, to listen to a strange story, quite as strange, perhaps, as your own:—

"I take it for granted, that you have heard people speak of the Hartz Mountains," observed Krantz.

"I have never heard people speak of them, that I can recollect," replied Philip; "but I have read of them in some book, and of the strange things which have occurred there."

"It is indeed a wild region," rejoined Krantz, "and many strange tales are told of it; but strange as they are, I have good reason for believing them to be true. I have told you, Philip, that I fully believe in your communion with the other world—that I credit the history of your father, and the lawfulness of your mission; for that we are surrounded, impelled, and worked upon by beings different in their nature from ourselves, I have had full evidence, as you will acknowledge, when I state what has occurred in my own family. Why such malevolent beings as I am about to speak of should be permitted to interfere with us, and punish, I may say, comparatively unoffending mortals, is beyond my comprehension; but that they are so permitted is most certain."

"The great principle of all evil fulfils his work of evil; why, then, not the other minor spirits of the same class?" inquired Philip. "What matters it to us, whether we are tried by, and have to suffer from, the enmity of our fellow-mortals, or whether we are persecuted by beings more powerful and more malevolent than ourselves? We know that we have to work out our salvation, and that we shall be judged according to our strength; if then there be evil spirits who delight to oppress man, there surely must be, as Amine asserts, good spirits, whose delight is to do him service. Whether, then, we have to struggle against our passions only, or whether we have to struggle not only against our passions, but also the dire influence of unseen enemies we ever struggle with the same odds in our favour, as the good are stronger than the evil which we combat. In either case we are on the 'vantage ground, whether, as in the first, we fight the good cause single-handed, or as in the second, although opposed, we have the host of Heaven ranged on our side. Thus are the scales of Divine justice evenly balanced, and man is still a free agent, as his own virtuous or vicious propensities must ever decide whether he shall gain or lose the victory."

"Most true," replied Krantz, "and now to my history:—

"My father was not born, or originally a resident, in the Hartz Mountains; he was the serf of an Hungarian nobleman, of great possessions, in Transylvania; but, although a serf, he was not by any means a poor or illiterate man. In fact, he was rich and his intelligence and respectability were such, that he had been raised by his lord to the stewardship; but, whoever may happen to be born a serf, a serf must he remain, even though he become a wealthy man: and such was the condition of my father. My father had been married for about five years; and by his marriage had three children—my eldest brother Caesar, myself (Hermann), and a sister named Marcella. You know, Philip, that Latin is still the language spoken in that country; and that will account for our high-sounding names. My mother was a very beautiful woman, unfortunately more beautiful than virtuous: she was seen and admired by the lord of the soil; my father was sent away upon some mission; and, during his absence, my mother, flattered by the attentions, and won by the assiduities, of this nobleman yielded to his wishes. It so happened that my father returned very unexpectedly, and discovered the intrigue.

The evidence of my mother's shame was positive; he surprised her in the company of her seducer! Carried away by the impetuosity of his feelings, he watched the opportunity of a meeting taking place between them, and murdered both his wife and her seducer. Conscious that, as a serf, not even the provocation which he had received would be allowed as a justification of his conduct he hastily collected together what money he could lay his hands upon, and, as we were then in the depth of winter, he put his horses to the sleigh, and taking his children with him, he set off in the middle of the night, and was far away before the tragical circumstance had transpired. Aware that he would be pursued, and that he had no chance of escape if he remained in any portion of his native country (in which the authorities could lay hold of him), he continued his flight without intermission until he had buried himself in the intricacies and seclusion of the Hartz Mountains. Of course, all that I have now told you I learned afterwards. My oldest recollections are knit to a rude, yet comfortable cottage, in which I lived with my father, brother, and sister. It was on the confines of one of those vast forests which cover the northern part of Germany; around it were a few acres of ground, which, during the summer months, my father cultivated, and which, though they yielded a doubtful harvest, were sufficient for our support. In the winter we remained much in doors, for, as my father followed the chase, we were left alone, and the wolves, during that season, incessantly prowled about. My father had purchased the cottage, and land about it of one of the rude foresters, who gain their livelihood partly by hunting, and partly by burning charcoal, for the purpose of smelting the ore from the neighbouring mines; it was distant about two miles from any other habitation. I can call to mind the whole landscape now: the tall pines which rose up on the mountain above us, and the wide expanse of forest beneath, on the topmost boughs and heads of whose trees we looked down from our cottage, as the mountain below us rapidly descended into the distant valley. In summer-time the prospect was beautiful: but during the severe winter, a more desolate scene could not well be imagined.

"I said that, in the winter, my father occupied himself with the chase; every day he left us, and often would he lock the door, that we might not leave the cottage. He had no one to assist him, or to take care of us—indeed, it was not easy to find a female servant who would live in such a solitude; but could he have found one, my father would nut have received her, for he had imbibed a horror of the sex, as the difference of his conduct towards us, his two boys, and my poor little sister, Marcella evidently proved. You may suppose we were sadly neglected; indeed, we suffered much, for my father, fearful that we might come to some harm, would not allow us fuel, when he left the cottage; and we were obliged, therefore, to creep under the heaps of bears' skins, and there to keep ourselves as warm as we could until he returned in the evening, when a blazing fire was our delight. That my father chose this restless sort of life may appear strange, but the fact was, that he could not remain quiet; whether from the remorse for having committed murder, or from the misery consequent on his change of situation, or from both combined, he was never happy unless he was in a state of activity. Children, however, when left much to themselves, acquire a thoughtfulness not common to their age. So it was with us; and during the short cold days of winter, we would sit silent, longing for the happy hours when the snow would melt and the leaves would burst out, and the birds begin their songs, and when we should again be set at liberty.

"Such was our peculiar and savage sort of life until my brother Caesar was nine, myself seven, and my sister five years old, when the circumstances occurred on which is based the extraordinary narrative which I am about to relate.

"One evening my father returned home rather later than usual; he had been unsuccessful, and, as the weather was very severe, and many feet of snow were upon the ground, he was not only very cold, but in a very bad humour. He had brought in wood, and we were all three gladly assisting each other in blowing on the embers to create the blaze, when he caught poor little Marcella by the arm and threw her aside; the child fell, struck her mouth, and bled very much. My brother ran to raise her up. Accustomed to ill-usage and afraid of my father, she did not dare to cry, but looked up in his face very piteously. My father drew his stool nearer to the hearth, muttered something in abuse of women, and busied himself with the fire, which both my brother and I had deserted when my sister was so unkindly treated. A cheerful blaze was soon the result of his exertions; but we did not, as usual, crowd round it. Marcella, still bleeding, retired to a corner, and my brother and I took our seats beside her, while my father hung over the fire gloomily and alone. Such had been our position for about half an hour, when the howl of a wolf, close under the window of the cottage, fell on our ears. My father started up, and seized his gun: the howl was repeated, he examined the priming, and then hastily left the cottage, shutting the door after him. We all waited (anxiously listening), for we thought that if he succeeded in shooting the wolf, he would return in a better humour; and, although he was harsh to all of us, and particularly so to our little sister, still we loved our father, and loved to see him cheerful and happy, for what else had we to look up to? And I may here observe, that perhaps there never were three children who were fonder of each other; we did not, like other children, fight and dispute together; and if, by chance, any disagreement did arise between my elder brother and me, little Marcella would run to us, and kissing us both, seal, through her entreaties, the peace between us. Marcella was a lovely, amiable child; I can recall her beautiful features even now—Alas! poor little Marcella."

"She is dead, then?" observed Philip.

"Dead! yes, dead!—but how did she die?—But I must not anticipate, Philip; let me tell my story.

"We waited or some time, but the report of the gun did not reach us, and my elder brother then said, 'Our father has followed the wolf, and will not be back for some time. Marcella, let us wash the blood from your mouth, and then we will leave this corner, and go to the fire and warm ourselves.'

"We did so, and remained there until near midnight, every minute wondering, as it grew later, why our father did not return. We had no idea that he was in any danger, but we thought that he must have chased the wolf for a very long time. 'I will look out and see if father is coming,' said my brother Caesar, going to the door. 'Take care,' said Marcella, 'the wolves must be about now, and we cannot kill them, brother.' My brother opened the door very cautiously, and but a few inches: he peeped out.—'I see nothing,' said he, after a time, and once more he joined us at the fire. 'We have had no supper,' said I, for my father usually cooked the meat as soon as he came home; and during his absence we had nothing but the fragments of the preceding day.

"'And if our father comes home after his hunt, Caesar,' said Marcella, 'he will be pleased to have some supper; let us cook it for him and for ourselves.' Caesar climbed upon the stool, and reached down some meat—I forget now whether it was venison or bear's meat; but we cut off the usual quantity, and proceeded to dress it, as we used to do under our father's superintendence. We were all busy putting it into the platters before the fire, to await his coming, when we heard the sound of a horn. We listened—there was a noise outside, and a minute afterwards my father entered, ushering in a young female, and a large dark man in a hunter's dress.

"Perhaps I had better now relate what was only known to me many years afterwards. When my father had left the cottage, he perceived a large white wolf about thirty yards from him; as soon as the animal saw my father, it retreated slowly growling and snarling. My father followed; the animal did not run, but always kept at some distance; and my father did not like to fire until he was pretty certain that his ball would take effect; thus they went on for some time, the wolf now leaving my father far behind, and then stopping and snarling defiance at him, and then, again, on his approach, setting off at speed.

"Anxious to shoot the animal (for the white wolf is very rare) my father continued the pursuit for several hours, during which he continually ascended the mountain.

"You must know, Philip, that there are peculiar spots on those mountains which are supposed, and, as my story will prove, truly supposed, to be inhabited by the evil influences: they are well known to the huntsmen, who invariably avoid them. Now, one of these spots, an open space in the pine forests above us, had been pointed out to my father as dangerous on that account. But, whether he disbelieved these wild stories or whether, in his eager pursuit of the chase, he disregarded them, I know not; certain, however, it is, that he was decoyed by the white wolf to this open space, when the animal appeared to slacken her speed. My father approached, came close up to her, raised his gun to his shoulder, and was about to fire, when the wolf suddenly disappeared. He thought that the snow on the ground must have dazzled his sight, and he let down his gun to look for the beast—but she was gone; how she could have escaped over the clearance, without his seeing her, was beyond his comprehension. Mortified at the ill success of his chase, he was about to retrace his steps, when he heard the distant sound of a horn. Astonishment at such a sound—at such an hour—in such a wilderness, made him forget for the moment his disappointment, and he remained riveted to the spot. In a minute the horn was blown a second time, and at no great distance; my father stood still, and listened: a third time it was blown. I forget the term used to express it, but it was the signal which, my father well knew, implied that the party was lost in the woods. In a few minutes more my father beheld a man on horseback, with a female seated on the crupper, enter the cleared space, and ride up to him. At first, my father called to mind the strange stories which he had heard of the supernatural beings who were said to frequent these mountains; but the nearer approach of the parties satisfied him that they were mortals like himself. As soon as they came up to him, the man who guided the horse accosted him. 'Friend Hunter, you are out late, the better fortune for us; we have ridden far, and are in fear of our lives which are eagerly sought after. These mountains have enabled us to elude our pursuers; but if we find not shelter and refreshment, that will avail us little, as we must perish from hunger and the inclemency of the night. My daughter, who rides behind me, is now more dead than alive—say, can you assist us in our difficulty?'

"'My cottage is some few miles distant,' replied my father, 'but I have little to offer you besides a shelter from the weather; to the little I have you are welcome. May I ask whence you come?'

"'Yes, friend, it is no secret now; we have escaped from Transylvania, where my daughter's honour and my life were equally in jeopardy!'

"This information was quite enough to raise an interest in my father's heart, he remembered his own escape; he remembered the loss of his wife's honour, and the tragedy by which it was wound up. He immediately, and warmly, offered all the assistance which he could afford them.

"'There is no time to be lost then, good sir,' observed the horseman; 'my daughter is chilled with the frost, and cannot hold out much longer against the severity of the weather.'

"'Follow me,' replied my father, leading the way towards his home.

"'I was lured away in pursuit of a large white wolf,' observed my father; 'it came to the very window of my hut, or I should not have been out at this time of night.'

"'The creature passed by us just as we came out of the wood,' said the female, in a silvery tone.

"'I was nearly discharging my piece at it,' observed the hunter; 'but since it did us such good service, I am glad I allowed it to escape.'

"In about an hour and a half, during which my father walked at a rapid pace, the party arrived at the cottage, and, as I said before, came in.

"'We are in good time, apparently,' observed the dark hunter, catching the smell of the roasted meat, as he walked to the fire and surveyed my brother and sister, and myself. 'You have young cooks here, Meinheer.' 'I am glad that we shall not have to wait,' replied my father. 'Come, mistress, seat yourself by the fire; you require warmth after your cold ride.' 'And where can I put up my horse, Meinheer?' observed the huntsman. 'I will take care of him,' replied my father, going out of the cottage door.

"The female must, however, be particularly described. She was young, and apparently twenty years of age. She was dressed in a travelling-dress, deeply bordered with white fur, and wore a cap of white ermine on her head. Her features were very beautiful, at least I thought so, and so my father has since declared. Her hair was flaxen, glossy, and shining, and bright as a mirror; and her mouth, although somewhat large when it was open, showed the most brilliant teeth I have ever beheld. But there was something about her eyes, bright as they were, which made us children afraid; they were so restless, so furtive; I could not at that time tell why, but I felt as if there was cruelty in her eye; and when she beckoned us to come to her, we approached her with fear and trembling. Still she was beautiful, very beautiful. She spoke kindly to my brother and myself, patted our heads and caressed us; but Marcella would not come near her; on the contrary, she slunk away, and hid herself in the bed, and would not wait for the supper, which half an hour before she had been so anxious for.

"My father, having put the horse into a close shed, soon returned, and supper was placed upon the table. When it was over, my father requested that the young lady would take possession of his bed, and he would remain at the fire, and sit up with her father. After some hesitation on her part, this arrangement was agreed to, and I and my brother crept into the other bed with Marcella, for we had as yet always slept together.

"But we could not sleep; there was something so unusual, not only in seeing strange people, but in having those people sleep at the cottage, that we were bewildered. As for poor little Marcella, she was quiet, but I perceived that she trembled during the whole night, and sometimes I thought that she was checking a sob. My father had brought out some spirits, which he rarely used, and he and the strange hunter remained drinking and talking before the fire. Our ears were ready to catch the slightest whisper—so much was our curiosity excited.

"'You said you came from Transylvania?' observed my father.

"'Even so, Meinheer,' replied the hunter. 'I was a serf to the noble house of —; my master would insist upon my surrendering up my fair girl to his wishes: it ended in my giving him a few inches of my hunting-knife.'

"'We are countrymen, and brothers in misfortune,' replied my father, taking the huntsman's hand, and pressing it warmly.

"'Indeed! Are you then from that country?'

"'Yes; and I too have fled for my life. But mine is a melancholy tale.'

"'Your name?' inquired the hunter.

"'Krantz.'

"'What! Krantz of —? I have heard your tale; you need not renew your grief by repeating it now. Welcome, most welcome, Meinheer, and, I may say, my worthy kinsman. I am your second cousin, Wilfred of Barnsdorf,' cried the hunter, rising up and embracing my father.

"They filled their horn-mugs to the brim, and drank to one another after the German fashion. The conversation was then carried on in a low tone; all that we could collect from it was that our new relative and his daughter were to take up their abode in our cottage, at least for the present. In about an hour they both fell back in their chairs and appeared to sleep.

"'Marcella, dear, did you hear?' said my brother, in a low tone.

"'Yes,' replied Marcella in a whisper, 'I heard all. Oh! brother, I cannot bear to look upon that woman—I feel so frightened.'

"My brother made no reply, and shortly afterwards we were all three fast asleep.

"When we awoke the next morning, we found that the hunter's daughter had risen before us. I thought she looked more beautiful than ever. She came up to little Marcella and caressed her: the child burst into tears, and sobbed as if her heart would break.

"But, not to detain you with too long a story, the huntsman and his daughter were accommodated in the cottage. My father and he went out hunting daily, leaving Christina with us. She performed all the household duties; was very kind to us children; and, gradually, the dislike even of little Marcella wore away. But a great change took place in my father; he appeared to have conquered his aversion to the sex, and was most attentive to Christina. Often, after her father and we were in bed would he sit up with her, conversing in a low tone by the fire. I ought to have mentioned that my father and the huntsman Wilfred, slept in another portion of the cottage, and that the bed which he formerly occupied, and which was in the same room as ours, had been given up to the use of Christina. These visitors had been about three weeks at the cottage, when, one night, after we children had been sent to bed, a consultation was held. My father had asked Christina in marriage, and had obtained both her own consent and that of Wilfred; after this, a conversation took place, which was, as nearly as I can recollect, as follows.

"'You may take my child, Meinheer Krantz, and my blessing with her, and I shall then leave you and seek some other habitation—it matters little where.'

"'Why not remain here, Wilfred?'

"'No, no, I am called elsewhere; let that suffice, and ask no more questions. You have my child.'

"'I thank you for her, and will duly value her; but there is one difficulty.'

"'I know what you would say; there is no priest here in this wild country: true; neither is there any law to bind; still must some ceremony pass between you, to satisfy a father. Will you consent to marry her after my fashion? if so, I will marry you directly.'

"'I will,' replied my father.

"'Then take her by the hand. Now, Meinheer, swear.'

"'I swear,' repeated my father.

"'By all the spirits of the Hartz mountains—'

"'Nay, why not by Heaven?' interrupted my father.

"'Because it is not my humour,' rejoined Wilfred; 'if I prefer that oath, less binding perhaps, than another, surely you will not thwart me.'

"'Well be it so then; have your humour. Will you make me swear by that in which I do not believe?'

"'Yet many do so, who in outward appearance are Christians,' rejoined Wilfred; 'say, will you be married, or shall I take my daughter away with me?'

"'Proceed,' replied my father, impatiently.

"'I swear by all the spirits of the Hartz mountains, by all their power for good or for evil, that I take Christina for my wedded wife; that I will ever protect her, cherish her, and love her; that my hand shall never be raised against her to harm her.'

"My father repeated the words after Wilfred.

"'And if I fail in this my vow, may all the vengeance of the spirits fall upon me and upon my children; may they perish by the vulture, by the wolf, or other beasts of the forest; may their flesh be torn from their limbs, and their bones blanch in the wilderness: all this I swear.'

"My father hesitated, as he repeated the last words; little Marcella could not restrain herself, and as my father repeated the last sentence, she burst into tears. This sudden interruption appeared to discompose the party, particularly my father; he spoke harshly to the child, who controlled her sobs, burying her face under the bed-clothes.

"Such was the second marriage of my father. The next morning, the hunter Wilfred mounted his horse, and rode away.

"My father resumed his bed, which was in the same room as ours; and things went on much as before the marriage, except that our new mother-in-law did not show any kindness towards us; indeed during my father's absence, she would often beat us, particularly little Marcella, and her eyes would flash fire, as she looked eagerly upon the fair and lovely child.

"One night, my sister awoke me and my brother.

"'What is the matter?' said Caesar.

"'She has gone out,' whispered Marcella.

"'Gone out!'

"'Yes, gone out at the door, in her night-clothes,' replied the child; 'I saw her get out of bed, look at my father to see if he slept, and then she went out at the door.'

"What could induce her to leave her bed, and all undressed to go out, in such bitter wintry weather, with the snow deep on the ground was to us incomprehensible; we lay awake, and in about an hour we heard the growl of a wolf, close under the window.

"'There is a wolf,' said Caesar. 'She will be torn to pieces.'

"'Oh no!' cried Marcella.

"In a few minutes afterwards our mother-in-law appeared; she was in her night-dress, as Marcella had stated. She let down the latch of the door, so as to make no noise, went to a pail of water, and washed her face and hands, and then slipped into the bed where my father lay.

"We all three trembled—we hardly knew why; but we resolved to watch the next night: we did so; and not only on the ensuing night, but on many others, and always at about the same hour, would our mother-in-law rise from her bed and leave the cottage; and after she was gone we invariably heard the growl of a wolf under our window, and always saw her, on her return, wash herself before she retired to bed. We observed also that she seldom sat down to meals, and that when she did she appeared to eat with dislike; but when the meat was taken down to be prepared for dinner, she would often furtively put a raw piece into her mouth.

"My brother Caesar was a courageous boy; he did not like to speak to my father until he knew more. He resolved that he would follow her out, and ascertain what she did. Marcella and I endeavoured to dissuade him from this project; but he would not be controlled; and the very next night he lay down in his clothes, and as soon as our mother-in-law had left the cottage he jumped up, took down my father's gun, and followed her.

"You may imagine in what a state of suspense Marcella and I remained during his absence. After a few minutes we heard the report of a gun. It did not awaken my father; and we lay trembling with anxiety. In a minute afterwards we saw our mother-in-law enter the cottage—her dress was bloody. I put my hand to Marcella's mouth to prevent her crying out, although I was myself in great alarm. Our mother-in-law approached my father's bed, looked to see if he was asleep, and then went to the chimney and blew up the embers into a blaze.

"'Who is there?' said my father, waking up.

"'Lie still, dearest,' replied my mother-in-law; 'it is only me; I have lighted the fire to warm some water; I am not quite well.'

"My father turned round, and was soon asleep; but we hatched our mother-in-law. She changed her linen, and threw the garments she had worn into the fire; and we then perceived that her right leg was bleeding profusely, as if from a gun-shot wound. She bandaged it up, and then dressing herself, remained before the fire until the break of day.

"Poor little Marcella, her heart beat quick as she pressed me to her side—so indeed did mine. Where was our brother Caesar? How did my mother-in-law receive the wound unless from his gun? At last my father rose, and then for the first time I spoke, saying, 'Father, where is my brother Caesar?'

"'Your brother!' exclaimed he; 'why, where can he be?'

"'Merciful Heaven! I thought, as lay very restless last night,' observed our mother-in-law, 'that I heard somebody open the latch of the door; and, dear me, husband, what has become of your gun?'

"My father cast his eyes up above the chimney, and perceived that his gun was missing. For a moment he looked perplexed; then, seizing a broad axe, he went out of the cottage without saying another word.

"He did not remain away from us long; in a few minutes he returned, bearing in his arms the mangled body of my poor brother; he laid it down, and covered up his face.

"My mother-in-law rose up, and looked at the body, while Marcella and I threw ourselves by its side, wailing and sobbing bitterly.

"'Go to bed again, children,' said she, sharply. 'Husband,' continued she, 'your boy must have taken the gun down, to shoot a wolf, and the animal has been too powerful for him. Poor boy! he has paid dearly for his rashness.'

"My father made no reply. I wished to speak—to tell all—but Marcella who perceived my intention, held me by the arm, and looked at me so imploringly, that I desisted.

"My father, therefore, was left in his error; but Marcella and I, although we could not comprehend it, were conscious that our mother-in-law was in some way connected with my brother's death.

"That day my father went out and dug a grave; and when he hid the body in the earth, he piled up stones over it so that the wolves should not be able to dig it up. The shock of this catastrophe was to my poor father very severe; for several days he never went to the chase, although at times he would utter bitter anathemas and vengeance against the wolves.

"But during this time of mourning on his part, my mother-in-law's nocturnal wanderings continued with the same regularity as before.

"At last my father took down his gun to repair to the forest; but he soon returned, and appeared much annoyed.

"'Would you believe it, Christina, that the wolves—perdition to the whole race—have actually contrived to dig up the body of my poor boy, and now there is nothing left of him but his bones?'

"'Indeed!' replied my mother-in-law. Marcella looked at me; and I saw in her intelligent eye all she would have uttered.

"'A wolf growls under our window every night, father,' said I.

"'Ay, indeed! Why did you not tell me, boy? Wake me the next time you hear it.'

"I saw my mother-in-law turn away; her eyes flashed fire, and she gnashed her teeth.

"My father went out again, and covered up with a larger pile of stones the little remnants of my poor brother which the wolves had spared. Such was the first act of the tragedy.

"The spring now came on; the snow disappeared, and we were permitted to leave the cottage; but never would I quit for one moment my dear little sister, to whom since the death of my brother, I was more ardently attached than ever; indeed, I was afraid to leave her alone with my mother-in-law, who appeared to have a particular pleasure in ill-treating the child. My father was now employed upon his little farm, and I was able to render him some assistance.

"Marcella used to sit by us while we were at work, leaving my mother-in-law alone in the cottage. I ought to observe that, as the spring advanced, so did my mother-in-law decrease her nocturnal rambles, and that we never heard the growl of the wolf under the window after I had spoken of it to my father.

"One day, when my father and I were in the field, Marcella being with us, my mother-in-law came out, saying that she was going into the forest to collect some herbs my father wanted, and that Marcella must go to the cottage and watch the dinner. Marcella went; and my mother-in-law soon disappeared in the forest, taking a direction quite contrary to that in which the cottage stood, and leaving my father and I, as it were, between her and Marcella.

"About an hour afterwards we were startled by shrieks from the cottage—evidently the shrieks of little Marcella. 'Marcella has burnt herself, father,' said I, throwing down my spade. My father threw down his, and we both hastened to the cottage. Before we could gain the door, out darted a large white wolf, which fled with the utmost celerity. My father had no weapon; he rushed into the cottage, and there saw poor little Marcella expiring. Her body was dreadfully mangled, and the blood pouring from it had formed a large pool on the cottage floor. My father's first intention had been to seize his gun and pursue; but he was checked by this horrid spectacle; he knelt down by his dying child, and burst into tears. Marcella could just look kindly on us for a few seconds, and then her eyes were closed in death.

"My father and I were still hanging over my poor sister's body, when my mother-in-law came in. At the dreadful sight she expressed much concern; but she did not appear to recoil from the sight of blood, as most women do.

"'Poor child!' said she, 'it must have been that great white wolf which passed me just now, and frightened me so. She's quite dead, Krantz.'

"'I know it—I know it!' cried my father, in agony.

"I thought my father would never recover from the effects of this second tragedy; he mourned bitterly over the body of his sweet child, and for several days would not consign it to its grave, although frequently requested by my mother-in-law to do so. At last he yielded, and dug a grave for her close by that of my poor brother, and took every precaution that the wolves should not violate her remains.

"I was now really miserable, as I lay alone in the bed which I had formerly shared with my brother and sister. I could not help thinking that my mother-in-law was implicated in both their deaths, although I could not account for the manner; but I no longer felt afraid of her; my little heart was full of hatred and revenge.

"The night after my sister had been buried, as I lay awake, I perceived my mother-in-law get up and go out of the cottage. I waited some time, then dressed myself, and looked out through the door, which I half opened. The moon shone bright and I could see the spot where my brother and my sister had been buried; and what was my horror when I perceived my mother-in-law busily removing the stones from Marcella's grave!

"She was in her white night-dress and the moon shone full upon her. She was digging with her hands, and throwing away the stones behind her with all the ferocity of a wild beast. It was some time before I could collect my senses, and decide what I should do. At last I perceived that she had arrived at the body, and raised it up to the side of the grave. I could bear it no longer, I ran to my father and awoke him.

"'Father, father!' cried I, 'dress yourself, and get your gun.'

"'What!' cried my father, 'the wolves are there, are they?'

"He jumped out of bed, threw on his clothes, and, in his anxiety, did not appear to perceive the absence of his wife. As soon as he was ready I opened the door; he went out, and I followed him.

"Imagine his horror, when (unprepared as he was for such a sight) he beheld, as he advanced towards the grave not a wolf, but his wife, in her night-dress, on her hands and knees, crouching by the body of my sister, and tearing off large pieces of the flesh, and devouring them with all the avidity of a wolf. She was too busy to be aware of our approach. My father dropped his gun; his hair stood on end, so did mine; he breathed heavily, and then his breath for a time stopped. I picked up the gun and put it into his hand. Suddenly he appeared as if concentrated rage had restored him to double vigour; he levelled his piece, fired, and with a loud shriek down fell the wretch whom he had fostered in his bosom.

"'God of Heaven!' cried my father, sinking down upon the earth in a swoon, as soon as he had discharged his gun.

"I remained some time by his side before he recovered. 'Where am I?' said he, 'what has happened? Oh!—yes, yes! I recollect now. Heaven forgive me!'

"He rose and we walked up to the grave; what again was our astonishment and horror to find that, instead of the dead body of my mother-in-law, as we expected, there was lying over the remains of my poor sister, a large white she-wolf.

"'The white wolf!' exclaimed my father, 'the white wolf which decoyed me into the forest—I see it all now—I have dealt with the spirits of the Hartz Mountains.'

"For some time my father remained in silence and deep thought. He then carefully lifted up the body of my sister, replaced it in the grave, an covered it over as before, having struck the head of the dead animal with the heel of his boot, and raving like a madman. He walked back to the cottage, shut the door, and threw himself on the bed; I did the same, for I was in a stupor of amazement.

"Early in the morning we were both roused by a loud knocking at the door, and in rushed the hunter Wilfred.

"'My daughter—man—my daughter!—where is my daughter?' cried he in a rage.

"'Where the wretch, the fiend, should be, I trust,' replied my father, starting up, and displaying equal choler; 'where she should be—in hell! Leave this cottage, or you may fare worse.'

"'Ha—ha!' replied the hunter, 'would you harm a potent spirit of the Hartz Mountains. Poor mortal, who must needs wed a were wolf.'

"'Out, demon! I defy thee and thy power.'

"'Yet shall you feel it; remember your oath—your solemn oath—never to raise your hand against her to harm her.'

"'I made no compact with evil spirits.'

"'You did, and if you failed in your vow, you were to meet the vengeance of the spirits. Your children were to perish by the vulture, the wolf—'

"'Out, out, demon!'

"'And their bones blanch in the wilderness. Ha!—ha!'

"My father, frantic with rage, seized his axe, and raised it over Wilfred's head to strike.

"'All this I swear,' continued the huntsman, mockingly.

"The axe descended; but it passed through the form of the hunter, and my father lost his balance, and fell heavily on the floor.

"'Mortal!' said the hunter, striding over my father's body, 'we have power over those only who have committed murder. You have been guilty of a double murder: you shall pay the penalty attached to your marriage vow. Two of your children are gone, the third is yet to follow—and follow them he will, for your oath is registered. Go—it were kindness to kill thee—your punishment is, that you live!'

"With these words the spirit disappeared. My father rose from the floor, embraced me tenderly, and knelt down in prayer.

"The next morning he quitted the cottage for ever. He took me with him, and bent his steps to Holland, where we safely arrived. He had some little money with him; but he had not been many days in Amsterdam before he was seized with a brain fever, and died raving mad. I was put into the asylum, and afterwards was sent to sea before the mast. You now know all my history. The question is, whether I am to pay the penalty of my father's oath? I am myself perfectly convinced that, in some way or another, I shall."

On the twenty-second day the high land of the south of Sumatra was in view: as there were no vessels in sight, they resolved to keep their course through the Straits, and run for Pulo Penang, which they expected, as their vessel lay so close to the wind, to reach in seven or eight days. By constant exposure Philip and Krantz were now so bronzed that with their long beards and Mussulman dresses, they might easily have passed off for natives. They had steered the whole of the days exposed to a burning sun; they had lain down and slept in the dew of the night; but their health had not suffered. But for several days, since he had confided the history of his family to Philip, Krantz had become silent and melancholy: his usual flow of spirits had vanished and Philip had often questioned him as to the cause. As they entered the Straits, Philip talked of what they should do upon their arrival at Goa; when Krantz gravely replied, "For some days, Philip, I have had a presentiment that I shall never see that city."

"You are out of health, Krantz," replied Philip.

"No, I am in sound health, body and mind. I have endeavoured to shake off the presentiment, but in vain; there is a warning voice that continually tells me that I shall not be long with you. Philip, will you oblige me by making me content on one point? I have gold about my person which may be useful to you; oblige me by taking it, and securing it on your own."

"What nonsense, Krantz."

"It is no nonsense, Philip. Have on not had your warnings? Why should I not have mine? You know that I have little fear in my composition, and that I care not about death; but I feel the presentiment which I speak of more strongly every hour. It is some kind spirit who would warn me to prepare for another world. Be it so. I have lived long enough in this world to leave it without regret; although to part with you and Amine, the only two now dear to me, is painful, I acknowledge."

"May not this arise from over-exertion and fatigue, Krantz? Consider how much excitement you have laboured under within these last four months. Is not that enough to create a corresponding depression? Depend upon it, my dear friend, such is the fact."

"I wish it were; but I feel otherwise, and there is a feeling of gladness connected with the idea that I am to leave this world arising from another presentiment, which equally occupies my mind."

"I hardly can tell you—but Amine and you are connected with it. In my dreams I have seen you meet again; but it has appeared to me as if a portion of your trial was purposely shut from my sight in dark clouds; and I have asked, 'May not I see what is there concealed?'—and an invisible has answered, 'No! 'twould make you wretched. Before these trials take place, you will be summoned away:' and then I have thanked Heaven, and felt resigned."

"These are the imaginings of a disturbed brain, Krantz; that I am destined to suffering may be true; but why Amine should suffer, or why you, young, in full health and vigour should not pass your days in peace, and live to a good old age, there is no cause for believing. You will be better tomorrow."

"Perhaps so," replied Krantz; "but still you must yield to my whim, and take the gold; If I am wrong, and we do arrive safe, you know, Philip, you can let me have it back," observed Krantz, with a faint smile—"but you forget, our water is nearly out, and we must look out for a rill on the coast to obtain a fresh supply."

"I was thinking of that when you commenced this unwelcome topic. We had better look out for the water before dark, and as soon as we have replenished our jars, we will make sail again."

At the time that this conversation took place, they were on the eastern side of the strait, about forty miles to the northward. The interior of the coast was rocky and mountainous; but it slowly descended to low land of alternate forest and jungles, which continued to the beach: the country appeared to be uninhabited. Keeping close in to the shore, they discovered, after two hours' run, a fresh stream which burst in a cascade from the mountains, and swept its devious course through the jungle, until it poured its tribute into the waters of the strait.

They ran close in to the mouth of the stream, lowered the sails, and pulled the peroqua against the current, until they had advanced far enough to assure them that the water was quite fresh. The jars were soon filled, and they were again thinking of pushing off; when, enticed by the beauty of the spot, the coolness of the fresh water, and wearied with their long confinement on board of the peroqua, they proposed to bathe—a luxury hardly to be appreciated by those who have not been in a similar situation. They threw off their Mussulman dresses, and plunged into the stream, where they remained for some time. Krantz was the first to get out: he complained of feeling chilled, and he walked on to the banks where their clothes had been laid. Philip also approached nearer to the beach intending to follow him.

"And now, Philip," said Krantz, "this will be a good opportunity for me to give you the money. I will open my sash and pour it out, and you can put it into your own before you put it on."

Philip was standing in the water, which was about level with his waist.

"Well, Krantz," said he, "I suppose if it must be so, it must—but it appears to me an idea so ridiculous—however, you shall have your own way."

Philip quitted the run, and sat down by Krantz, who was already busy in shaking the doubloons out of the folds of his sash. At last he said—

"I believe, Philip, you have got them all now?—I feel satisfied."

"What danger there can be to you, which I am not equally exposed to, I cannot conceive," replied Philip; "however—"

Hardly had he said these words, when there was a tremendous roar—a rush like a mighty wind through the air—a blow which threw him on his back—a loud cry—and a contention. Philip recovered himself, and perceived the naked form of Krantz carried off with the speed of an arrow by an enormous tiger through the jungle. He watched with distended eyeballs; in a few seconds the animal and Krantz had disappeared!

"God of Heaven! would that thou hadst spared me this," cried Philip, throwing himself down in agony on his face. "Oh! Krantz, my friend—my brother—too sure was your presentiment. Merciful God! have pity—but thy will be done;" and Philip burst into a flood of tears.

For more than an hour did he remain fixed upon the spot, careless and indifferent to the danger by which he was surrounded. At last, somewhat recovered, he rose, dressed himself, and then again sat down—his eyes fixed upon the clothes of Krantz, and the gold which a on the sand.

"He would give me that gold. He foretold his doom. Yes! yes! it was his destiny, and it has been fulfilled. *His bones will bleach in the wilderness,* and the spirit-hunter and his wolfish daughter are avenged."

The shades of evening now set in, and the low growling of the beasts of the forest recalled Philip to a sense of his own danger. He thought of Amine; and hastily making the clothes of Krantz and the doubloons into a package, he stepped into the peroqua, with difficulty shoved it off, and with a melancholy heart, and in silence, hoisted the sail, and pursued his course.

"Yes, Amine," thought Philip, as he watched the stars twinkling and coruscating; "yes, you are right, when you assert that the destinies of men are foreknown, and may by some be read. My destiny is, alas! that I should be severed from all I value upon earth? and die friendless and alone. Then welcome death, if such is to be the case; welcome—a thousand welcomes! what a relief wilt thou be to me! what joy to find myself summoned to where the weary are at rest! I have my task to fulfil. God grant that it may soon be accomplished, and let not my life be embittered by any more trials such as this."

Again did Philip weep, for Krantz had been his long-tried, valued friend? his partner in all his dangers and privations, from the period that they had met when the Dutch fleet attempted the passage round Cape Horn.

After seven days of painful watching and brooding over bitter thoughts, Philip arrived at Pulo Penang, where he found a vessel about to sail for the city to which he was destined. He ran his peroqua alongside of her, and found that she was a brig under the Portuguese flag, having, however, but two Portuguese on board, the rest of the crew being natives. Representing himself as am Englishman in the Portuguese service, who had been wrecked, and offering to pay for his passage, he was willingly received, and in a few days the vessel sailed.

Their voyage was prosperous; in six weeks they anchored in the roads of Goa; the next day they went up the river. The Portuguese captain informed

Philip where he might obtain lodging; and passing him off as one of his crew, there was no difficulty raised as to his landing. Having located himself at his new lodging, Philip commenced some inquiries of his host relative to Amine, designating her merely as a young woman who had arrived there in a vessel some weeks before but he could obtain no information concerning her. "Signor," said the host, "to-morrow is the grand *auto-da-fé*; we can do nothing until that is over; afterwards, I will put you in the way to find out what you wish. In the mean time, you can walk about the town; to-morrow I will take you to where you can behold the grand procession, and then we will try what we can do to assist you in your search."

Philip went out, procured a suit of clothes, removed his beard, and then walked about the town, looking up at every window to see if he could perceive Amine. At a corner of one of the streets, he thought he recognised Father Mathias, and ran up to him; but the monk had drawn his cowl over his head, and when addressed by that name, made no reply.

"I was deceived," thought Philip; "but I really thought it was him." And Philip was right; it was Father Mathias, who thus screened himself from Philip's recognition.

Tired, at last he returned to his hotel, just before it was dark. The company there were numerous; everybody for miles distant had come to Goa to witness the *auto-da-fé*, — and everybody was discussing the ceremony.

"I will see this grand procession," said Philip to himself, as he threw himself on his bed. "It will drive thought from me for a time; and God knows how painful my thoughts have now become. Amine, dear Amine, may angels guard thee!"

Chapter Forty

Although to-morrow was to end all Amine's hopes and fears—all her short happiness—her suspense and misery—yet Amine slept until her last slumber in this world was disturbed by the unlocking and unbarring of the doors of her cell, and the appearance of the head gaoler with a light. Amine started up—she had been dreaming of her husband—of happiness! She awoke to the sad reality. There stood the gaoler, with a dress in his hand, which he desired she would put on. He lighted a lamp for her, and left her alone. The dress was of black serge, with white stripes.

Amine put on the dress, and threw herself down on the bed, trying, if possible, to recall the dream from which she had been awakened, but in vain. Two hours passed away, and the gaoler again entered, and summoned her to follow him. Perhaps one of the most appalling customs of the Inquisition is, that after accusation, whether the accused parties confess their guilt or not, they return to their dungeons, without the least idea of what may have been their sentence, and when summoned on the morning of the execution they are equally kept in ignorance.

The prisoners were all summoned by the gaolers from the various dungeons, and led into a large hall, where they found their fellow-sufferers collected.

In this spacious, dimly-lighted hall, were to be seen about two hundred men, standing up, as if for support, against the walls, all dressed in the same black and white serge; so motionless, so terrified were they, that if it had not been for the rolling of their eyes, as they watched the gaolers, who passed and repassed, you might have imagined them to be petrified. It was the agony of suspense, worse than the agony of death. After a time, a wax candle, about five feet long, was put into the hands of each prisoner, and then some were ordered to put on over their dress the *Sanbenitos*—others the *Samarias*! Those who received these dresses, with flames painted on them, gave themselves up for lost; and it was dreadful to perceive the anguish of each individual as the dresses were, one by one brought forward, and with the heavy drops of perspiration on his brows, he watched with terror lest one should be presented to him. All was doubt, fear, and horror!

But the prisoners in this hall were not those who were to suffer death. Those who wore the Sanbenitos had to walk in the procession, and receive but slight punishment; those who wore the Samarias had been condemned, but had been saved from the consuming fire, by an acknowledgment of their offence; the flames painted on their dresses were *reversed*, and signified that they were not to suffer; but this the unfortunate wretches did not know, and the horrors of a cruel death stared them in the face!

Another hall, similar to the one in which the men had been collected, was occupied by female culprits. The same ceremonies were observed—the same doubt fear and agony, were depicted upon every countenance. But there was a third chamber, smaller than the other two, and this chamber was reserved for those who had been sentenced and who were to suffer at the stake. It was into this chamber that Amine was led, and there she found seven other prisoners, dressed in the same manner as herself: two only were Europeans, the other five were negro slaves. Each of these had his confessor with him, and was earnestly listening to his exhortation. A monk approached Amine, but she waved him away with her hand: he looked at her, spat on the floor, and cursed her. The head gaoler now made his appearance with the dresses for those who were in this chamber; these were Samarias, only different from the others, inasmuch as the flames were painted on them *upwards* instead of down. These dresses were of grey stuff, and loose, like a waggoner's frock; at the lower part of them, both before and behind, was painted the likeness of the wearer that is the face only, resting upon a burning fagot, and surrounded with flames and demons. Under the portrait was written the crime for which the party suffered. Sugar-loaf caps, with flames painted on them, were also brought and put on their heads, and the long wax candles were placed into their hands.

Amine, and the others condemned, being arrayed in these dresses, remained in the chambers for some hours before it was time for the procession to commence, for they had been all summoned up by the gaolers at about two o'clock in the morning.

The sun rose brilliantly, much to the joy of the members of the Holy Office, who would not have had the day obscured on which they were to vindicate the honour of the Church, and to prove how well they acted up to the mild doctrines of the Saviour—those of charity, good-will, forbearing one another forgiving one another. God of Heaven! And not only did those of the Holy Inquisition rejoice, but thousands and thousands more, who had flocked from all parts to witness the dreadful ceremony, and to hold a jubilee—many, indeed, actuated by fanatical superstition, but more attended from thoughtlessness and the love of pageantry. The streets and squares through which the procession was to pass were filled at an early hour. Silks, tapestries, and cloth of gold and silver, were hung over the balconies, and out of the windows, in honour of the procession. Every balcony and window was thronged with ladies and cavaliers in their gayest attire, all waiting anxiously to see the wretches paraded before they suffered; but the world is fond of excitement, and where is anything so exciting to a superstitious people as an *auto-da-fé*?

As the sun rose, the heavy bell of the cathedral tolled, and all the prisoners were led down to the grand hall, that the order of the procession might be arranged. At the large entrance-door, on a raised one sat the Grand Inquisitor, encircled by many of the most considerable nobility and gentry of Goa. By the Grand Inquisitor stood his secretary, and as the prisoners walked past the throne and their names were mentioned, the secretary, after each, called out the names of one of those gentlemen, who immediately stepped forward, and took his station by the prisoner. These people are termed god-fathers; their duty is to accompany and be answerable for the prisoner, who is under their charge, until the ceremony is over. It is reckoned a high honour conferred on those whom the Grand Inquisitor appoints to this office.

At last the procession commenced. First was raised on high the standard of the Dominican order of monks, for the Dominican order were the founders of the Inquisition, and claimed this privilege by prescriptive right. After the banner, the monks themselves followed, in two lines. And what was the motto of their banner?—"Justitia et Misericordia!" Then followed the culprits, to the number of three hundred, each with his godfather by his side, and his large wax candle lighted in his hand. Those whose offences have been most venial walk first; all are bareheaded and barefooted. After this portion; who wore only the dress of black and white serge, came those who carried the Sanbenitos; then those who wore the Samarias, with the flames reversed. Here there was a separation in the procession, caused by a large cross, with the carved image of our Saviour nailed to it, the face of the image carried forward. This was intended to signify, that those in advance of the crucifix, and upon whom the Saviour looked down, were not to suffer; and that those who were behind, and upon whom his back was turned, were cast away, to perish for ever, in this world and the next. Behind the crucifix followed the seven condemned; and, as the greatest criminal, Amine walked the last. But the procession did not close here. Behind Amine were five effigies, raised high on poles, clothed in the same dresses, painted with flames and demons. Behind each effigy was borne a coffin, containing a skeleton; the effigies were of those who had died in their dungeon, or expired under the torture, and who had been tried and condemned after their death, and sentenced to be burnt. These skeletons had been dug up and were to suffer the same sentence as, had they still been living beings, they would have undergone. The effigies were to be tied to the stakes, and the bones were to be consumed. Then followed the members of the Inquisition; the familiars, monks, priests, and hundreds of penitents in black dresses, which concealed their faces, all with the lighted tapers in their hands.

It was two hours before the procession, which had paraded through almost every important street in Goa, arrived at the cathedral in which the further ceremonies were to be gone through. The barefooted culprits could now scarcely walk, the small sharp flints having so wounded their feet, that their tracks up the steps of the cathedral were marked with blood.

The grand altar of the cathedral was hung with black cloth, and lighted up with thousands of tapers. On one side of it was a throne for the Grand Inquisitor, on the other, a raised platform for the Viceroy of Goa, and his suite. The centre aisle had benches for the prisoners and their godfathers; the other portions of the procession falling off to the right and left to the side aisles, and mixing for the time with the spectators. As the prisoners entered the cathedral, they were led into their seats, those least guilty sitting nearest to the altar, and those who were condemned to suffer at the stake being placed the farthest from it.

The bleeding Amine tottered to her seat, and longed for the hour which was to sever her from a Christian world. She thought not of herself, nor of what she was to suffer: she thought but of Philip; of his being safe from these merciless creatures—of the happiness of dying first, and of meeting him again in bliss.

Worn with long confinement, with suspense and anxiety, fatigued and suffering from her painful walk, and the exposure to the burning sun, after so many months' incarceration in a dungeon, she no longer shone radiant with beauty; but still there was something even more touching in her care-worn yet still perfect features. The object of universal gaze, she walked with her eyes cast down, and nearly closed; but occasionally, when she did look up, the fire that flashed from them spoke the proud soul within, and many feared and wondered, while more pitied that one so young, and still so lovely, should be doomed to such an awful fate. Amine had not taken her seat in the cathedral more than a few seconds, when, overpowered by her feelings and by fatigue she fell back in a swoon.

Did no one step forward to assist her? to raise her up, and offer her restoratives? No—not one. Hundreds would have done so, but they dared not: she was an outcast, excommunicated, abandoned, and lost; and should any one, moved by compassion for a suffering fellow-creature, have ventured to raise her up he would have been looked upon with suspicion, and most probably have been arraigned, and have had to settle the affair of conscience with the Holy Inquisition.

After a short time two of the officers of the Inquisition went to Amine and raised her again in her seat, and she recovered sufficiently to enable her to retain her posture.

A sermon was then preached by a Dominican monk, in which he portrayed the tender mercies, the paternal love of the Holy Office. He compared the Inquisition to the ark of Noah, out of which all the animals walked after the deluge, but with this difference highly in favour of the Holy Office, that the animals went forth from the ark no better than they went in, whereas those who had gone into the Inquisition with all the cruelty of disposition, and with the hearts of wolves, came out as mild and patient as lambs.

The public accuser then mounted the pulpit, and read from it all the crimes of those who had been condemned, and the punishments which they were to undergo. Each prisoner, as his sentence was read, was brought forward to the pulpit by the officers to hear it, standing up, with his wax candle lighted in his hand. As soon as the sentences of all those whose lives had been spared were read the Grand Inquisitor put on his priestly robes, and followed by several others, took off from them the ban of excommunication (which they were supposed to have fallen under), by throwing holy water on them with a small broom.

As soon as this portion of the ceremony was over, those who were condemned to suffer, and the effigies of those who had escaped by death, were brought up one by one, and their sentences read; the winding up of the condemnation of all was in the same words, "that the Holy Inquisition found it impossible, on account of the hardness of their hearts and the magnitude of their crimes, to pardon them. With great concern it handed them over to secular justice to undergo the penalty of the laws; exhorting the authorities at the same time to show clemency and mercy towards the unhappy wretches, and if they must suffer death, that at all events it might be without the *spilling of blood*." What mockery was this apparent intercession not to shied blood, when, to comply with their request, they substituted the torment and agony of the stake!

Amine was the last who was led forward to the pulpit, which was fixed against one of the massive columns of the centre aisle, close to the throne occupied by the Grand inquisitor. "You, Amine Vanderdecken," cried the public accuser. At this moment an unusual bustle was heard in the crowd under the pulpit, there was struggling and expostulation, and the officers raised their wands for silence and decorum—but it continued.

"You, Amine Vanderdecken, being accused—"

Another violent struggle; and from the crowd darted a young man, who rushed to where Amine was standing, and caught her in his arms.

"Philip! Philip!" screamed Amine falling on his bosom; as he caught her, the cap of flames fell off her head and rolled along the marble pavement. "My Amine—my wife—my adored one—is it thus we meet? My lord, she is innocent. Stand off, men," continued he to the officers of the Inquisition, who would have torn them asunder: "stand off, or your lives shall answer for it."

This threat to the officers, and the defiance of all rules, were not to be borne; the whole cathedral was in a state of commotion, and the solemnity of the ceremony was about to be compromised. The Viceroy and his followers had risen from their chairs to observe what was passing, and the crowd was pressing on, when the Grand Inquisitor gave his directions, and other officers hastened to the assistance of the two who had led Amine forward, and proceeded to disengage her from Philip's arms. The struggle was severe. Philip appeared to be endued with the strength of twenty men; and it was some minutes before they could succeed in separating him and when they had so done, his struggles were dreadful.

Amine, also, held by two of the familiars, shrieked, as she attempted once more, but in vain, to rush into her husband's arms. At last, by a tremendous effort, Philip released himself; but as soon as he was released, he sank down helpless on the pavement; the exertion had caused the bursting of a blood-vessel, and he lay without motion.

"Oh God! Oh God! they have killed him! monsters—murderers!—let me embrace him but once more!" cried Amine, frantically.

A priest now stepped forward—it was Father Mathias—with sorrow in his countenance; he desired some of the bystanders to carry out Philip Vanderdecken, and Philip, in a state of insensibility, was borne away from the sight of Amine, the blood streaming from his mouth.

Amine's sentence was read—she heard it not, her brain was bewildered. She was led back to her seat, and then it was that all her courage, all her constancy and fortitude gave way; and during the remainder of the ceremony, she filled the cathedral with her wild hysterical sobbing; all entreaties or threats being wholly lost upon her.

All was now over except the last and most tragical scene of the drama. The culprits who had been spared were led back to the Inquisition by their godfathers, and those who had been sentenced were taken down to the banks of the river to suffer. It was on a large open space, on the left of the custom-house, that this ceremony was to be gone through. As in the cathedral raised thrones were prepared for the Grand Inquisitor and the who, in state headed the procession, followed by an immense concourse of people. Thirteen stakes had been set up, eight for the living, or the dead. The executioners were sitting on, or standing by, the piles of wood and faggots, waiting for their victims. Amine could not walk she was at first supported by the familiars, and then carried by them, to the stake which had been assigned for her. When they put her on her feet opposite to it, her courage appeared to revive, she walked boldly up, folded her arms and leant against it.

The executioners now commenced their office: the chains were passed round Amine's body—the wood and faggots piled around her. The same preparations had been made with all the other culprits, and the confessors stood by the side of each victim. Amine waved her hand indignantly to those who approached her, when Father Mathias, almost breathless, made his appearance from the crowd, through which he had forced his way.

"Amine Vanderdecken—unhappy woman! had you been counselled by me this would not have been. Now it is too late, but not too late to save your soul. Away then with this obstinacy—this hardness of heart; call upon the blessed Saviour, that he may receive your spirit—call upon his wound's for mercy. It is the eleventh hour, but not too late. Amine," continued the old man with tears, "I implore you, I conjure you. At least, may this load of trouble be taken from my heart."

"'Unhappy woman!' you say?" replied she, "say rather, 'unhappy priest:' for Amine's sufferings will soon be over, while you must still endure the torments of the damned. Unhappy was the day when my husband rescued you from death. Still more unhappy the compassion which prompted him to offer you an asylum and a refuge. Unhappy the knowledge of you from the *first* day to the *last*. I leave you to your conscience—if conscience you retain—nor would I change this cruel death for the pangs which you in your future life will suffer. Leave me—*I die in the faith of my forefathers*, and scorn a creed that warrants such a scene as this."

"Amine Vanderdecken," cried the priest on his knees, clasping his hands in agony.

"Leave me, Father."

"There is but a minute left—for the love of God—"

"I tell you then, leave me—that minute is my own."

Father Mathias turned away in despair, and the tears coursed down the old man's cheeks. As Amine said, his misery was extreme.

The head executioner now inquired of the confessors whether the culprits died in the *true* faith? If answered in the affirmative, a rope was passed round their necks and twisted to the stake, so that they were strangled before the fire was kindled. All the other culprits had died in this manner; and the head executioner inquired of Father Mathias, whether Amine had a claim to so much mercy. The old priest answered not, but shook his head.

The executioner turned away. After a moment's pause, Father Mathias followed him, and seized him by the arm saying, in a faltering voice, "Let her not suffer long."

The Grand Inquisitor gave the signal, and the fires were all lighted at the same moment. In compliance with the request of the priest, the executioner had thrown a quantity of wet straw upon Amine's pile, which threw up a dense smoke before it burst into flames.

"Mother! mother! I come to thee!" were the last words heard from Amine's lips.

The flames soon raged furiously, ascending high above the top of the stake to which she had been chained. Gradually they sunk down; and only when the burning embers covered the ground, a few fragments of bones hanging on the chain were all that remained of the once peerless and high-minded Amine.

Chapter Forty One

Years have passed away since we related Amine's sufferings and cruel death; and now once more we bring Philip Vanderdecken on the scene. And during this time, where has he been? A lunatic—at one time frantic, chained, coerced with blows; at others, mild and peaceable. Reason occasionally appeared to burst out again, as the sun on a cloudy day, and then it was again obscured. For many years there was one who watched him carefully, and lived in hope to witness his return to a sane mind; he watched in sorrow and remorse—he died without his desires being gratified. This was Father Mathias!

The cottage at Terneuse had long fallen into ruin; for many years it waited the return of its owners, and at last the heirs-at-law claimed and recovered the substance of Philip Vanderdecken. Even the fate of Amine had passed from the recollection of most people; although her portrait over burning coals, with her crime announced beneath it, still hangs—as is the custom in the church of the Inquisition—attracting from its expressive beauty, the attention of the most careless passers-by.

But many, many years have rolled away—Philip's hair is white—his once powerful frame is broken down—and he appears much older than he really is. He is now sane; but his vigour is gone. Weary of life, all he wishes for is to execute his mission—and then to welcome death.

The relic has never been taken from him: he has been discharged from the lunatic-asylum, and has been provided with the means of returning to his country. Alas! he has now no country—no home—nothing in the world to induce him to remain in it. All he asks is—to do his duty and to die.

The ship was ready to sail for Europe; and Philip Vanderdecken went on board—hardly caring whither he went. To return to Terneuse was not his object; he could not bear the idea of revisiting the scene of so much happiness and so much misery. Amine's form was engraven on his heart, and he looked forward with impatience to the time when he should be summoned to join her in the land of spirits.

He had awakened as from a dream, after so many years of aberration of intellect. He was no longer the sincere Catholic that he had been; for he never thought of religion without his Amine's cruel fate being brought to his recollection. Still he clung on to the relic—he believed in that—and that only. It was his god—his creed—his everything—the passport for himself and for his father into the next world—the means whereby he should join his Amine—and for hours would he remain holding in his hand that object so valued—gazing upon it—recalling every important event in his life, from the death of his poor mother, and his first sight of Amine, to the last dreadful scene. It was to him a journal of his existence, and on it were fixed all his hopes for the future.

"When! oh when is it to be accomplished?" was the constant subject of his reveries. "Blessed indeed will be the day when I leave this world of hate, and seek that other in which the weary are at rest."

The vessel on board of which Philip was embarked as a passenger was the Nostra Señora da Monte, a brig of three hundred tons, bound for Lisbon. The captain was an old Portuguese, full of superstition, and fond of arrack—a fondness rather unusual with the people of his nation. They sailed from Goa, and Philip was standing abaft, and sadly contemplating the spire of the cathedral, in which he had last parted with his wife, when his elbow was touched, and he turned round.

"Fellow-passenger, again!" said a well-known voice—it was that of the pilot Schriften.

There was no alteration in the man's appearance; he showed no marks of declining years; his one eye glared as keenly as ever.

Philip started, not only at the sight of the man, but at the reminiscences which his unexpected appearance brought to his mind. It was but for a second, and he was again calm and pensive.

"You here again, Schriften?" observed Philip. "I trust your appearance forebodes the accomplishment of my task."

"Perhaps it does," replied the pilot; "we both are weary."

Philip made no reply; he did not even ask Schriften in what manner he had escaped from the fort; he was indifferent about it; for he felt that the man had a charmed life.

"Many are the vessels that have been wrecked, Philip Vanderdecken, and many the souls summoned to their account by meeting with your father's ship, while you have been so long shut up," observed the pilot.

"May our next meeting with him be more fortunate—may it be the last!" replied Philip.

"No, no! rather may he fulfil his doom, and sail till the day of judgment!" replied the pilot, with emphasis.

"Vile caitiff! I have a foreboding that you will not have your detestable wish. Away!—leave me! or you shall find, that although this head is blanched by misery, this arm has still some power."

Schriften scowled as he walked away; he appeared to have some fear of Philip, although it was not equal to his hate. He now resumed his former attempts of stirring up the ship's company against Philip, declaring that he was a Jonah, who would occasion the loss of the ship, and that he was connected with the Flying Dutchman. Philip very soon observed that he was avoided; and he resorted to counter-statements, equally injurious to Schriften, whom he declared to be a demon. The appearance of Schriften was so much against him, while that of Philip, on the contrary, was so prepossessing, that the people on board hardly knew what to think. They were divided: some were on the side of Philip—some on that of Schriften; the captain and many others looking with equal horror upon both, and longing for the time when they could be sent out of the vessel.

The captain, as we have before observed, was very superstitious, and very fond of his bottle. In the morning he would be sober and pray; in the afternoon he would be drunk and swear at the very saints whose protection he had invoked but a few hours before.

"May holy Saint Antonio preserve us, and keep us from temptation," said he, on the morning after a conversation with the passengers about the Phantom Ship. "All the saints protect us from harm," continued he, taking off his hat reverentially and crossing himself. "Let me but rid myself of these two dangerous men without accident, and I will offer up a hundred wax candles, of three ounces each, to the shrine of the Virgin, upon my safe anchoring off the tower of Belem." In the evening he changed his language.

"Now, if that Maledetto Saint Antonio don't help us, may he feel the coals of hell yet! damn him, and his pigs too; if he has the courage to do his duty, all will be well; but he is a cowardly wretch, he cares for nobody, and will not help those who call upon him in trouble. Carambo, that for you!" exclaimed the captain, looking at the small shrine of the saint at the bittacle, and snapping his fingers at the image; "that for you, you useless wretch, who never help us in our trouble. The pope must canonise some better saints for us, for all we have now are worn out. They could do something formerly, but now I would not give two ounces of gold for the whole calendar; as for you, you lazy old scoundrel—" continued the captain, shaking his fist at poor Saint Antonio.

The ship had now gained off the southern coast of Africa, and was about one hundred miles from the Lagullas coast; the morning was beautiful, a slight ripple only turned over the waves, the breeze was light and steady, and the vessel was standing on a wind at the rate of about four miles an hour.

"Blessed be the holy saints," said the captain, who had just gained the deck; "another little slant in our favour, and we shall lay our course. Again, I say, blessed be the holy saints, and particularly our worthy patron, Saint Antonio, who has taken under his peculiar protection the Nostra Señora da Monte. We have a prospect of fine weather; come, signors, let us down to breakfast, and after breakfast, we enjoy our cigarros upon the deck."

But the scene was soon changed; a bank of clouds rose up from the eastward with a rapidity that to the seamen's eyes was unnatural, and it soon covered the whole firmament; the sun was obscured, and all was one deep and unnatural gloom; the wind subsided, and the ocean was hushed. It was not exactly dark, but the heavens were covered with one red haze, which gave an appearance as if the world was in a state of conflagration.

In the cabin the increased darkness was first observed by Philip, who went on deck; he was followed by the captain and passengers, who were in a state of amazement. It was unnatural and incomprehensible. "Now, holy Virgin, protect us!—what can this be?" exclaimed the captain in a fright "Holy Saint Antonio, protect us!—but this is awful."

"There—there!" shouted the sailors, pointing to the beam of the vessel. Every eye looked over the gunnel to witness what had occasioned such exclamations. Philip, Schriften, and the captain, were side by side. On the beam of the ship, not more than two cables' length distant, they beheld slowly rising out of the water the tapering masthead and spars of another vessel. She rose, and rose, gradually; her topmasts and topsail yards, with the sails set, next made their appearance; higher and higher she rose up from the element. Her lower masts and rigging, and, lastly, her hull showed itself above the surface. Still she rose up, till her ports, with her guns, and at last the whole of her floatage was above water and there she remained close to them, with her main yard squared, and hove-to.

"Holy Virgin!" exclaimed the captain, breathless; "I have known ships to *go down*, but never to *come up* before. Now will I give one thousand candles, of ten ounces each, to the shrine of the Virgin, to save us in this trouble. One thousand wax candles! Hear me, blessed lady, ten ounces each! Gentlemen," cried the captain to the passengers, who stood aghast; "why don't you promise?—promise, I say; *promise*, at all events."

"The Phantom Ship—the Flying Dutchman," shrieked Schriften; "I told you so, Philip Vanderdecken; there is your father—he, he!"

Philip's eyes had remained fixed on the vessel; he perceived that they were lowering down a boat from her quarter. "It is possible," thought he, "I shall now be permitted!" and Philip put his hand into his bosom and grasped the relic.

The gloom now increased, so that the strange vessel's hull could but just be discovered through the murky atmosphere. The seamen and passengers threw themselves down on their knees, and invoked their saints. The captain ran down for a candle, to light before the image of St. Antonio, which he took out of its shrine and kissed with much apparent affection and devotion, and then replaced.

Shortly afterwards the splash of oars was heard alongside, and a voice calling out, "I say, my good people, give us a rope from forward."

No one answered, or complied with the request. Schriften only went up to the captain, and told him that if they offered to send letters they must not be received, or the vessel would be doomed, and all would perish.

A man now made his appearance from over the gunnel, at the gangway. "You might as well have let me had a side-rope, my hearties," said he, as he stepped on deck; "where is the captain?"

"Here," replied the captain, trembling from head to foot. The man who accosted him appeared a weather-beaten seaman, dressed in a fur cap and canvas petticoats; he held some letters in his hand.

"What do you want?" at last screamed the captain.

"Yes—what do you want?" continued Schriften, "He! he!"

"What, you here, pilot?" observed the man—"well—I thought you had gone to Davy's locker, long enough ago."

"He! he!" replied Schriften, turning away.

"Why, the fact is, captain, we have had very foul weather and we wish to send letters home; I do believe that we shall never get round this cape."

"I can't take them," cried the captain.

"Can't take them! well, it's very odd; but every ship refuses to take our letters. It's very unkind; seamen should have a feeling for brother seamen, especially in distress. God knows, we wish to see our wives and families again; and it would be a matter of comfort to them if they only could hear from us."

"I cannot take your letters—the saints preserve us!" replied the captain.

"We have been a long while out," said the seaman, shaking his head.

"How long?" inquired the captain, not knowing what to say.

"We can't tell; our almanack was blown overboard, and we have lost our reckoning. We never have our latitude exact now, for we cannot tell the sun's declination for the right day."

"Let *me* see your letters," said Philip, advancing and taking them out of the seaman's hands.

"They must not be touched!" screamed Schriften.

"Out, monster!" replied Philip; "who dares interfere with me?"

"Doomed—doomed—doomed!" shrieked Schriften, running up and down the deck, and then breaking into a wild fit of laughter.

"Touch not the letters," said the captain, trembling as if in an ague fit.

Philip made no reply, but held his hand out for the letters.

"Here is one from our second mate to his wife at Amsterdam who lives on Waser Quay."

"Waser Quay has long been gone, my good friend; there is now a large dock for ships where it once was," replied Philip.

"Impossible!" replied the man; "here is another from the boatswain to his father, who lives in the old market-place."

"The old market-place has long been pulled down, and there now stands a church upon the spot."

"Impossible!" replied the seaman; "here is another from myself to my sweetheart, Vrow Ketser—with money to buy her a new brooch."

Philip shook his head. "I remember seeing an old lady of that name buried some thirty years ago."

"Impossible! I left her young and blooming. Here's one for the house of Slutz and Company, to whom the ship belongs."

"There's no such house now," replied Philip; "but I have heard that, many years ago, there was a firm of that name."

"Impossible! you must be laughing at me. Here is a letter from our captain to his son—"

"Give it me," cried Philip, seizing the letter. He was about to break the seal, when Schriften snatched it out of his hand and threw it over the lee gunnel.

"That's a scurvy trick for an old shipmate," observed the seaman. Schriften made no reply, but catching up the other letters which Philip had laid down on the capstan, he hurled them after the first.

The strange seaman shed tears, and walked again to the side. "It is very hard—very unkind," observed he, as he descended; "the time may come when you may wish that your family should know your situation." So saying, he disappeared. In a few seconds was heard the sound of the oars retreating from the ship.

"Holy St. Antonio!" exclaimed the captain. "I am lost in wonder and fright. Steward, bring me up the arrack."

The steward ran down for the bottle; being as much alarmed as his captain, he helped himself before he brought it up to his commander. "Now," said the captain, after keeping his mouth for two minutes to the bottle, and draining it to the bottom, "what is to be done next?"

"I'll tell you," said Schriften, going up to him: "that man there has a charm hung round his neck; take it from him and throw it overboard, and your ship will be saved; if not, it will be lost, with every soul on board."

"Yes yes, it's all right, depend upon it," cried the sailors.

"Fools," replied Philip, "do you believe that wretch? Did you not hear the man who came on board recognise him, and call him shipmate? He is the party whose presence on board will prove so unfortunate."

"Yes, yes," cried the sailors, "it's all right; the man did call him shipmate."

"I tell you it's all wrong," cried Schriften; "that is the man: let him give up the charm."

"Yes, yes; let him give up the charm," cried the sailors; and they rushed upon Philip.

Philip started back to where the captain stood. "Madmen, know ye what ye are about? It is the holy cross that I wear round my neck. Throw it overboard if you dare, and your souls are lost for ever;" and Philip took the relic from his bosom and showed it to the captain.

"No, no, men;" exclaimed the captain, who was now more settled in his nerves; "that won't do—the saints protect us."

The seamen, however, became clamorous; one portion were for throwing Schriften overboard, the other for throwing Philip; at last, the point was decided by the captain, who directed the small skiff hanging astern to be lowered down, and ordered both Philip and Schriften to get into it. The seamen approved of this arrangement, as it satisfied both parties. Philip made no objection; Schriften screamed and fought, but he was tossed into the boat. There he remained trembling in the stern-sheets, while Philip, who had seized the sculls, pulled away from the vessel in the direction of the Phantom Ship.

Chapter Forty Two

In a few minutes the vessel which Philip and Schriften had left was no longer to be discerned through the thick haze; the Phantom Ship was still in sight, but at a much greater distance from them than she was before. Philip pulled hard towards her, but although hove to, she appeared to increase her distance from the boat. For a short time he paused on his oars, to regain his breath, when Schriften rose up and took his seat in the stern-sheets of the boat. "You may pull and pull, Philip Vanderdecken," observed Schriften; "but you will not gain that ship—no, no, that cannot be—we may have a long cruise together, but you will be as far from your object at the end of it, as you are now at the commencement.—Why don't you throw me overboard again? You would be all the lighter—He! he!"

"I threw you overboard in a state of phrenzy," replied Philip, "when you attempted to force from me my relic."

"And have I not endeavoured to make others take it from you this very day?—Have I not—He! he!"

"You have," rejoined Philip; "but I am now convinced that you are as unhappy as myself, and that in what you are doing, you are only following your destiny, as I am mine. Why and wherefore I cannot tell, but we are both engaged in the same mystery;—if the success of my endeavours depends upon guarding the relic, the success of yours depends upon your obtaining it, and defeating my purpose by so doing. In this matter we are both agents, and you have been, as far as my mission is concerned, my most active enemy. But, Schriften, I have not forgotten, and never will, that you kindly *did advise* my poor Amine; that you prophesied to her what would be her fate, if she did not listen to your counsel; that you were no enemy of hers, although you have been and are still mine. Although my enemy, for her sake I *forgive you*, and will not attempt to harm you."

"You do then *forgive your enemy*, Philip Vanderdecken?" replied Schriften, mournfully, "for such I acknowledge myself to be."

"I do, with *all my heart, with all my soul*," replied Philip.

"Then have you conquered me, Philip Vanderdecken; you have now made me your friend, and your wishes are about to be accomplished. You would know who I am. Listen:— When your father, defying the Almighty's will, in his rage took my life, he was vouchsafed a chance of his doom being cancelled, through the merits of his Son. I had also my appeal, which was for *vengeance*; it was granted that I should remain on earth, and thwart your will. That as long as we were enemies, you should not succeed; but that when you had conformed to the highest attribute of Christianity, proved on the holy cross, that of *forgiving your enemy*, your task should be fulfilled. Philip Vanderdecken, you have forgiven your enemy, and both our destinies are now accomplished."

As Schriften spoke, Philip's eyes were fixed upon him. He extended his hand to Philip—it was taken; and as it was pressed, the form of the pilot wasted as it were into the air, and Philip found himself alone.

"Father of Mercy, I thank thee," said Philip, "that my task is done, and that I again may meet my Amine."

Philip then pulled towards the Phantom Ship, and found that she no longer appeared to leave; on the contrary, every minute he was nearer and nearer and at last, he threw in his oars, climbed up her sides and gained her deck.

The crew of the vessel crowded round him.

"Your captain," said Philip; "I must speak with your captain."

"Who shall I say, sir?" demanded one, who appeared to be the first mate.

"Who?" replied Philip: "tell him his son would speak to him, his son, Philip Vanderdecken."

Shouts of laughter from the crew followed this answer of Philip's; and the mate, as soon as they ceased, observed with a smile.

"You forget, sir, perhaps you would say his father."

"Tell him his son, if you please," replied Philip; "take no note of grey hairs."

"Well, sir, here he is coming forward," replied the mate, stepping aside and pointing to the captain.

"What is all this?" inquired the captain.

"Are you Philip Vanderdecken, the captain of this vessel?"

"I am, sir," replied the other.

"You appear not to know me! But how can you? you saw me but when I was only three years old; yet may you remember a letter which you gave to your wife."

"Ha!" replied the captain; "and who, then, are you?"

"Time has stopped with you, but with those who live in the world he stops not; and for those who pass a life of misery, he hurries on still faster. In me behold your son, Philip Vanderdecken, who has obeyed your wishes; and, after a life of such peril and misery as few have passed, has at last fulfilled his vow, and now offers to his father the precious relic that he required to kiss."

Philip drew out the relic, and held it towards his father. As if a flash of lightning had passed through his mind, the captain of the vessel started back, clasped his hands, fell on his knees, and wept.

"My son, my son!" exclaimed he, rising and throwing himself into Philip's arms; "my eyes are opened—the Almighty knows how long they have been obscured." Embracing each other, they walked aft, away from the men, who were still crowded at the gangway.

"My son, my noble son, before the charm is broken—before we resolve, as we must, into the elements, oh! let me kneel in thanksgiving and contrition: my son, my noble son, receive a father's thanks," exclaimed Vanderdecken. Then with tears of joy and penitence he humbly addressed himself to that Being, whom he once so awfully defied.

The elder Vanderdecken knelt down: Philip did the same; still embracing each other with one arm, while they raised on high the other, and prayed.

For the last time the relic was taken from the bosom of Philip and handed to his father—and his father raised his eyes to heaven and kissed it. And, as he kissed it, the long tapering upper spars of the Phantom vessel, the yards and sails that were set, fell into dust, fluttered in the air, and sank upon the wave. The mainmast, foremast, bowsprit, everything above the deck, crumbled into atoms and disappeared.

Again he raised the relic to his lips and the work of destruction continued—the heavy iron guns sunk through the decks and disappeared; the crew of the vessel (who were looking on) crumbled down into skeletons, and dust, and fragments of ragged garments; and there were none left on board the vessel in the semblance of life but the father and son.

Once more did he put the sacred emblem to his lips, and the beams and timbers separated, the decks of the vessel slowly sank, and the remnants of the hull floated upon the water; and as the father and son—the one young and vigorous, the other old and decrepit—still kneeling, still embracing, with their hands raised to heaven, sank slowly under the deep blue wave, the lurid sky was for a moment illumined by a lightning cross. Then did the clouds which obscured the heavens roll away swift as thought—the sun again burst out in all his splendour—the rippling waves appeared to dance with joy. The screaming sea-gull again whirled in the air, and the scared albatross once more slumbered on the wing. The porpoise tumbled and tossed in his sportive play, the albicore and dolphin leaped from the sparkling sea.—All nature smiled as if it rejoiced that the charm was dissolved for ever, and that " *The Phantom Ship*" *Was No More* .